Quiet Blood

Plantation to Prison

Lionel Stewart, Jaime Stewart,
& Demar Brazil

Library of Congress Control Number:		2011901397
ISBN:	Hardcover	978-1-4568-6072-1
	Softcover	978-1-4568-6071-4
	Ebook	978-1-4568-6073-8

This is a work of fiction. Names, characters, places and incidents either are the product of the author's imagination or are used fictitiously, and any resemblance to any actual persons, living or dead, events, or locales is entirely coincidental.

This prepublication draft is not to be copied, quoted, or referenced; the forthcoming publication version will contain significant changes and improvements.

This book was printed in the United States of America.

To order additional copies of this book, contact:
Xlibris Corporation
1-888-795-4274
www.Xlibris.com
Orders@Xlibris.com
89474

Dedicated to

Nikki Giovanni,

one of the most brilliant, beautiful, strong, and courageous persons that this world has ever had the honor and privilege to meet.
God bless you.

I love you.

—Lionel Stewart

Young men, hear an old man to whom old men hearkened when he was young.

—Augustus Caesar

Acknowledgments

From Lionel and Jaime Stewart

Special thanks to the students of the Black Americana Studies Department at Western Michigan University and the Department of English and Literature at the University of Michigan who, over the years, gathered invaluable information for this book.

Many thanks to Paul Zieger (Proper Paul), a musician with the Jackson Symphony Orchestra, whose professional work product on his computer supplied so much of everything and continuously surprised everyone associated with *Quiet Blood*.

The thousands of incarcerated minority men and women across the nation and their families and friends who provided transcripts of racially disparate sentences from coast to coast. The men of Jackson Inside and the guards who worked there, for stories and detailed documentation of everyday life as lived in that place known as the Killing Grounds. Thanks to all of you.

Detroit Free Press reporter Jeff Gerritt, who wrote an article (prompted by Penny Ryder, director of American Friends Service Committee, and Sandra Girard, executive director of Prison Legal Services of Michigan, on my father's failing health that compelled the Michigan Department of Corrections to immediately address the matter, resulting in my father regaining his health. It's not often that a reporter's newspaper article will save someone's life. In this case, that is precisely what happened. Thanks from the Stewart clan, Jeff.

Kisses and hugs for my father, Lionel Stewart, whose strength and unwavering love for me over the decades was the inspiration for it all. Thanks, Dad.

A standing ovation for Betty Lou and David Lawson, my father's mother and stepfather, better known as my grandparents, who financed this entire project.

An African dance of celebration for all of you.

From Demar Brazil

I would like to thank Lionel Stewart, who did the lion's share of the work for this masterpiece, for allowing me to take part in this excellent and necessary exploration of several unacknowledged social maladies. This has been an unforgettable experience, which I pray we will explore together again.

Many thanks to my father, Daniel Brazil, who supported me throughout all my trials and during my darkest hour. You are my inspiration and my rock. Without you, I can't imagine where I would be.

To my dearest cousin, Myrtis Brazil, who sacrificed much to walk with me through my personal troubles; thank you from the bottom of my heart.

To the rest of my friends and family who believed in me, my gratitude overflows for you.

All of you who supported our efforts by reading our humble work, I thank you also. If you enjoy this work, rest assured that there will be more to come.

Special Acknowledgements

All authors would like to give a very special note of thanks to Sarah Kunstler, the daughter of the great late William Kunstler. She allowed us to use an excerpt from her father's speech, "The Terrible Myth," to make this work even more gripping and engaging.

We would also like to give a special acknowledgement to the godmother of verse, Dr. Maya Angelou, for her inspiring poetry.

Foreword

This book is written by one of our finest, brightest, and most capable black males. For whatever reasons, Lionel Stewart is a product of two of our finest educational institutions: the university and the prison.

Lionel went to prison soon after graduating from college. It was not supposed to be that way. Our hopes were to take young people, refine their skills, help to cultivate values, give direction, then send the finished products into the world. This time, under this particular set of facts, the educational system failed. Events inside the university, the community, and the streets shaped Lionel's life in another most tragic way. Most assuredly, had I known, I would have locked him up, imprisoned him inside my small university office, screaming to him, "Don't do this, but do this. That is not how it is done."

This story, this life account, was recorded inside our Michigan prison system by a well-trained, educated university graduate. An account of and by one of the smartest, ablest students I have taught, who has taken his academic skills, fine-tuned, polished, and tempered them in nearly three decades on the front lines of the state's judicial and penal system wars, dissecting both razor sharp cuts interrupted by rough edged knife thrusts.

This is a powerful story. A must read for anyone who wishes to study today's black man, today's judicial, penal, inner city, public school systems or man's inhumanity toward man. This book is also for those who don't have appointments to keep, who can unplug their phones, retire to comfortable chairs, and enjoy a damned good read.

A doctor friend of mine, after having read the manuscript, said this work isn't for the squeamish or weak. It isn't.

I, along with other reviewers of the earlier versions of the manuscript, told Lionel that he had two books here, a story and a factual/statistical presentation. Perhaps it would be better to divide the work, we advised him. Lionel responded that a mere factual/statistical presentation could not portray the moral or emotional experiences of blacks in the judicial and penal systems, the frustrations, fears, terror, and blatant racism that incarcerated black men as well as their women, experiences in every prison, in every state, across the nation.

Figures and facts cannot adequately tell of the sorrow, the pain, and the rage a black man feels when discovering many young black low-income inner city youth who look upon prison as being the natural course in the black man's life.

There's the resilience of the human spirit. Is this not worth mentioning? A black spirit that will not die.

"What about the tears?" Lionel asked. Shouldn't someone mention something about the tears? "Reach out and grab one in a hand," he told us. Hold on to it. Let it roll around in your palm, and get a feel of it. Listen closely. Each tear has its own story to tell.

"It's vital to present all of the material, at least to some extent," Lionel continued. He reminded us of the nineteenth century writer who wanted to portray the untold horrors and injustices of slavery but found that she could not do so by presenting a mere factual/statistical report because such a work would be too dry for reading, leaving out far too many necessary ingredients that could only be brought out in story form. The writer, Harriet Beecher Stowe, penned the melodrama *Uncle Tom's Cabin*, a book that recreated the slaves' characters, dreams, hopes, scenes, and incidents with humor and realism, analyzing the institution of black slavery in the south in a way that a factual/statistical presentation could never do. The same is true of *Quiet Blood*. Stowe's star character, Uncle Tom, was around when blacks made cotton king. Stewart's star character, George, says that today blacks have made prison king. I cannot help wondering how Uncle Tom and George would have related to each other during the slave years and during the latter part of this century, a period that George calls the prison years.

In my role as a young naive university professor and department head, imagine the sting I felt when one of the best students I ever taught wrote to me from inside one of the country's highest maximum-security prisons. Right away I felt a bit guilty for not having done enough for Stewart and, at the same time, created a way initially to distance myself, my teaching, and my beliefs system from Lionel Stewart 148666. Before I visited to see his face, I was certain no. 148666 was tall, slim, college groomed, and smart. Lionel was a bit of a smart aleck in class. He did read and understand text but offered remarks that reflected little tolerance for problems. Now well informed and knowledgeable about the inside of several maximum penitentiaries, Stewart has carefully and scholarly put his experiences into hard copy. The story is just one account of how people who keep others locked up act and how inmates who are locked up act.

At first, I didn't know whether I did not like the content or whether it was the fact that one of my "prize" students was locked up inside the maximum penitentiary. It took a second reading to accept the fact that I like neither.

Let me be clear. I don't like what happened to Stewart. I don't like prisons. I don't even like the historical accounts in *Quiet Blood*. Mainly because as a scientist and a wise old professor at six decades plus six years, I want to see what, how, and why family values, institutions, and socioeconomic conditions produce products/students. How arrogant of me to think that a few hours of teaching a young adult three hours per week for twelve weeks would be enough. Where did I—the director of an entire department, a teacher proud of his teaching abilities that have been measured by student successes, along with the backing of a major university, some of the country's best and brightest instructors and teachers underneath me, by my side and bringing up the rear—go so wrong? I found many of the answers in this novel.

Yet *Quiet Blood* is more than a novel. It is a life created in many ways molded by our best institution into a teaching module, a self-instructional module.

Long before the last page of *Quiet Blood* is turned, one question becomes paramount: where does fact end and fiction begin? Nearly every factual scene can be verified, Lionel explained, by researching prison records, published case laws of Michigan Courts, medical reports, university papers, along with Michigan Department of Corrections annual statistical reports, newspaper articles, and Michigan State Police files. Everything didn't necessarily happen in the sequence as told in *Quiet Blood*. "You must understand," Lionel said, "what we have here is a situation where an old adage holds true—'If it looks like a duck and if it walks like a duck and if it talks like a duck, buddy, you've got yourself a damned duck.'"

This is one of the best novels that I have ever read. It is the most comprehensive work on racial disparity in sentencing, parole practices, and prison classifications that I have ever seen. Stewart has taken in-depth research into drugs, poverty, crime, prisons, and the deplorable inner city public school system and shows these variables to be direct reverberations of slavery that have snaked their way through generation after generation after generation, only to sink their fangs into black people in another way.

Jaime, the daughter. I know her too. A university graduate, a psychologist, and a scholar in her own right. This father-daughter team has put together a work that will be around long after the walls of the world's largest walled prison have disappeared.

Dr. Leroi Ray Jr.

> Contrary to the myth held by many white Americans, the ghetto is not a monolithic unit of dope addicts, alcoholics, prostitutes and unwed mothers. There are churches in the ghetto as well as bars. There are stable families in the ghetto as well as illegitimate. Ninety percent of the young people of the ghetto never come in conflict with the law.
>
> —Rev. Martin Luther King Jr.

Chapter 1

Detroit 1964. Black people in Detroit were talking about the year's events: Nelson Mandela was found guilty of conspiring to overthrow the white apartheid government of South Africa and sentenced to life imprisonment; independence was won by the former colony of Northern Rhodesia, creating Zambia; Malawi proclaimed independence; the United States began bombing North Vietnam while President Lyndon B. Johnson signed the 1964 Civil Rights Bill; congress gave the president authority to use American troops to aid any state in SE Asia, thus entering a blood war where over 5,700 young black soldiers were killed; the reverend Dr. Martin Luther King Jr. was awarded the Nobel Peace Prize in Oslo, Norway, for his work toward racial integration in the United States; Malcolm X resigned from the Nation of Islam; thousands of civil rights workers traveled to Mississippi, America's boilerplate of racist hell, for Freedom Summer, the mammoth voter registration drive; brutalized bodies of three civil rights workers—James Cheney, Andrew Goodman, and Michael Schwerner—were found embedded in an earthen dam near Philadelphia, Mississippi, and the killers were Chief Deputy Sheriff Cecil Price and Sam Bower, Imperial Wizard of the Klu Klux Klan; there were race riots in Harlem, Rochester, Jersey City, Patterson, and Philadelphia; Dr. Anna Julia Cooper, the black educator and author of *Voice From the South: By A Woman from the South*, a work addressing racial problems in 1892, died at 105 years old; a twenty-two-year-old named Cassius Clay became the second youngest in boxing history to win the heavyweight crown when titleholder Sonny Liston failed to answer the bell at the beginning of the seventh round, causing the young man from Louisville to shout, "I am the greatest!"; Cassius Clay joins the Nation of Islam and changes his name to Muhammad Ali; Bob Hayes wins the title of the World's Fastest Human by winning two gold medals at the Olympics in Tokyo; Ray Charles is arrested at Logan Airport in Boston for possessing heroin; Sam Cooke was shot to death under mysterious circumstances; Sidney Poitier becomes the first black to win an Oscar for Best Actor for his performance in *Lilies of the Field*; four black women from Detroit's east side ghetto who called themselves the Supremes rocked the music industry by topping the charts three times in less than five months; another black woman from Detroit's east side ghetto, Martha Wells, grabbed music's top spot with "My Guy"; Marvin Gaye jazzed everyone with "How Sweet It Is"; Louis Armstrong soothed a nation in turmoil with "Hello, Dolly!"

Blacks in Detroit were talking about black-on-black crime; about the influx of drugs, especially heroin, entering the black communities; about how the drugs were turning black life into black death.

A recent University of Michigan study showed three factors that would come to play a significant role in the life of a ten-year-old black girl named Mary Evans. First, the study showed that children raised in poverty have a less enjoyable childhood. Second, that prolonged exposure to poverty decreases a child's chances of success and happiness later in life. Third, that a child's development is seriously hampered most by prolonged exposure to poverty.

Not only was the little Evans girl born to a family in poverty, but even worse, she was born behind the eight ball. The girl lived in a completely impoverished neighborhood. Her generation comprised the third of the Evans family born and raised poor.

Brewster Projects, an old federally funded low-income housing complex on Detroit's east side. The ghetto. All black. All poor.

Mary was born in the Brewster Projects, on the first floor, to an alcoholic mother too drunk to make it to the hospital or to the phone. A local madam delivered the baby. Mary's father had died before her birth of a drug overdose, Mexican heroin, a.k.a. Mexican dog food, black tar, mud.

The little girl was too young to understand the exact nature of poverty and too young to understand that a one-parent family was out of the norm—as many families in the neighborhood had only one parent—but these harsh facts, however, would soon attack this tiny ghetto child.

Mary had three brothers: Gerald died at birth, two years prior; eight-year-old Harold died earlier that year, caught in the cross fire of a shoot-out between neighborhood drug dealers, his death adding one more grim statistic to support the high trend of black adolescent death.

Sixteen-year-old George was the child's only living brother. An energetic youth, George spent his free time in the Kronk Gym or the Brewster Center boxing, trying to imitate the flamboyant style of his hero, the young Muhammad Ali.

George, quite big for his age, stood about five-eight, weighed in at around 175 pounds with sharply chiseled muscles. Next week he would fight for the city's Golden Gloves championship in the light heavyweight division, with a two-hundred-dollar purse going to the winner and fifty dollars to the loser. Talk of the fight had reached every ear in the city, and hundreds of people had already bought tickets. George had been training hard for the fight, and he was going to win it. Even though his opponent, a kid from Detroit's west side who called himself the Bone Crusher, was strong, quick, and tough, George was stronger, quicker, and much tougher. He had the fight in the bag, and he knew it. The fight would end in the first round; a straightforward power punch, his best shot, would end it quickly.

George planned to take his winnings and buy his sister some school supplies, clothes, underwear, and a couple pairs of shoes. He'd do something for his mother too, probably pay to have her hair done. She'd like that. With the remainder, he thought he'd buy some hamburger meat, buns, pickles, and a pumpkin pie. Mary loved hamburgers and pumpkin pie. He'd have to cook the burgers himself, which was no problem because he had been cooking for his sister for so long, he couldn't remember anyone else ever having done it. Every day he cooked for her, making sure the food was hot, nutritious, and on time. Anyone who knew him knew that he cherished his little sister more than anything. Often, he would wash dishes in a nearby restaurant just to make sure he had enough money to buy good-quality food. Then at other times, after he'd won a few dollars boxing, he would use most of it to buy something for Mary. He enjoyed taking care of her. He loved washing and ironing her clothes, all the things a big brother was supposed to do.

The principal of George's high school, knowing his circumstances, allowed him to leave his last period fifteen minutes early every day so he could run over to Mary's school to meet her when she got out and walk her home.

George felt his sister wasn't safe roaming the mean streets of Detroit's east side ghetto, and after changing into his workout clothes (a pair of sweatpants, a T-shirt, and a sweat shirt, which he kept in a duffel bag slung over his shoulder), he reflected on their life as he jogged and shadowboxed all the way to the local elementary school.

Too many drugs and gangs clogged the corners of the east side of Detroit, too much alcohol and violence, prostitution and ignorance, apathy and indifference. He hated their neighborhood. Things were terrible there for everyone—especially the children. Too many children looked up to the drug dealers, gamblers, pimps, and every other scum that represented the exact opposite of what role models should be.

Then he thought of how much sorrow and pain infected the ghetto: two monsters that had wormed their way into the bones of so many people, melting them, seeping into the very marrow, then finally crippling their spirits to the point of desperation. This black ghetto.

Of course, he remembered good times and good people in the ghetto. Yet common sense said that the ghetto was not the best place to raise a child. No reasonable, intelligent, or well-to-do person had ever chosen a black ghetto as the ideal place to help his or her child succeed in life.

George knew good people in Brewster also. Like Mr. Clark, the old black man who owned and ran a corner grocery store. He was a great man. He gave food to poor people on credit when he knew they'd never be able to pay and treated every one of them with dignity and respect.

Fred Parker, who also lived in Brewster with his wife and nine children, George considered another great man. Fred worked two jobs; he never drank nor used drugs. Every Sunday the people of Brewster would watch Fred Parker and his family walk to a nearby church. The children, always clean and dressed in their Sunday best, sported smiles that said, "Despite our situation, we know we're blessed." George viewed Fred as somewhat of a hero. The Fred Parkers of the world were rare in Brewster.

Even Fred's wife was the ideal woman, a true role model. A beautiful lady who not only took care of her nine children but also cared for many of the other children who seemed to linger around the Parker home when dinner time approached. The children knew the food would be there and it would be good. They also knew that Mr. and Mrs. Parker never turned away a hungry child. "Against God's law not to feed a hungry child," Fred would sometimes say.

Despite that, George still hated a lot of things about the ghetto, particularly the public school system. He believed deeply in education. A quality education—genuine, not tailored—was the golden key that unlocked doors.

At sixteen, George recognized and respected the value of a good education. Why couldn't other people understand? Or did they? Certainly, grown-ups couldn't be that stupid, so why didn't they do something? Why so much talk from the government about better education but nothing ever being done to make it happen, no progress whatsoever? If they were serious about improving the quality of life for the poor, why didn't they put more money into education?

The poor quality of the public school system was a major concern for George. He had to find a way to get his sister out of the system and pay her way through a private school. His little sister simply had to have the best education possible, and he decided to do everything in his power to make it happen. Her present school wouldn't cut it. A lot of the children who had gone through elementary, junior high, and high school still couldn't read or write like they should. And the teachers, society, and parents of the children were all to blame.

Many problems, and money was just one of them, infected the public school system. The schools didn't have enough staff, and they didn't pay the few staff they hired nearly enough. The buildings were in desperate need of repair. When sinks and toilets broke down, it took weeks for any to get fixed. Gangs demanded lunch money from the weak; students had sex, drank alcohol, smoked cigarettes and marijuana in the bathrooms, and fought in the hallways and in the classrooms. Many of the books and study materials were outdated. These, along with many other serious problems, brought with them an air of hopelessness so overpowering, it suffocated the dreams of many of the children, most of them looking upon their school as no different than hell itself.

For that, George intended on finding a way to pay for his sister's tuition through private school. He had even gone so far as to investigate a few of the better schools, actually making appointments with admissions officers, interviewing teachers, talking to children walking down hallways and in the school yards. He even took tours and sat in on a few of the classes. The list of schools narrowed weekly. A choice had to be made soon; Mary's school was getting out of control.

Today, as George headed for Mary's classroom, her teacher stepped out of door and stopped George in the hallway. She told him that a man had come to her class to get his sister out of school, claiming that there was an emergency at home. At least that was the story the strange man tried to feed her. The man said he was Mary's father. The teacher thought the girl's father was dead, so she decided to take him to the principal's office to compare his story with the child's file. While checking the file room, the man left the office, walked down the hallway, snatched Mary out of her class, and disappeared. That was about half an hour ago. They were waiting for the police now.

George ran all the way home, stopping people on the way walking down the sidewalk, asking them if they had seen Mary. An old man said that he'd seen the boy's sister in a big car. He thought it was a fairly new Cadillac, maybe three or four years old, with a shady-looking man wearing a big hat, driving. "He's a drug dealer and a pimp," said the old man, pointing toward Brewster Projects. George took off. He noticed a car fitting the description the old man gave him parked in the lot out front as he approached his building. He quickly glanced inside on his way by heading straight for the front door.

He snatched open one of the doors to Brewster and paused in the doorway a moment to catch his breath. He sucked air in ragged gasps, his lungs not wanting to open fully from the exertion of the all-out sprint and the anxiety he felt for the plight of his baby sister. He used that brief respite to collect his thoughts and prepare for a fight if it came to that.

Pimps in every ghetto had the same endgame: to trick or force poor young girls into using heroin. The drug was so addictive, it usually took only one injection to string them out. After the addiction took hold, in order to support their new habit, the girls would sell their bodies and hand the money over to their pimps, who would give them more heroin. A coldhearted play and little Mary would fall to it next.

Mary lay on her back in the center of the living room floor. The big hatted stranger straddled her with a knee in her stomach, one hand around her neck, with the other hand holding a syringe. He struggled trying to hold the girl's right arm still so he could inject the drugs into her veins.

The terrified little girl had been wrestling with man for ten minutes, and the effort of resisting was taking its toll. Little fight remained in her, and the syringe inched closer. The needle hovered a hair's breadth from her soft skin. A wicked smile of triumph spread across the strange man's face when he noticed her weakening. A bone-chilling scream erupted from little Mary's chest.

The boy was still sweating, though his breathing had just about returned to normal, as he arrived at the door to his family's apartment. That was when the first scream rang out. It was a loud, long, shrill sound, brimming with pure terror—a sound that cut at George's heart like a knife.

George's hand froze on its way to the doorknob when he heard the scream. He stepped back, raised his right foot, and kicked out with devastating force. The door exploded inward with a loud crash.

The young boy rushed into the room and stopped right when a sloppy fat naked man staggered into the living room from his mother's bedroom door. The portly man stopped, swayed, and tried to focus his eyes on the scene in the center of the room.

"Where's dat little girl? Said you'd bring me a little girl. I paid ya, Mack." The bloated man grunted, squinting his eyes as he looked at Mary on the floor. He took a step forward, bent over, and tried to focus on Mary. "Is dat dere my little doxie? Done finished the mama. And what's all this damned noise?" he slurred.

"Over here," a cold voice stated.

"Huh?" the slob said, dumbfounded, just noticing the presence of someone else in the room. "Who're you? Gotta little girl for me? I already paid Mack here, but I might have a little extra. How much ya charge anyway?"

"Yeah, I got something for you right here," George growled as he took three steps toward the fat man. The boy's right fist sunk deep in the man's fleshy stomach, doubling him over, then a lightning-quick right uppercut broke his jaw, laying him out.

George turned, and the other man dropped the syringe and stood.

"You must be George," he said, smiling. "Your sister's had so much to say about you. About how mad you'd be. Well, ain't shit to be mad about here. I got some of this heroin for you too if you want it. Didn't think I'd leave my mellow out, did ya? How much you want? What ya say, young'in? You wanna walk around broke all your life, or do you wanna start making some money, some real money? I might have a job for a strong boy like you. If—"

Something in the boy's eyes made the man stop talking. He didn't notice it at first, but it was definitely there. He had learned to recognize it over the years surviving in the streets. Strange, he thought, that it could be in one so young: the desire to kill. What was that all about? Certainly the youngster couldn't have been that mad about him feeding his mother dope and pimping her out. She'd already been selling her body for years. Maybe the boy was upset because he was trying to turn his little sister out. But they were all just sluts anyway. Bitches and hos. What did he think they were here for anyway?

The man would have to tread lightly with this one. He eyed George. "Easy. Easy now, fella."

"What kind of a man are you?" George forced words past clenched jaw muscles. "You sell my mother poison, string her out on that bullshit, and for what? So she can sell her body and make you even more money?

"Then you have the nerve to put your motherfuckin' hands on my little sister? She's only ten years old! You've got to be a sick son of a bitch. You and that perverted fat-ass trick over there. I hate pedophiles with a passion, but you I despise more than any because you turn babies out and have them strung out on dope, killing them before they even have a chance to live. You're worse than any murderer or rapist or child molester. You're heartless, and all you're about is destroying black people. It's men like you who need to be buried under the jail. You're not even human, you're a disease. You don't even care about your own people. You're nothing but the devil in black skin."

The stranger began to relax a little. Perhaps he'd read the boy wrong. If he was willing to do all this talking, maybe he could be reasoned with after all. He was just a little ignorant. No problem. "You still livin' in the dark ages, boy?" he started. "Let me tell you a little something about black life and about this black ghetto we live in.

"Life for blacks is a jungle, boy, and it started long before you and I were born.

"We weren't all kidnapped from Africa by the white man. Sometimes we were sold to the white man by our own black brothers. Hungry and sick, they laid us in the hulls of ships, side-by-side, each slave's body fitted snugly against the next, spoon fashion, belly to back and groin to rump. Chains and shackles, the whole nine. And it was like this that we sailed the ocean to get to this great country.

"When we arrived in this new world, they sold us like cattle, made us work in the fields where we made cotton king. It wasn't always the white man in the field making sure we worked. It was more often another black slave cracking the leather whip on our backs.

"We were slaves in the deepest and darkest sense of the word. There were times when some tried to escape, only to be caught by the white man and his dogs. They were rewarded for their efforts with a lopped-off foot to serve as an example to others who would consider running. To add insult to injury, many times the white master sent other black slaves to chase down and catch the escaped slaves.

"On the plantation, it was blacks who did the white man's dirty work. Slaves made sure the other slaves worked from dusk to dawn in the cotton fields under the burning sun, who selected women and young girls from among other slaves to satisfy the master's perverted sexual desires, who took care of the master's children while neglecting their own, and they did other degrading and humiliating things to the more miserable slaves. These slaves were considered drivers or house niggas because they often lived in the master's home. They had the best clothes, the master's hand-me-downs, and the best food, scraps from the master's table.

"They considered blacks who worked in the fields the field niggas or field hands. The master gave them the cruelest, most backbreaking jobs imaginable.

"Ain't shit changed. Look around you. Slavery ended about a hundred years ago, but you still got your house niggas and field niggas around.

"Slavery lasted for hundreds of years, and after it was over, it just changed names from the plantation to the ghetto. That's where you and I are now, on the modern-day plantation.

"We've had the filthiest jobs and the filthiest life. The last to get hired and the first to get fired. It's an old story and you've heard it before. For every step the white man takes, the black man has to take two, and we still end up one step behind. That's because black people don't try hard enough. Blacks are too timid and too afraid to play the white man's game.

"But I'm of a different breed. I'm smarter than most, and that's why I have more than most. I'm the new *house nigga*: still productive and still comfortable. Don't look down on me because I slang dope and pimp hos. I'm doing what I gotta do. I didn't make yo mamma buy heroin. She came to me. She offered herself and ya sister to me for a little of this white powder that will give her a few hours of escape from this hell. Who the fuck are you to deny her escape? Who appointed you God?

"The drug game is supply and demand, bucko, and I'm a businessman, like your black brothers who sold our black brothers and sisters to the white man for slaves. Profit, baby, nothing personal. Capitalism, it's the American way. Every man for himself. I have no problem placing my feet on the backs of my so-called people to get my hands on the all-powerful American dollar. Why not? No black man has ever done shit for me. Why not sell 'em dope? I don't know about the rest of these niggas, but I'm not my brother's keeper.

"If I don't supply the demand for the people, then someone else will. So you can preach that bullshit to someone else. I've been around for a long time, my man. I know the real."

When the drug dealer stood to confront George, Mary had scuttled backward, gotten to her feet, and run into her mother's bedroom. She tried to wake her mother but couldn't, so she just stood there staring blankly, petrified.

The man's eyes never left George as he continued his tirade. "And for your information, I hate my mother. I always have and always will. My mother beat the fuck out me. She would tie me to a pipe in the closet whenever she left the house and cuss me out every goddamn day. And when I was no more than a few feet tall, she left me. She left me in a condemned house, all alone without food, family, or friends. I was left to survive in the cold by a coldhearted bitch.

"I ended up in a Catholic orphanage ran by bitches and the ass whippin's, and the cussing started again. What's even more fucked up is one of them bitches molested me. In class they tried to teach us what hell was according to the Bible, but I knew I was in hell already.

"All women are bitches and hos, and they ain't worth shit on a stick. And black bitches are the worst. They complain that they can't find a good black man and that black men get 'em pregnant then leave 'em alone to raise the babies. They forget to mention the fact that they wouldn't've got pregnant if they'd kept their fuckin' legs closed.

"They ain't good for shit but three things: suckin' dick, makin' money, and havin' babies. Have you—"

A penetrating scream blared from the direction of the mother's bedroom, severing the man's tirade midsentence. Both the boy and the man raced headlong into the bedroom.

Mary stood next to the bed, trembling. An eerie, hollow noise issued from her throat; despair tied her stomach in knots. Terror threatened to consume her, pushing the strength of her young mind to its limits.

It had all started when the strange man forced her into the big car. She didn't want to go. Her brother had told her to never talk to or to go anywhere with strangers. She knew her brother would be angry with her, but it wasn't her fault. The man said her mother was in the car and that she was sick and that she needed her. When they got into the car, the man screamed at her and slapped her and said if she didn't do as he said, he would kill her. When they arrived at Brewster, she told him about George, about how angry George would be. He laughed at her. But he wouldn't have laughed if he knew her big brother.

When they arrived and entered the apartment, the man told her she was going to have sex with another man and that her mother wanted it that way. Then came the awful needle: the heroin. She knew George would get him for that. Her brother had broken a man's jaw once because he cussed in front of her.

She fought desperately when the man tried to put the needle into her arm. She tried acting brave, but she was so scared. Her cries and protests came out as incoherent sobs, but still, she fought the man courageously. Her big brother would have been proud of her because she did hit the man with her fist, holding it as tight as she could, just like he had taught her.

The tiny child was so frightened that her legs had given out on her, and she tripped and fell several times in her struggle to escape. She crawled frantically when she couldn't walk, her lungs wouldn't take in enough air, urine streamed down her leg, and her body shook uncontrollably. And it continued to quiver as she stood next to her mother's bed.

Mary placed her soft trembling hands on each side of her mother's face and jostled her gently.

"Mamma! Mamma!"she whispered nervously, but the little girl's mother did not respond.

"Mamma! Mamma, please wake up, Mamma!" She began to shake her more violently, warm tears pouring from the girl's eyes.

Mary pulled back the covers, intending to place an ear to her mother's chest to listen for a heartbeat like she had seen someone do on TV. She found, instead, a syringe protruding from the bend in her mother's right arm.

When Mary saw the needle, she knew mamma wouldn't wake up. She moaned, heartbroken; the blood receded from her skin and tightened over the bones of her face just as she released a shriek borne of grief and misery.

George stopped at the foot of the bed and looked at the naked lifeless body of his mother. The syringe, the heroin, his mother was dead.

When the man turned to confront a stupefied George, his hand concealed a straight razor. He knew that there would be nothing more to talk about.

George took two steps to the side, crouched low for a left jab when a razor appeared suddenly and slit him open from beneath the left side of his chin up to his brow—a hurt that would have felled the average sixteen-year-old.

The razor cut deep, cleaving a gaping wound that burned fiercely, and made the boy falter. The razor continued its pernicious work, cutting rapidly, slashing his left hand, his neck, then back to his face. Finally, George's left jab connected, with a right-left-right combination following, and the razor went flying across the room. George pinned the stranger in the corner and reigned blow after blow to the man's person. He could hardly see through his own blood flowing into his eyes, but George kept on punching. He had never hit so hard for so long in his life. His mind went blank with rage. He couldn't even hear his sister's anguished howling, but he could hear the bones in the man's face and in his own hands breaking under the force of every blow. Because he knew he had to destroy this wicked man before he could go free to keep destroying the whole damned black community, he pounded harder and harder. When the man fell, George immediately dropped to his knees, straddled him, and continued drilling his face with unrelenting blows.

Suddenly, strong hands gripped his waist from behind as he continued to flail away at the object of his wrath. Abruptly, he was facedown on the floor with the weight of a powerful man on top of him.

A few seconds passed before George could wipe the blood from his face. When his vision finally cleared, he could see Mary's teacher standing in the bedroom and a policeman over him with a knee in his back trying to restrain his free hand. The officer handcuffed George, read him his rights, escorted him in the ambulance to the hospital, then took him to jail. He was charged with open murder.

At the sixteen-year-old's trial, the teacher and the policeman testified that when they arrived on the scene, they saw George astride a man who was prone on his back. George's fists were pummeling the man's bloody face. The prosecutor insisted that George's fists were lethal weapons. The jury found George guilty of murder in the second degree, and the court sentenced him to life in prison.

Fred Parker's family took Mary in when George went to jail, raising their tally to ten children to foster. When the Parker family could afford it, they piled into the family car and took Mary to the enormous prison in Jackson to visit her brother. They continued to take her to visit her brother for seven years until Mary was seventeen when she discovered two lumps in her left breast. Mary was diagnosed with malignant breast cancer. Mary died at the tender age of seventeen.

On the day that Mary died, George locked himself in his cell and cried. That was the first time in his life he could remember ever crying. He stayed in his cell for seventeen days, drinking water and eating what little food other prisoners brought him. On the eighteenth day, he walked from his cell down the catwalk. Almost heedlessly, he descended four flights of stairs and crossed the base and opened one of the massive doors leading out of four-block. At once, as he stepped outside into the hypocritical sunlight, he fell against the iron railing and tears began to fall anew.

These prisons have always borne a certain resemblance to Dachau and Buchenwald, places for the bad niggers, Mexicans, and poor whites.

—George Jackson

Chapter 2

Jackson Penitentiary 2008. The State Prison of Southern Michigan (SPSM) was the world's largest walled prison. Opening in 1926 and located on the outskirts of the city of Jackson, the prison was one of the community's largest, most secure sources of employment, providing jobs for 1,286 of the 18,000-person workforce of Michigan Department of Corrections (MDOC) in the form of correctional officers (guards), administrative staff, healthcare workers, maintenance workers, food service personnel, etc.

Jackson Prison was a maximum-, close-, medium-, and minimum-security penitentiary that housed approximately 5,000 men, who lived in fourteen cell blocks, many of which were located inside the huge brick walls of the prison. Everyone referred to the area within the walls as Jackson Inside.

The men living inside the walls were classified as the most dangerous of the state's most dangerous. Their security levels were close and maximum. Men classified as medium lived in one-, two-, and three-blocks. Adhering to penal experts' reports that Jackson Inside was too big to manage, the MDOC cemented shut the doors of all three blocks leading inside the prison in late 1977 and opened the exit doors leading outside the prison. The prison erected a fifteen-foot-tall concertina wire fence and installed a perimeter detection system about five hundred yards out from the blocks, connecting the ends of one- and three-blocks, creating a new prison called the Charles Egeler Facility. The minimum-security prisoners were housed completely outside the walls in an area known as Trustee.

The housing blocks inside the walls were extremely long, many over three hundred feet and four galleries high, where all the men lived in tiny cells called cages and sometimes "houses" or "dummies." Within the small space of the cells stood a tall locker—for the prisoner's allowable personal property—a bed, a desk with a steel chair, and a worn, filthy, porcelain toilet and sink with a small glass mirror above it. The majority of mirrors had been broken over the decades, the prisoners breaking them to use the broken pieces as weapons to cut other prisoners. The pieces of mirrors that remained were less than one inch by one inch. The remaining space had to accommodate the rest of the prisoner's property that didn't have to be stored in the locker, like a TV, radio, footlocker, or typewriter.

Aside from the sheer ruthlessness and savagery of life at Jackson Inside, the prison was renowned for its enormous, towering walls. The monstrous red-brick barricade encompassed the entire prison. In every direction, their vastness dominated the skyline. For those encased within them, there was no escaping those unforgiving barriers.

For over sixty years, the huge walls lay exposed to nature's harsh elements. The surface of the walls, originally rough and uneven, had been worn nearly smooth. The bricks, once sought after by builders for their attractive deep red hue, the weather turned gray and black, giving them a haunted, foreboding appearance.

There were hundreds of windows situated in rows the length of the blocks. The windows were small with bars built directly in front of them. So ingrained into the steel, the rust of many decades had warped and chewed at the bars, leaving them as decrepit looking as centuries old bones.

The original thin panes of glass that the builders had placed into the window frames during the late twenties stood directly behind the corroded bars. Decades prior, some power-struck administrator had ordered all the windows painted a lifeless dark green. No one knew exactly why they did it, but the green paint, now peeled and quite gray, remained nonetheless. Countless wayfarers passing through Jackson over the years had broken out many of the windows, leaving holes that permitted all forms of inclement weather to enter upon the men living in the corresponding cells. In the summer, flies, mosquitoes, and other insects insisted on becoming the cell mates of the prisoners. Some of the breaches inmates stuffed with old newspapers and garbage bags while others were left exposed, many prisoners not caring one way or the other.

Today, the wind blew hard and carried with it a light mingling of rain and snow. The men hoped it would be the last snow of the season. The little snow that remained on the ground had a dirty, sooty hue. Small snowbanks melted alongside the long winding road.

The yard at Jackson Inside, one of the largest in the world, contained fifty-seven and a half acres of open space for men to socialize. In the corner of three- and four-blocks, thirty steel card tables, cemented into the ground, speckled the north yard. Each table had four steel arms protruding from its base at right angles with flat round plates on the ends that served as seats. Two baseball diamonds, several sets of bleachers, a weight pit, a tennis court, four basketball courts, and a small cement stage for activities such as prisoner bands, talent shows, and religious services tried in vain to clog the rest of the vast compound. The grass clung to existence in sparse patches bordering the walls. Mostly dirt, sand, fences, and vast stretches of cement decorated the floor of the yard.

Men called Jackson Inside the Killing Grounds. An unnerving epithet reminiscent of Pol Pot's infamous Killing Fields of Phnom Pehn, Cambodia.

No sidewalks graced the grounds of Jackson Inside. The rules prohibited prisoners from walking on the grass and confined them to the cement road and the dirt. Dilapidated concrete, just wide enough for a car or small truck to travel on, made up the old road. The road snaked around the back of one—all the way to eight—plus eleven- and twelve-blocks, then crooked around the chow hall and past the prison gymnasium. It continued bending right, running behind the back dock of the kitchen. Another right and it skirted around the front of the theater and the infirmary, finally ending at the entrance to the subhall.

The prison compelled all prisoners, guards, and other personnel to walk this road to and from their various work assignments, housing blocks, school, etc. Whenever the blocks opened for chow, men amassed in groups as large as five hundred—small pilgrimages to the Big Top (chow hall)—stepping rapidly. Thousands made the trek every meal, three times a day.

The road stayed muddy in the spring. Many puddles, some two inches deep, the result of melting snow, rain, and forever-clogged drains, spotted the road and had to be waded through. A portion of the hundreds of cigarette butts men carelessly flung along the road each day, gum wrappers, paper cups, and pounds of other trash filled the stagnant, squalid puddles.

Blood was always present and visible somewhere on the yard. Prisoners constantly beat, clubbed, or stabbed both one another and even the prison guards. Whenever a man stabbed another on the yard, the victim had to lie still until either help arrived or until he died. Either way, there would be a puddle of blood left behind as a cold reminder of the brutal life inside the walls.

However, if the wound was not too serious, the victim sometimes walked or even ran down one of the roads to the prison infirmary, leaving a trail of blood in his wake. Often, in order to locate the scene of the assault, guards would leave the infirmary and follow the trail of blood.

If the victim could not walk to the infirmary, one of the guards on the yard or in one of the gun towers called over the mobile radio for the prison ambulance. The ambulance, dubbed the Meat Wagon, resembled an oversized two-seater golf cart, with a stretcher latched to its side, which a male nurse usually drove with a female nurse seated in the back and one or two guards running alongside. Because the ambulance had no top, whenever it rained or snowed, the patient had to endure the harsh elements along with the agony of his wounds.

When a man stabbed another outside in the winter, the blood of the victim soaked into the snow like thick cherry syrup spread over a snow cone. Today, as the temperature rose, the snow began to melt and the blood merged with the mud and water that spotted the roads. A guard spotted the blood and reported it to his supervisor. Soon, within a matter of minutes, a prisoner would come and clean up that blood. During a fierce blizzard this past winter, two stabbings in the midst of an ongoing gang war had occurred dead in the center of the road in front of one-block during a heavy snowstorm. The rival gangs battled to determine who exactly would control the drugs on the south yard. One of the victims died. That morning, the puddle was thick with blood, and nearly all who walked the path saw it. Most people who approached the scene, staff included, veered off onto the sooty snowbanks to avoid the bloody mess while others who were aware but indifferent splashed their way through it stolidly.

One man named Manuel Scotts stomped through the water blithely, sloshing the foul concoction onto the hem and shoes of a female nurse passing by. Caught off guard, the nurse turned and glared at the man. Their eyes locked for just an instant. That instant was all it took for the nurse to realize that something was not quite right with the man. She tore her gaze away and continued on her way, faster now, which was a wise decision, because the man, known as Mr. Scotts, had been sentenced to eight consecutive terms of life in prison for eight separate counts of murder in both the first and second degrees. Up to that point, he had served over thirty-four years in prison and, somewhere along the way, had fallen apart. Now, everyone considered him a bug: not the kind found in restaurant soup bowls at times but the infamous caste of deranged prisoners whose souls prison had successfully claimed. The sad state of Mr. Scotts was a far cry from the high-ranking position he held with the unscrupulous, merciless, dreaded franchise killers.

Mr. Scotts began stomping more forcefully, almost maniacally. Several prisoners swore at the man, who in response carried on unaffectedly as if no one had said a word, bellowing at the top of his lungs "Onward, Christian soldiers! March on!" to no one in particular.

Less than twenty yards away from where the madman frolicked in the rancid puddle stood a small building where employees of a giant pharmaceutical company injected prisoners with experimental drugs. The prisoners earned anywhere from ten to two hundred dollars per trial. A tall young thirty-year-old, whom everyone knew as Ice, exited the building at the exact moment Mr. Scotts muddied the nurse's dress. Because no one could get close enough to him to find out his real name, people simply called him Ice because of his ice-cold demeanor.

The board had denied Ice's parole two years ago because at the time, a round of experimental drugs had hindered his ability to walk, caused him perpetual nosebleeds, and left him partially blind in one eye and deaf in one ear. He traveled the compound in a wheelchair for an entire year before his condition had improved enough for him to walk on his own. Over the last year, all his faculties had slowly returned to him. Maybe now the parole board would release him.

Ice stepped out of the entrance, paused a second, looked around, then strolled down the winding road.

The nurse watched as Ice swaggered by, noticing that he walked on a direct collision course with the lunatic playing in the mud. She kept her vision straight for a while after Ice went by then stopped and turned to watch the showdown. She knew that both men would not willingly give ground to anyone.

The nurse wasn't the only person who noticed the impending showdown. Every man near the scene stopped, attention divided between Ice and Mr. Scotts. A test of wills between psychopaths, always an unpredictable event.

Ice—eyes front, focus distant, stalking resolutely—pressed forward without giving any indication of altering his course. Mr. Scotts continued to splash joyously fifty feet away. Ice's approach slowed not a pace—Mr. Scotts may as well not have been there. As Ice closed in, Mr. Scotts seemed not to have noticed him. The spectators inhaled as Ice approached ground zero. Scarcely a few feet beyond the splash zone, Ice plowed on. When he stepped within inches of being splashed, Mr. Scotts abruptly wheeled sideways, kicked his right leg out to the side, slammed it flush against his left, swung rigid fingers to his forehead, and saluted an indifferent Ice as he strode on by.

Some of the men watching smirked, shook their heads, and walked on. The nurse huffed "Yeah right," turned, and continued toward her destination.

An old adage maintained that if a man lived in a house long enough, he'd begin to look like that house. Perhaps there was some truth to that, as the collective face of the prisoners at Jackson Inside was a reflection of the winding road snaking its way through the compound. That was not to say that their individual faces appeared dirty, pockmarked, and filthy; rather, the collective face of the population looked old, bedraggled, cold, weathered, scarred, cracked, and crooked just like the old road that stretched beneath the putrid water.

Men often said that Jackson Inside was the ugliest place in the world in the springtime, probably because Jackson Inside *was* the ugliest place in the world in the springtime.

It was springtime at Jackson Inside now, early March, and it was ugly.

It is said that no one truly knows a nation until one has been inside its jails.

—Nelson Mandela

Chapter 3

Four-block. Maximum security. A large rectangular spine-type block, where the cells faced outward, located on the southwest corner of Jackson Inside. The penitentiary was old in years and design. The constructors of the prison erected most of the housing blocks with a spine-type skeleton while others had an open-block design, where the cells faced one another from opposite walls with an area of relatively empty space in between.

A set of two doors at each end of the building opened four-block up to the rest of the prison. The set of doors closest to five-block led to the back of five-block, and the doors closest to three-block opened out to the yard. Like all other spine-type blocks, hundreds of small windows covered both the facade and the rear of the building. A dull green paint covered the rear windows, obscuring the prisoner's view to the outside world. On the face of four-block, men had broken out or cracked many of the windows over the years. The same dreary green paint that coated the rear windows covered half of those that remained whole on the front. Still, it wasn't often that the men looked through those windows anyway, because the view of the prison yard, the chow hall, and the other blocks only deepened the misery.

At three minutes to morning shift change, which took place at 0600, Angela Brown, one of thirty black female guards working at Jackson Inside, swung open the heavy steel door that covered the outside entrance of four-block to begin her eight-hour shift. She stood on base where fifty-six cells extended consecutively nearly the entire length of the large block. The five cells nearest to the guard station, which consisted of two wooden desks and some padded chairs at the end of the base, had been converted into one communal shower area. The block rose four galleries high, and each gallery contained fifty-one cells.

To qualify to become a Michigan Department of Corrections (MDOC) correctional officer, an applicant must possess a GED or a high school diploma; he or she must pass a civil service examination, a physical examination, and a drug screen. The department also imposed a minimum requirement of fifteen credit hours or twenty-three term hours in either psychology, sociology, or criminal justice.

If all those qualifications are met, then the candidate must complete a month of training at the DeMarse Corrections Academy (named after prison guard Earl F. DeMarse, killed in September 1973 by prisoner Richard Goodard in the Marquettte Branch Prison) MDOC academy in Lansing—the state's capital. Furthermore, they had to undergo two months of on-the-job training at one of the state's numerous prisons, then he or she is returned to the academy for one more month of training. Many of those who began the process dropped out before completing the requirements. However, if the department hired them, the new employee remained on probation the entire first year on the job.

Brown turned right and walked toward the guard station at the end of the block. Knowing that normal operating procedure placed the more disruptive, recalcitrant, suicidal prisoners in the cells on base under close observation, guard Brown kept a respectable distance between them and herself. The prisoners in those cells were apt to do anything. Someone might grab her, pull her to the bars, grope her, or worse. Others might throw urine or feces. Prisoners called it dressing out the guard. Though she never experienced it herself, she knew plenty of people who had, and she knew it was one experience she could live without. Nevertheless, walking away from the bars was only the lesser of two evils. The catwalk to the first gallery extended out only so far, and it served as a protection from the objects flung blindly by prisoners on the upper four galleries. Many times before, men who were out of their cells had dropped paper, garbage, cigarettes, piss, shit, and mop buckets on guards walking out from under the protection of the catwalk.

Brown heard no signals—the prisoners on the base and lower galleries made distinct noises to signal to those above that a guard was in range—and doubted that any of the men in the block would throw anything on her anyway. She had never had any problems with any of them.

Her male coworker came through the door seconds behind her. The two guards being relieved stood as Brown approached and handed her and the other guard their keys and mobile radios. The third-shift guards briefly explained that nothing problematic happened in the housing block but that an incident transpired out near food service. There was very little prisoner movement during the 2200 to 0600 shift, as this period was considered lockdown.

All staff possessed small personal protection devices (PPDs), which they kept clamped to their belts. The small box had two methods of activation: first, a white button in the middle of a shallow depression, to help prevent triggering it accidentally, could be pressed, or else, a plug tethered to a short string or chain could be pulled from the bottom of the device. The guards used the PPDs whenever fights broke out, when they or another guard was assaulted, or for any potentially violent situation. The button set off a manned alarm in the control center that instantly gave the number and location of the activated PPD. An immediate announcement blared over the mobile radios for a predesignated response team to report to the area of the disturbance also known as a Code Blue.

In 1996, prisoner Clarence Herndon murdered storekeeper Tammy Serels at the Huron Valley Men's Facility. At the time, she was not wearing her PPD. Since that incident, the department made it mandatory for all staff to wear their PPDs at all times.

The male guard sat at the desk and made his first entry into the logbook. He wrote his name next to guard Brown's signature, the time and date, then settled back and began reading the logbook entries for the previous two shifts. All noteworthy occurrences within the block or prison during the last sixteen hours, staff recorded in the logbook.

Brown got up to make her rounds. She walked down base and each of the four galleries, checking each cell to make sure a live body was present. If the cell was empty, she marked it on her count board—a thin board seven and a half inches long and seven inches wide with the names, prison numbers, and cell numbers of all 246 men locking on that side of four-block. At the end of her rounds, she checked the work details to find out the whereabouts of the absent prisoners. To find a cell empty that early likely meant that the prisoner worked in the kitchen. Some kitchen details began at 0430 hours.

Toward the ceiling at the end of each block hovered a single-manned gun tower. Three holes in the metal walls of the towers, no more than eight inches across—just enough to look and shoot through—split the walls of the tower. While Brown made her rounds, the guard in the tower sat on a small stool, watching her through one of the holes. The guard acknowledged Brown's wave by holding up the two-finger peace sign.

George heard the guard making rounds on third gallery. Because the block usually remained quiet at that time of morning, the jingling of the guard's keys—which, when not in use, hung securely from a belt clip—chimed throughout half the block. Regardless, George slept lightly anyway. Over four decades in prison had taught him to sleep with an eye and an ear open. On more than one occasion, a man had caught one of his enemies sleeping and, with a hand clutching a spray bottle filled with a flammable liquid, slipped an arm through the bars. It took the guards at least five minutes to extinguish the blaze. Other times, men had held excrement in the palm of a hand or on a folded piece of paper then stuck it through the cell bars of a slumbering adversary and smashed it in his face.

George pulled the heavy dark blue state-issued wool blanket from his face when he heard the guard push the keys into the lock of his door. While unlocking George's door, guard Brown told him that shift command wanted him to clean up a blood spill near the chow hall. About an hour ago, one kitchen worker had chased another out of the chow hall with a knife—and caught him.

George had the highest-paying job in the prison and one of the most dangerous jobs inside the walls. His work detail read as such:

GEORGE EVANS #97855

BLOOD-BORNE PATHOGEN CLEANUP. 24 HOURS A DAY, 7 DAYS PER WEEK. WITH PRIOR SHIFT COMMAND APPROVAL, INMATE IS ON CALL WHERE BLOOD-BORNE PATHOGENS MAY EXIST.

> ALL CALLOUTS MUST BE APPROVED BY SHIFT COMMAND/CONTROL CENTER PRIOR TO INMATE REPORTING TO CLEANUP SITE.

The MDOC initiated the Blood-borne Pathogens Exposure Control Plan in December of 1992. The warden himself had volunteered George for the job, providing him with training in blood-borne pathogens awareness and furnishing him with the HBV vaccine.

George cleaned up blood on the yard, in the blocks, and anywhere else blood spilt, or sometimes the administration called him to dispose of hidden or discarded syringes. Each shift paid him a dollar and fifty-four cents, just as long as he worked on that shift.

In one fluid motion, George flung the full length of the blanket to the floor. He made sleeping with the blanket over his head and throwing it aside when he woke a habit because nightly, cockroaches would crawl up the legs of the bed or fall off the walls or ceiling onto the surface of the blanket. Thus, like many others, George slept completely enshrouded in the wool blanket to avoid the onslaught of the pests.

Wearing only his undershorts, George sat up, swung his legs over the side of the bed, and absently slipped his feet into the shower shoes he kept in the same spot every night. With the exception of the few times, he went to the hole (i.e., solitary confinement, a.k.a. punitive segregation); he had lived in that small cell for a little over forty years. Every detail of his cell stained his memory like sunspots: the cracks in the floor, the walls, the ceiling, the layers of paint that coated the walls for the past forty years. Without looking, he could retrieve anything in his cell and not fumble. Just as many animals had a primal sense of their lairs, George knew his cell; if something changed, he'd feel it.

George stood, grabbed the blanket from the floor, slid open his door, and stepped onto the catwalk. He leaned over the three-foot iron railing that ran down the length of the catwalk, spread the blanket, and shook off the roaches.

Returning to his cell, he made his bed in the obligatory military fashion, stood at the toilet twelve inches from his bunk, relieved himself, flushed, then turned to the sink and washed up.

Before coming to prison, George had always harbored a deep love for his black people, and forty years in prison had not changed that. Even still, George didn't like all black people, specifically those blacks who exploited other blacks, and Jackson Inside housed those in abundance. He held a keen dislike for black drug dealers. In fact, his dislike bordered on pure hatred. Several times his hatred had led to fights out on the prison yard, in one of the cell blocks, and in the school building. In some fights, he battled up to four men at once.

Two decades of boxing at Jackson Inside had never gifted George with a serious injury, but on the yard, dope pushers had broken his nose, his jaw—twice—his ribs, and a hand. He had even been stabbed and cut a few times.

George fought on account of younger, weaker blacks seeking protection from drug dealers, loan sharks, or extortionists they owed money, or those seeking protection from sexual predators. Owing to such, some men viewed George as a one-man vigilante squad.

George belonged to none of the religious organizations that now flooded the system, like the Moorish Science Temple of America—arguably the largest black religious organization in the MDOC, which many staff considered nothing more than a gang—the Melanics (another gang according to some staff members) or the Muslims, Catholics, Christians, etc. He never joined any of the numerous gangs either. Yet he remained one of the most respected men in the MDOC. Men knew him for his integrity, his nonconformist attitude, and for speaking the truth and holding his own. Most considered him one of the best jailhouse lawyers in the state penal system. In fact, many attorneys and state and federal judges claimed that he was one of the best jailhouse lawyers in the nation.

All prisons issued each man entering the system a set of"prison quartermaster"—three pairs of blue pants, three blue shirts, a plastic blue coat, nine pairs of briefs, two pairs of orange shorts, and six pairs of gray or white socks. Most men used to wear free-world clothes sent by family or friends or purchased from a catalog. Recently, the department had discontinued the policy of allowing family or friends to send prisoners clothes, which reduced inmates to purchasing everything out of a catalog. That meant that the prisoners had to spend their own money. Since most prisoners had no money, they no longer had clothes. Now, nearly everyone wore prison blues.

Detailed work assignments required all prisoners to wear prison blues. George slipped into his before he stepped from his cell and slid the door shut behind him. Giving the other prisoners as much respect and privacy as he could, George walked down the catwalk without once glancing into any of the other forty-nine cells he passed. Men had fought, at times to the death, because a passerby had looked into the cell of another man.

As he approached the end of the catwalk, George slowed his pace. He sensed danger. When he turned the corner and stepped onto the secluded bulkhead, there stood a group of five men, all wearing sweaters with the hoods pulled snugly over their heads and dark-shaded glasses covering their eyes. Those blind spots concealed many stabbings and murders over the years. The configuration of the blocks left over 95 percent of the bulkhead hidden from view of the gun tower and the guard station. A prisoner crossed the bulkhead alone.

All five men wore kitchen uniforms—white pants, white shirts, and black shoes—under their hooded sweaters. Guard Brown had unlocked the cell doors of the kitchen workers while making her rounds. They were supposed to be on their way to work. Had the guards known that men huddled on the bulkhead, they would have ordered them to disperse and head to their work assignments.

The motives of men, positioned as they were, couldn't be guessed. A man risked death or serious injury if he chose to cross the bulkhead under these circumstances. Most men would turn around, return to their cells, and wait for the men to leave voluntarily. George didn't. Instead, he walked so close to one of the men that their shoulders brushed. The man turned, briefly locked eyes with George, then turned his attention back to the group. Well into his fifties, George still remained an imposing figure at just over six feet, with a frame thickened by solid, time-hardened muscle. The prisoners at Jackson Inside knew George, and they knew not to play games with him.

George proceeded a ways, turned right, and descended the steps to second gallery, then again to first gallery. Just before he walked across first gallery bulkhead, he heard someone call his name.

"Hey, George, over here. I need to see you a minute."

George stopped and peered down first gallery catwalk. He saw a leathery dark old hand holding a small rectangular plastic mirror through the cell bars with the pinched reflection of an elderly black man in it. The man had used his plastic mirror, known as a hawk, to watch George descend the second gallery steps.

George walked over to face the man in the first cell.

"What's up?" he asked.

"I've been working on my appeal, and I'm stuck on this issue," explained Kenneth Marshall, sixty-seven, whom the courts had sentenced to life imprisonment in 1969 for armed robbery. With a face as black as coal, Kenny Marshall, or Hoot Owl as he was known throughout the system, sat on the edge of his bed with legal papers strewn everywhere.

"I'm preparing a sentencing issue," the old man continued, "and as part of it, I'm claiming ineffective assistance of counsel, but I can't find any cases that say I'm entitled to effective assistance of counsel at sentencing. I got the standard for ineffective assistance of counsel before and at trial, but I want something more specific. I need something that deals directly with the sentencing phase. You got anything?"

"Pencil and paper."

After Kenny Marshall handed George a pencil and a piece of paper, George knelt, laid the paper on the floor, and wrote the following:

> Defendant was entitled to the effective assistance of counsel at sentencing. US Const Am VI, XIV; Mich Const 1963, art 1, 20; Strickland v Washington, 466 US 668 (1984); People v Dye, 6 Mich App 217 (1967)

George stood and handed the paper and pencil through the bars. "Start there," he instructed.

Kenny Marshall glanced down at the paper then looked up to thank George, but he had disappeared onto the first gallery bulkhead, on his way to the blood spill.

George descended the last set of stairs and, without even glancing at the two guards behind the desk, crossed base, pushed open one of the massive doors, and stepped onto the yard. He crossed the winding road just in front of four-block, walked through the card tables, and across Peckerwood Park. After reaching the far side of the winding road, he went up the ramp and into the subhall, past gate 15, and exited the other side of the subhall onto the south yard.

He spotted the blood spill right off. The blood had mixed thickly with a puddle of water in the middle of the winding road.

Completing his examination of the area, George returned through the subhall, this time following the crooked road to the small shed in front of four-block. He took a key from his pocket, unlocked the shed, and removed a wheelbarrow. In it he placed two large plastic bags. Each bag had a wide red strip around it with Contaminated stenciled on it in large black letters. He threw in two more large garbage bags full of rags. Lastly, he placed three one-gallon plastic containers of bleach solution into the wheelbarrow, a long pole with a hooked tip, and a shovel.

To keep from contaminating his state-issued blues, he pulled on a pair of rubber boots and two pairs of disposable nonsterile vinyl examination gloves. He hung a plastic apron, the last of the protective gear, around his neck and tied the loose strings around his waist. The apron started at his neckline and ended about an inch from the ground.

At about 0715 hours, George pushed the wheelbarrow down the crooked road.

"Open yard" meant that any man who wanted to could leave his cell and go out onto the yard for recreation to go to the store or just to hang out. Open yard began at 0700 hours. About a hundred men lingered on the yard when George pushed the wheelbarrow back up the winding road and through the subhall to the blood spill.

On his way he spotted a middle-aged black man, whom he recognized as Sucker Punch, walking toward him. George stopped. Sucker Punch earned the name because he habitually walked up to men, no matter if he knew them or not, and without words or warning, sucker punched them in the face and walked away. Sucker Punch walked to the middle of the road, impeding the progress of the wheelbarrow, and stood and stared at George. George stared back unimpressed but ready. After a moment, Sucker Punch turned and walked away. George continued on his way.

As always, men stopped and watched as he pushed the wheelbarrow. Because they knew his job consisted of cleaning blood spills, they knew that him pushing the wheelbarrow meant that someone had lost a lot of blood. Everyone gave George a wide berth. His work involved blood, which meant it also involved HIV and AIDS. In other words, his job involved death. George had all the room he needed.

When he parked the wheelbarrow to the right side of the blood spill, everyone immediately stepped to the opposite side of the road and moved next to the building. The men didn't move so much out of respect for George as for the blood.

George emptied one of the bags of rags into a puddle, stood to the side, and with the pole, he plunged the rags into the water, thoroughly saturating them, then hooked them one at a time and carefully—because the outside of the bag had to remain free of any contagion—put each inside one of the bags marked Contaminated. It took over an hour to absorb all the bloody water. George then broke the ice on the road with a shovel and scooped it into another one of the bags.

Once the blood was removed and the entire area cleaned, George sprayed the bleach solution all over the spill site and let it stand for ten minutes. He followed the same procedure to absorb the solution as he did with the bloody water. Now satisfied, he pushed the wheelbarrow to the dumpster near the back dock of the kitchen, lifted the lid, removed the first set of gloves—turning them inside out as he did—and placed them into one of the red-striped bags. He knotted all the bags and tossed them into the dumpster.

After he pushed the wheelbarrow back in the shed, George took a hose and sprayed everything down, first making sure the drain in the center of the floor wasn't plugged. Before locking the door, he sprayed everything again with the bleach solution.

He reached through a small hole, just big enough for a hand, in a box nailed to the outside of the door of the shed that contained smaller versions of the contamination bags he used to clean up the blood spill, and brought one out. In it he placed his rubber boots, apron, and the second pair of gloves, tied the bag, and dropped it into a garbage can next to the shed. When he returned to his cell, he washed his hands and forearms vigorously for twenty seconds using hot water and strong soap.

George missed breakfast that morning. He lay in bed staring at the ceiling with his hands clasped behind his head, thinking. About two months prior, a battle between two rings of black drug dealers ignited over which gang would control the drugs in certain areas of the prison. George recalled the incident well. It was during the middle of the week, shortly after lunch, when the violence erupted.

Snow fell hard that day, and visibility was less than two feet, hiding the confrontation from all except the combatants. The stabbing resulted in the death of one man and left two more seriously wounded; one of the wounded had lost an eye. The warden had locked down the prison for investigation by the state and county police. Most prisoners knew who did the killing, but an unwritten law kept tongues still, eyes closed, and ears shut. They never discovered the killer. Since the storm had thoroughly concealed the blood, the next day-shift command had told George to wait until the snow melted to clean it up.

If a man stayed on the front lines long enough, he'd become battle hardened and his system would become immune to the killing. That was a fact of war—or so it was supposed to be. As George lay on his back, he knew that he was the exception. Each new killing affected him in the same way that the first killing did.

As he continued to lie there, George's thoughts about the killing led to thoughts about people dying in prisons across the nation, especially blacks. Aside from state executions, society at large didn't hear about the black men and women who died in prisons at the hands of other prisoners or staff or from natural causes. The deaths of black prisoners weren't worthy of the obituary columns, nor did any of the countless news programs broadcast them on their television specials. Even the black media, black organizations, black churches, and all other black caucuses refused to talk about the daunting number of deaths of blacks in jails and prisons across the nation.

People in the free world didn't care to hear about the deaths of black men and women behind bars, be they violent deaths, suicides, drug overdoses, deaths from medical indifference, or natural causes. Their deaths remained silent; their blood ran quiet.

As George drifted off to sleep, the last words he heard came from thirty-six-year-old Eric Bailey, a black prisoner known throughout the system as Truth. An eccentric introvert, Truth built a reputation of talking to everyone while conversing with no one. Night after night, while everyone remained locked inside their cells, Truth would stand at the front of his cell and read an excerpt from a book, magazine, or newspaper clipping of what he believed to be important information pertaining to black people. He also did this on the yard, after approaching groups of black prisoners unsolicited. After finishing his recitation, he turned and walked off, not waiting for a response, nor did he seem to expect one.

Tonight, Truth stood at his bars two galleries below George and read from a January 22, 2007, *USA Today*. "State prison inmates, particularly blacks, have lower mortality rates on average than people on the outside, the Justice Department's Bureau of Justice Statistics said Sunday. For black inmates, the rate was fifty-seven percent lower than among the overall black population."

> I have begun everything with the idea that I could succeed, and I never had much patience with the multitudes of people who are always ready to explain why one cannot succeed. I have always had a high regard for the man who could tell me how to succeed.
>
> —Booker T. Washington

Chapter 4

The Black Think Tank: a group of black prisoners who consider themselves duty bound to help rectify the destruction their crimes and criminal lifestyles had wrought on the black community.

George and a friend of his, who called himself Samuel Davis, founded the group, which consisted of eight full members and an undetermined number of associate members who, over the years, had contributed research skills, money, time, and input they believed the Black Think Tank could use. The group clearly defined their objectives and procedures in eighteen pages of bylaws that they amended occasionally by a majority vote of all full members.

The men of the Black Think Tank, well-known throughout the Michigan Department of Corrections by prisoners and staff alike, who eventually gave it the nickname BTT, endeavored to use their brains to identify, analyze, and recommend solutions to the issues that caused good, intelligent, upstanding people to conclude that the black community was in a state of crisis. Once BTT researched and clearly defined a solution to a particular issue, George prepared a thorough and systematic written presentation and mailed copies to black-community activist groups across the nation. George referred to these written presentations as the works of the Black Think Tank. During the six years of its existence, more than thirty-five community groups from major cities such as Harlem, Detroit, Chicago, Miami, Houston, Denver, Philadelphia, and South Central Los Angeles had sent positive responses to BTT for its work.

Fellow prisoners viewed BTT as a select, highly intelligent, independent group of black men who constantly struggled to do the right thing and also considered them worthy role models for prisoners and black men in general. Many staff members looked at BTT as a positive organization striving for positive change, yet other staff and administrators had labeled BTT as potentially dangerous and a group to be carefully watched. The Michigan Department of Corrections had them listed as one of the "black activist groups," along with the Moorish Science Temple of America, the Melanics, Sunni Muslims, and the different inner city street gangs.

A full-time member of BTT had to possess a GED or be in the process of gaining one. He also couldn't smoke; use or sell drugs; make, drink, or sell homemade wine (otherwise known as spud juice); engage in homosexual activities; or use profanity. Each full member had to formulate and use regularly his own exercise program, maintain respectable hygiene, keep his clothes clean and ironed at all times, stand straight and look people in the eye while talking, and tell no lies. He had to go to the library at least three times per week to study current events and at least once on a different day to work on a project for BTT. Before leaving his cell each day, he had to look at himself in the small mirror and say, "I will work to be a better man today than I was yesterday."

Their ages ranged from nineteen to early sixties. The scope of their crimes ranged from drug dealing, home invasion, and extortion to armed robbery, contract killings, and multiple murders. Generally, BTT met once a week at 0700 hours every Sunday in the outside weight pit behind the back dock of the kitchen. This was the most convenient time and place for the meetings because their separate work schedules allowed them to exercise in the pit as a group every Sunday morning. In fact, many of the men who worked out regularly and belonged to organizations would schedule their meetings in the weight pit while working out. The weight pit was not only a place where one could find a sense of individual and group privacy but was also an uplifting atmosphere.

A fence enclosed the small weight pit, which boasted a maximum capacity of thirty men, and contained enough weights for everyone. Of the seventeen men occupying the pit—as they called it—this morning, eight of them were members of BTT. The eight men of BTT regularly arrived earliest to the pit, frustrating the latecomers because there ended up being no room left for many of the hundreds of men that would come out to the yard during the next few hours. As soon as the guard unlocked the wire door, the eight men walked in and headed straight to the squat rack in the far right corner of the pit.

At the end of every Sunday meeting, the men chose the topics of discussion for the next Sunday. The subjects dealt with every aspect of the lives of black people. Last Sunday, the men had decided today would be an open-discussion day, meaning that anyone could begin speaking on any topic.

After gathering the needed equipment—a long forty-five-pound Olympic barbell, various weighted metal plates, and safety clamps—two of the men loaded the bar for their warm-up. George walked up to the squat rack, gripped the bar with both hands, stepped beneath it, and hefted the 135 pounds of steel off the rack, letting the barbell rest across the backs of his shoulders. He backed up three steps from the rack and, with eyes forward, squatted as far down as he could. Their routine consisted of ten sets of a decreasing number of repetitions and increasing amounts of weight.

The squat, the most demanding resistance-training exercise, worked the entire body, including the cardiovascular system. Even men who lifted weights regularly made excuses for not doing squats; the only true reason was that squats taxed the body to its limit.

As the men waited for their set, a few of them watched George while the rest stretched.

"I want to tell you what happened to the black movement of the sixties." George Murphy, or Good-bye George to those who knew him, introduced the first topic for discussion. Prisoners began calling Murphy Good-bye George because of his tendency to return to prison so fast that the only thing his family had the chance to say to him outside the prison walls was "Good-bye, George!"

Whenever the MDOC released him, before boarding the Greyhound bus, Good-bye George would call his family and tell them he was on his way home. Within a few hours, most of his family, both children and adults, would end up jumping out of their cars in front of his mother's house and running down the sidewalk just to be able to wave and yell "Good,-bye George" as he sat handcuffed on a long prison-transport bus headed right back to prison. With every new felony conviction for which a man received a fresh prison sentence, the MDOC appended an alphabetical prefix to his number, beginning with *A* for a first-time offender. Good-bye had a *J* prefix.

At the age of forty-seven and nearly six feet tall, Good-bye weighed around 220 pounds, kept his head shaved, and had a complexion the color of lightly creamed coffee. The courts sentenced him to serve ten to fifteen years for manslaughter this time.

"I'm talking about the black movement of the sixties," continued Good-bye, stretching, getting prepared for his set.

"Run it down," George said over the loud clang of metal against metal as he sat the weight back onto the rack.

"Remember how it was in the sixties? The black movement? It was stronger than ever. A revolution in black pride—we marched, we sat in, we boycotted, we protested. It was the day of Rev. Dr. Martin Luther King Jr., Malcolm X, Huey Newton, Stokeley Carmichael, Charles Hamilton, Eldridge Cleaver, Fred Hampton, Dick Gregory, Rosa Parks, Julian Bond, Nikki Giovanni, and all the other great black men and women who played their part." Good-bye paced back and forth behind the squat rack. "Black awareness: the afros, the dashikis. This wasn't something confined to any one particular place either. It spanned from coast to coast."

Another member of the group completed his set.

"Haven't you ever wondered what happened to it, the clenched fist?" Good-bye asked as he prepared to squat. He stepped beneath the bar and centered it on his back, lifted it from the rack, and backed up. "Bullets and bombs," he resumed as he executed his squats, "jails and prisons. The shooting of Medgar Evers, the jailing of Martin Luther King Jr. and the protestors. The civil rights workers, fire hoses, police dogs. The bombing of the Sixteenth Street Baptist Church, and so on and so forth. Nothing could stop the black movement. But drugs did. I—"

"You mean the blacks leading the movement began selling and using drugs?" interrupted Never Black, George's friend, a spirited nineteen-year-old with a bone-thin frame of about five-seven, 135 pounds.

"No, no," replied Good-bye, annoyed. He just couldn't figure this young man out. The boy was so damn weird. He broke his own mirror, took a piece of it, and carved Never Black in large deep letters across his forehead. Plus, the young boy looked like a girl. The boy's face was prettier than some of the women Good-bye had been with, even *with* the scars on his forehead. For that reason alone, a lot of predators pressed him for sex. A few of them had even tried paying him money for sex, but George watched over him like a guardian angel.

"Just listen for a minute, this is important," Good-bye said, glancing at Never Black."The government saw that it couldn't control the black movement and couldn't stop it through conventional means. So what it decided to do was introduce drugs into black communities all across the nation. The government brought in and then turned a blind eye while others imported almost every drug you could imagine into the United States, from heroin to cocaine, from LSD to marijuana, even morphine and opium—bringing in the highest quality and practically giving it away. The black movement became the black drug game. The black nonconformists conformed by abusing drugs. The government's answer to the black movement was drugs of every kind—and plenty of them. I remember reading that a Harvard student task force estimated the size of the heroin-abuser population in Boston and found that there was a tenfold increase in the ten-year period of the sixties. Coincidence? Don't think so. And our people didn't even act. Instead, we reacted. We became victims. We didn't know it at the time, but we sold out. We sold our dreams and our lives and the dreams and the lives of our children."

Every man in the group knew that the black movement of the sixties came to an abrupt end, but they never imagined drugs as being the cause. Good-bye's point of view brought thoughtful looks to the rest of the men's faces. The fact that Good-bye had very close ties with some of the top drug dealers in the state and that he had himself been deeply involved in the drug game all his life added a considerable amount of weight to his words.

"That's what happened to the black movement of the sixties," breathed Good-bye after finishing his set and stepping away from the squat rack, trying to catch his breath. "The black movement was killed by drugs. Most of them allowed in and supplied by the government."

"I'll take it from there," announced Samuel Davis, a mixed man of black and Puerto Rican heritage. For a man in his early sixties, he possessed a 229-pound frame. A half-inch shy of five-ten, his rugged appearance confessed a harsh and brutal past despite his soft-spoken demeanor. Samuel Davis, an ex-Vietnam vet still sporting his close-cropped military haircut and awarded ten times for valor, had experienced intense military combat in the Dominican Republic, 82nd Airborne Division, Company B, 2nd Battalion, 508th Infantry on his very first tour of duty. He toured the Republic of Vietnam, 101st Airborne Division, Company C, 2nd Battalion, 501st Infantry, Reconnaissance for his second.

"Most people don't understand the depth of the government's involvement in bringing drugs into the United States and into the black communities, but I know some of the ways." Samuel Davis continued while beginning his squats. While in Vietnam, Samuel Davis had been assigned to one of the elite "headhunter squads"—strike force units consisting of less than ten men, whose mission was to operate on both sides of the demilitarized zone between North and South Vietnam.

The headhunter squads received orders only sporadically. Whenever helicopters dropped crates of supplies to the units, the squads found maps inside with specific areas circled. Their orders were simple: destroy everything within the circles—men, women, children, animals—anything breathing. Because the squads had exceeded the armed forces' expectations, and after the My Lai incident in March 1968, the Pentagon recalled the squads. However, Davis's unit refused to cooperate. American troops and CIA agents vainly tried to hunt the special strike force unit around the Mekong Delta. Eventually, the countries called for a truce, and Davis's unit hijacked a military plane to Japan and then another to McGuire Air Force Base in New Jersey. Pentagon officials conducted extensive negotiations with them, and after turning themselves in, the rogue squad underwent the most contemporary psychiatric evaluation techniques before finally being released into society.

War hero Samuel Davis had difficulty adjusting to civilian life. Of the 5,711 black soldiers killed in the Vietnam War, Davis had witnessed the deaths of nineteen of them.

While being transported to court by the police on a minor charge, a shoot-out erupted (it was alleged at trial that a member of Davis's death squad unit had planted a weapon in the courthouse for Davis). The fallout left one federal marshal and one Detroit police officer dead and a civilian wounded. Davis received a sentence of double life without the possibility of parole for the murders and fifty years for shooting the pedestrian.

"I'll give you an example," Davis said as he sped through his set. Although not by a great deal, overall, Davis was unquestionably the strongest man in the group and stronger than any man over fifty within the MDOC. "Recently, the antidrug unit of the CIA let a ton of almost-pure cocaine into this country." Having completed his set, Davis stood next to the rack as another man began his set.

"It worked like this. First, you have to understand that there are two kinds of shipments of drugs that the antidrug units make in order to gain the confidence of the drug dealers. One type is the controlled shipments that end with arrests and the confiscation of the drugs, then there are the uncontrolled shipments, the ones where the drugs are let through to the streets. The incident I'm talking about was an uncontrolled shipment. The failure to seize it, the CIA claimed, was to allay all suspicion so as to gather as much intelligence as possible about members of the drug gang. When—"

"But how did the public find out about the incident you're talking about?" someone broke in.

"I watched a broadcast of *60 Minutes*. In 1990, at Miami's international airport, the US Custom Service workers seized a thousand-pound shipment of nearly pure cocaine and found that it had been shipped by members of the Venezuelan National Guard. A Venezuelan undercover agent who had been working with the CIA told the US drug agency that the shipment had been approved by the US government. The investigation crippled the drug agency's operation in Venezuela, but the cocaine was still allowed to go through."

"I read something about it myself," interjected Billy Brown, a coal black fifty-three-year-old from Miami serving a twenty- to forty-year sentence for breaking and entering. Billy Brown, the inventor of a new type of art called Billy Art, had never drawn or painted in his life before enrolling in an art class taught by master artist Herschel Turner. Within two years of enrollment, he invented Billy Art, which shortly thereafter became sought after by art collectors across the country. "The government is backing operations such as this in Bolivia, Peru, Colombia, and several other countries that are home to heavy drug smugglers."

"Whose communities do you think the drugs end up in?" asked George.

"Ours," several men answered in unison.

"And just who do you think paid for this cocaine?" George asked while adding seventy-five more pounds to the bar. The only men besides George who could handle the 385 pounds now on the rack were Samuel Davis, Billy Brown, and Ed Hill. The rest of the men would have to strip off much of the weight for their set.

"US tax dollars paid for it," answered Never Black.

"If you take one ton of pure cocaine and cut it down to street use, how many addicts will be served, how much crack cocaine can be made?" asked Billy.

"You could probably put one cut on it, double it to two tons, and it would still be the best cocaine in town. You could serve thousands upon thousands of crack addicts. Ten to fifteen people would probably die before all of it could be consumed, and that wouldn't even include the stillborn crack babies. Then you have the drug-related crimes. For example, over one hundred homes would be broken into, ten or so automobiles would be stolen, robberies, assaults, and the list goes on," replied Ricky Snowden, a tall young light-skinned man from Chicago, now serving a five- to fifteen-year sentence for armed robbery out of Kalamazoo.

For the next hour, the men continued their discussion on the destruction of the black movement of the sixties, the government's involvement in drugs entering the black communities, and the destruction of those communities by drugs.

Near the end of their workout, the men loaded 650 pounds on the 45-pound bar, totaling 695 pounds. George prepared for his set. He sat on a small iron bench and wound gold wraps tightly around both knees. He then stood and cinched his large leather squat belt around his lower back, pulling it as tight as he could.

Two men, George's spotters, stood securing each end of the bar in case something went wrong as he stepped up to the rack and underneath the bar. Directly behind George stood another spotter, who placed his arms around George's upper torso without actually touching him, ready to grab and help George safely complete the rep if necessary.

Everyone in the weight pit and several others walking outside the pit stopped to watch George. No one else in the prison could squat this much weight. George's legs and back were his most powerful attributes. On a good day, he could actually squat up to 735 pounds.

George got under the weight so the bar rested on the top of his shoulders, focused straight ahead, and with only a brief hesitation, smoothly broke the weight from the rack. He backed up slowly with short, controlled, but slightly tremulous steps, the obscenely heavy poundage taxing every muscle in his body.

All the way out of the rack, George stopped; his spotters tensed. Eyes widening, face straining into a grimace of unbreakable concentration, George ever so slowly descended with the weight. Inhaling on his way down, he squatted until the tops of his thighs broke parallel to the floor. When George, holding his breath and with extraordinary force, reversed directions, the fourteen forty-five-pound metal plates on the bar clinked and jingled against one another like wind chimes in a light breeze. Slowly and laboriously, George climbed toward the starting position. Veins stood out of his neck like steel cables and throbbed in his forehead like snakes trying to escape captivity. Halfway up, George exhaled (and so did many of the spectators who didn't know they were holding their breath until they let it out), and with a sudden bullish display of might, he shot upright. The nearly seven-hundred-pound load bounced on his shoulders in protest to the abrupt change in momentum. George quick stepped the barbell back to the rack and eased it down.

"Let me tell you where the government miscalculated," resumed Ed Hill, one of the first men to join BTT, while removing weights from the bar. Ed, midforties, brown skinned, of average height, and serving life for armed robbery, hailed out of Ann Arbor. One of the stronger members of the group, he was now working on his twenty-sixth year in prison. "You see, certain elements of the government were pleased that the plan was working so well. Then the police started raiding some of the homes of ghetto drug dealers and found money in closets stacked from floor to ceiling. They saw black teenagers riding around in new Mercedes and wearing gold chains and Rolex watches.

"That left a bad taste in the mouths of government officials," Ed continued as he squatted four hundred pounds down until there was no room to squat any further, "seeing all of those young black men with all that money. So what do you think they did about it?"

"I know exactly what they did," declared Richard Smith, also in his midforties, originally from Detroit, light skinned, barrel-chested, with huge biceps, serving twenty to forty years for possession with intent to deliver controlled substances. "The government came up with yet another scheme. This one designed to kill not just two but many birds with one stone. Here, check this out."

Richard reached into his billfold and pulled out an article cut out of the *USA Today* his wife had sent him. "The title of the article is 'War on Drugs a War Against Minorities?'

> If you are black in America, you are four times as likely to be arrested on drug charges than a white person. If you live in Minneapolis, you are twenty-two times as likely. In Columbus, Ohio, eighteen times; in Seattle, thirteen times. Although law enforcement officials say blacks and whites use drugs at nearly the same rates, a *USA Today* computer analysis of 1991 drug arrests found that the war on drugs has, in many places, yielded a disproportionate rate of arrests for blacks.
>
> At the same time, critics charge, the decade-old war against drugs, the largest and costliest mobilization against crime in U.S. History, has focused less attention on drug use and dealing where it happens most: among whites.
>
> "It's just astonishing" said Allen Webster, president of the National Bar Association, the nation's largest black legal group. "Basically, it's a war against minorities."
>
> "It's racist, that's the bottom line," said Representative Charles Rangel, N.Y., head of the House Narcotics Abuse Caucus.
>
> In a study four years ago, *USA Today* found that blacks—about twelve percent of the population—made up almost forty percent of those arrested on drug charges in 1988, up from thirty percent in 1984.

The men went on squatting while Richard read the newspaper article.

> The new analysis found that by 1999, the proportion of blacks arrested for drugs increased to forty-two percent. Among other key findings: In the Midwest, blacks are eight times as likely to be arrested on drug charges, compared

> with four times as likely in the Northeast and West, and five times as likely in the south.
>
> In at least thirty major cities, from Little Rock, Arkansas, to Yonkers, New York, from Peoria, Illinois, to Lubbock, Texas, blacks are at least ten times as likely to be arrested for drugs as whites. In many of those cities, the disparities are much greater. In the suburbs, blacks are most at risk of arrest on drug charges—six times as likely as whites. In sixty-seven of the nation's one hundred and ninety-five largest cities, from Hartford, Connecticut, to San Bernardino, California, the likelihood of blacks being arrested on drug charges, though below the national average, is still greater than whites.

"So what we have here is the government's attempts to quash the black movement by pouring drugs into black communities then enacting drug laws that target and lock up the black youth, which, in turn, fills prison and jail cells and creates employment and job security for lawyers, judges, secretaries, prison guards, etc., most of whom are white." Richard's face screwed up more and more as he talked on, knowing he spoke about his own life.

If there was one thing constant about violence in this nation's prisons, it was that whenever it struck, it often did so without warning and with the suddenness of an earthquake. Violence paid Jackson Inside a visit early that Sunday morning while the men were discussing the rippling effect of drugs on black communities, how dope had destroyed individuals, entire families, entire communities, and in the end, at least for now, an entire movement.

Near the front of the weight pit, a tall nineteen-year-old black man stood doing front overhead military presses with seventy-five pounds on the straight bar. As Richard concluded his point, and at the peak of one of the young man's lifts, another black man strode up and ruthlessly plunged a homemade knife with an eight-inch blade, into the left side of the young man's stomach, just below the rib cage, and quickly gripped the handle with both hands and jammed it upward.

His assailant left the knife protruding from the young man's stomach as he stepped out of the weight pit and vanished into the crowd. The whole grim ordeal lasted no longer than seven seconds.

Paralyzed from shock, the young man balanced the weight over his head for a second longer, then the bar crashed to the floor.

A couple of the men from BTT witnessed the entire incident. Still, not until the young man dropped the weight did George look around. At first George didn't notice the knife jutting from the boy's stomach, but he recognized immediately the horrified expression on his face, the look of a reluctant dead man. George also spotted a different kind of fear, the fear of experiencing the most dreadful death imaginable: dying in prison.

The young man collapsed to his knees and, with desperately sad eyes, looked out into the flow of heedless faces passing by. "You didn't have to kill me, man," he whispered to no face in particular.

Then the dying man turned and saw George. On his knees, he began inching toward him. He had never spoken with George, but he knew his face and heard men talking about him. This man was known for helping black people. Yes, by the squat rack, the black brother that helped black people. Maybe things will be all right after all.

Jumping a bench and nearly tripping over some weights, George caught himself and bolted toward the boy. When the boy could advance no more, he lifted his head and muttered painfully, "My brother." Time seemed to thicken as George scrambled through the maze of cast iron equipment. He watched as a tear fell from a large sorrowful eye, rolled off a cheek and with a tiny quiet splash, hit the cold rough concrete of the weight-pit floor.

"My black brother, I need your help." A crooked smile spread across the boy's face, blood spurted from the corners of his mouth before he fell forward, just as George arrived to catch him in strong arms. He shook against George for a moment, and then his body stilled and went slack in George's embrace. The boy died with neither family nor friend to mourn his passing.

The boy was murdered because earlier in the week, he had stolen three stamps from the man who killed him, a black man who had a long history of crimes against his own people. BTT labeled men like him sweepers—blacks who preyed on the black community, whose ceaseless intraracial crimes often swept from black communities' social developmental factors such as self-respect, self-esteem, dignity, aspirations, and ethnic pride: the ingredients necessary in structuring a healthy community and creating successful citizens. Sweepers left in their wake self-hate, dissension, and confusion, stifling progress and self-actualization.

Justice
That Justice is a blind Goddess
Is a thing to which we black are wise:
Her bandage hides two festering sores
That once perhaps were eyes.

—Langston Hughes

Chapter 5

"Have you ever heard the joke about the man who was sellin' brains?" asked Never Black. He had searched around the entire yard for George and had just found him walking in front of four-block. Never Black told George that he had spent most of the day in the visiting room with his wife and two children for the third time that week.

George said nothing regarding Never Black's visit. Never in his nearly four decades in prison had George befriended anyone to the extent that he had Never Black. Their lives mirrored each others in a lot of ways. Both men grew up in Brewster Projects before coming to prison, and both had mothers who died from heroin overdose. Also, they both possessed the same drive and determination to improve themselves and black people in general, and they each hated drugs.

Never Black, Frederick Brown by birth, a nineteen-year-old high school dropout, former alcoholic, self-proclaimed corner-hustling crack dealer, married at the young age of seventeen, the father of two girls, insisted that he'd started dealing drugs at the age of eleven. In the city of Detroit drug dealers had begun selecting young boys around that age to sell their drugs because the boys were too young to go to jail when caught. The organization had gotten so big, and the money started flowing in such enormous quantities, they began calling themselves Young Boys Incorporated. YBI, the shortened, more familiar title, quickly evolved into one of the most notorious and dangerous street gangs Detroit had ever played host to, and before coming to prison, Never Black claimed he had been in the thick of it.

In coming to prison, a man's time would either flow by easily or it stumbled along, afflicted by unpredictable hardships. For Never Black, it seemed that the coin toss just didn't go his way. His youth, feminine features, and soft and subdued speech may as well have been a flashing beacon above his head. Homosexual predators swarmed like hyenas stalking an injured gazelle. They tried running their con games and strong-arm tactics on Never Black before he could even put down his bedroll. He fought nine times in the first four weeks, losing every time, yet managing to duck any sort of sexual assault.

In one confrontation, while Never Black stood taking a shower, two men approached him and demanded sex. When he refused, one of the men grabbed him, wrestled him down, turned him over, gripping the back of his neck with brutishly strong fingers, and pressed his face to the filthy shower floor while the other man pried his legs apart.

Even though the men outnumbered Never Black two to one, both men weighing at least twice as much as him, the bad boy from Detroit's east side would not just lie down. He thrashed on the floor, kicked, twisted, and fought with everything he had to save his manhood. Somewhere above him, he heard a loud crack, a sound that reminded him of a sledgehammer connecting with the skull of a pig at slaughter.

One of the men released his legs before the sound died away, and soon after, the other man let go of his neck. Before he could even scramble to his feet, he heard another crack. He looked over and saw two men on the floor.

As Never Black started to get up, another strong but more gentle hand swallowed his upper arm and pulled him upright. That was the first time Never Black had met George. From that unexpected encounter, there developed a friendship stronger than either man had ever known.

The same night the men tried to rape him in the shower was the night that Never Black broke a small piece of his mirror off the wall and, while everyone else slept, looked into the fragment of mirror left on the wall and carved the words Never Black deep into the span of his forehead. He never knew and no one ever told him that the words Never Black could not be read face to face and that only looking into a mirror could the words be read. Then he pushed the ashes of some burnt bark he took from the tree in Peckerwood Park into the wounds so the letters would heal dark and distended. Never Black remembered from an article in National Geographic how the Dinka of Nigeria darkened and raised decorative scars on their bodies.

The next morning, the bleeding still had not stopped, and while George walked him to the infirmary, Never Black explained to him why he had done it.

"It's about reincarnation," Never Black began, holding a white prison-issued face towel to his forehead. "I've read a couple of books about reincarnation, about how on the other side we get the choice of what we want to be when we come back. It's written that we can look back at all of our past lives before we choose. If that's true, then when I look at my past lives and see myself in this century, on this day, I'll see the words Never Black written across my forehead. There's no way in hell I can miss these big-ass letters carved right into my own forehead. When I see them, I'll remember. I'll remember that my name is Never Black, and I'll know that when I come back, I can come back as any man, or any animal for that matter, but I cannot and will not come back as a black man. I'll come back as a white man, an Italian, a Jew, a Chinese, or I'll even come back as an alley dog, but I'll not come back as a black man. Life is just too hard for the black man.

"I hope that you can understand, George. Everyone is not as strong or as intelligent as you. I know I'm not. I can only take so much of this hard, poor black life before I begin to fall apart. Bit by little bit, the cruelty of being black grinds away at me, and it grinds and grinds and grinds until there's not so much of me left. And when I look around me, George, I see a lot of other blacks being ground down from the harshness of our lives. Life has ground down even the rich blacks, famous blacks, and intelligent blacks right along with the poor, uneducated, stupid blacks like me. Certain parts of my armor have worn thin, and I cannot be the man I could've or should've been.

"Take a look at yourself, George. You've devoted most of your life to fighting racial injustice. Just think of all the things you could've accomplished if you focused all your time and energy in another direction. Really think about it, George. I'm giving you the real.

"Tell you what, how 'bout I get that piece of mirror I used to carve these words into my forehead, and tonight you can carve them into yours too?"

George shook his head, partly empathizing with the lost young man. "So you say you would rather come back white than black? Life would be much easier that way, huh?"

"Hell yeah, it would, George!" exclaimed Never Black.

"Maybe you could come back as one of those rich white men, standing in the front of the crowd, awaiting the first shot at buying me off the slave block," George offered.

Never Black slowed to a halt. He looked up and met George's stern, serious gaze.

"Would you buy me, Frederick," George continued. "I'm big and strong. The biggest and strongest slaves were the most valuable and went for top dollar."

George paused, and Never Black said nothing. He could say nothing. He felt trapped by those deep-set, grave eyes.

"Or would you put me on a breeding plantation instead? A big bull like me with the right heifer could produce some valuable suckers. If you didn't know, that's what the slave masters and traders called black babies born on breeding plantations: suckers."

Never Black could see the anger and the hurt in George's eyes.

George was angry because he hated seeing such weakness in young black men. Frederick, or Never Black as he now wanted to be called, was a reflection of a good percentage of the black youth today. He was hurt by the tears sliding silently down the young man's face. He knew they were tears of pain, tears George had intentionally caused, tears that he wanted to share. They were tears that he dared not share. He had to be strong, for if his strength failed, he would have failed his people. Without strong black individuals, life would steamroller over the black race, leaving them flat and lifeless as the asphalt. Life would relegate them to a position so low that other races would trample over them, spit on them; even birds would shit and piss on them. That, George could not let happen. He had to remain an unflinching force against the darkness called despair trying to swallow his people.

None of the other men on the yard that day could understand the reason why George held the young boy in his arms in front of the infirmary. Several of the men would have sworn that they saw

George kiss Never Black on the ear when he brought his mouth close to the youth's ear and whispered, "I'm sorry, my friend. I'll be your crutch until you can stand up on your own."

"No, I haven't heard it. Go ahead and tell me about the man selling brains," said George.

"Well, it goes like this," started Never Black.

Since that day in front of the infirmary, George had supplied Never Black with all the books he needed to become familiar with his history, to gain some perspective on his history. He learned about things he had no idea about. He learned that there had been empires in ancient Africa with kings and queens, emperors and empresses, and both male and female pharaohs. He had never before even heard of his namesake, Frederick Douglas.

"There was this small shop in the market place that sold human brains. Three jars sat on top of a stand in the front of the shop. The first jar was labeled White Man's Brain, and it had a price tag of ten thousand dollars. The second jar was labeled Chinese Brain and a price tag that said ten thousand dollars. The third jar said Black Man's Brain, and it sold for five hundred thousand dollars. Now the customer asks the storekeeper, 'Why so much money for the black man's brain?'" Never Black paused dramatically and looked at George with barely concealed mirth.

With no guess forthcoming, Never Black blurted, "The shopkeeper answered, 'Because it's hardly been used.'"

Both men broke out laughing and kept laughing until the loudspeaker blared, "Evans, 9-7-8-5-5. Evans, 9-7-8-5-5, report back to your housing unit."

"I wonder what that's about?" George thought out loud. "There must be a blood spill that I have to clean up." Then George and Never Black turned and headed back toward four-block.

As the two men crossed the yard, George noticed several men furtively glancing in Never Black's direction. He noted the faces and decided he would have to have a talk with them later.

Prisoners had a choice of whether they wanted their legal mail opened in their presence or delivered with the regular mail during the afternoon count between 1610 and 1650 hours, when most prisoners, aside from a few kitchen workers, were locked in their cells. George preferred to have his legal mail opened in his presence. Most prisoners chose the same route to prevent staff from reading their legal mail, while others did so to either make themselves feel important or simply because everyone else did it.

At the four-block officer's station, Never Black stood by as George, after signing for it, took out and read the letter handed to him by the officer. It wasn't a letter but a court order from the Wayne County Courthouse in Detroit. It ordered George to appear before the court eight weeks from the date of the order. The court granted the request for an evidentiary hearing on a motion for new trial George had prepared and filed nearly a year ago. Oral arguments would take place during the hearing.

The motion George had prepared cited several different constitutional violations that occurred during his original trial. If the court granted the motion for a new trial, that would open the door for a potential plea bargain for a shorter sentence or maybe even for time served.

The court would appoint George an attorney if he couldn't afford to retain one for himself, the order concluded.

If people thought news traveled fast in small towns, it was because they had never seen it spread in a maximum-security prison. By the day's end, everyone from prisoners to the warden knew that George had finally fought his way back into court. What made the accomplishment so admirable was that at sixteen, a black boy from a Detroit ghetto, with a ninth-grade education, entered the prison system with a life sentence shackled around his neck and earned his GED and, a couple years later, an associate's degree. On his own, he studied criminal law for four decades, researched and discovered the errors in his own case, compiled and filed pleadings, and won an opportunity to stand again before a judge—a stunt not often achieved by licensed attorneys. Damned right it was big news.

For the rest of the day, George had to suffer hundreds of congratulations, handshakes, and slaps on the back from both prisoners and guards. To the guards, their wishes of good luck stemmed from nothing more than a sense of familiarity with prisoner Evans's number 97855. But for the prisoners, especially the black men at Jackson Inside, George embodied hope. For him to fight against all odds and come so close to freeing himself from a place that relegated freedom to obscurity drew forth a surge of hope from the breasts of men who nearly forgot how to hope in a place built to crush hope.

Despite that, George knew that if he succeeded in freeing himself, he would simply be adding to the list of the great achievements of other black prisoners like Ron LeFlore. While inside the walls of Jackson, Ron LeFlore, determined to do something positive while serving a sentence for robbery, not only studied the game of baseball, he also trained religiously—physically and intellectually—in the field, eventually signing a contract with the Detroit Tigers, a club that ended up being instrumental in securing his release. He played with the Detroit Tigers from 1974 through 1979 and later watched the release of a movie based on his life.

Fritz Hale, serving a short sentence for attempted armed robbery, picked himself up and took up writing. A manuscript of his later appeared as a published work titled *The Detroit Connection*. The last George had heard of Fritz, he was singing, songwriting, and counseling drug abusers.

George couldn't forget Donald Goines. Sentenced to the Michigan penal system for running an illegal still, Goines wrote a book while at Jackson titled *Whoreson*, a fictionalized but deeply personal account of his youth as a pimp on the street corners of Detroit's ghetto. Goines went on to have eleven more books published after the first had been published while he slept at Jackson Inside.

The memories of men coursed through his mind like a litany of praise. Arthur Hamilton, founder of Fathers Behind Bars, Inc., the first program of its kind in the country addressing the problems incarcerated men have in making a difference in the lives of their children, also authored a book titled *Father Behind Bars*; Willie X. Harris, after serving nearly twenty years and teaching himself reading and oratory skills while at Jackson Inside, went on to become executive director of the Michigan Conference on Crime, Corrections, and Criminal Justice; Leon Baker, the first person in Michigan, and perhaps the country, to establish a publishing company while incarcerated, penned a published book of poetry; Mann Lewis, a self-made songwriter, producer, arranger, and album coordinator, in 1986 helped produce an album and cassette recorded live in the Jackson Inside auditorium in cooperation with United

Sounds, Mark Farner, and Pack 3 Studios, which contained six songs performed by him, titled *I'm Gonna Reach My Goal;* and Blue Lewis, a great boxer who swept through Jackson Inside, eventually, after his release, squared off with Muhammad Ali in Ireland.

Perhaps the most prolific author George remembered coming through Jackson was Antoinne Evans, who wrote *Welcome Back to Self,* a collection of short stories and poems culturally inspired by his African American/Caucasian heritage.

George had met all these men on the yard at one time or another throughout his incarceration. He recognized within them a kindred spirit. They shared a spirit of survival, a spirit of fearless daring. Not one of them cared to admit or even hear of limitations. Each one of them believed that to stop meant death. Stepping into Jackson Inside, their spirit carried them through the fight of their lives. They all fought, bled, and suffered, as almost every other prisoner had to do, but their struggles ended in victory. Their amazing legacies bespoke the dogged strength of the black race, a race George loved dearly.

Because of the fortitude these men showed, George refused to give way to any excuse or shortcoming. He witnessed miraculous turnaround after turnaround and, for that reason, dismissed any notion of retreating.

George visited the law library the week he arrived at Jackson Inside. There he met a black prisoner named Lee Dell Walker, who began teaching George how to utilize the law books. From bits of information gleaned from conversations with the man and with other prisoners and from correspondence with James R. Nuehard, head of the State Appellate Defender's Office, George knew that Lee Dell Walker was serving a life sentence for first-degree murder since sometime around 1954. The prosecution tried and convicted him on meager evidence. Lee Walker had little to no education entering Jackson, not having even completed grade school. While at Jackson Inside, though, he earned his GED certificate and partook in several college courses.

Eventually, Mr. Walker became a self-taught jailhouse lawyer, who, in the words of James R. Neuhard in a letter written to George, "filed and won many, many, many cases for fellow inmates. In point of fact, the case he filed on his own behalf, *People v. Walker*, 374 Mich 331 (1965), was decided by the Michigan Supreme Court and established what is known in the state as a 'Walker Hearing,' which tests the voluntariness of confessions at a non-trial hearing."

George recalled some of the other things James Neuhard wrote of Lee Dell Walker:

> While pursuing releases for other inmates, he established his own law library, which was more current than the existing law library at Jackson prison. He became known throughout the prison system as the best. He was well known for being an extremely early riser and his schedule each day consisted of vigorous exercises followed by work on the hundreds of cases he was handling for other inmates. Ultimately he was released from prison based on a motion for new trial at which he had several lawyers representing him followed by a massive celebration which many lawyers, friends, and well wishers attended, for he had become quite well known.
>
> He worked at our office for several years following his release, during which time he continued not only to perform his job, but to urge and obtain voluntary counsel to represent in court many of the inmates he had represented while in prison. This, he continued for many friends both inside and outside the institution. He was a man of extreme good will and cheer. He never had a bad word to say about anyone and, consequently, had a smile on his face and a handshake and encouragement for anyone who was working for the defendant in the criminal justice system.
>
> "The legacy he left behind inside the institutions created many self-styled jailhouse lawyers but at a minimum he was an example that said to inmates it can be done, therefore, let's do it. It was his accomplishments that directly lead to the formation, by the Young Lawyers of the State Bar of Michigan, of the Prison Inmate Legal Services Program whose objective was training inmates to be better jailhouse lawyers. The fact that he had done so well and achieved so much, made it possible that such a program could succeed.
>
> I am sure my remarks do not do justice to the man.

Thoughts and memories of how much respect and admiration he possessed for Lee Dell Walker reminded him of a more recent phenomenon in jailhouse lawyering: Ron L. Jordan. Ron had come to prison sometime around 1969 on a first-degree-murder conviction out of Detroit. He spent years diligently studying criminal and civil law, and he had helped several prisoners gain their freedom and others win numerous monetary awards.

Several Michigan law firms had contracted Mr. Jordan to handle criminal appeals for them. So professional was his work, Mr. Jordan once found himself on the receiving end of a complaint filed with the Attorney Grievance Commission. The complainant, who just so happened to be an attorney himself, claimed that Mr. Jordan was withholding portions of his client's trial transcripts until the attorney paid him for services rendered. Mr. Jordan responded by stating that one could not file a complaint against him with the Attorney Grievance Commission because such grievances could only be filed against attorneys, and he was not an attorney. The commission concluded that Mr. Jordan's command over the law was equivalent to that of an attorney and he should, therefore, abide by the rules of ethics governing the conduct of attorneys. The commission ordered Mr. Jordan to relinquish the transcripts.

That night, George lay in his small bunk, staring at the ceiling, seeing nothing, his mind a flurry of activity. He thought of all the black men who stood and fought. How, instead of fighting against the system, they found a way to fight within the system. And all of them won; they won against overwhelming odds.

Still, George knew that he was not yet a free man. Many individuals had returned to court for evidentiary hearings, but very few left triumphant. These hearings could go either way. The court could either find that your claims were substantiated and grant you a new trial or deny your claims altogether. The fact that he had the law on his side, did not guarantee victory.

For what seemed like hours, George lay there thinking of how he would handle himself in the courtroom, what arguments the prosecutor might use to counter his legal proofs, with what could he provide his defense counsel in order to fend off the prosecutor's attacks. As he drifted off to sleep, his mind continued grinding through different legal strategies and the scenes that could and would play out in the court room—but not before first pulling the covers over his head in order to fend off the roaches.

> I was sleeping and someone put a pillow over my face. I struggled and a fist hit me in the stomach, and I was told to shut up and quit fighting. Duct tape was placed over my mouth and eyes. They raped me repeatedly. They think I don't know who they were, but I recognized the voice of one of them. He was a guard that worked the yard. This was the seventh time that happened to me this year. Now I sleep in a fetal position, with a fourteen inch shank clutched in my hands. The tip rests against the skin beneath the left side of my ribs. The next time someone wakes me at night, I'll ram the shank up and into my heart. I'd rather be dead, than go through that again.
>
> —excerpt from a letter written to author from a black female prisoner

Chapter 6

Black men are four times more likely to be imprisoned in the United States than black males under South Africa's old apartheid system. The current rate of incarceration for black males in the United States is 3,370 per 100,000, compared to 306 per 100,000 whites. Michigan ranks number 6 in the United States for imprisoning more people per capita, and compared to the national average of money spent on prisons, Michigan spends 43 percent above that average. The prison population in Michigan has more than doubled since 1980. Roughly 56 percent of all Michigan prisoners are black males. There are about 1,000 black female prisoners compared to 365 white female prisoners.

The weather was nippy in the prison, and the men on the yard wore sweatshirts and their state-issued blue plastic coats while they performed their daily activities of reporting to their work assignments, going to their health care appointments, just hanging out on the yard, or doing whatever it was to be done today. There were no more than a hundred men on the yard right now.

It was an early Sunday morning that found BTT in the weight pit working arms and having its weekly discussion. The topic: the number of prisons in the United States and the number of blacks in them.

Samuel Davis finished his set and began talking about the economics of blacks in prison. He insisted that the incarceration of blacks in the twentieth and twenty-first centuries had worked to enrich society in the same manner as the enslavement of blacks did during the seventeenth, eighteenth, and nineteenth centuries.

"And just as slavery was legal up until the Emancipation Proclamation, the mass incarceration of blacks for extremely long periods of time will be legal up until the point where laws are enacted to prohibit such racial incarceration."

While Samuel spoke, George sat on the incline bench, grabbed the ninety-pound dumbbells, lay back, and curled them alternately for six repetitions on each arm—an extraordinary feat for even the strongest of men. Inhaling and holding his breath on the up stroke, he exhaled slowly as he lowered the weight. Thick veins bulged through the skin of his twenty-inch guns. During every repetition, he thought about his impending court date. The possibility of being set free sent adrenaline coursing through his veins, and the usually challenging weight, for the moment, felt as light as baby rattlers.

"As I see it," Ed Hill chimed in while Billy Brown replaced George on the incline bench, picked up the fifty-pound dumbbells, and performed his set of curls, "the problem here is threefold. First, we have the black man or woman committing the crime. The moment that person violates one of the laws of society, he or she virtually signs their name on the penal system's roster. Therefore, the black criminal's the first obstacle that must be dealt with. Eliminating the criminal mind set in blacks will considerably reduce the number of those incarcerated.

"Secondly, we have judges who, for the same or similar crimes, systematically hand down far longer sentences to blacks than to whites. If one understands this, then the enormity of the problem becomes at least somewhat obvious even to the casual observer. Creating sentencing guidelines that delineate the length of sentences for each crime in all categories will quickly eliminate this problem."

Whenever BTT had meetings on any preplanned subject, it was a standing rule that anyone who intended on joining in on the subject had done their homework and had their facts together supporting their arguments. That required researching materials in the library or from whatever source they could gather the information. Ed Hill had done his homework.

"Lastly, we have a penal system or, more accurately, a parole board that assumes jurisdiction over prisoners' sentences when their minimum expires. Blacks are more likely to get denied parole more times than whites with the same sentence, thereby increasing their incarceration by years. For instance, if a white person and a black person are sentenced to five to ten years in prison, the system generally makes the black person serve one or two more years in prison. Statistics also show that in the federal prison system, blacks serve 20 percent more time than whites for the same crime. Furthermore, in the summer of 1983, the RAND Corporation did research into sentencing disparities and found similar results. Laws can and should be enacted, which would make it mandatory for the penal system to release all prisoners at the conclusion of the sentence handed down by the court.

"Then you have—"

Ed Hill quieted as three black men—all of them sweepers—walked into the weight pit and approached Ricky Snowden.

Two of the men stood slightly behind the unspoken leader. The one to the left—short and wide as a bull with a compressed torso that carried a chest as wide as his stomach was big, with arms that hung from thick shoulders like mule legs—tried to hide his wariness below a skin-thin layer of nonchalance. The one to the right, tall and slim, with a leanness not stemming from frailty, had taught sinews and solid muscle in his forearms and a stance that betrayed the quickness of an experienced brawler. The man out front, whom George recognized as John Walker out of Wayne County, standing six feet and weighing around 225 pounds, serving a fifteen- to forty-year sentence for robbery, was rather unremarkable, except for a baleful look in his deep-set disturbingly green eyes. When he spoke, his voice smacked of perfidy and poorly disguised hostility.

"E'eryting's a'right, just need a few words wit'ya boy 'ere," Walker declared, holding up a placating hand as George stepped up next to Ricky. "E'eryting's cool."

George grabbed Ricky by the shoulder and tugged him to the back of the weight pit.

"What's up with them Ricky? Why're you dealing with guys like that?"

"Don't worry about it, George," Ricky assured him. "I just needed some squares a couple weeks ago, and I borrowed a pack from Walker. I just need to see if the fellas got a couple packs I can borrow until next week. If not, then I'll just run back to the block and get a couple."

Ricky walked away, and George hung back awhile watching the exchange. Ricky asked the rest of BTT if they had any cigarettes he could borrow, but no one did. The three other men stood waiting, seemingly hoping that Ricky would come up short.

"George," Ricky yelled, "I'll be right back. I've gotta run back to the block for a minute."

George felt uneasy as he watched the men exit the weight pit behind Ricky. He considered following, but then he remembered that Ricky could take care of himself. It was nothing but a couple packs of cigarettes anyway.

Ever since word got out about the approach of George's court date, the scum of the prison started harassing his friend Never Black. Just the other day, the biggest homosexual predator at Jackson Inside, a young black man nearly six and a half feet tall and almost three hundred pounds of hard fat and solid muscle, nicknamed Scrap Iron, made sexual advances toward Never Black.

Scrap Iron was serving four life sentences: one for raping his eleven-year-old daughter, another for sodomizing his thirteen-year-old nephew, and the last two for murdering them and leaving their bodies in a pile of scrap iron in one of Detroit's junk yards. The men at Jackson Inside considered Scrap Iron the strongest and most dangerous man in the prison. He currently held the championship title in the Golden Gloves heavyweight division. He also led a gang of prisoners who specialized in drug selling, extortion, and murder-for-hire inside the prison.

When George found out that Scrap Iron approached Never Black, he confronted the big man on the yard and told him, without equivocation, to stay away from his friend. Scrap Iron smiled unconcernedly and walked away. Word of the brief encounter between George and Scrap Iron circulated through the compound like a wayward breeze. Prisoners wondered how far Scrap Iron could push George. Others wondered whether George had the courage to battle Scrap Iron.

Now George wondered if others were trying to test the waters, trying to cross boundaries they normally wouldn't come near otherwise. He forced the thought out of his mind. *Maybe I'm just being paranoid,* he chided himself as he strolled back over to where the rest of BTT had resumed exercising.

"What about the black woman?" asked Billy Brown, picking up a straight barbell loaded with 110 pounds and curling it, as George rejoined the group."I read an article in an issue of *Essence* about black women doing time in prison. It read that in May of 1994, there were approximately fifty thousand women in prison nationwide, and 49 percent of them were black."

Ricky Snowden strolled down the third-gallery catwalk of four-block, asking the men in each cell if he could borrow some cigarettes until the following week. So far he hadn't found any. Walker and the other two men stalked no more than three feet behind Ricky.

All three of the men trailing Ricky claimed membership in a recently formed loan-sharking ring, from which Ricky had borrowed a pack of cigarettes two weeks prior and agreed to pay two packs in return a week ago. Ricky delayed payment because he didn't have the money at the time.

"I read the same article," said Richard D. while Never Black, the weakest among the group, curled the forty-five-pound barbell."And if I remember correctly, it stated that between 1980 and 1989, the female prison population increased by a percentage nearly double that of males. It also said that approximately 43 percent of all incarcerated women were victims of sexual and physical abuse and grew up depressed, frightened, and confused."

Ricky reached the end of the gallery and had not come up with one pack. He couldn't believe that not one person on the whole gallery had a pack of cigarettes. He turned to the men behind him and spread his hands palms forward."Sorry, brothers, I guess it's not going to happen today. At the end of next week I'll double it and give you four packs. I'll probably have them—"

Before Ricky could finish his sentence, Slim's sharp knuckles crashed against his exposed front teeth. His teeth yielded and Ricky jumped up from the floor, holding his mouth, trying to balance himself against the stabbing pain in his face and head.

"What the hell you do that for?" Ricky murmured past a hand full of blood.

"It don't work like that, my man," Slim stated. "You already a week late. Niggas'll think we're weak if we keep lettin' you slide. You pay now, muthafucka."

Still holding his mouth, Ricky leaned his head against the bars of the last cell and squeezed his eyes shut, trying to ease the throbbing. Blood poured through his fingers in a steady stream.

"By the time the women reach the prison gates," said Good-bye George, "nearly three-fourths of them are mothers. So what about the thousands of black children who must be shuffled around to grandparents and other kinfolk?

"In some states, the children are forever lost in the foster care system, because those particular states will initiate the process of terminating parental rights if the child stays in foster care for over a year. The children catch the worst of it though. Some reports state that there are over 167,000 motherless children because the mothers are incarcerated in either a federal or state penitentiary. The majority of those children are black, and the mothers were the families' primary wage earners. About 9 percent of incarcerated women were pregnant when arrested and gave birth while locked up.

"Look, the majority of the affected children's families had only one parent, which was the mother, and when the mothers get sent to prison, the children are left with nothing and no one. The children grow up thinking that their mothers don't love them, because if they did, they wouldn't have gone away."

A man in one of the last few third-gallery cells pushed a white linen bath towel through the bars at Ricky, who accepted it gratefully and immediately held it against his swollen, battered lips and aching, mangled gums, trying to halt the flow of blood. Fear and panic swelled inside Ricky's chest as he and the three men ascended the steps to the fourth gallery, his final chance.

"Most of the women prisoners are either drug offenders or were involved in drug-related crimes, usually property crimes," put in Never Black. "There should be more alternatives to imprisoning women, both black and white. I'm sure such alternatives could be provided at lower cost with less disruption to the families."

As Ricky stepped past the tenth cell on fourth gallery, he still hadn't come upon any cigarettes. Most of the men in the cells took one look at the blood pouring from Ricky's mouth and the men trailing him and turned their backs, not wanting to get involved.

Ricky felt the situation going critical. The men wouldn't even let him go back down to base or the first two galleries to see if he could find the cigarettes. By now, Ricky could see that the men intended to make an example out of him. He just wondered how far were they willing to go.

Blood loss stole the strength from Ricky's legs, and fear turned his bones to ice. He looked up toward the gun tower; there was no one there. *Damn, the guard must be on break.* He furtively glanced over the rail to gauge the distance: about sixty feet. Could he jump and survive? he wondered.

"I'll tell you, one thing that really pisses me off," George declared, "is the fact that there's no difference between black women behind bars and black women in slavery. I'm talking about the sexual aspect of imprisonment. Just as the slave master and his sons used to stop and demand sex from any slave at any time, so do the male guards demand sex, at any time, from the black female prisoners, who are themselves nearly powerless to refuse.

"Remember Joan Little from the early seventies? The sheriff demanded sex from her, and while she was down doing what he commanded, she killed him and escaped. I don't like this nonsense at all, but it's going on in all the jails and prisons in the state that house black women. Not to say that it isn't being done to white women as well, I just want to make it clear that there is a correlation between the rape of black women now and when they were raped during slavery. And it's not restricted to Michigan's prisons either, it's nationwide."

The rest of BTT had stopped exercising to listen closely to what George had to say. They knew that the exploitation of black women—by anyone, especially the guards in jails and prisons—was a bitter source of distress for George.

"It's an atrocity!" George yelled as his pitch and tone reached a thunderous peak. "In 1992, the *New York Times* reported that over one hundred women were raped and sodomized in one women's prison in Georgia. In that particular incident, a deputy warden and male *and* female guards were arrested for raping and sodomizing black women.

"Just like on the slave plantations, where the black women were being passed from one white slave owner to another or to a son or nephew or to whoever, black women in prison are being passed from white guard to white guard. Nothing is being said or being done about it except in a few isolated incidents. The rapes are kept silent, the blood from their torn vaginas and anuses and bruised faces run quiet, as does the blood of the black men in this country's prisons.

"A black woman in one of Michigan's prisons wrote me a few years ago, telling me she had been stripped, tied to the concrete floor, and raped. A friend of hers was made to stand, tied to the bars, and raped. This depraved wickedness goes on every single day in women's prisons all over the nation. Black women are being extorted for sex in exchange for favorable reports to the parole board or for better prison jobs and so on.

"Raping black women has become an accepted part of the decorum in the jails and prisons of this nation. Sex with black women is like a fringe benefit that comes with working in a women's prison. Just as half-breed babies were born on plantations, black women are giving birth to half-breed babies in prisons as we speak. And that's only for the lucky few. The majority of those prison pregnancies are being aborted.

"To tell you the truth, it's not too much different in the men's prisons. Of course there is no physical rape, but these white women come into these prisons and have sex with any black man damn near anytime they want to—in prisons from coast to coast. It shocked me when I first came to prison and witnessed this, but after realizing that a lot of the men had been locked up for a decade or more, I understood how a white woman could just point and the black man would strip and perform like a stud on a stud plantation. And to hear of some of the things these women make the men do for them sexually, it's beyond disgusting. I can't even describe the kind of sick perversion that goes on."

Only thirty-two cells to go, and still Ricky acquired not one pack of cigarettes.

"Prisons cost millions upon millions of tax dollars to build and maintain. Just take a look at the number of people who benefit from prisons. There are, first and foremost, the contractors who are hired to build them, the electricians who wire them, the companies who manufacture the desks, chairs, and lockers."

"There's the food producers and suppliers," threw in Ed Hill.

"You also have the people who construct the fences and perimeters," commented Never Black. "Millions of dollars were made by both those who made the fences and those who put them up for the forty or more prisons in this state. When—"

"Then you have the gas stations around the prisons," interjected Good-bye George, "that make a ton of money from all of the guards commuting to and from work. The local restaurants, bars, banks, and all that make money off the employee traffic and the thousands of visits a year that the prisoners get."

"Then, in order to get the prison bunks filled," George picked up, "you have the police, the lawyers, and the judges. To keep them running, you need the administrators from the wardens down to the secretaries, the health care workers, the routine maintenance crews, the photocopy machine and computer manufacturers, along with the Web companies that provide the Internet service for the institutions. The number of people dependent on Michigan's prison industry is overwhelming. This state has well over a 1.6-billion-dollar so-called corrections budget."

"The real money comes in with the revenues accumulated from institutional collect calls. Nearly all the major phone companies come wagging their tails trying to offer the best incentives to the MDOC in the form of kickbacks of a percentage of the revenues." Billy Brown had researched the topic thoroughly and memorized the facts. He, like the rest of BTT, spent hours each week studying to prepare themselves for the Sunday morning discussions.

"In 1993," he continued, "prisoners made over two million dollars worth of collect calls from Jackson Inside, with the MDOC's cut totaling 540,000 dollars. Prisoners made one million dollars worth of calls across the street at the G. Robert Cotton Prison and 930,000 dollars worth in one-, two-, and three-blocks, otherwise known as the Egeler facility. The five hundred richest people in the world do not have to pay those types of phone prices, only the families who have no choice but to accept collect calls from their family members who are incarcerated find themselves in that dilemma. That's called exploiting the poorest of the poor."

With only a few cells left, and in them his last hopes of possibly walking away from this situation unbroken, Ricky thought furiously for another way out. He knew that there would be no talking. This was it. If he had any chance at all, he had to take the initiative. He couldn't let them get the drop. Even though the situation unnerved Ricky, the south side of Chicago didn't produce cowards. If it had to go down, he would give just as much as he got. There'll be no one-way ass kickin' this way.

Ricky had already made his decision by the time he came to the last cell and saw that it was empty. Before the two henchmen had time to react, Ricky spun 180 degrees, and with every ounce of strength he had left, scooped Slim up, one arm through the crotch, the other hand clutching his shoulder, and heaved him over the catwalk rail. Slim had no time to react as he plunged headfirst sixty feet to the base. Since Ricky wheeled back around to prepare for the rush he knew would follow, he didn't get a chance to see Slim's head cave and neck shatter against the unforgiving concrete. He died instantly.

Men in the cells up and down the face of the block roused at the sounds of the commotion. The mortal scream that pierced the air as the condemned man fell to his death jolted nearly the entire block out of their stupor. Some of the men shook their cell bars and hollered madly, while others just watched, completely fascinated by the gruesome display.

Rick caught Bulldog looking out over the rail as his friend fell, and smashed a right hook to the side of his head, knocking him to the catwalk. The adrenaline coursing through his veins seemed to expel all sense of fatigue and wooziness from his conscious thoughts and muscles.

The white prison guard manning the gun tower had just returned from his lunch when he saw one black man toss another over the fourth gallery. "Hot damn, we got us a good one this morning," he chortled, amused, slapping his knee. He picked up the 30.30-caliber rifle, but instead of firing a warning shot as was departmental procedure, he watched the show right along with the population. His daddy always said that the only good nigger was a dead nigger.

The two guards at the officer's station couldn't see the disturbance from their vantage point and thought nothing of the clamor they accepted as a part of the job. It didn't help that they were bent over an old radio with bad reception, engrossed, trying to follow the progress of a NASCAR race. If they would've looked up for just a second, they would've noticed a man's brains spilling out onto the base less than forty yards from where they sat.

Walker pulled a knife from beneath his shirt. Ricky had nowhere to run and not much room to dodge, which left him the choice of either letting Green-eyes get set and allowing Bulldog time enough to recover, or striking first, hoping to overwhelm his opponents enough to escape down the bulkheads to base. It was one thing to fight heads up—hell, he was even willing to fight two on one; however, it was an entirely different story, fighting against a weapon fashioned to kill.

Fist first, Ricky lunged at Walker.

George had begun to worry after Ricky hadn't returned. It didn't take this long to go get some cigarettes. He left the rest of the men in the weight pit and quick stepped back to four-block. A disturbing feeling gnawed at his gut.

One of the guards noticed that some of the noise sounded like cheering, which usually indicated a fight. He looked up, and when he saw the bloody mess down on base, he jostled his partner while depressing the white button in the middle of his PPD. The second guard jumped up on the desk to get a better view of the situation. He immediately saw the two men struggling up on the fourth gallery. He sprang to the floor into a sprint toward the stairs leading up to the galleries, while the first guard called over the mobile radio to four post—the gun tower in four-block. Two warning shots cracked thunderously throughout the block.

George swung open one of the heavy doors and stepped into four-block. The constant racket inside of the prison blocks took on different qualities depending on the circumstances. The eager roar smacked of trouble beyond the threshold. As he stepped through the door, the image of a man lying dead in the middle of base assaulted his vision, his uneasiness mushrooming into full-blown alarm. Then two shots from the tower rifle rattled his ear drums. He looked up to see the two unit guards racing for the stairs, taking them two at a time. He stepped forward out of the doorway, as if on cue, at the same moment eight members of the response team came surging through.

Up in the gun tower, the guard shook his head ruefully. There was no need to run now; the fight was over. The light-skinned nigger who tossed the black one over the rail had to be dead. He put up a good fight, though, until that other nigger caught him in the stomach with that long shank. After that, there was no more fighting. The high-yellow nigger straddled him and punched at least twenty more holes in him. That boy's goose was cooked.

The sun had fallen beneath the horizon hours since by the time George pushed the wheelbarrow, for the fourth time, down the winding road to the dumpster. There had been so much blood. It didn't seem natural for a body to hold as much blood as spilt from the man on base. The blood had dried in a large uneven circle by the time shift command had summoned him to the spill. The local coroner and other investigators had taken hours examining the scene on base and on fourth gallery after pronouncing both men dead on arrival.

George flowed through the process without much thought. After making sure he sprayed everything down before closing the shed, he doffed the safety equipment, secured it all in one of the contamination bags, and disposed of it in the can next to the shed.

Exhausted, sighing wearily, the old boxer set off at a slow trudge back to where one of his partners had lost his life. Ricky's death pained George deeply. He wondered if there was something more he could've done. Probably not. He knew that Ricky's death wasn't his fault but still couldn't help thinking that if he would've just went with him, he could've gotten the cigarettes himself. No, he had to stop thinking along that line. It was not his fault. It was Walker who murdered Ricky; that was all there was to it.

It was a slow and painful walk to the shed where George had to get into his blood-cleaning clothes and equipment. Afterward, several men on the yard expressed their grief as George pushed the wheelbarrow down the crooked road to clean up his friend's blood and the blood of the man he had killed.

When George arrived back at his cell, he washed up, drank a tall mug of cold water, and lay down. Fatigue threatened to drag him under. He had missed lunch and dinner and really didn't have much of an appetite now anyway. As tired as he was, still, he would not find rest so easily. No sooner than his eyelids touched closed, he heard the jingling of the guards' keys as they slid in and clicked the lock open on his door.

"Up and at 'em, Evans. No rest for the weary. You got a blood spill on the yard in front of the theater, another one on the south yard eight-block entrance, and one in the infirmary lobby. Let's go, chop, chop."

What a day, George thought.

We're having problems finding the political will to spend $4,500 per kid for education, but we have no problem finding $30,000 per year for a convict . . . . We're closing schools and opening prisons, and I don't think one voter would say these are proper budget priorities.

—Rep. Kirk Profit, D-Ypsilanti, MI

Chapter 7

Even from beneath the blankets, the stench of human feces and urine turned his stomach. George tossed the covers off and swung his legs to the floor. Standing over his stool, he saw it full of another man's waste.

The plumbing system at Jackson Inside was terrible. When the stool in one cell flushed, the waste usually surfaced in the toilet of the adjacent cells. Last night, the human waste from the cells on each side of George had risen into his stool, filling the room with a horrible odor. George flushed the stool five times before the water finally cleared. Then his neighbor began flushing. They continued flushing back and forth until both toilets cleared.

George held down the cold water button on the sink and watched the running water. As usual, the water gushed out a rust orange color, smelled awful, and tasted damn near just as bad. He kept his finger on the button for a few minutes until it began to run colder and clearer. He drank and washed up with the cold water, avoiding the hot water because it was just too filthy and wouldn't clear up for all the running in the world. He even took cold showers. They sold fresh water in the prisoner store, but he couldn't afford the cost.

Pollution overwhelmed nearly everything in the ten Jackson-area prisons. In 1989, George read a report in one of the local papers about a food chain contamination. It stated that the prison used sludge containing cadmium from the wastewater treatment plant as fertilizer for the prison farms to grow oats containing the cadmium—an element resembling tin, used in plating and making certain alloys—from the soil, which, in turn, they fed to the livestock they raised and eventually butchered to feed to the prisoners. The same report also stated that the prison used improper pesticides on the farms, that the prison factory workers dumped toxic dyes and chemicals on the workplace floor regularly, and that sixty tons of DDT and other toxic chemicals were dumped in a landfill on the prison property: a site not prepared to handle hazardous waste.

The state Department of Natural Resources (DNR) reported that Jackson Prison housed the state's largest assortment of toxic messes. The DNR further said that the grounds lodged an illegal storage of DDT and Agent Orange, and that tainted sewage sludge, applied over a forty-year period, contaminated the ground water. The illegal storing and dumping of toxic wastes by the prison was responsible for the corruption of the soil, drinking-water wells, wetlands, and food grown on the prison farms.

Back around 1993, the state attorney general defended the prison by persuading the federal government to vacate a 33,000-dollar fine for the mislabeling of capacitors that contained the cancer-causing PCBS at the prison. A DNR agent found a swampy blue quagmire of solvents beneath the prison. Toxic sludge containing various known cancer-causing chemicals suffused over three thousand acres of prison farmland over a forty-year period.

In the late eighties, a prisoner working on one of the farms had been treating acres of corn with anhydrous ammonia and five different herbicides. While walking through the fields, the contaminants in the dirt burned through his athletic shoes, causing severe burns to his feet.

Damn right, George thought to himself, *I'll keep this button held down for as long as necessary before I drink a drop of it or put it on my skin.* After he finished washing up and brushing his teeth, he slipped on some clean clothes and stepped from his cell.

Today was the third Monday of the month: the day George walked the yard and socialized with other prisoners, giving advice, answering questions, or just engaging in some form of meaningful conversation. Before he got started, though, he stopped by the prisoner store to buy what things he could afford to take with him and hand out as gifts while visiting the sick in the prison infirmary.

When George pushed open one of the big heavy doors of four-block, the light drizzle of a chilled spring morning buffeted the dark tempered skin of his face. The cold wind and rain kept most of the prisoners in their cells that morning. No more than fifty men milled around the yard, with ten or so sitting at the metal tables.

George looked across the yard and recognized old man Baker sitting alone at one of the tables. The thick leathery skin of his face seemed the impenetrable jet-black color of the blackest coal dug from the deepest mines. Old man Baker surrendered a long time ago. He surrendered his quest for freedom and his life. The toothless man no longer washed or changed his clothes, took showers, nor washed his face.

George sat at the table across from Baker. "How's it going this morning, old man?"

"Not bad, pal, not too bad." His voice crackled as the old man spoke.

"Anything new on the heavyweight scene?"

"Watch that young boy Mike Tyson. Don't think he's done yet. Gotta lot of fight left in 'im."

Since George sat at the table, Baker hadn't even glanced in his direction. He was too busy cleaning, clipping, and filing his fingernails. Baker held up his hand, turned it over, and examined the fingernails from every angle. In the other hand, he held a small set of fingernail clippers and had two more sitting on the table.

Ted Baker took pride in having the cleanest and best-groomed fingernails of any man on the compound. Cleaning, clipping, and filing them was all that he did, and he did it for hours a day. The old man's immaculately cleaned and trimmed fingernails was his final attempt at being a respectable member of the human race.

The first day George walked into Jackson Inside at the age of sixteen, he'd asked one of the first men he saw if they boxed at the prison. The man pointed at a big building and George headed there.

Ascending the steps then opening the door, George found himself in a big gym, and in the center of the gym was a boxing ring, with a small group of men encircling it watching two others box.

George walked over to the ring and joined the spectators. Both fighters were in their midtwenties, big men, weighing around two hundred pounds each. Some of the men standing near the ring were placing bets on one fighter or the other. After a few minutes, George walked over to them.

"Somebody back me and I'll get into the ring and whip either one of these guys. When it's over, send in the other man, and I'll whip him too. We can split the take."

The men turned and looked George up and down. A couple of them laughed. "But you still got milk around your mouth, boy. Where's your mamma anyway?" a short pudgy man, quipped.

"I'll tell you what," George replied as he took off his state-issued coat, dropping it on the chair. "Give me two to one odds and I'll either knock both of them out or chase them out of the ring."

The boxers were between rounds, and one of them caught a snatch of the conversation. He looked over at George and addressed the crowd, "Spot the boy, two to one odds and I'll spank him in the first round."

"Right here, I got a spot. A hundred bucks. Two to one odds says the boy here can whip them both by knockout or he can make 'em leave the ring, back to back." A dark-skinned man named Ted Baker held up a hundred-dollar bill.

Everyone fell silent. Men in the weight pit at the back of the gym abandoned their workouts and began walking over to the ring. A basketball game was even called because the players wanted to see what was going on.

After much squabbling, two men pulled a hundred dollars each from their pockets and gave them to another man who also held Baker's wager.

George took off his shirt and laid it on a chair then climbed into the ring. He didn't have any boxing shoes or gym shoes, so he took off his heavy state shoes and stepped barefoot into the center of the ring. Baker climbed into the ring and helped George with the boxing gloves.

Once George was ready, before Baker stepped from the ring, he whispered to the boy, "Listen, pal, neither of them are quick, and they're tired, so take your time and wear them down with body punches for a couple of rounds, then move in for the kill."

What Baker didn't know was that George had no intention of taking the time to wear anyone down. Too much time in the ring always heightened the risk of injury. Avoiding injuries was the boy's second concern; his primary concern was getting some cash. Mary needed money, and he needed money for an attorney.

The bell rang, and the big man and the boy walked into the center of the ring. Emulating his hero, he did the Ali shuffle, bringing a surge of laughter from everyone including the big man in front of him. While his opponent's attention was intent on George's footwork, he, just a second too late, detected a blur with his right eye. George's left jab caught him flush on the chin. The big man staggered, and before he could regain his balance, a right-left-right combination gave George his first KO at Jackson Inside.

The other big man fared no better, and the duration of both fights was less than sixty seconds.

From that point on, Ted Baker became George's trainer, backer, and friend. For the next eighteen years, George ruled the ring at Jackson Inside.

George and the old man sat in the rain for a good fifteen minutes, talking. While the old man reminisced about some long-ago fight, George pulled a five-dollar silvery token—the currency of the penitentiary—from a coat pocket and laid it on the table. Before George could pull his hand back completely, black fingers with very clean fingernails snatched the token and deftly slid it into an inside pocket. Then the same hand picked up a different pair of nail clippers from the table—the pair that had a file attached—and the incessant grooming resumed.

It wasn't until George had risen from the table to leave that the old man stopped cleaning his nails and lifted his gaze to him. "Heard they got one of your boys yesterday. All we seem to do is kill each other while the man sits back and laughs. You watch yourself boy. This new breed don't seem to care about anything but selling crack and victimizing other blacks. Now that you're going back to court, you're a prime target for these thugs running around here. Don't lose sight of your goal, pal. Stay focused."

George didn't even have time to reply before the old man again engrossed himself in his manicuring—one hand stretched in front of his face, flipping it from one side to the other. Unfortunately, because the cloudy sky allowed only the least bit of light to filter through, hindering his scrutiny, the old man sighed, picked up another pair of clippers, and began filing again.

George felt a pang of sympathy for the old man and others like him. It was certain that he was going to die in prison; the most horrible death imaginable would be the fate of his old friend.

Officially, Michigan was supposed to be a state that didn't impose the death penalty, but George knew better. Though Michigan did not utilize the gas chamber, firing squad, lethal injection, electric chair, or hanging by the neck, Michigan, like other states that claimed to have no death penalty, killed prisoners by attrition: holding them in prison until they die of natural causes. Death by attrition, a punishment employed by many of the nation's prisons, the system inflicted upon black prisoners for every crime from murder to petty theft. Though society didn't recognize this death penalty—instead choosing to turn its collective back on its existence—black prisoners faced the ugly possibility of falling victim to this death each day they existed within this nation's penal system.

As George walked through the small group of tables, he noticed three young black men standing near the outside stage in front of three-block. They were standing around talking and listening to a large radio sitting on the stage. The radio had a clear plastic garbage bag over it to protect it from the light rain. As George approached, the men fell silent.

"What's up, bro?" the tallest of them asked when George stopped in front of the group.

"Not a whole lot," George responded, "just walking around trying to find some good conversation. Never know who I might learn something from."

"There's nothing new here man, just chillin'," one of the men said as he began slow dancing, eyes closed, arms embracing a woman who wasn't there. "Just chillin' on out."

"Listen, let me ask you brothers something. What are you doing in here to pass your time? I mean, what positive things are you doing with your life?"

"Got my GED, man," answered one.

"Me too," said another.

"Me? I ain't got nothin', man," replied the one on the dance floor.

"But what about when you get out, brothers, how are you preparing yourself for the current job market? How are you going to support yourself?" asked George.

"Got me an ol' lady, man. She's my support." The young man stopped dancing, opened his eyes, and looked at George squarely. "I'm a player, my man. I play the women. Anything wrong with that?"

"To be quite honest, there's a lot wrong with it." As George spoke, he reached over and turned down the radio, drawing several frowns from the small crowd. "Listen, a man is supposed to make a living for himself, not live off a woman. Yes, it's wrong without question. When a man sets out to live off of a woman, he abandons the common decency standard of humanity and adopts the standard of the parasite and the bloodsucker."

"Hold on now," the dancer declared, pulling his tinted glasses down to the tip of nose, sizing George up from feet to forehead, yet being careful not to seem too aggressive. Most men in the prison knew George's reputation for the longest stint as Golden Gloves champ at Jackson Inside. "What you tryin' to say about me?" he said aloud, trying to maintain some of his swagger though his uncertainty showed plainly.

"I'm not trying to say anything about you, my brother. This is a reality check."

"But I'm a player, man, you know the score: a woman's money or no money. Play or die," he stated, smiling as if that one phrase should be enough to end the debate.

"Besides," he continued anyway, "I know a lot of brothers who got they GED and tried to get into one of them vocational trade classes, but the racist-ass classification director denied 'em. You walk around and all you see is black faces in prison. But you look in them classrooms, you might see three or four black faces outta twenty. If they don't want to let us in, I say fuck 'em. I'll play the hos."

A long time ago, George had learned that a wise man didn't argue with, belittle, or demean a man in a group setting. That was one of the quickest ways to provoke violence. Even the biggest coward in the world just might fight to the death if challenged in a group setting. Though the young man with the tinted glasses was smiling, George didn't think it went beyond the muscles in his face, not after George challenged his manhood. Still, George had to make what he believed to be an important point. Point being made, it would be foolish to continue on that line.

"Listen closely." George now spoke to the entire group. "All of you are going to get out someday. My question is, what are you going to do out there? Matter of fact, don't even bother answering. I'll tell you what's going to happen. First, if you don't have marketable skills to enter the current job market, you're going to discover a hostile world. One where you don't have the means to put a roof over your head or food in your mouth. Secondly, you'll end up needing some quick, easy cash, which far too many times is only obtained through drugs, robbery, burglary, et cetera. You see what I'm getting at?"

"I'm taking advantage of one of the vocational programs," one of them said. "I thought that since I've always been good with my hands, I might as well enroll in the building-trades program. I've got children out there, man, children that need me. I've got to make it when I get out. I don't have a choice.

"This," the man swept his arm around in a semicircle indicating the entire prison, "is no choice. This is nothing! This is death! It's my first time in prison, and what landed me here is exactly as you said: a need for quick, easy money.

"Jobs are already hard to find for a black inner city male, then on top of that, to have 'high school dropout' written on your resumé, you've nearly sealed your fate. Hell, I'm talking about before I came to prison. Now when I get out, add 'ex-convict' to my resumé, and I can virtually kiss my ass good-bye, excuse my language.

"But I'm no dummy, see," he continued, tapping his temple with his index finger. "I know how to use this. I don't need to continue banging my head against a wall. So I enrolled in the building-trades program. I'm at the top of my class. I've established a workable plan that I'll implement upon release."

"I'm in the paralegal program here," one of the others chimed in on the other man's heels. "I'll become a paralegal and get a good job in a law firm when I go home. I've got a son out there. The state just closed the school my son attended, and we've got to find another one for him. I've got to get out and support him and his mother. I've got to show my son the right way. I don't want him to pass through the prison system or to die in prison. I'll make it when I get out. I know the consequences if I don't. If I don't succeed, I'll end up in prison again or in someone's cemetery.

"But I'm going to make it for another reason too. I want to set an example for young black boys. I want to show them that success can be achieved by someone from the black ghetto. I want to be in a position where I can tell them that selling drugs is not only criminal, but it's immoral. The bottom line is that I need to teach youngsters that crime is simply the wrong thing to do. Period. There's a need to show young blacks that working inside the system as opposed to outside of it is not only morally correct, but it's the manly thing to do."

George was very impressed with the last two of the three young men in the group. If the two made it when they got out, then two out of three wasn't bad because over 70 percent of black males between the ages of seventeen and thirty who are released from prison return with new convictions and longer sentences, perpetuating the vicious and deadly cycle of black man in prison, then on parole, then in prison again, back out on parole, and right back in prison.

Before George left, one of the young men asked him to leave them with something to think about. "You've been around for a long time, and you're known as a man who really tries to help prisoners, especially blacks. Leave us with some of that knowledge and wisdom you've gained over the years, something that we can work with."

George smiled and looked at the young man. "It's very simple, just live your life the right way. All of you know what's right and what's wrong. It's right to do good and wrong to do evil. Each morning when you wake up, you must do so with a life plan already in place. It must be a positive plan that will contribute to moving your life forward.

"When you get out of bed, know that for this entire day, you intend to take the best within you and give it to the world. Giving your best means giving your best in everything you do, without exception. No act is too big and no act is too small when it comes to giving your best. Giving your best means living your life the right way, be it brushing your teeth, washing your face, reading a book, talking to a person, or even sitting in a chair.

"Contact your dentist, get a checkup, get your teeth cleaned. While you're there, find out the best way to brush your teeth. Find out what's considered overbrushing and what's considered underbrushing. You should brush your teeth every time you finish eating, no matter what it is. However, seeing as this is not very practical, try at least brushing your teeth thoroughly in the morning and before you go to bed and flossing your teeth on a daily basis. The best order for cleaning is to brush first and floss afterwards to prevent loose particles from being pushed down under the gum line by the floss, which can lead to gum disease. And don't neglect the backs of the teeth. Make sure you use a soft-bristled brush, with minimum pressure, brush in a circular motion, and keep the bristles angled toward the gum line to prevent damaging the gums.

"When washing your face, don't just splash water on it, use soap and a clean washcloth. Wash gently and in circular motions. When you're done, splash cold water on your face to close the pores.

"When you read, always try reading a book that will leave you feeling better and perhaps with a bit more knowledge. When reading, try concentrating and don't let your mind wander. Focus on what you're reading. Not only will this improve the quality of your reading, it's also good mental exercise. Likewise, try improving your speed. All of this raises the quality of your reading skills.

"When you talk to people, don't swear. Instead, try using proper language. Learn to listen to the person you're conversing with: you just might learn something useful. Don't waste time talking about nonsense, but try keeping to subjects that have substance. Make yourself known as a wonderful conversationalist—this will make cultured individuals want to seek you out and dialogue with you. Wise men always surround themselves with people of substance.

"Pay careful attention to your posture. Poor posture often leads to back pain, inhibits your breathing, and fatigues several muscle groups. Good posture should be practiced at all times because it protects and supports several parts of the body and it displays vitality. Having correct posture means keeping your tendons, bones, and ligaments in their natural positions. This reduces stress on your back. While standing, correct posture is demonstrated by keeping your head high, chest forward, while slightly pulling in your shoulders and behind. And tuck your chin.

"There is even proper posture for sleeping. The best position for sleeping is to sleep on your side with your legs bent and drawn up slightly with a pillow or some type of cushion between your knees. If you sleep on your back, you should put a pillow or cushion under your knees to keep a slight bend in them. Sleeping on your stomach is the worst position, but if you must, you should most definitely sleep with some form of cushion under your abdomen.

"You should wear proper-fitting shoes, as poorly fitting shoes can cause posture problems. Tell the women you know that high-heeled shoes can affect good posture."

George took a few steps over to the stage and sat. His conversation was so captivating, which was not often found in prison, they hung on every word. They found his speech inspiring and profound, and despite the fact that several minutes had passed since he started speaking, they were in no hurry.

"When sitting in a chair, don't slouch. Not only does it look bad, slouching is bad for you. Sit upright. It shows class, and it is good for your back. Your thighs should be parallel to the ground, and your head should not be slumped forward. An upright position also works the lower abs and makes them stronger, so you may as well get whatever benefit you can from it since you're doing nothing but sitting anyway. Accepting anything free that moves you forward is intelligent. Exhibiting intelligence is a sign that one is putting forth his best efforts. A man who puts forth his best efforts is a man who is living the right way.

"Basically, I have this to say, if you put forth your best effort in everything you do, your life will move forward prosperously. Each day and several times during the day, say to yourself, 'I shall live a life of excellence. Regardless of the obstacles and pitfalls in my way, I will exercise prudence and fortitude. I will live life the right way.'

"Confront all barriers with your best fight. Do not permit yourself to backslide.

"Do not—and this is important to remember—do not engage in every fight that is brought to your doorstep. Some fights are not worthy of your attention. For example, do not fight a fool. Remember, Jesus could cure the leper, he gave sight to the blind, he could even return the dead to life. Yet the fool he could not help. Do not attempt what Jesus could not accomplish. Some fights can only be won by walking away.

"Understand what it means to be an individual. Be your own man. When you make a choice, be certain that the choice is yours and not what someone else wants of you. Do not bend to peer pressure. Do not let anyone pull your strings. Be no man's puppet. When you are your own man, you are what real men call a man's man. A man's man can only exist if he lives life the right way."

When his speech was over, the men felt compelled to shake his hand. One man went so far as to give him a partial embrace and thanked him for the inspiring words.

Later, George found another group of young men who never really did figure out how the conversation turned from basketball to enrolling in the narcotics, alcoholics, and assaultive offenders' psychotherapy programs. The conversation was, nevertheless, quite fulfilling. One of the men even asked him to stay for a while.

On his way to the prisoner store, someone pounced on George's back, arms clutching his neck and legs, clinging to his waist. George fell to his knees and twisted sideways to the asphalt, pinning his attacker to the ground.

It was Never Black, continuing a game he'd started almost a year ago. Sneaking up behind George had become a favorite pastime of the young man. George abhorred playing games, especially the physical type, which could provoke the guards into assuming the men were fighting. If that happened, the guards would come running to break it up and, despite the fact that they were just fooling around, put both him and Never Black in the hole. Regardless, the game was harmless in itself, and George rather enjoyed the short break in his austere existence.

"I got you this time," chortled Never Black as George pinned him in the grass. "I could've had you."

"Not hardly. I heard you coming." Which was true. George knew Never Black's footsteps even when he half heard them; the game had been going on for so long. He heard his steps quicken and was fully aware of what Never Black was up to.

"Where are you going, George?" asked Never Black as they stood brushing the grass and dirt off their clothes.

"To the store and then to the infirmary."

"Oh, that's right. Today *is* Monday, and you're making your rounds. Let me roll with you? You never let me go when you do your goodwill thing."

Never Black's voice grew excited as the thought of making rounds with George turned over in his head. He really wanted to tag along because he liked being around George. Not only was George his best friend, but George's stature inside the prison increased the respect Never Black received from other prisoners. Men who would have never noticed him otherwise knew and admired the fact that George took him as a friend. Never Black, proud to have a friend as intelligent and knowledgeable as George, took complete advantage of the fact that George was willing to share that knowledge with him. George had told him once that a man with knowledge had a duty to share it with others.

Of all the prisoners at Jackson Inside, only George had ever obtained permission to visit prisoners inside the new prison infirmary called Duane Waters. George had always gone to the old infirmary and visited the prisoners there, taking them what little odds and ends he could afford. Once the prison constructed the new hospital, the procedure carried over. The guards at the new infirmary were the same guards that worked the old infirmary. They never asked George for a pass, knowing he'd not have one. They also knew that if they called the control center, it would give the okay anyway. So whenever George entered the hospital with a bag of groceries, the guards just waived him through the gates.

Except this time Never Black wanted to accompany him. After he and Never Black left the prisoner store, they headed toward the control center to try to obtain permission.

The two men strolled down the middle of the old road engaged in casual conversation. The prisoner store was annexed to the back of the gym in a building that also housed the quartermaster and a small warehouse. They followed the winding road as it curved to the back of the gym and walked for about twenty yards to the wire gate. Never Black opened it and let George through to a short sidewalk that they followed to a large steel door leading to the waiting area of the prisoner store.

As George and Never Black stepped into the small room, they faced nine men standing around. One of them was Scrap Iron, whose huge back was toward the two friends. Upon sensing the new arrivals, Scrap Iron turned around, eyeing the two men distrustfully. He scrutinized, slowly and seductively, up and down the full length of Never Black's body then leered menacingly into his eyes. There, Scrap Iron instantly recognized weakly concealed fear. Scrap Iron smiled lewdly.

George immediately sensed the wrongness of the situation. He glanced down the hallway and noted the empty store line. Prison policy did not allow for an occupied waiting room absent a full store line.

The nine men occupying a room that should've been clear made George and Never Black halt, unmoving. It took only a moment for the two men to comprehend the danger. The very horror of the scene made Never Black want to weep. Instead, his mouth filled with bile seconds before his last meal painted the floor in front of him.

When I think of the profundity of the injustices done to black people in America, I feel horror I cannot easily describe. I would not be a man if I believed that blacks are not justified socially in treating any and all white people in this society with violence and hatred. Even as I write this I am aware of white boys being raped and murdered in prisons.

—Jack Abbott, *In the Belly of the Beast*

Chapter 8

It was a scene from one of the most twisted corners of hell. A human auction—young white men being sold to the highest bidder. Young blacks would face the same fate too, but that was rare. Today's word on the prison yard: whites only.

Often, when attractive young white males entered the prison system, gangs of extortionists, drug dealers, homosexuals, or whoever could get to them first would try to stake their claim. The predators would approach one and declare bluntly that he belonged to them, and as their property, he'd perform sexual favors at their whim, turn over any and all money he received, and do anything else they asked of him. If the young man refused to cooperate, he'd be forced to fight. Many of the young men who fought in the beginning eventually succumbed in the end. Nevertheless, there were those who fought too hard and for too long, leaving the gangs no choice but to give up the chase. Southern poor white trash, otherwise known as the hillbillies, were those who continued to fight. When some of the hillbillies merged into cliques, even large gangs dealt with them cautiously, knowing they could turn dangerous at a moment's notice.

Then there were the white killers. No matter the youth or the apparent susceptibility—whether due to feminine features or boyish figures—the white killers would yield their manhood to no one. Not long ago, a black man by the name of Milton "Dickie" Hunt had tried pressing John Jack Mackay—the wrong white guy. One day, while Dickie slept in his cell in four-block, Mackay doused him with gasoline, tossed in a match, and burned over half his body, confining him to a wheelchair for several years. From that point on, everyone called Dickie the Krispie Kritter.

At five in the morning, Scrap Iron roused himself from a restless slumber. He washed up, ate three bowls of oatmeal, and lay back on his bed, hands clasped behind his neck.

Scrap Iron was anxious. There was nothing on earth more exhilarating, more satisfying, or more vindictive than the event that was set to take place later that morning. The auction. The selling of slaves: tender young white boys.

The big fellow had extorted men, sold drugs, and loan-sharked for the past year, with the sole purpose of hoarding enough money to dominate the auction. He scrimped up on a nice little sum of twelve hundred dollars worth of prison tokens and hundred-dollar bills.

Scrap Iron was the first out of the block when the guards called breakfast. He couldn't swallow fast enough and damn near choked a time or two as he shoveled buttered toast and bran flakes down his throat. As he exited the Big Top, he met up with two of the most dangerous members of his extortion ring: serial killer Kenneth Spears and Gerrel Barnes, killer of food service supervisor Doris Taylor at Lapeer Correctional Facility in 1998, the day before she was to retire. Together they walked the back-forty (the huge yard behind the building housing the prisoner store), waiting to get the signal that the auction was to begin. Scrap Iron watched a man with green sweatpants as he stepped through the yard gate and immediately started jogging toward them. As the jogger neared, Scrap Iron's pulse quickened. The man trotted past and, without directly addressing anyone, announced,"Waiting room. Prisoner store. Five minutes."

Scrap Iron and his men could barely keep themselves from breaking into a reckless dash.

When they arrived at the store, they saw four men already there, two black and two white. Before Scrap Iron could even make it half way across the room, the door crashed open behind him, and two more black men ambled through. One of the new arrivals hustled past Scrap Iron and his boys, yelling, "I want this here white boy," pointing at one of the young white men cowering in the corner. "I got top dollar. He's mine. Let's go, boy,"he finished, wrapping a ham fist with a vicelike grip around the boy's upper right arm.

The young white boy was nineteen-year-old Charles Mason, serving a two- to fifteen-year sentence for breaking and entering. A black man and a Mexican had raped Mason in the county jail, all the while telling him that it was payback for the hundreds of years of wickedness and humiliation heaped on blacks during slavery.

"You just calm down and wait till the bidding gets started," interrupted Scrap Iron. He'd be damned if anyone bought one these fine-ass young boys before he even got the chance to bid.

"Hold on now," a tall medium-built black man began, "no need to argue. I'm the auctioneer, and the bidding begins now. First up."

No one budged. The auctioneer grabbed Mason by the arm and jerked him to the middle of the floor directly beneath an overhead light. One of the bidders stepped forward and told the auctioneer to have the boy drop his pants for inspection.

"Yeah, make him drop them drawers," yelled Scrap Iron, with an intoxicated grin on his face, his enthusiasm bubbling over.

The young man stood motionless. The auctioneer slapped the young man across the face, but he still remained paralyzed. Scrap Iron's huge palm reared back and connected flush against the boy's cheek, knocking him violently to the floor. Without hesitating, Scrap Iron reached down, entangled his fingers in the young boy's hair, and hefted him effortlessly to his feet. The boy unbuckled his belt and dropped his pants.

"The shorts, off with 'em!" an eager bidder barked.

All dignity lost, the boy removed every scrap of his clothing and stood there on showcase, naked as the day he was born.

The crowd had swelled slightly since the auction had commenced, and a tall inky-black newcomer, John Allen, nicknamed Mississippi, lifted the young man's penis then his testicles, inspecting for *something* he knew but not sure of what exactly *it* was. Earlier in the week, when he first got word of the upcoming auction, he decided to go to the library and read up on slave auctions. He studied the procedure the white slave masters used, and this was one of the more humiliating. He never found out what exactly they were looking for; he was just ecstatic at having the opportunity to spread the love. He hated anything dealing with white people, and a chance to literally buy a young white boy seemed like the fulfillment of a fantasy. His plan was to pimp him out, turn his miserable existence into a waking nightmare, and eventually, kill him. After what white people had done and continued to do to his people, killing the white boy didn't even tickle his conscience.

Mississippi spun the young man around, bent him over, and made him spread his cheeks.

"We'll start the bidding at a hundred."

"Right here, I got it," blurted the broad-shouldered brown-skinned man who first laid claim to the boy.

"A hundred. Do I hear one fifty?"

"One fifty, right here!"

"I've got three," hollered Scrap Iron.

Broad shoulders frowned then angrily said, "I'll raise it a hundred dollars."

"I'll pay seven fifty," Scrap Iron pronounced arrogantly; he knew it would be a hard bid to match.

Hard indeed, because the other men scarcely drew breaths after that bid. Scrap Iron handed over the money with no hesitation. Without being told, Mason dressed and walked over and stood at Scrap Iron's side.

As the next white youth stepped under the light, a man approached Scrap Iron and whispered to him that George and some other guy were approaching the store. Scrap Iron told him to let them in.

A few moments later, George and his friend walked through the door. Scrap Iron turned around to see that Never Black was the guy with George. A lurid smile spread across Scrap Iron's face. Never Black was a much more desirable prize than the white boy. Word was that George was going back to court soon, and Scrap Iron couldn't wait; Never Black would be all his then.

Something seemed to be wrong with Never Black. His face sagged as he grabbed his middle, doubled over, and hurled puke everywhere. Scrap Iron quick stepped to the side, dodging the splatter. "Come on, let's get this shit finished before it starts to stink in here," Scrap Iron said, laughing as he turned his attention back to the auction.

After Never Black finished vomiting, George told him to go back to the block and get cleaned up, while he went to the store and bought what they needed for the patients in the infirmary, and to meet him in the subhall.

By the time Never Black reached the subhall, George had already obtained authorization from the captain for them to go to the infirmary, but only after he agreed to make rounds in five-west. The hole.

"The hole?" George had asked. That was something new. The thought of visiting the hole was not a pleasant one. Bedlam was the only word to describe it. Nevertheless, George was forced to accede because the Captain had given him plenty of leeway in being able to continue his regular rounds through the infirmary. Sometimes the piper came to call.

George and his companion each held a bag of provisions as they approached the doorway to the hole. The captain removed his bundle of keys from his belt and unlocked the door. The two men stepped through, and at once, the heavy door clanged shut behind them.

The noise from the keys turning the lock had just finished echoing down the hall when a wad of newspaper came soaring over the top gallery railing. The ball hit the ground with a heavy thud, and the newspaper exploded in a spatter of human feces. A shit bomb."Welcome to hell, you sons of bitches!" the culprit shouted in greeting.

Five-west was a spindly block where the cells faced outward toward windows that never opened wide enough. Without further goading, George and Never Black stepped under the first gallery overhang that doubled as protection from thrown or dropped projectiles.

The two cells the two men stepped in front of—cell numbers 1 and 2—were the only quiet cells at Jackson Inside. The hole for people already in the hole. Instead of bars, each cell had a thick steel slab as a door, which opened up to a small four-foot-long antechamber, at the end of which stood another steel door that gave access to the cell itself. Each quiet cell was soundproofed. The lights within the cells—which, because of the cells' punitive nature, were rarely turned on—could only be operated from the outside by the guards. There was no running water, no chairs, and no beds. The unfortunate occupant had to sit and sleep on the filthy, grimy floor. A small round hole in the middle of the room, for men to relieve themselves in, interrupted the solidarity of the cold stone floor.

The quiet cells were the foulest cells in the entire state penal system. Years would pass between cleanings. Feces, urine, vomit, mucus, and blood covered every square inch of the six-by-nine-foot cell. Cockroaches infested them by the hundreds. The stench was altogether intolerable. The prison stripped the inhabitants of their clothing, thereby compelling them to lie unprotected while the cockroaches swarmed over their naked bodies.

George shuttered as his back brushed against the outer doors of the quiet cells.

"Come on, Never Black," shouted George as he broke into a sprint for the safety of the officers' station just a few meters away. *Splat, splat, splat!* Three more shit bombs just missed their mark.

"Look at these niggas run! You should see this shit!" howled a man in one of the cells on base. His laughter overtook him, tears streaming down his face. He had to clutch the bars in order to keep from falling off the edge of his bed. The sight of George and Never Black rushing toward the officer's desk damn near split him in two with hysterical laughter.

The bombers were on the fourth gallery. They never really knew—nor did they care—who it was they were bombing; they knew only that it took eight steps to pass from beneath the protection of the overhang out into the open area on base after hearing the door shut and lock. The two miscreants throwing the missiles had been confined in segregation for over two years and had the timing down to the second. The reason: boredom; it was merely recreation.

The guard station was constructed with a tin roof to protect them from the unending rain of debris. The roof took a considerable amount of damage, and the inmate porters were left with cleaning the unthinkable off it every day.

George and Never Black left their bags at the guard station then darted right back for the protection of the overhang.

Most of the men at the end of the block on base and first and second galleries were up watching the spectacle. Laughter flooded the block. Shit slingers seemed to have an endless supply of the revolting bombs.

Three steps from the overhang, a shit bomb detonated on the top of Never Black's head. The laughter roared to an impossible level. Even the guards were doubled over.

Other than the two quiet cells, those remaining on base were punitive cells where the prisoners remained without mattresses, blankets, or pillows, with rigid sheets of metal welded on top of four metal legs cemented into the floor as bunks. Nine columns of holes punctured the length of the metal sheets in rows of three, spaced evenly apart. The torches that carved through the metal left burrs behind, burrs that frequently drew blood from the vulnerable bodies of prisoners. On a few prisoners, the burrs had remained in the skin to fester for years, burrowing deeper and deeper over time, finally causing large brown cysts to develop that only surgery could remove.

Prison maintenance could have easily removed the burrs from the bunks beforehand. A small welder's hammer, made specifically for that purpose, could have done the job within a few hours. Regardless, the burrs would remain as further recrimination for men already in the hole for punishment.

As George and Never Black stood in front of one of the cells on base, Never Black thought about his first hole experience. He shivered imperceptibly. The place was genuine misery. Years of food and shit bombs caked the walls. Birds flew into the cells, perched on windows, and added their own measure of droppings to the situation. The entire building was a cloud of suffocating smoke. Prisoners wadded up paper, ignited it, and tossed it out over the catwalks. There were about fifteen small fires burning or sputtering out down the length of the base. One man had squeezed his mattress through the bars, somehow got it to burn, and managed to pitch it over the rail down onto the base.

Many of the men in the cells on base had small strips of sheet—most likely from the only sheet given to them—tied around their lower faces to help filter the smoke. Some prisoners, however, had become used to the smoke and needed no protection.

The noise level was deafening. Men hollered from gallery to gallery, talking and preaching about everything from religion to politics to money. George had to put his mouth an inch away from Never Black's ear in order to be heard. "Let's begin by walking down base and work our way up to the fourth gallery," he said as he started for the nearest cell.

The first cell was empty, but they found an old dark-skinned man sitting on the edge of the bed in the second cell with his hands folded in his lap and his chin resting on his chest. He looked up as George came into view. "Hello, George," he mumbled.

"Why, Mr. Brown," George exclaimed, surprised to see the old man in the hole, "what in the world are you doing in here?"

Mr. Brown was nearly eighty years old, and when he spoke, his voice stayed low and the words came slow and deliberate, as if he had to form each word before he released it.

"Well," he intoned, "you remember my cousin, Louis Shelton?"

"Yeah, I heard he died a week or so ago."

"Well, it's true. He died, and the prison buried him in Cherry Hill." Cherry Hill was the cemetery for Jackson Inside, just outside the wall at the far corner of four-block. The prison reserved the cemetery for prisoners who had no money and no family or friends who could claim the body. Tiny markers listing the first initials and last names of the dead men, along with a plot and burial number, identified the men buried in Cherry Hill.

"The strange thing is that he was all set to go home a few days after his death. My family was anticipating it and had a party all planned out for the day he was supposed to make it home. There were quite a few people at the house for the surprise party, and when he didn't show, they called the prison and found out that Louis had died and had been buried in Cherry Hill. I—"

"You mean the prison didn't even contact his family?" Never Black interrupted, eyes widening in shock.

"They say they did," Mr. Brown resumed, "but they lied. There's always someone at the house, and there was no call. My family said they'll have to pay four thousand dollars for the embalming and the vault. That don't even cover the cost of having his body transported to West Virginia, where he'll be buried with the rest of his family. They shouldn't have buried him in Cherry Hill without contacting the family."

"But how did you get in the hole?" asked George.

"I went to one of the guards, and I guess I was pretty upset, and we began arguing, and he threatened to write me a ticket for cussing. I got angrier and angrier, and he said he felt threatened by my tone, and he said that I verbally threatened him. So I was dumped in the hole for threatening behavior on staff."

George and Mr. Brown spoke for a few more minutes before George and Never Black departed. They stopped at the small sink on the bulkhead, and Never Black put his head beneath the running water. The toilet paper he'd been given by one of the men would not cut it. He could still smell the shit bomb.

Never Black dried his head with his shirt, and the two men ascended to first gallery. There, the cells, like the cells on the rest of the galleries, had mattresses and blankets but no pillows, desks, lockers, TVs, radios, tape players, or reading materials. Most of the men did not want to be bothered and had no problem in telling them so. One of the men even spit on Never Black.

George didn't expect many of the men to be eager to chat. Most of them just waved the two men down the catwalk. A number of them resented George and Never Black for being in general population and having the nerve to come to the hole and taunt them. The two men were heckled and cursed at nearly every other cell.

In April of 1993, the state charged eight black inmates with the stabbing of four white prison guards in four-block. The prosecutor claimed it was racially motivated, and the trial stretched the longest in the history of Jackson County. The jury returned guilty verdicts against less than half the defendants. One of the men the jury found guilty, known as Double R, still sat in the hole. He was the next to stop George.

"What's up, my brotha?" he beckoned.

"I'm doing all right," replied George. "And yourself?"

"They've got me locked down here for that '93 guard stabbing. I'll probably end up doing twenty years for it." The man stood gripping the cell bars. "I won't say whether I did it or not, but if this racism throughout the penal and judicial systems doesn't disappear or at least decrease, the violence will only get worse.

"Remember when Jack Budd was killed?" Jack Budd, a white prison guard assigned to work in that very same hole, had complaints filed against him repeatedly by the black prisoners in the hole at the time. The black prisoners complained that he singled them out for harassment; he spit through the bars at them and even spit and pissed in their food before pushing it to them through the slot. Finally, one of the black prisoners, James Lamont Miller, a.k.a. Killer Miller or Money Mont, snapped. When one of the guards opened his door for showers, Miller pounced on Jack Budd's back and, with a homemade knife, commenced stabbing him in the head and neck area, fatally wounding him. "The racial tension that was present then is still here today. Perhaps even more so.

"I know a lot of the men around here don't agree with your antidrug and self-help messages, but I believe in them. I believe that blacks should quit pointing fingers at white people all the damned time and start doing things for themselves. I'm from Cincinnati, Ohio. There, we had an all-white ghetto called Lower Price Hill, which is probably still there. Anyway, like blacks, people stereotyped the whites living there as being lazy and stupid. Most had bad teeth, some say bad genes, and they spoke broken English. They were what people considered poor white trash. Their ghetto was no different than a black ghetto: same high school dropouts, same drugs, same misery. Basically, the same old garbage lifestyle. But there was one thing about them I admired, that I respected. During my school days, growing up with them, never once did I hear them claim that their circumstances was the government's fault or anyone else's. One of them once said to me, 'I point the finger at myself. My father taught us to blame ourselves and that it was us and only us that could get ourselves out from beneath this bullshit.'

"Now I only mention this to you, George, because I know you're about doing the right thing, about this self-help thing. I say keep it up because you do make a difference. Matter of fact, I think anyone who helps blacks who are this far down in hell makes a difference. The men who are booing you today are also loving you today. They're just a bit confused and don't know how to express what their hearts feel or need. So just keep at it, my brother."

George and Never Black stopped at a few more cells and had a few more enlightening conversations. They spoke with a white prisoner named Richard Goodard, who killed a guard in Marquette Branch prison in the Upper Peninsula during the early seventies. He had been in the hole for a few months past the thirty-year mark. The cell next to Goodard housed Killer Miller, the infamous killer of Jack Budd the prison guard. Next to Killer Miller was a black man named Gerrel Barnes, who killed black food-service worker Doris Taylor at Thumb Correctional Facility in Lapeer County. All three men were on lifetime lockdown. These weren't the only guard killers on life lockdown, but they were the only ones housed in consecutive cells.

Finally, George and Never Black reached the beginning of fourth gallery, the gallery that housed the notorious throwers of the shit bombs. The shit slingers were angling mirrors out of their bars to spot who was coming up the catwalk. George saw the telltale flicker of light off the mirrors and stopped. He knew for certain that they were going to get shit bombed the moment they stepped in range.

Both men turned around and went back the way they had come. Once they reached the bottom of the last bulkhead, they ran full out across base to the guard station. This time, George took a shit bomb to the right shoulder.

The man who had been laughing uncontrollably when Never Black got blasted on the head fell into hysterics once again. He couldn't even stand. He was on all fours looking out his bars at George and Never Black, face flushed, tears streaming down both cheeks. He was laughing so hard he could barely draw breath. He tried yelling at the top of his lungs, but it came out as a harsh whisper. "You good running ass niggas, I love ya!" Realizing that he couldn't be heard at all, the man pushed his face right up in between the bars and tried barking at them. Still, his laughter was so debilitating even his barking emerged as hoarse coughs, which, in turn, spurred another bout of gut-wrenching laughter. Never in his life had he laughed so damn hard for so damn long.

Quand'il servo il signor d'aspra catena Senz'altra spume in carcer tien legato, Volge in tal uso el suo misero stato Che liberta domanderebbe appena. (When the Lord keeps the slave bound by a cruel chain in prison without hope, he becomes so used to his pitiful state that he scarcely demands his freedom.)

—Michelangelo

Chapter 9

The black man lying in bed had full blown AIDS. John, they called him, a twenty-eight-year-old man expected to die before the end of the week. He contracted HIV while sharing a needle with a fellow drug abuser and homosexual lover. The latter succumbed to complications from AIDS, in the same infirmary, two months prior.

George and Never Black, having returned to their cells and washed and changed clothes, now stood bedside John, who lay with his head propped up on a pillow. George wore a white T-shirt with Love Black emblazoned across the front. A humanitarian club in Harlem had gifted the shirts to him as part of an award ceremony. The club awarded him the Golden Handshake award, bestowed annually on unsung heroes who embody the true spirit of giving to, working for, and empowering others. "George has enriched the lives of all races," the club wrote, "in and out of prisons across the nation with his unselfish spirit, unfettered creativity and exceptional good nature. He is a true ambassador of good will."

George could feel nothing but sympathy for the man lying before him. John once weighed in at around 200 pounds, but his frame had withered, and his emaciated body would now barely tip the scale at 120. A fever, which wracked his body with chills, and chronic diarrhea drained him of what little energy he had remaining and left him perpetually fatigued.

George leaned his ear down to better hear the man's enfeebled speech.

"I'm not going to be here much longer, George," John whispered weakly. "I survived a lot, but I can't duck this one." He tried to smile at his own attempt at lightheartedness.

"Before my condition got so bad," he continued, "I read up on AIDS. Within the next two years, AIDS will be the number 1 killer of black men between the ages of twenty-five and forty-four."

A grimace of pain abruptly twisted his face; he paused, closed his eyes, and swallowed with difficulty before he composed himself enough to continue. "Basically, I believe that the steady rise in the amount of heroin and cocaine flooding into black communities has boosted intravenous drug use, compounding the spread of AIDS . . . I was ignorant. I simply didn't know. I thought I couldn't catch AIDS because it was a disease for gay white men."

His voice trailed off, and all George could make out was incoherent mumbling.

From his own research, George knew that since mid-1994, black males accounted for 80 percent of the reported AIDS cases in Michigan. Of all statewide cases, black males comprised half. Michigan State University's Walker Institute reported that black males accounted for 35 percent of all AIDS-related deaths.

Never Black, who had been standing by observing the exchange between the dying man and George, proffered the open bag and asked if John wanted some cigarettes or candy. He declined, explaining that he could only smoke in the day room, and he was too tired to get out of bed. The candy he would only vomit back up.

As George, trailed by Never Black, departed, he heard the doomed man's senseless murmuring diminish. That would be the last they would ever hear from John. He passed away three days later, a new resident of Cherry Hill, for his family refused to claim the body.

The next room held Lloyd Byron Martell. The judge sentenced Lloyd to one to four years for fleeing a police officer, and today, he was scheduled for release. Sitting in the corner of his room, a dilapidated wheelchair the MDOC provided for him bore on its tattered seat a cardboard box containing thirty days' worth of colostomy bags and morphine.

Lloyd was forty-one years old with less than one year to live. Cancer had spread from his colon to his chest. He was dying because the Correctional Medical Services Inc. (CMS) of Missouri, a private commercial medical company contracted by the MDOC for seventy million dollars a year to provide medical care for its prisoners, found and diagnosed, but failed to treat for twenty months, a colon polyp. Had CMS properly cared for Lloyd, the cancer would likely have regressed.

"Lloyd, how's it going?" George asked.

"I'm good, man." He stood as he talked, going through personal papers, setting some to the side and discarding others. "I'm going home today. After the *Detroit Free Press* editorialist Jeff Gerritt called the parole board, they moved up my hearing date, and now they're letting me go. I'm leaving in a few minutes by bus. It's a relief because now I don't have to worry about dying in prison.

"But you know something, George? The court gave me one to four years in prison, but the MDOC and CMS instead executed me. God, I hate these motherfuckers with everything in me."

After a minute of idle chat about Lloyd's plans for when he made it home, the two visitors shook hands and embraced Lloyd briefly before bidding him farewell and good luck. George and Never Black watched the hapless man limp down the hallway, steadied on the rear grips of his wheelchair.

The next room sheltered a forty-six-year-old black man named Pete. Pete suffered from a terminal case of prostate cancer.

"Hello there, George. Who's your friend?" asked Pete, sitting in a chair next to the bed, holding open a paperback book.

"This is my friend, Never Black." George answered as Never Black took Pete's extended hand. "How you doing today?" asked Never Black.

"Not good, actually, with this prostate cancer and all, they say I have only a few months to live."

"Well, I know this isn't much, but we brought cigarettes and candy if you'd like some." Never Black opened the bag and let Pete reach in. He chose a pack of Midnight Special cigarettes, menthol, and a Snickers bar. "Thanks," he said gratefully, immediately tearing the wrapper of the candy bar with his teeth. After a few minutes, George and Never Black said good-bye and moved on.

In the next room, a black man who had recently returned to prison for violating parole lay prone on his back, stark naked. His parole officer ordered him sent back because his urine tested positive for heroin and also for suspicion of selling crack cocaine.

Out of the cell wafted a putrid odor, and the closer George got, the more apparent became the source of the foul stench. Covered from feet to neck with large pitted sores, he lay on top of a cotton sheet stained with blood and greenish fluids. His feet and ankles had swelled so severely, recognizing them as human appendages was nearly impossible, for they had the most concentrated collection of the reeking, oozing cavities.

George remembered all too well what caused those abscesses. His mother had experienced the same thing before dying over four decades ago.

George pulled himself back to the present when Never Black moved closer to the room to peer closely at the man's wounds. Maggots crawled around the hollows of some of the lesions. Never Black elbowed George and pointed toward what he saw. George indicated the bottle full of maggots stored on the shelf to the left of the bed.

George visited that room regularly over the past several months and knew that the man was supplied with the maggots for medicinal purposes. The insect larvae lived inside the festering pits, feeding off the dead flesh in order to slow the spread of decay and infection. In spite of all that, a few days later, the doctors amputated both legs.

His name was Freddy Flowers, another fine product of Detroit's underworld, a heroin dealer and abuser, another sweeper. He used to move into abandoned houses, set up shop selling heroin for no more than a week, then packed up and found another abandoned house. If he stayed in one hovel for too long, he knew the police would eventually get wind of his unauthorized presence. He tried to avoid the police at all costs.

The houses were always run down and uninhabitable. Frames held no windows, all plumbing had been long since plundered, and heat and furnishings were luxuries not even thought about. Abject misery, the state of a contemptible soul. Freddy held no illusions of getting his life in order. He would not abandon the heroin—had never even considered it. As soon as he was released, even dismembered, he planned to continue finding abandoned houses so he could sell and shoot heroin into his veins. He seemed fated to wheel through alleys and slither into abandoned houses just to find his next fix for the rest of his pitiful existence.

George grabbed two candy bars from one of the bags, entered the room, and left them on the shelf next to the maggots.

Before he gripped the handle of the door to the next room, George stopped and regarded Never Black. He wondered if Never Black might be a little too sensitive for what lay beyond this door. "You might not want to come with me into the next two rooms. The men and the rooms are in pretty rough condition. I'm not trying to scare you, but they have some issues with aggression too."

Never Black stared back at George for a moment then shrugged his shoulders and turned the knob to the door. George smiled inwardly at the young man's show of heart. Before Never Black could enter, George hurriedly grabbed for the brown paper bags, remembering that these two men were permitted nothing. He set the bags outside the door and followed Never Black into the room.

The room was just as bare as the man lying bound to the stripped hospital bed where the mattress normally lay. Devoid of linen, pillows, mattress, and all forms of decoration, the room felt more like a dungeon than a hospital cell. Long black leather straps encircled the man's ankles then stretched and knotted around the metal bed posts. His arms were double strapped to his sides and again to the bed. The straps that cinched his arms to his sides braced his upper arms, while two other straps extended from his wrists to the two upper bed posts. Finally, two enormous leather bands, one at the legs and another around the upper torso, affixed his body firmly to the hospital bed. The strapping confined his movement to turning his neck to either side and lifting his head off the bed slightly. Four-point restraints plus.

Dexter Tolliver was a mutilator. For years, he had taken solid objects and mangled his own flesh with them. On nearly a dozen occasions, he had acquired objects sharp enough to rupture his abdominal wall and extract his intestine. He used discarded razors, nails, tacks, ink pens, or broken shards of glass. Several times, he managed a small breach just above the navel, inserted the index and middle fingers of each hand, and tugged and yanked at the breach until he rent a gaping hole in his middle. He howled and shrieked for the nurses only after he succeeded in once again pulling his guts out.

Tolliver had slashed his wrists and neck, mangled the backs of his hands, stabbed through his lips and tongue, and gored the roof of his mouth. Once, he had opened a heavy steel door as wide as he could, positioned his penis in the area where the locking mechanism caught the door jamb, and slammed the door with all his might, nearly severing his penis from his body. After the doctor had sewn it back together and before it could finish healing properly, the disturbed man took a dense metal padlock, laid his still injured penis on a table, and pounded it to a bloody mess. After allowing the trauma of that episode to heal completely, he unfolded a large paper clip and shoved the entire length of it into his urethra.

Tolliver had only been in prison for about eight years. He was convicted in his hometown of Saginaw and was serving a lifetime sentence for a 1984 first-degree murder. As a teenager, he did odd jobs around the neighborhood to earn extra cash. One day, at the age of fifteen, after cutting eighty-four-year-old Peter Jacobi's grass, he went to the door to collect his fifteen dollars' pay. A dispute ensued over what the job was worth, and when the old man only paid Tolliver ten instead of fifteen, the young boy stormed off. A short while later, Tolliver returned to the house with a gun in hand. When the pastor answered the door, Tolliver shot him point blank to his death. The boy thought that shooting a man in cold blood would earn him respect and that people would view him as tough and not to be played with. The sad state he now lay in exemplified precisely what all his peers thought of him: as the weakest man in the penitentiary. Tolliver feared returning to general population because men all over the system knew and despised him for what he did. He believed that those same men would kill him for it—of that, he was certain.

The nauseous stench seemed to penetrate all of George's and Never Black's senses. The rankness of urine and defecation thickened the air. George knew that once every hour, a porter would stop in to feed the bound prisoner and, if necessary, clean the filth from his body and bed.

Tolliver didn't have much to say, and George and Never Black were eager to be away from the sickening odor. The tag was missing from the next door. Department policy mandated that all penal institutions label every cell or bunk in the system with the prisoners' last names and inmate numbers. Obviously, they had made an exception for the prisoner of this cell. The administration wanted his identity kept from staff and prisoners. Rumor had it, he was the man who had killed his wife and their five children. However, around Jackson, he was known as KM or King Mutilator.

KM lay in the same manacled position as the man in the previous room, except that a leather contraption, which was fastened around his head by a strap tied around his neck, masked his face. A large leather strap threaded through two holes in the forehead of the contraption secured his head to the cement bunk. He could only move his tongue and eyes.

When he first arrived at the prison, King Mutilator and Tolliver began trading tales of self-mutilation. KM considered Tolliver a punk and a weakling and told him as much. "For example," he had begun explaining to Tolliver one day, "the day you opened out that big paperclip and pushed it up your piss hole, they took you straight to the hospital, done some x-rays, and pulled it right out. What you should've done was hook and sharpen the end and then pushed it up in there so they couldn't pull it straight out. To get it out, they would have had to cut your dick open. If you're going to do something, do it right."

KM wasn't just running his mouth either. He spoke from experience. While in the county jail, he shoved two large paperclips, with both ends hooked and sharpened, into his penis. He had one testicle, the other he removed after butchering his own scrotum. He had one kidney, the other having been surgically removed after he pierced it with a long knife. He sawed one of his nipples from his chest and chewed and swallowed it. From the neck down, he flaunted a grisly mass of jagged, pinched scars.

Never Black stood next to the bed and gawked openly at the leather mask concealing the man's face. He thought it looked identical to what Dr. Hannibal Lecter wore in *Silence of the Lambs.* The department had modified the mask so that it would restrict the movement of his mouth, because with any freedom of movement, KM posed a danger to himself and those around him.

One day while being escorted somewhere by two guards, they were moving past another prisoner when, without warning, KM attacked. His teeth clamped down on and tore the other prisoner's jugular vein so viciously the victim nearly died from blood loss before health care could stabilize him. On a different occasion, while in session with a prison psychiatrist, he abruptly seized his arm and bit down with such force that the doctor's bone had fractured in several places. Another time, while four guards were escorting KM somewhere, he turned his head and ripped his own shoulder open with his teeth, leaving a wound that required eighteen stitches.

Never Black saw that KM had fixed his eyes on him, but it took awhile for the youngster to realize that the device prevented KM from speaking. When he noticed the tongue moving but only heard strained gurgles coming from the disturbed man, he asked, "Is he trying to talk, George? What's he trying to say, 'cause I can't understand him."

"We can't understand what you're trying to say, KM," George said, addressing the bound man. "We're just going to pray for you."

George and Never Black prayed for the ill-fated man and left.

As they walked into the next room, George stopped and shook his head in disgust before he took his third step. George had known the medium-built light-skinned patient sitting in the corner chair for about thirty years but still did not know his real name. All he knew was that everyone called him Red Bone. Red Bone was about fifty years old with one prosthetic leg, which George noticed was nowhere in sight after quickly surveying the room. The leg's absence, the source of George's disgust, implied that Red Bone had pawned it to a heroin dealer. Again. To get the leg back, George knew Red Bone had to first pay the money he owed, a back-and-forth exchange that had been in play for the last two years.

On more than one occasion, Red Bone had skipped on his one good leg all the way from three-over to four-block to beg George for twenty-five or fifty dollars to get his leg out of pawn, swearing to pay him back. George had not seen a dime paid back yet.

Red Bone was in the hospital because he could not walk to and from the chow hall. The prison administrators knew that he had pawned his leg for drugs again, and they told him that they were not going to issue him another leg, crutches, nor a wheelchair. He had been housed in the infirmary for five days without word of what the administrators were going to do; apparently, they were going to do nothing.

"What's up, George," Red Bone uttered languidly, scratching underneath his chin.

George noticed the rawness under Red Bone's nose from scratching and the drooping lids of his bloodshot eyes: Red Bone had recently gotten a fix. Somehow he had managed to get his hands on some right here in the hospital. Again, George shook his head in disgust.

"Hey, Red Bone," George responded. "What happened, old friend, dope man got your leg again?"

"You know how it goes," he replied, scratching the smooth tightened skin of his stump. "Nigga gotta do what a nigga gotta do."

"Just can't seem to get off that horse, can you?"

"Naw, man. I tried though. Lord knows I tried. Shit's too strong, man, I can't fight it."

"Well, we choose our own path. You seem to be set, your road pretty well-defined."

"Yeah, you right. If . . . Hold up, what did you say, my road is pretty well traveled?"

"No, I didn't. I said your road is pretty well-defined."

"What's that supposed to mean, my road is 'pretty well-defined'?"

"I'm just saying that if you've given your life up to being a heroin addict, then anyone can pretty much see the road you'll travel. For example, everyone can pretty much take for granted that this isn't the last time you'll pawn your leg, and that's probably why you won't get another one. They know you'll just go straight back to the dope man. The same goes for money: if I paid to get your leg back, we both know you wouldn't pay me my money back. Whatever money you get, you'd just buy more drugs. When—"

"Hold up, George. I know I owe you. Dammit, man, you my nigga. How many times have you got my leg back for me? I gotta lotta love for you, George. I'm gone pay you back every cent I owe you, just do me this one more solid. If I don't get you back this time, I'll never ask again. Have a little compassion on a one-legged brother who left his other leg back in Nam, fighting for this piss-ass country."

"Well, old friend," George sighed, feeling a mix of amusement and annoyance at the same old dope-fiend game Red Bone tried running every time he wanted something from George, which, he didn't know, never worked on George. George knew, in getting his leg out of pawn for him, he was throwing money to the wind. Because George felt compassion for the man, he had been willing to give him a chance. He talked to Red Bone each time he got his leg back, with Red Bone promising to quit, not pawn it again, or pay George back. George had a feeling that it would come to this eventually, but he didn't have to like being right. "I'll give it to you straight, the same way you like your dope. Can you mainline a little truth today?

"Yeah, I've gotten your leg back for you a few times, and each time I did it, you walked it straight back to the dope man to get more heroin. You're fifty years old, and your only goal in life is to get high. If I keep getting your leg back for you, you'd still need more money to get your fix, and the only thing you'd have to work with is your leg. You said it yourself, the stuff is too strong for you. I won't do it this time. They say, 'Friends don't let friends drive drunk.' As a friend, I won't let you walk around high."

George knew that the man thought he had a good thing in George, and now he knew that his run was up. There was nothing else he could say, and when George handed him the brown paper bag, he took out a pack of cigarettes and a candy bar and thanked George for the gifts and for everything he had done for him. The three men shook hands, and George and Never Black turned for the door.

"I still love you, man," Red Bone uttered to George's back.

George looked over his shoulder at the broken man. "I love you too, but I'll not help you walk that road again, my friend."

Before entering the next room, George and Never Black stopped as they heard several voices coming from inside. Both men stepped to the window and peered in. Guards and nurses stood coldly in a semicircle around the bed. On the bed, a young white prisoner lay stiffly. His face and body had that dreadful aspect of emptiness, as if body and soul no longer occupied the same space. *Another casualty of a foul health care system,* George thought.

The scene brought to mind the list of prisoners victimized by Michigan's notoriously inadequate prison health care. The most adequate form by which these victims could be listed was best set forth by James Baldwin in *The Evidence of Things Not Seen.*

Bring out your dead:

> Steven Boals, fifty-two-year-old, died in June '06 "of lung cancer two months after complaining of fatigue, weight loss and a lump on his chest. During the last two months of his life, he suffered in pain as a prison doctor

repeatedly failed to examine him or order treatment" (Shellenbarger, Sept. 24, 2006. p. A1).

Jefferey David Clark was found dead on July 24, 2002, "after spending four days alone in a hot observation cell. According to a U.S. Court of Appeals ruling, Clark, thirty-nine,'lay naked on the floor, in full rigor mortis, with eyes open and vomit encrusted on his mouth. The water to Clark's cell was turned off at least part of the time, and Clark was seen drinking from the toilet"(Gerritt, Sept. 22, 2006. p. A).

Larry Evans, sixty-one-year-old "bled to death in his cell two days after complaining to the medical staff about abdominal pain. The prison doctors didn't order a simple test that could have detected a bleeding ulcer" (Shellenbarger, 2006. p. A1).

Joseph Griffen, unable to convince doctors he needed medical care, died May 9, 2005, after "five months of suffering with a swollen right arm and legs so bloated he could no longer walk . . . . After suffering a stroke, a doctor noted Griffen 'speaks gibberish'" (Shellenbarger, 2006. p. A1).

Unnamed inmate, in 2002, a seventy-six-year-old man "with a history of heart disease, emphysema, diabetes, and hypertension died while walking to his prison job during a heat wave. Despite evidence of a worsening heart condition and getting repeated requests for help, prison medical staff failed to treat the inmate and required him to walk outside to his prison job on a blistering August day. He died hours later"(Gerritt, June 19, 2006, p. A10).

John McRae, seventy-year-old, died August 2006 "in his cell after the prison's medical staff failed to follow an outside doctor's instructions on caring for his many health problems, including heart failure, diabetes and internal bleeding"(Shellenbarger, 2006. p. A1).

Hakim Muhammad, forty-five years old, died February of '06"of non-Hodgkin's lymphoma, untreated for months as a doctor repeatedly ignored requests to examine him. When he complained of severe pain in his hip and legs, the doctor canceled his medication and took away his wheelchair" (Shellenbarger, 2006. p. A1).

Jeffery Muller, fifty-one-year-old, died March 23, 2003, of liver failure. Before that, he had "sued the state, [and] the University of Michigan Medical Center agreed to put him on the list [liver transplant] if he remained drug free." A prison guard, a few days after that, came to collect a urine sample for testing from Muller, which came back positive for THC, the active ingredient in marijuana, prompting the hospital to drop him from consideration for a transplant. Muller insisted that the test was wrong. The U of M law students asked that they be allowed to have the urine sample tested, but corrections officials maintained that it no longer existed. "But the law students tracked it to a Texas laboratory and had the DNA compared with a sample of Muller's blood. The test showed the urine was not Muller's. His attorneys claimed someone deliberately switched the urine sample to keep Muller off the transplant list" (Shellenbarger, 2006. p. A1).

Carla Ringleka, a fifty-six-year-old woman, died in prison August 20, 2006, "of breast cancer, which had spread to her liver and lungs . . . . Family and friends say Ringleka did not get treated for breast cancer until nearly a year after she was diagnosed in 2001." *Detroit Free Press*, 9-18-06. "Health care dismissed a lump in her right breast as "fatty tissue" (Shellenbarger, 2006. p. A1).

Timothy Joe Souders, twenty-one years old, spent most of his last four days naked, without physician or psychiatric care, his arms and legs bound to a steel bed in four-point restraints, i.e., wrist and ankles strapped down. "He was in a bare, all-steel isolation cell about the size of a walk-in closet . . . . He lay in urine 'agitated, disoriented, psychotic' as the temperature in the cell rose to 106 degrees." The "MDOC . . . has turned down a Free Press request under the Freedom of Information Act for documents and records related to Souder's death, including a videotape of his last few hours that show him, court records report, staggering from the bed and trying to drink water from a toilet." An

> expert in court called Souder's death "death by torture" (Gerritt, Sept. 22, 2006. p. A10).
>
> Shawn Townsend's health care failed to check thirty-five-year-old Shawn's "testicles during an incoming physical," then when they did, it was too late; he was diagnosed with testicular cancer and given six to twelve months to live. "Townsend has lost a testicle, most of his hair, and at least 70 pounds. He has a tumor in his penis. He hasn't had pain medication in two weeks" (Gerritt, Sept. 18, 2006, p. A8).
>
> Dr. Robert Cohen, "appointed by U.S. District Judge, Richard Enslen, to monitor health care in the Jackson prisons, cited numerous examples of inmates suffering and dying due to under staffing, mis-diagnosis, and delays in treatment . . . without naming patients, Cohen detailed case after case of men who suffered and some died for lack of proper care" (Shellenbarger, 2006. p. A1). Bring out your maimed:
>
> Martinique Stoudemire, twenty-seven years old, had both legs amputated below the knees after "doctors ignored her severe chest pains and body swelling . . . even though they knew she had a history of lupus and blood problems" (Gerritt, Aug. 21, 2006, p. A8).

George had seen so many people maimed and amputated throughout his forty years in prison, he could fill a book with their names and circumstances.

As George and Never Black moved to enter the next room, a guard called to him. The guard told him that Sandra Girard, whose offices were annexed to the law library in the subhall, had called and wanted him to report to her office immediately.

Slavery has been fruitful in giving itself names. It has been called the "peculiar institution," "the social system," and the "impediment . . ." It has been called by a great many names, and it will call itself by yet another name; and you and I and all of us had better wait and see what new form this old monster will assume, in what new skin this old snake will come forth next.

—Frederick Douglass, May 9, 1865

Chapter 10

"The Michigan Court of Appeals failed to address my issue of ineffective assistance of counsel on my appeal. The court held that my attorney's failure to mention the claim anywhere in the brief, except in the argument itself, was an abandonment of that issue. Is that true? Can they do that?" asked a man from a back table.

"While you're appealing by right or by delayed or timely application for leave to appeal, the Michigan Rules of Court require the appellant to include all issues on a separate document called the statement of questions. Your attorney's failure to include the ineffective assistance claim there rendered the issue abandoned. Your claim is worthless. *People v. Wilkins*, published in volume 184 of the Michigan Appeals Reporter, or Mich App for short, starting on page 443, in the year 1990. Also *People v. Mackle*, 241 Mich App 583, (2000)," answered George.

"The strongest issue on my appeal was denied because my trial attorney failed to object during the course of the trial. I was denied three weeks ago, and now I'm preparing my argument for the Michigan Supreme Court. Can you give me some information on how I should frame the appeal?"

This question came from a stern-faced clean-shaven young man sitting at a table in the second row. This table, and an additional one next to it, each held five members of the Nation of Islam. Most men in the large study area of the library, which stood in the subhall, clustered according to their chosen religion. The room contained a total of fifteen long tables arranged in three columns of five and one desk at its head. The Sunni Muslims occupied two tables near the front, and the Catholics and the Christians occupied one apiece. The members of the Moorish Science Temple of America, or MSTA, filled four tables. Scattered over the rest of the room were members of various prison gangs and a few nonaffiliated men.

"The Michigan Rules of Court, or as most people refer to it, the MCR, bars appellate review if the appellant made no objection during the trial court level. However, there are two ways to get around that. First, the court will review any error if failure to do so would result in a manifest injustice, in other words, for example, the continued incarceration of an innocent man. Secondly, a full panel of the court can review a constitutional issue that was not preserved through objection. Cite *People v. Handley*, 415 Michigan Reports, or Mich for short, page 356, 1982, for the first, then *People v. Martin*, 393 Mich 145, 1994, and *People v. Harris*, 95 Mich App 507, 1980, for the latter."

George paced the front of the room between the desk and the tables answering each man's question in turn. Never Black sat behind the desk reading the comics out of a *Detroit Free Press* he found in the hallway. In the far front corner of the room sat Sandra Girard, whom everyone called Sandy, director of Prison Legal Services of Michigan or PLSM. In the late seventies, George and Lee Dell Walker, along with several members of the State Bar of Michigan, founded PLSM, the original purpose of which was to educate prisoners somewhat on the basics of criminal appellate law and procedure. State and federal grants and court order had kept PLSM functioning in the past, and now a number of the Prisoner Benefit Funds of different institutions subsidized the organization. Sandra Girard had been the director of PLSM for more than twenty years.

When George and Never Black entered Sandy's offices, after leaving the infirmary, Sandy informed George that the attorney whom the administration had hired to lecture on the new procedural laws affecting criminal appeals had canceled. The population had been anticipating the event for months, and now, more than fifty oblivious men sat waiting in the library. Sandy asked George to fill in.

After finishing telling the men about the new procedural laws, George, for the last half hour, patiently answered the men's questions. Actually, the abrupt change of plans did not disappoint George's audience. The men actually preferred having George address them regarding the law instead of an attorney. However, because George was not an actual attorney, and even though they knew he was more than competent, the administrators did not want to be liable for any damage caused by inaccurate information.

Every day George left his cell, he met with a barrage of legal questions: in the law library, on the yard, in the shower, wherever. Though he answered as many questions as he could, he had to turn most men away; else his days would pass without him accomplishing anything else.

It didn't take long for the news of the substitution to surge through the prison grapevine. Because many of the men felt that they had to get as much assistance from George as possible, as his action in court could push him out of the system altogether, prisoners packed the hallway outside of the study room, hoping for the chance to put their criminal appeal questions before George. They remained despite Sandy's order to disperse. In order to prevent the crowd from disturbing the proceedings, Sandy had locked the door to the study room. Some of the men were so desperate they wrote their questions in large letters on pieces of paper and tried to get the attention of one of the participants, hoping someone would put the question before George on their behalf. Men continued trickling out of their blocks, gathering outside of the windows of the law library, also holding questions on paper to the window just like the men outside the door of the study room.

As soon as George answered a question, the inquirer clambered from his seat and began turning the pages in one of the hundreds of law books lining the walls from floor to ceiling. Sandy had expected George to at least occasionally consult some of the law books, but up to that point, he hadn't hesitated on any of the numerous questions pitched at him.

Sandy sat passively in the corner with her left leg crossed over the right, studying George intently. She had never met anyone with a knowledge base as extensive and accessible of the state and federal criminal systems as George possessed. The confidence and proficiency with which he cited cases and referenced legal sources astounded her. As an attorney, Sandy knew that in order to be considered an accomplished attorney, it wasn't necessary for one to memorize the intricacies of the manifold and ever-changing laws. One simply had to be soundly familiar with the different sources of the law. George excelled in both areas. If she wasn't mistaken, she would bet that George knew more about the law than all of the lawyers and paralegals employed by the prison combined—herself included.

Like most of the staff, Sandy had a lot of respect for George—more so as a man but also as a prisoner. She especially believed him to be an exceptional role model for the other prisoners. Years ago, Sandy encountered a poem George had written when he had entered the prison at age fifteen. The piece moved her so much, she sent it to a professional printer, had it blown up to poster size, framed, and then bolted high up on the front wall of the study room. She glanced out into the audience and saw some of the men who were waiting their turn to question George reading the passage behind him. Following their eyes, she read the passage again, as she had done many times before:

I Walk as a Man

I know that mountains are climbed,
Though only by the strong.
I know the dream of the caged bird
And that it sings the freedom song.
I know that roads get rough,
That strength will pave the way.
I know the pinnacle shall be staked
By the man who fears naught the day.
I know man will be knocked to the ground,
A scarred and bloody face.
I know it's the strong and courageous heart
That lifts and puts him back into the race.
I struggle, parry, and struggle more,
As I trudge this land.
Be I my own North Star,
I walk as a man.

—George Evans (1964)

"Can I file a habeas corpus into the Michigan Court of Appeals?" one man asked as Sandy refocused on the session.

"Yes, check the *Michigan Compiled Laws Annotated* or *MCLA*, chapter 600.4304 and MCR chapter 7.203 section C subsection 3," George answered.

"I just lost a civil action in the lower court. How long do I have to get into the Court of Appeals?" asked another.

"Twenty-one days. Check MCR chapter 7.204 section A subsection 1a."

"How many copies of my application do I send to the clerk of the Court of Appeals?" Another man.

"Five copies. MCR chapter 7.205 section B subsection 1."

"I need information on a motion to remand from the Michigan Court of—"

"MCR 7.211 section C subsection 1." George cut short a man in the back.

"Peremptory reversal?" blurted a husky, gravel-voiced old black man seated at a middle table.

"MCR 7.211 section C subsection 4," George shot right back.

"I need something more extensive, more detailed on Michigan Appellate Procedures, something better than the MCR. Do you—"

"*Michigan Appellate Handbook* by Carl L. Gromak, John A. Lydick, and Nancy L. Bosh, published by the Institute of Continuing Education in Ann Arbor, copyright 1992, with updated supplements." George preempted a white Christian man at a front table.

"I've never been in the trial court on a motion for relief from judgment, and I've been out of court for more than twenty years. Is it too late to go in now?" sputtered an older black man by the window.

"No, it's not too late. You are entitled to one such motion after August 1, 1995. MCR 6.502 section G."

"I'm serving a natural life sentence for first-degree murder. I have about twenty-five years in. I need something on misidentification. Do you have any issues already prepared in brief form? My eyes are bad, and they don't have the strength to do all of this research. Going through all of these books is just too much for me," asked a rough-skinned light-complexioned black man Sandy knew as Nelson Pitts. Nelson Pitts seemed one of the grungiest prisoners Sandy had ever met. Even though the prison provided brand-new quartermaster at no cost, Pitts refused to take advantage of it. His clothes held no wrinkles, not because of a good press job, but because the fabric of his clothes was so worn and flimsy, it couldn't even hold a crease for too long. He kept his salt-and-pepper hair kinked up in repulsive dreadlocks with a winter cap—or for him, an all-year cap—draped over them like a dead blue squirrel. His face was unshaven, and his eyes sagged lethargically. Psoriasis beset his skin, and gingivitis his mouth. His voice seeped out of his throat so quietly, the room went completely silent when he began to speak, and Sandy still had to strain to catch most of the question.

Sandy, along with almost every prisoner in population, knew that Pitts wasn't trying to appeal his case. The courts allowed prisoners two shots only at appealing their conviction, and after that, the door was closed for good. Pitts had already exhausted one of his chances. As long as one remained, he still had hope. It was a hope that just one law might change in his favor someday, a law that just might free him. That hope kept him going, even when in reality, the convicted murderer's chances of regaining his freedom lay one among a trillion: the gambler's linchpin and noose. Hope, the last inhabitant of Pandora's box, roused in the man enough energy to wake up every day. Hope had dragged Pitts to the law library today.

"No," answered George. "I don't have an issue briefed on misidentification." George nodded to the next man.

"They did me wrong, man. They say I killed three people, man. They straight-up lied on me. Got any cases where they lied on a man?" asked Willie Talley, a black man from Detroit's notorious Cass Corridor section of the city's east side ghetto. He and his two half brothers kidnapped, robbed, and killed a man leaving a drugstore not far from Cass Corridor in the early eighties. They took his money, ID, and key chain then traveled to the apartment that held the victim's wife and infant child a few blocks away. Threatening to kill the baby, the men demanded a ridiculous amount of cash. The woman had no money. Despite the woman's pleas for mercy, Talley and his half brothers killed the baby then raped and killed her. Now Talley and his brothers wanted out of prison. No amount of social injustice suffered by this man and his brothers could excuse or mitigate the vileness of their crimes. God put them right where they belonged. They'd die at Jackson Inside. Even if George did actually know a way of helping them, he wouldn't do it. Some men deserved a fate worse than death.

Willie Talley had approached George years ago asking for help on his case. Instantly, George had made it unmistakably clear that he would not help him and bluntly told him why: that his deeds were born in hell and that he should be dead instead of in prison. Despite seeing George on the yard hundreds of times after that, Talley had never approached George again regarding his case. Presently, perhaps because of the setting, Talley thought that George would feel pressured enough to offer some type of assistance. *Hmph, whatever,* thought George then looked away and nodded for the next man to voice his question.

"This guard named Mike Richardson wrote me two major tickets last month," started a young Mexican gangbanger sitting at a table with four other bandana-draped Chicanos. "One was an outright lie, and the other was an out-of-place for not having my ID on me on my way to the shower. Guard Richardson is racist as a muthafucka, homes. I think he's one of the 'good ol' boys.' How can I beat these bogus tickets?"

Any staff member who witnessed a prisoner breaking a rule or violating a policy directive could write a major or minor misconduct—otherwise known as a ticket. Minor tickets, the less severe of the two, staff usually wrote for small noncritical infractions, like not having your bed made between designated hours throughout the day. On the other end, staff wrote major tickets for the more serious infractions like fights, assaults—sexual or physical—threatening behavior, insolence, and so on. Generally, before a guard or staff wrote a ticket, if the violation was not too serious, they warned the prisoner verbally. Nevertheless, a few of them still wrote tickets at the slightest provocation.

The hearing officer, an attorney not under the supervision of the MDOC, conducts the hearing within fourteen business days after staff had given notice of the misconduct to the prisoner. If found guilty, the prisoner automatically either lost seven days of accumulated disciplinary credits—days earned for good behavior—for the month in which he committed the infraction, which extended his sentence, or because of the truth-in-sentencing statute, it added disciplinary time (time added for poor behavior) onto his sentence. Additionally, for an extremely serious infraction, the warden forfeited some or all the disciplinary credits earned for the period served prior to the violation. This usually added three to four years onto the prisoner's sentence and heightened the probability of the parole board delaying his release for twelve, eighteen, or twenty-four months.

On average, a guard wrote about four major tickets per year; guard Richardson averaged about 450—the vast majority of them aimed at minorities. The institution had conducted several investigations into allegations of racial discrimination, and in every instance, it cleared him of all wrongdoing.

"That's a bit of a tough one there," George answered after a moment of thought. "As you know, Richardson has been investigated for racial discrimination and cleared many times. Rumor has it that he and three or four other racist white officers have cliqued up over the years and decided to see who could write the most major misconducts on minorities: the 'good ol' boys,' like you said. There really are no checks and balances within the MDOC regarding misconducts. Your only recourse is to appeal them and then, perhaps, file it in the state courts for judicial review." George nodded to another table.

"I'm serving a thirty-year sentence for armed robbery. It was my first offense, with no prior record, and no one was hurt during the incident. I know personally several white prisoners, including my codefendant, who's actually at home already, with the same crime and criminal record. None of them were given more than three years in prison. Do you have anything on racial disparity in sentencing?"

When the man began speaking, George stopped pacing, faced the man, and folded his huge arms across his chest. Unlike the other men in the room, the questioner stood before making his inquiry after George acknowledged him. The men to his immediate left, those who escorted him to the library, were, like him, very sober individuals. They all had thick neatly trimmed beards. Their prison attire they kept neat—pants and shirt sharply pressed, shoes spotless. Down to a man, they kept their posture rigid and heads held proudly, if not brazenly. These men were Muslims, and the man speaking was their leader: the Imam.

"In your particular case, I would—"

"I don't speak only on my behalf. My case is only an example. I speak on behalf of all blacks incarcerated," the Imam articulated, sweeping both arms out to his sides, indicating the entire room and beyond, "and all minorities."

"Yes, of course," George resumed. "I understand. Now in Michigan, they—"

"I speak not only on behalf of those incarcerated in Michigan," the Imam continued, "but for blacks and minorities in prisons and jails across the nation." He turned to his left and nodded toward the man next to him. The man stood, lifted and unzipped a leather satchel, then upturned the contents onto the table. Hundreds of letters splayed out across the surface, some of them sliding off the table, floating to the floor.

Without taking his eyes off of George, the Imam searched the pile with his left hand and pulled out a white envelope. He removed a letter and read a highlighted section. "'I'm a black prisoner here at the Pelican Island prison in California. I'm serving a life sentence for stealing a pizza from a store. White prisoners don't get more than a year for this crime in California, regardless of their criminal records. Can you help me? There are thousands of us in this situation.'"

The Imam grabbed another letter and opened it. "'I'm a black man serving a twenty-year sentence. I have several prior convictions, but white prisoners with worse criminal records than mine don't get anywhere near the amount of time that I got. It's like this all over Florida."

The Imam stood there for half an hour reading letter after letter, all of them from black men and women incarcerated across the nation. The complaints were the same—racial disparity in sentencing. George stood patiently, waiting for the man to finish.

"When a person commits a crime against society, I see nothing wrong with him being sent to prison. Society cannot function in any other manner. But when judges use the sentencing laws to give minorities sentences two, five, ten, or even twenty times those given to whites for the same crimes, then it's no longer a matter of punishment. Instead, it becomes a new form of slavery. Lawyers, judges, law clerks, paralegals, prison guards, health care workers, and others benefit from racial disparity in sentencing. From the plantation to prison, this is where we're at today."

Sandy squirmed a bit in her seat and adjusted the legal notepad she held on the knee of her left leg. She felt uneasy when groups of prisoners got together and discussed racial disparity in sentencing. The topic was a sore spot for men in every prison across the nation and their families.

As the Imam continued talking, George glimpsed one of the Muslims get up, walk toward the window, and stand atop a chair.

Just as George glanced over to check out the commotion outside the window, the man leapt to the floor and bolted for the exit. The rest of the Muslims, including the Imam, sprinted out after him.

No sooner than the man stood up on the chair, Never Black was on his way to the window. When the man ran out the door, Never Black hurried the rest of the way to the window and jumped onto the chair. "It's a boy!" Never Black yelled at the top of his lungs, excitedly jumping up and down on the chair, pointing out of the window frantically. "It's a little black boy!" Never Black turned to find George no longer at the front of the room. Looking around, Never Black caught a flash of the back of George's massive shoulders just as they disappeared out the door.

"All the children are our children," Hillary sweeps her hand around the church. She segues into the theme of her book, community support: "It may be going next door and saying to that young single mother, 'Why don't you take a break and go out for awhile, and I'll look after your child.'"

—Gail Sheehy, writing about Hillary Clinton, in Sheehy's book *Hillary's Choice*

Chapter 11

George sprinted until he reached the ever-growing crowd of men clogging the old road. He shoved his way to the hub of the riveted spectators. Upon arriving in the center, George stopped cold, jolted by what he saw. A ripple of disbelief left a tingling sensation on the surface of his skin. There in the middle of the road stood a little black boy no more than four and a half feet tall and looking to weigh about sixty-five pounds with clothes on. And he was wearing a state-blue prison uniform.

Michigan's get-tough-on-crime laws enabled prosecutors to charge and try juveniles of any age for serious felonious offenses. Proponents of the law maintained that it was a clear measure to curb the steady increase of violent crime and to punish serious felony offenders. Criminal justice experts said it was the strictest law of its kind in the nation. Civil rights activists called the law unconstitutional and inhumane. Black activists deemed the law to be racist, insisting that under it, only black children were being sent to prison. China, Afghanistan, and a few other Middle Eastern countries—countries that the United States and European countries considered barbaric for the beheading and maiming of offenders for noncapital offenses—declared that these same get-tough laws of Michigan were directed at blacks and identical to the old apartheid laws of South Africa. Experts predicted that the law would spread across the nation like wildfire in the dry season.

Nathaniel Abraham, a sixty-two-pound eleven-year-old black boy, was the first to be convicted under the get-tough law. With a .22-caliber rifle, the boy shot and killed eighteen-year-old Ronnie

Lee Green. Today, eleven-year-old Nathaniel stood in the center of the old road that snaked its way through Jackson Inside with a look of abject terror and utter confusion on his face.

"You can let go of him now. We'll find his cell." It was the Imam talking. He too stood in the center of the road, feet apart, rooting himself firmly in front of the boy. Four other Muslims flanked him, two to each side, shoulder to shoulder.

The crowd had swollen to about fifty men and kept growing by the second. Men from all sections of the prison rushed to have a look. In its nearly eighty years of existence, Jackson Inside had never imprisoned a child so young—until today.

Immediately to the boy's left stood Scrap Iron—holding the young boy's hand. Scrap Iron had been walking hand in hand with the boy up the old road when the Imam stepped directly in his path, bringing him and the boy to an abrupt halt.

"Get the fuck out my way," growled Scrap Iron, taking a step forward, seething hatred and restrained violence contorting his monstrous face. The five men in his way did not waver.

One punch was all it would take, thought Scrap Iron. He could knock the Imam out and was pretty sure he could take the rest of them.

"I said let him go!" hollered the Imam.

"Nigga, you don't tell me what the fuck to do! Mind your own fuckin' business!" Scrap Iron roared back at him.

The Imam raised his balled fists to chest level, preparing to lunge at the huge demon.

Scrap Iron looked around for the rest of his crew but saw no one.

"What's going on here?"

Prison guard Mike Richardson plowed his way to the center of the crowd, the same guard whom the young Hispanic spoke of, one of the 'good ol' boys.'

Richardson, about forty years old, stood about the same height as Scrap Iron. He wore his black MDOC cap turned backward on his clean-shaven head. His hands rested on his hips as he stood in front of the little boy, searching the faces of the men in the crowd. A wave of silence had followed Richardson to the center of the gathering, and now the crowd stood as quiet as a graveyard. The Terrorist—what most prisoners called him—had arrived.

Richardson fixed his icy blue gaze on Scrap Iron. Looking down, he focused for a second on the tiny hand buried inside Scrap Iron's giant mitt. Richardson looked into Nathaniel's eyes. A sick, disdainful grin split his face."And just who might you be, with your cute brand-new little uniform on?"

Nathaniel's eyes dove for the ground. He didn't respond but just stood there whimpering.

Richardson pulled a notepad from his front shirt pocket and scratched down the prison number stenciled down the side of Nathaniel's pant leg."You just got yourself your first major misconduct for disobeying a direct order. Yep, you refused to give your name when ordered," Richardson smirked, returning the notepad to his shirt pocket.

"Why don't you just leave him alone?" asked the Imam, trying with everything he had to keep the irritation and belligerence out of his voice.

Richardson turned and faced the Imam, wintry eyes boring holes through the man's head. Again, he retrieved the notepad. "You just got yourself a ticket for interfering with administrative rules,"he told the Imam as he retrieved the notepad from his pocket and scrawled his prison number right below Nathaniel's. "Now," Richardson continued,"any more of you boys want to get on my notepad?" He brandished the notepad at hip level as if it were a six-shot pistol. No one said a word. Nearly a hundred pairs of eyes glared pure hatred at the overzealous prison guard.

"That's what I thought."The guard looked around the crowd and shook his head."No backbone at all. None of you.You're just a bunch of welfare-chasing, drug-dealing, women-beating, baby-making piss ants. God, do I hate the goddamn lot of you!

"And now look at this new little thing here,"he declared, flinging his hand toward Nathaniel."You no-parenting pieces of shit! Your goddamned stinking children are coming to prison, and now we gotta take care of them too. Lord have mercy, I swear you blacks are forever the white man's burden," Richardson finished, spitting onto the ground, giving the crowd one last sneer before turning his attention back to little Nathaniel Abraham.

Richardson reached toward his belt and, from a black vinyl pouch, removed his chrome-plated handcuffs. Dangling them in front of Nathaniel's face, he said, "I'll ask again. What's going on here? Don't answer me this time, boy, and you're going straight to the hole. You've got two seconds to answer."

"I don't think so," declared a feminine voice from amid the crowd.

Everyone turned to watch the young law student, Tina Brown, from the University of Michigan's school of law, step through the crowd.

Tina regularly conducted classes on the second floor of the subhall. Today was officially her day off, but she'd decided to come in and catch up on some work. While walking by a window in her classroom, she had noticed the prisoners amassing in the center of the old road. Initially, she thought that it had to be a fight or a stabbing or some such. However, when she looked closer, she had noticed the tiny figure in the middle of the gathering.

By the time she approached and began wading through the crowd, Richardson had already begun his tirade. She stopped as she neared the core of the gathering and listened to the last few remarks Richardson made to the prisoners. What she heard turned her stomach. She couldn't believe this man had the audacity to say such things. She knew that guards and other staff members regularly made inappropriate remarks to prisoners when they thought other staff members weren't around, but this was just ridiculous. This crowd was going to explode at any second, she thought.

For now, the law student was not concerned about Richardson's safety; she'd get to him later. Presently, she focused on the little boy. For months she had followed the little boy's trial. She knew that the courts had sentenced him as an adult and that he would someday soon reach prison. The eleven-year-old's case had been the main topic of most of the criminal law classes at the university, even making national and international headlines. The unthinkable had finally become a reality: little children being sent to prison to be preyed upon by ruthless child predators.

Any other time, Tina wouldn't have hesitated at all before going to intervene for the frightened child. Except this time, there loomed Scrap Iron. The sight of him made her blood run cold. Before accepting the position at Jackson Inside, she, as with all other prospective staff employees, had to read the files of the fifty most dangerous criminals at Jackson Inside. Scrap Iron was in the top ten.

She became physically ill before she had even read half the contents of his prison file. The man's crimes were inhuman.

Tina stood trembling for seconds, seconds that ticked with the harsh slowness of an IV drip. She jammed her hands in her pockets so that any prisoner watching wouldn't see them shaking. Every day she came to work, she asked herself why. Why not stay at home with her two-year-old son? Why not quit and perfect the moves of that new African dance she was trying to learn? After all, she was a professional dancer, and it was one of her life's passions.

Today, as with each day she walked through Jackson's doors, she had to steel herself. She had to remind herself of her first passion: justice. Her need to feel that she was making a little bit of a difference in an unjust world. The little boy in front of her needed someone at this moment. She wouldn't dare abandon him now. Richardson's last comment shook her from her brooding. She watched Richardson jingle his handcuffs in the boy's face then stepped between the few men in front of her. "I don't think so," she announced with authority. The disdain with which he addressed these men gave her courage and strengthened her resolve. She no longer trembled. Scrap Iron, for the moment at least, became just another obstacle to be overcome.

Her first order of business was to defuse the situation. The moment she breached the inner ring of men, she assessed the scene. The huge monster that held the little boy's hand and the racist Richardson, she had already taken stock of. Next, she saw the Muslims standing solidly in the pedophile's path. Without looking at any of the other prisoners, she tramped straight toward Richardson. She could see the barely concealed scorn in his expression, but she could also detect a tinge of apprehension. Two feet away from Richardson, Tina crooked her finger for him to lean his ear over to her. She cupped her hand over her mouth and brought it up next to his ear. "Give me your notepad, and leave the area without another word. Otherwise, I'll report your conduct and have you fired."

Richardson's first instinct was to tell her exactly what he really thought of her. Although prudence was not one of his strong points, anything that threatened his job set off what little sense of caution he had. He hated this woman. She had been trying to get him fired for the last year. Yet, even though she now had the evidence, she was about to let him walk away. He wondered why. *Probably something to do with this little black bastard. Hah, figures. Damn nigger women have always been awfully attached to the little ones. No matter, she can have the little shit.*

Richardson eyed Tina malevolently while he reached and took out the notepad. He handed it over with a little more force than was necessary then disappeared into the throng of men.

Tina Brown retreated a step away from Scrap Iron and nearly bumped into a former student of hers, George Evans. Next to him stood that light-skinned young man with the scarred forehead she always saw with George.

At six feet with long straight dark-brown hair streaked with ochre hanging to the middle of her back, Tina had the body of a fitness trainer. Her ebony skin was flawless, and her hazel eyes sparkled like gold whenever the sun shone on them at just the right angle. Wherever she went, her stunning beauty captivated onlookers. Men, women, and children had been gaping at her since she was fifteen. Her exotic beauty—a cross between the Euro-American standard of superlative beauty and a seductive pop-culture allure—overlaid a remarkable intelligence that was just as captivating.

Just taking in the sight of Scrap Iron made Tina want to hurl. His clothes were wrinkled and stained with every sort of filth. In his hair, which clung matted to his head like avocado skin, nested a rainbow of lint particles and clumps of dandruff and dirt. Scars and severe acne grossly disfigured an already repulsive face. Yellowish white pus leaked from lumps on his bulbous nose, and gobs of gummy white curds lodged in the four corners of his flat, intensely malicious black eyes. His appearance was just the first obstacle. If she could make it past that, she still had to contend with the overpowering stench that wafted off him in nauseating waves.

Still not completely over her dread of the pedophilic murderer, Tina took another step back."Let go of his hand,"she demanded.

"No,"Scrap Iron said flatly; his raspy voice sent the word tumbling through the expectant crowd.

"I'm giving you a direct order to let go of the boys hand,"Tina said with what she hoped was a little more authority. However, as soon as she finished the sentence, she knew that she had forever lost any mental advantage she could have gained. Major misconducts meant nothing to a man serving as many life sentences as Scrap Iron.

"Fuck a ticket. Write the muthafucka." Scrap Iron was also a misogynist. And he had a particular dislike for Tina Brown. This bitch thought she was better than him. All caught up on her looks 'n shit. He could imagine just sloshing acid in her face, snatching her hair out with his bare hands, gutting her, and then leaving her dead body in a garbage dump. He wondered how pretty she would be then.

Scrap Iron tightened his grip on Nathaniel's hand. The boy yelped and struggled vainly to snatch away.

"Let him go, you bastard!" screamed Tina, taking a small step forward, clinching her fist.

"Fuck you!" The putrid odor and spittle that shot from the pedophile's fetid mouth nearly made Tina stagger.

"You have no right!"

"I got to 'im first!"

"There *is no* 'first'!'" Tina said, grabbing for the boy's other arm, trying to jerk him free of the monster's viselike grip.

"He's mine!" roared Scrap Iron, snatching at the little boy's other arm. Some of the men in the crowd cringed when they heard a sickening snap as the boy's shoulder dislocated.

Nathaniel wailed wretchedly as his body sagged to the ground.

Before she could think, Tina's open palm flew in a wide arc, connecting loudly with the left side of Scrap Iron's face, knocking his head sideways. Just as Scrap Iron's face returned to bare on Tina, her left hand clouted the other side.

Scrap Iron released the boy's hand and in a flash launched his rugged-knuckled fist at Tina's vulnerable face. He imagined his fist crashing through the bones and cartilage of her face. He saw the blood and teeth flying from her tattered lips. The moment she hit the ground, he was astride her, pummeling her face into the concrete road. He saw all this the instant before his blow stopped jarringly mere inches from its target. Puzzled, he looked and saw his fist trapped in the powerful grip of another giant gauntlet.

"What the . . ." Incredulously, Scrap Iron's reptilian eyes crawled the length of the arm holding his fist, up the neck, and finally came to rest upon another face he despised: George Evans. Scrap Iron stared pure loathing into George's unperturbed brown eyes.

"Move," he demanded, breathing heavily.

A conspicuous noise like clinking silverware drew the horrendous giant's attention. Only moving his eyes, he glanced and saw that one of the Muslims had two knives—one in each hand—and stood tapping the blades together dangerously. Then more clinging started from behind him.

Scrap Iron let the grimace on his face melt away and smiled. He snatched his fist back and unballed it. He turned in a circle, taking in the crowd, bobbing his head slowly. "A'right, a'right," he said, patting the air in resignation.

Without warning, Scrap Iron wheeled around and fixed his gaze on the little boy clinging to Tina Brown with one arm as the other hung limply at his side. Then Scrap Iron looked up into the law student's eyes. Slowly, he leaned over, and when his face was two feet away from hers, he reached up and stretched his fleshy lower lip until it touched the bottom of his chin. The move was so unexpected it caught everyone, including George, off guard.

Peering into Scrap Iron's mouth, Tina saw a wasteland. Almost every single tooth he had in his mouth was decayed, those that he hadn't sharpened to wicked points. Plaque and tartar caked his gum line; oozing sores and swollen abscesses infested the lining of his lips and jowls.

Suddenly, Scrap Iron hissed loudly. His putrid breath knocked Tina back two steps, and she screamed involuntarily. Scrap Iron threw his head back and boomed with laughter. His mirth still reverberated throughout the crowd as he shoved his way off the old road.

Tina and George rushed Nathaniel to the infirmary. Tina remained with him while the doctor treated his injuries. It was dark when the doctor finished with Nathaniel. The guards had already locked George and the rest of the prisoners in their cells for the night by the time Tina escorted the young boy across the yard. When they reached four-block, Tina told the boy how to get to his cell and that he would be okay and then turned to leave. Nathaniel's good arm circled her waste, hugging her tightly.

"No, no," he cried, "please don't make me go."

Tina turned back and hugged the boy's head to her stomach. "It's going to be all right, Nathaniel," she said, wanting so bad to believe her own lie. Again, she turned to go.

"Please, oh please, no," the child begged. "I'll be good. I swear." Nathaniel fell to his knees, hooked his good arm around Tina's leg, and sobbed harder. At that moment, Tina Brown was no longer a law student, no longer a staff member: she was a mother with a child.

The child's despair rent her heart in two. Her blood flowed painfully from the injustice of it all. Anguished tears welled up in her eyes and spilled over. Yet she felt so powerless. What could she do? She felt as if she were up against some intangible beast. Because there was nothing that she could do, she pried the boy's arm from her leg and turned again to go.

Nathaniel fell facedown in the dirt, promptly reattaching himself to Tina's ankle like a magnet. "Please, lady. Don't . . . leave . . . me," the boy blubbered through distressing sobs.

Finally, Tina bent over, lifted the boy off the ground, embraced and hefted him in her arms. Carrying him to a nearby bench, she sat down and laid his head across her lap.

"What happened to your life, my child?" she asked the wind while caressing Nathaniel's face gently, tears steadily streaming down her face.

Hours passed and still they sat there. Nathaniel had cried himself to sleep but still clung tightly to Tina. Tina knew that the institution would take count again soon and that Nathaniel would have to be in his cell at that time. She turned and looked at the entrance to four-block, then she looked at the entrance to the subhall, then her vision drifted to the enormous walls surrounding them. "I don't know what to do," she whispered sorrowfully.

As Tina sat comforting the boy, a hymn came unbidden to her mind. A song that helped to ease the feelings of impotence and despair that threatened to consume her. She started to sing. The verses flowed from her beautiful lips like the wind across taffeta:

We shall overcome.
We shall overcome,
Someday.
Oh, deep in my heart,
I do believe that
We shall overcome,
Someday.

We'll walk hand in hand.
We'll walk hand in hand,
Someday.
Oh, deep in my heart,

I do believe that
We shall overcome,
Someday.

We are not afraid.
We are not afraid.
Oh, no, no, no,
'Cause deep in my heart, I do believe that
We shall overcome,
Someday.

[The Negro Past] of rope, fire, torture, castration, infanticide, rape; death and humiliation; fear by day and night, fear as deep as the marrow of the bone; doubt that he was worthy of life, since everyone around him denied it; sorrow for his women, for his kinfolk, for his children, who needed his protection, and whom he could not protect; rage, hatred and murder, hatred for white men so deep that it often turned against him and his own, and made all love, all trust, all joy impossible.

—James Baldwin

Chapter 12

Though it wasn't yet ten in the morning, George was already tired. The sergeant that worked third shift had roused George at 0400 hours and asked him to help his neighbor, Andrews, pack and move all his property to eight-block, south yard—the farthest part of the prison. When they got there, George had to help carry the property up four flights of steps to Andrews's new cell on fourth gallery.

Once the cell next to George in four-block was empty, he had to scrub it down and prepare it for its next occupant. Before that, though, on his way back from eight-block, the guard at the desk had told him that up-front had called and said they needed him to clean a blood spill at the gym entrance. George decided that if he was going to do anybody any good, he had to steal some sleep from somewhere. Fifteen minutes was all he needed, a short power nap. He went into his cell and lay down immediately.

About thirteen minutes later, after shaking off the drowsiness, George splashed water on his face, drank a mug of lukewarm water, and stepped from his cell. As he walked by the neighboring cell, he glanced in and saw little Nathaniel curled up fetuslike in the middle of the bunk. The cell door was still open, so George closed it as quietly as possible so the boy wouldn't blindly fall into trouble.

Tina Brown had arranged the move. Last night she phoned the warden at home, waking him from his sleep, and explained what had happened and firmly suggested that the boy would be safer living next to George. The warden ordered the move at once.

George walked on. After finishing the cleanup, he ran into Never Black on the yard. Never Black told George that within the hour, he was expecting to be called for a visit that would last the rest of the day.

"I have to hurry and go hop in the shower and change clothes. My wife and daughters should be here any minute," Never Black told George. He also asked George for some picture tickets so that he could take pictures with his family. George said he didn't have any. Never Black looked perplexed for a moment because although it may have been true that George had no photo tickets, Never Black knew that George could easily get some. Several times, Never Black had asked George for some photo tickets, and George never gave him a single one. Never Black determined to ask George about that right after he returned from his visit. For now, he had to get ready. He said good-bye to George and took off toward his block.

George lingered for a minute watching his young friend make his way back to his block. He looked up when he noticed a rifle-toting guard running along the railing on top of five-block. The guard stopped in the middle of the block and aimed the rifle directly at the old road in front of the building. Moments later, a second guard joined the first. Nearly twenty more guards burst through the steel doors of the subhall, rushing for the area the armed guards on the roof had their rifles trained on.

When the emergency lockdown siren sounded, prisoners from the back-forty baseball diamond outside weight pit made their way along the old road, eventually merging with the hundreds of prisoners exiting the subhall. Over a thousand prisoners made their way to the scene of the disturbance.

George focused on the same area. To head in that direction, he turned left at the intersection. Had he been a bit more vigilant, he would've noticed the ruthless atrocity taking place beneath the bleachers off to the right, less than fifteen yards ahead.

That morning, as Scrap Iron and five of his men strolled the back-forty, all six men surveyed the yard in every direction. The men tried to look as if they were simply walking and talking, and to the casual observer, they were probably convincing. However, for someone who knew what to look for, the tension in the men's faces, their determined stride, and the fact that they barely even glanced one another's way would have put all five and maybe even a sixth sense on alert. These men had murder on their minds.

Johnnie Hanks, the leader of a small gang of eight men from Chicago's Cabrini Green Housing Projects, was their target. Hanks was serving sixty years for murder. For the last few months, Scrap Iron and his henchmen had been trying to assimilate Hanks and his men into his already bloated gang. So far, nine small gangs had linked up with Scrap Iron, totaling fifty-seven men in all. Hank's refusal spurred Scrap Iron to take action. If Hanks wouldn't join him, he had to die.

Hanks jogged nonchalantly around the track outlining the back-forty. He passed by Scrap Iron and his gang several times. Each time he lapped them, he couldn't help but laugh to himself. Who this fat-ass black piece of shit think he was, trying to press him into handing his gang over, Hanks thought. He'd be damned if he'd pay homage to this flabby muthafucka.

Although Scrap Iron's reputation preceded him, Hanks was no angel either. At nine years old, in the Cabrini Green Projects, he sliced a thirteen-year-old boy's throat from ear to ear. He killed the boy to get the gym shoes he had on. The son of a convict and an alcoholic mother, Hanks never got caught. That was the start of a ruthlessly violent life. After living on the edge of death for nine more years, Hanks's luck ran out in an alley on the east side of Detroit, where a plainclothes detective witnessed Hanks brutally beat and rob a man. The judge showed no mercy and even enhanced the sentence recommended by statute, handing him down a sixty-year prison sentence.

Scrap Iron and his boys were not the only ones with murder on their minds. Hanks had planned, for Saturday, a killing of his own: he intended to sneak up behind Scrap Iron in the theater and, with both hands, plunge a nine-inch shank through the top of his ugly skull.

Scrap Iron decided to let Hanks jog by one more time. His next lap would be his last. Scrap Iron motioned for his boys to be patient. He had to keep them from scaring the rabbit away. Just one more lap, he thought, then he would see what little Johnnie was made of.

As Hanks bent the corner and hit the stretch directly in front of Scrap Iron and his crew, he made it just within ten feet when the emergency lockdown siren erupted. Hanks jogged right by his would-be assassins, stopped at the gate, and walked off the yard. Scrap Iron cursed the undulating alarm as its shrill cry suffocated the perpetual din inside the prison. All he needed was twenty fuckin' seconds, he spat silently.

Still fuming at the injustice of it all, he and his crew exited the yard through the same gate as Hanks, heading toward four-block. Even though the crowd was beginning to thicken like cold chicken grease, Scrap Iron spotted Hanks through the throng, talking with someone in front of the store. A plan suddenly slammed into Scrap Iron's treacherous mind. He quickly issued orders to his men, sending four of his toughs jogging to blend in with the sluggish crush of men returning to the block. Everyone else waited for Johnnie to leave.

When Hanks broke off from the other man and began walking back toward his block, Scrap Iron and the rest of the men followed not too far behind. The insane hunters stalked their prey down the old road and past the gym, past the small Jaycee store, and past the chow hall, then past the exit doors of the chow hall to the four-way intersection. At this point, Johnnie took a right heading toward three-block.

Hanks walked under the bleachers that stood next to the old road to cut some distance off the walk back to his block. Scrap Iron and his men exploded into motion. The four men Scrap Iron sent ahead with the crowd appeared, it seemed, out of nowhere, and by the time Johnnie spotted them, a knife had already sunk inches into his gut. Reflexively, Johnnie wrapped both hands around the knife so his assailant could not extract it and carry out his murderous intent.

Before Hanks could find a way to defend himself, one of the men shadowing him from the rear crept up and caved the back of his skull in with a concrete cinder block. Johnnie crumpled to the ground.

The crowd on the road moved a mite faster now, everyone taking pains not to look in the direction of the bleachers. Yet prison eyes saw everything in all its horror.

The blow from the brick had smashed all resistance out of Johnnie; nevertheless, the man with the knife straddled his legs and continued hacking away at his abdomen, while Johnnie's other killer pulverized his face as he repeatedly raised the cinder block over his head and slammed it down full force to the sound of crunching bone.

Johnnie's executioners rose from his lifeless corpse and fused with the flow of men along the old road.

George plodded along with the rest of the men until he reached the spot along the old road where the guards on the roof had their guns leveled. George couldn't believe what he saw. Four decades of witnessing the worst in man laid bare was not enough to dampen the shock he felt from the scene in front of him.

Namen Travis, a ruggedly handsome dark-skinned man, at the age of thirty-five, stood about five-eight and weighed 160 pounds, without an ounce of fat marring his sculpted frame, had taken center stage today. Of the 51,000-plus prisoners warehoused in the state, the director of the MDOC ranked Travis as the number 1 threat to the department's safety. Not only because he led the largest gang within the department, but more so for his revolutionary mind set. He devoted his time to mastering the tactics of guerrilla warfare. He diligently studied the philosophies of Mao Tse-Tung, Niccolo Machiavelli, Alexander the Great, V. I. Lenin, Genghis Khan, and Che Guevara.

A very charismatic man and a superb orator, Namen Travis stole people's attention. More than one mental health expert referred to him as a black Adolf Hitler. And Travis was violently insane.

Many prisoners and staff members considered Travis to be the most racist man they had ever met. A smoldering hatred for white people shaped his every thought, impacted his every emotion, and motivated his every action. He constantly spoke of slavery. He spoke of slavery not in the past tense but in the present. He just could not comprehend why all black people did not hate all whites.

The few times George had seen Travis smile, Travis had either just brutally beaten a white prisoner or he had just found out that more white soldiers got killed in Iraq. Other than that, Travis did not smile. Or laugh.

Travis was dressed in clean, neatly pressed army fatigues, spit shined black boots, and a black tam tipped to the side. Pursuant to his orders, all his top men were dressed in the same fashion.

Travis was dragging an unconscious white man down the old road. He gripped the ankle of the four-block case manager in his left hand. The unconscious man's head left a bloody trail in Travis's wake. Fifteen members of his rugged gang surrounded him like the secret service, with a thick ring of guards encircling them all.

The captain of the guards stood near the circle of men surrounding Travis, trying unsuccessfully to talk over the siren. In frustration, he snatched the radio from his belt and roared for the control center to shut off the alarm. A palpable residue from the blaring siren saturated the sudden quiet. The crowd of men marching back to the blocks halted slowly, except for the men near the bleachers; they kept moving, knowing that locked in their cells was a safer bet than staying on the yard.

"Captain, why don't you and your men just clear out," Travis's deep voice rumbled over the backs of his men as he walked, gripping the case manager's ankle firmly, dragging the unconscious man's head back through the same potholes, stones, and filth the case manager had just maneuvered around on his way to work in four-block that morning. "I've taken it easy on this racist bitch, and you know it. I could've easily killed his ass, but I didn't. I just banged him around a little bit. He'll live."

About thirty minutes earlier, as Travis walked back toward his block, he spotted some of his crew parleying at one of the metal card tables. He stopped for a quick second to tell them that he'd just been called off the yard and that he might be getting transported to Henry Ford Hospital to see his father, who was deathly ill. He told them that the case manager, whom they all knew was one of the most racist staff members at Jackson Inside, might be playing games with him. As he moved away from the table, he yelled back over his shoulder for his men to follow just in case the situation got nasty.

Nasty indeed. When Travis stepped into the case manager's office, the case manager, sitting behind his desk, looked up and said, "Well, I got your off-grounds transport approved. To be truthful, they approved it last week. I just haven't had the time. I had a lot of other things to do."

Travis knew the cracker was lying. Every day and several times a day for the past two weeks, he had stopped in to check on the status of his request. This slimy piece of shit had the chance to tell him then, but no, he wanted to play little bitch games. No matter, he could look past it, because all he wanted was the chance to see his father before he passed on.

"When will I be transported?" he asked instead of calling the racist bastard on his lie.

"You can leave today," the case manager replied. "However," the case manager uttered as Travis turned to leave, "there's one small problem. It's true that we're ready to transport you, but it doesn't appear that your father's ready. About an hour ago, the hospital called to inform me that your father had passed away. Now should you want to attend the funeral, we can—"

"Hold the fuck up. You telling me my father is dead, white man?" Travis asked with a voice so cold the temperature in the room seemed to plummet a few degrees. "And don't play no more fuckin' games with me because you might be playing with your life."

Namen's eyes flared maliciously. The case manager knew he might have pushed the man a little too far, but he refused to back down now. He swiveled to his left and rose out of his chair. "Listen here, buddy," he intoned, "don't you try intimidating me. I'll throw your black ass in the hole. It's not my fault your goddamn daddy is dead." As he finished, he depressed the button on his PPD.

The case manager tried to move past Travis, but Travis stepped in front of him, expressionless, rigid determination in his eyes. With a powerful shove, he sent the case manager sprawling against two file cabinets. Quickly, he stuck his head out the doorway, barked orders to his men to barricade the door, then turned back just as the case manager regained his footing. The case manager raised his fist, preparing to defend himself. Travis stepped forward and sent a right cross shooting past the man's defenses and broke his jaw. The case manager sagged to the floor.

Grabbing the man's ankle, Travis tugged the man to the doorway. Again, he peeked out and asked his men if everything was cool. He saw two guards standing in front of his men, pleading for cooperation.

"Everything's perfect out here," answered a dark-skinned giant, "handle yo' business." A behemoth looming close to seven feet, with his two front teeth missing, he stood with his hands crossed in front of his waist.

With all faith in his men, Travis turned back to the case manager. Still holding the left ankle aloft, he slammed the steel toe of his right combat boot squarely in between the case manager's legs. "Bitch," he growled as he landed another kick. And another.

"You racist . . . white . . . devil . . . son of a . . . bitch," he continued in time with several more kicks. Travis saw blood begin to soak through the crotch of the case manager's pants. By now, Travis had worked the unconscious man all the way to the other side of the office, the manager's neck crooked up against the wall. Blood flowed freely from the man's groin, and the smell of urine and feces bloomed in the small office.

Travis turned, hefted the case manager's left ankle upon his shoulder, and began dragging the listless man. "Let's roll," he commanded his soldiers, "we goin' to the control center." A few more of the response-team guards had trickled into the block out of breath. None of them wanted a direct confrontation with the group of fierce men, so they just paced alongside them, pleading and threatening every step of the way.

As the impromptu lynch mob started up the winding road, the siren sounded. When he heard the alarm, Travis dropped the ankle, turned, and stomped the case manager's mouth, knocking out all his front teeth. "Bitch," he grunted. Travis picked the leg up again and continued his trek toward the control center.

The obscenely rotund captain of the guards walked alongside Travis's men. He knew that in his line of work, there was always a chance of this happening. He still hated when it happened on his watch. He had to treat this situation very delicately and try to stop it from getting further out of control. He and his guards had the prisoners outnumbered with rifles on the roof to boot. But if they tried to rush in on Travis and his men, there's no doubt bloodshed would follow. And some would probably die. Each and every one of Travis's men probably had a knife or two on them, and it was too risky for him to order the guards on the roof to shoot because the case manager or an officer on the ground might get hit. Although it'd been thirty years, no one had yet forgotten the guards killed by friendly fire in 1971 in the midst of the Attica prison riot. As it stood, there was only one man's life in danger, and the captain had his hands full trying to come up with a way to keep him alive.

The captain decided it would be best to keep talking. The officers that apprized him of the situation had no idea of what went wrong back in four-block, but they could get to that later. He had the *now* to deal with. The case manager probably had let his tongue flap a little too loosely. This guy was the most racist colleague the captain had ever had the displeasure of working with. Whatever transpired, he probably had it coming anyway. Yet he had to do what he could.

The captain ordered the siren shut off so that the man in the center could hear him clearly. They exchanged a few words, but the men kept moving slowly toward the control center. He had already given orders for the state police to be called, so he hoped they would be there to fortify the control center security.

As the procession arrived at the entrance to the subhall and turned left, Travis dragged the case manager up the ramp and yelled "Unlock the gates" to the guards beyond.

"They're unlocked," blurted the captain.

One of Travis's men pushed open the steel gates and led in the rest of the legion. Travis dragged the miserable man ten more yards to the end of the hall then stopped and turned to the right where he faced another hallway. Through gate 15, which led to the control center, he saw a pack of medical personnel shifting around anxiously.

In what seemed like one swift motion, Travis dropped the case manager's leg, bent and flipped him over on his stomach, clutched the seat of his pants, and seized a fistful of blood-clotted hair. With insane strength, Travis heaved the limp man over his head and launched him down the hallway. "Get this garbage out of here!" he shouted as the case manger's body smacked the ground with a brutal thud.

Two doctors and two nurses dashed for the downed man and immediately fell to their knees around him. Two more nurses hastened from a room off the hallway wheeling a gurney. In less than twenty seconds, the case manager was on the gurney and on his way out the front door of Jackson Inside into a waiting ambulance ready to rush him to Foote Memorial Hospital.

After the case manager's safe departure, the captain immediately reactivated the emergency lockdown siren. Namen Travis and his boys surrendered without further incident. The guards handcuffed them and escorted them to the hole. The rest of the population eventually made it to their cells, and the prison seemed to be fairly under control, except for one small problem: the number of prisoners locked in their cells didn't match the institutional roster; the total was off by one.

The captain ordered the guards to conduct an immediate search of the grounds. Five minutes later, a female guard, who had only been on the job for six months, stumbled upon the mutilated body of Johnnie Hanks. The macabre scene proved too much for her delicate senses and sent her spiraling into a near-catatonic state. She drifted almost mindlessly back to the control center. No one had yet cleaned up the case manager's blood, and before she realized it, her feet fled from under her, her back slamming heavily onto a semicoagulated puddle. When she finally reached shift command, she reported, as best she could, where she found the prisoner's remains. Thereafter, she unclipped her work keys, radio, PPD, and handcuffs, laid them all before the window of the control center, and walked straight out the front door. She never returned to work. She never picked up her final paycheck. And she never told anyone about the incident that induced the nightmares that haunted her from that day forward.

We have all heard the doomsday cries as to how fetid our schools are today. The baleful reports are all in, and we have been called,"A Nation at Risk."We have written about our education problems. We have more studies than we know what to do with. What about solutions? The solutions to these problems—that is my dream. My dream, actually, is many dreams, that all come under the giant rainbow arch of"A Better World For Our Children,"a world that I believe begins in our schools.

—Marva Collins

Chapter 13

The assault of the case manager and the murder of Johnnie Hanks put the entire prison on total lockdown. George spent the last eighteen hours going over his briefs and motions, making sure that everything was in order. He made sure that not one typographical error escaped his detection and that every case he cited still remained functional precedent. He checked again to ensure that he had complied with all court rules and state statutes. Completely confident, he put everything away and lay back on his bunk. Sleep overtook him, and he drifted off momentarily. What seemed like seconds later, he sprung awake on alert, eyes gaping. There in front of his bars stood a burly black man. The man had reached inside the bars and prodded George's leg.

Initially, George thought of how strange it was for a prisoner to even be out of his cell during a lockdown, let alone on fourth gallery. As his head cleared, he recognized the man in front of his cell.

The man, Big Frank it turned out, must have recognized the tightening of George's expression, because before George could say anything, Big Frank explained, "Listen, George, I know you and I don't really talk and that we're at odds on the way we think. You don't approve of me sellin' dope and stuff and of me using black women for money, and I can feel where you comin' from on that. But I come to you humbly as a man. I need help, brotha."

George looked and saw his bloodshot eyes, the area around them swollen from crying. George knew that most men considered it a sign of weakness to cry and judged it even worse to let another man witness it. Big Frank had status among the prisoners at Jackson Inside. In order to survive in the profession he chose, he could not show weakness and then expect to succeed. Seeing this man as broken as he was, George knew that something serious had him out of sorts.

George softened his expression, swung his legs to the floor, looked Big Frank in the eyes, and waited for him to continue. Big Frank backed up and leaned against the catwalk railing.

"I received a telegram two days ago and haven't been myself since. A few moments ago, I showed the telegram to one of the guards and told him flat out that if he didn't let me out to talk to you, I would probably lose my mind. I told him that they would have to open my door eventually, and I couldn't say what I would end up doing. They musta knew I was serious because they gave me permission to come talk to you.

"Here's the situation. I'm doing seven to thirty years for delivering a controlled substance, or basically, for selling crack. I got four years before I see the parole board. I was living happily with my wife and two sons when I got arrested. My oldest son is ten and the other is nine. Last week, I called my wife, and she told me my ten-year-old was being pressured by other kids to sell drugs, but he refused. The telegram I got two days ago said that the same kids ended up shooting him in the face with a sawed-off twelve-gauge shotgun. I mean, damn, man, they were all kids,"he trailed off as tears streamed slowly down his dark brown face and into the three-day growth of stubble on his cheeks.

It took a moment for him to regain his composure enough to resume his story. "I need your help, man. I still got a nine-year-old, and I need to know how to raise him and how to stop him from gettin' caught up in the streets. Once in it, our kids can't see beyond the ghetto life. It blinds them to the rest of the world. They begin to see the system as the enemy. They are taught that the only way to be successful is to break the law. It's not hard for even a grown man to think that way because every day we see the system not working for us. How much easier would it be for a little boy's mind? I don't have much money, but the guys in here say that you know ways of working within the system. I need to know how to raise my son to live a decent life. I don't want to lose my last child to the streets or to prison or to the graveyard. Can you help me?"

George thought for a second, but before he could respond, Big Frank started again. "I just wish I was out there right now, man. These white folks have fu—, I mean, messed up our lives so much that I just want to grab an AK and take it to 'em, and—"

"Hold it! Stop right there," George blurted intensely. He stood and stepped to the cell bars. "That's your first problem, Frank, blaming white people. White people didn't make you sell crack in your own neighborhood. You did that with your own black hands. Your children's father is not at home because you tried to take a shortcut in life. White people had nothing to do with that." George's eyes blazed fiercely.

"White people didn't try to make your son join a gang and sell drugs," George plowed on. "They didn't aim a shotgun at your son and shoot him in the face. One of the main problems we have today is that we continue to blame white people for our actions. I know that there's racist whites who go all out to make life miserable for blacks, but they are the exceptions. The majority of white people don't care one way or the other, and you even have some who try to help. Anyone who tells you that all whites are racist is either a fool, a liar, or your enemy.

"On more than one occasion, I've heard you talking about disparity in sentencing and how white people are responsible for giving us lengthy sentences. Yet I've never seen you in the law library working on your case to try and rectify this wrong. All I've ever seen you do is watch television; soap operas and videos is how you're living your life. I've never seen you do anything constructive towards seeking your freedom. Do you understand what I'm saying? You say the state gave you a long sentence. What did you do about it except complain?

"There are many blacks in the ghetto who constantly complain and then do nothing to have those complaints addressed. They say life is unfair and that life is too hard and that the deck is stacked against them. Life is unfair for invalids too. Life is hard for the blind, the deaf, the mute. The deck is stacked against many people. In spite of this, you hear every day stories of handicapped people overcoming obstacles or people born with hearts too large for their bodies, living way past the two years the doctor projected. Life seems to have played a cruel joke on thousands of people, but they have gone on to be successes, have gone on to be happy.

"The 1906 San Francisco earthquake registered at 8.1 on the Richter scale. In the earthquake's aftermath, San Francisco nearly burned to the ground. The 2004 tsunami in Southeast Asia killed over 200,000 people. Over 300 people died in 2005 from the fallout of hurricane Katrina. The deadliest tornado in history killed 689 men, women, and children in Illinois and Indiana in March of 1925. Hurricane Fife hit Honduras in 1974 and killed 8,000. Can you imagine how unfair life seemed to those people during those times of crises? Can you fathom the hell they went through? Try to conceive a picture of the devastation left by flood waters in 1988 that killed sixteen hundred and left 25 million homeless in Bangladesh. And don't forget about the families and friends of the 32 student and faculty victims of the April 2007 bloody massacre by Seng-Hui Cho at Virginia Tech.

"I've often heard you yelling to men in other cells about this or that on the television. A man's intellect cannot grow when his brain is forever locked in to the latest hit TV program or the hottest new rap or R & B video. Turn your TV off and start studying your history. Read biographies and study the characters of men. I guarantee you'll learn something you didn't know before.

"My point is this: many people are dealt a bad hand in life. If you look at those same societies today, you probably couldn't even tell that a disaster had recently swept through and destroyed the lives of hundreds. You know why? Because they didn't sit back and complain and blame others for their misfortune. Instead, they gritted their teeth until it was over, held each other and cried. They nursed the wounded, buried their dead, and then rebuilt. They continued living. James Brown, the Godfather of Soul, put it best: 'When you fall down on your face, you pick yourself back up and get into the race, because that's life.'

"Can you see where I'm going with this? Blacks have many obstacles to overcome. One way to overcome them is by not blaming whites for all of our problems. Blacks must be more realistic because our situation is too grave. We should throw blame at no one but ourselves. We have to say to ourselves, 'I am to blame, and I must pull myself up out of the mud.' As long as blacks complain and do nothing about resolving those complaints, we'll continue being the doormats of the world.

"If you want some insight on how to raise a black child in a way that he becomes a success as opposed to a drug addict or dealer, an alcoholic, a convicted felon, a menial-subsistence wage earner, an odd-job man, or a young corpse in the local morgue, then drop all of the racist nonsense. It's nothing but a cop-out.

"Blacks must be stronger and more intelligent than that. We must get on about the business of moving forward. Ask yourself, can you get beyond the blaming of white people for all of your problems?"

The tears on Big Frank's stout cheeks had dried up, and he had sat listening intently to George's lecture. He nodded his head despondently. Although he no longer cried outwardly, he still felt the sharp sting of loss.

George peered into Big Frank's eyes and got a glimpse of his soul. He saw no desire for debate or objection. The man abased himself to stand before George. He came beseeching help because he saw nowhere else to turn. At this moment, Big Frank was in such a fragile state that George would have to temper his usual brusque approach, because he could end up crushing him. George had seen so many other black men crumble in prison over the years, he didn't know how many more he could witness before his soul began to crack.

George sat down on the edge of the bunk inches away from the bars. "Frank," he began in a voice he hoped was more gentle, "listen closely. In two words I'll give the best defense in saving your son from misery and death and the best offense for propelling him to success and life: quality education."

"Quality education? What do you mean, like, sending your kids to better schools?" asked Big Frank.

"Quality education is much more than sending your child to a better school. A quality education is sending your child to the very best school. There's a big difference. Too often society's definition of better schools is simply schools with the most modern buildings, the most current textbooks, and the most expensive audiovisual and computer equipment. Here is where the bulk of society misses the mark. Marva Collins said it best. 'Teachers teach, not buildings.'"

George bent over and retrieved a dusty large old cardboard box laden with an assortment of neatly organized papers from underneath his bed and pulled out a manila folder containing lots of newspaper clippings. He leafed through the folder, snatched out one clipping, and laid the folder to the side. He unfolded the clipping in his hand and spread it out on the bed so that Big Frank could see it.

Big Frank pushed off of the railing and knelt in front of the bars. He reached through and pulled the article as close to the bars as possible. He saw several different charts and graphs. Over the top, a few of the charts had written the captions Reading, Math, and Science. There were listings below those headings for grades 4, 7, and 10 and then 5, 8, and 11. In a column alongside, the article listed the names of the regional school districts.

"The best, the worst," George read, indicating the title of the article. "This is a *Detroit Free Press* study on the learning gap. The computer analysis examined the scores of 648,147 students who took the Michigan Education Assessment Program test or the MEAP test. It ranked over five hundred school districts and thirty-two hundred buildings. It scrutinized the performances of students based on gender and ethnicity, in other words, black, white, Hispanic, and Asian boys and girls. Every year, the districts administer the tests to fourth, fifth, seventh, eighth, tenth, and eleventh graders, and the results are used by many experts as evidence to support various theories and hypotheses. The experts uncover and identify for society the most disadvantaged schools and students. Parents and teachers rely on the test to determine in what areas their children and students are lacking.

"Experts also use the results to demonstrate the poverty connection. They postulate that high scores have nothing at all to do with the quality of the schools. Rather, they believe that test performance is a reflection of community wealth and that achievement goes hand in glove with social status. Furthermore, they argue that poor students perform poorly because of the disadvantages of their station in life. For example, they say that the poor spend their time demanding more meals at school per day for their children, health clinics in school, longer academic days and years, and recreation centers and educational programs for the parents of children instead of being concerned about the school curriculum. On the other hand, you have the experts who use the tests to show the spending connection. They claim that school districts spending the most money per student have higher scores. These experts, depending on which side they're on, either want no change in the status quo or want more money per student for the poorest school districts.

"I myself use the test results to identify the target areas that produce the overwhelming majority of drug dealers, drug addicts, criminals, convicts, high school dropouts, and just flat-out losers. Here, take a look at these charts." On his knees, with his shoulder against the bars, George held the article so that he and Big Frank could read it together. With his index finger, George skimmed down the column under Wayne County and stopped at the row labeled Grosse Points.

"Here," George said, "we have a wealthy all-white district. Now here in 1993," he said, pointing to the columns specifying the dates and continuing over to the next column, "you see this 66.6? It's under the fourth-grade Math column, and it means that 66.6 percent of the students did satisfactory work on the test.

"Now let's go down the column and check out the poverty-stricken predominately black district of Highland Park and compare its fourth-grade math section. Only 8.3 percent had satisfactory results on the test. Notice that I have the Highland Park area marked in yellow. That's because Highland Park is a target area. All the yellow you see are my targeted areas.

"But let's not stop there." George, forever passionate about this particular subject, began to get excited. His large finger glided from figure to figure, pointing out example after example. "The percentage for math for tenth-grade Grosse Points students in 1993 is 65.8 percent compared with 2.5 percent in Highland Park. Same year, seventh-grade reading, Grosse Points, 78.7 percent. Highland Park, 28.3. Huge disparities here, high-target areas.

"Let's switch up and contrast a couple more districts. Look here. We have the middle- and upper-middle-class all-white Manchester district in Washtenaw County for 1993 tenth graders in reading. It says 55.4 percent satisfactory. Now up here, the lower- to middle-class predominantly black Detroit school district in Wayne County for the same year, same grade: 20.6 percent. Again, big gaps, high-target areas."

George's fingers skimmed over the paper so fast, Big Frank could barely keep up. "Let's go back a few years and down a few grades. Manchester, 1991, fourth-grade math, 59.5 percent. Detroit, 16.4. Manchester, 1992, eighth-grade science, 80 percent. Detroit, 29.5. The entire city of Detroit is a target area. However, there are a few schools there that are pretty decent, but we'll get to them in a minute.

"Let's go over here to Oakland County's all-white middle- to upper-class Birmingham, which had a 69.2 percent satisfactory rate in 1993 for tenth-grade reading, overshadowing the Ypsilanti district in Washtenaw County, which contains the county's largest concentration of lower-class black people at 35.2. Another big gap, yellow highlight, target area. Now—"

"Hold up a minute," interrupted Big Frank. "Let me digest some of this. The target areas you're pointing to are predominantly black or Mexican, right?"

"Yes," answered George, pushing himself erect off the bars and turning to face Big Frank. Big Frank had returned to the catwalk railing. "I grew up in a couple of these high-target areas and have friends and family who grew up in others. Did you know that at least half of the students in the target areas qualify for free or reduced-price lunches? We're talking about the poor blacks here. And here, look over here."

Big Frank returned to the bars. He reached through the bars and pointed, his finger settling on the highlighted school, Finney High, in Detroit. "I went to Finney," he declared. "Just the other day, I was in the shower with about five other guys, and there was eight more waiting to get in. It was like a high school reunion because out of the fourteen of us, five went to Finney around the same time.

"Come to find out three other people we went to school with, which are in the fed joint for sellin' dope, three others had overdosed on heroin within the last five years, and three chicks we knew are cracked out and out there hookin' on street corners."

"On the tenth-grade math and eleventh-grade science tests," George continued, "Finney had the poorest performance of any regular high school of any regular high school in Michigan. Out of all of the students at Finney, there was not one tenth grader who performed at a satisfactory level on the math test."

George stared at the man in front of his bars for a moment, to let the point sink in. "Now do you understand that the lowest scores on the MEAP test are the target areas?"

"Yeah, I can see that," answered Big Frank.

"All right, let's move another step forward."

George snatched up another folder and removed a copy of an opinion issued by the United States District Court for the Eastern District of Michigan. He flipped through the case until he found what he sought, folded the rest of the pages over, and handed it to Big Frank.

"Remember how in grade school the teacher taught us how to calculate math equations and then calculate them another way to check the answer?" asked George.

"I remember."

"Well, I'm going to recalculate the target areas I've discovered from using the MEAP test to make sure they're correct. You're holding a class-action lawsuit Michigan prisoners filed against the MDOC for various civil rights violations. The name of the case is *Hadix v. Johnson*, in 694 of the *Federal Supplement*, page 259, published in 1988. Look at the place I've highlighted, starting at the bottom right-hand corner of page 269, where it says 'The Acute Problem of Illiteracy.' Let me quote what it says about the problem of illiteracy for all prisoners at Jackson Inside.

"I don't need it," George said, waving off the photocopies Big Frank tried to hand back through the bars. "I committed it to memory years ago. It states, 'Illiteracy or an inability to use, that is, read and write, and understand the English language precludes twenty to fifty per cent of the inmates from using any law library materials . . . . Status as an illiterate person is based upon an inmate's reading level, that is, as demonstrated by the results of the standard achievement tests administered upon intake into the Central Complex . . . .

"'Based on the results of McIntyre's examination, the average reading level, that is, ability to comprehend, of the sample of inmates was grade six to six and one-half . . . .

"'Approximately twenty per cent of the inmates tested were "actually" illiterate, that is, capable of reading only below the fourth grade level.'

"So we can conclude from the MEAP test administered to grade school, junior high, and high school students and the standard achievement test administered to prisoners that those who score the lowest on the tests make up the overwhelming majority of prisoners, drug dealers, drug addicts, criminals, and such, while those who score highest make up the successes in society: the doctors, bankers, stock brokers, CEOs, and so forth. Undoubtedly, there are exceptions, but they are few.

"Big Frank, compare the lowest results of the MEAP test with the results of the standard achievement tests administered to all prisoners upon intake into Jackson Inside, and you'll again end up with the same target areas. It's simple: with this procedure, you can demonstrate the authenticity of the danger those areas face."

"So what you're saying is," Big Frank reasoned, "the way to get my son into a high-quality educational system is to stay away from those target areas, right?"

"No, that's not quite what I'm saying," George replied, "but that does bring me to my final point. Let me tell you about a black woman from Chicago named Marva Collins. She's a teacher who other professionals call the Super Teacher.

"In the mid seventies, Marva Collins taught with the Chicago school system. Soon after, she left the system to start a school named Westside Prep, located in Chicago's West Garfield Park ghetto. She began teaching students of ages four through thirteen, with books rescued from a garbage bin. She not only taught poor students from the community but also students that other teacher's billed as unteachable. She taught a great deal of vocabulary and classic reading with endless drills and daily essays.

"She was adamant about teachers always believing in their students and never giving up on them. Marva Collins demonstrated how children should and must be praised for their efforts and taught that they can do anything. The students from West Side Prep are considerably further ahead of the national average for children of the same grade level in subjects like reading, writing, and arithmetic. West Side Prep students learned to love learning for its own sake, and they loved it so much they often refused to take recesses and hated to see holiday vacations arrive. The graduates go on to Ivy-sponsored institutions such as the Hotchkiss School and Phillips at Andover.

"In short, Marva Collins walked resolutely into one of Chicago's target areas and turned failures into successes. Now—"

"But there's no schools like that in Michigan, are there?" Big Frank interjected.

"Michigan already has some very notable schools. For example, Detroit's McColl Elementary School is excellent. However, the question is, what happens to the students after McColl Elementary?

Our educators need to commit to a great deal of follow-up work with them and not just push them through the rest of their education and hope for the best. But yeah, I'm basically saying that our educators should start schools such as the West Side Prep in the target areas. And people shouldn't worry so much about the money aspect. Marva Collins didn't have the money she needed, but she had the brains and the true desire to see our children educated, and that's all she needed. Once society begins to understand that it has to truly care about the education of its children, then everything else follows necessarily.

"Recently, black males earning doctorates has declined drastically. This must stop," George said fervently, slicing the air pointedly with a huge hand. "And it's close to impossible to find black male teachers, despite the fact that it's very important for black children to see black men at the front of the class teaching. A recent study by the Federal Education Department showed that only about 10,000 of the country's 1.2 million elementary school teachers are black males and only about 26,000 of the country's 1.3 million junior high and high school teachers are black males. Somehow, we must reverse this trend. Black children need role models in the classrooms and hallways of their schools so they can actually see how education pays off.

"To quote the Super Teacher, 'It's not the audiovisual equipment. It's not how impressive the building is. Places don't teach. Things don't teach. Teachers teach.' Many of the teachers in the schools today should be fired, and other teachers should be paid more. The teachers who coast through their careers have students who coast through their classes. Some teachers even go so far as to tell their students that it doesn't matter whether or not the students refuse to learn because the teachers will get paid anyway. The legislature should enact a law prohibiting schools from hiring teachers with this attitude and punishing those already employed.

"If people were to see a mother bird push her chicks out of the nest and watch them tumble to their deaths without first having taught them to fly, they would call the mother crazy. Yet society repeatedly sends its children into the world without having taught them to live.

"Simply put, we cannot send our children to school to die. Because society has created rules that mandate children attend schools, society must be responsible for what happens to the children who attend those schools.

"At any rate, now you have an outline to follow in order to prevent your child from dropping out of school, living a life of crime, coming to prison, abusing drugs, and so forth. Once again, it's simple: quality education, target areas, schools, role models. Get your life right, become a role model for your son."

A couple hours had passed since Big Frank, feeling hopeful and rejuvenated, returned to his cell. The institution remained locked down, offering the prisoners another cruel meal—a paper plate with cold baked beans and a plastic cup of warm Jell-O. George refused the proffered paper plate when the food-service worker tried sliding it through the slot in the bars. He opened up a bag of potato chips, devoured them, then cleaned his cell, washed up, and brushed his teeth.

The sun had set again, leaving the block dark and hushed. Only the cockroaches went about their nightly business. George lay in bed, feeling kind of pleased with the day despite the circumstances. Maybe, just maybe, Big Frank will hold on to the information George gave him. A man can always hope, George thought, right before he drifted off into another heavy dreamless slumber.

One man that has a mind and knows it can always beat ten men who haven't and don't.

—George Bernard Shaw

Chapter 14

A guard standing in front of his cell calling his name stirred George from his slumber. George snatched the cover from over his head and stared questioningly at the guard. He didn't recognize the face. It didn't surprise him though. Because of the prolonged lockdown, the institution ordered that guards from every shift work overtime. This guard probably worked as a regular at the minimum security prison next door.

"Flash memo from the Warden," the guard blurted and then began reading the memo. "'Writ issued from the Circuit Court of Wayne County to Warden of Jackson Inside. Prisoner Evans to report to control center immediately for transport to the circuit court for the county of Wayne. Deputies from Sheriff's Department of Wayne County await transport in control center. Transport detail states that Evans is maximum-security prisoner and is to wear state blues, black state shoes and socks, along with standard belly chains, handcuffs, and leg shackles.' Evans, you have thirty minutes to get ready for court and step onto the catwalk for escort to control center." The guard unlocked George's cell door as he finished.

George was up and moving before the guard had made it halfway through the memo. He grabbed his toothbrush and toothpaste, his soap dish and a washcloth, and his bath towel and some body lotion. He hustled down the gallery steps to the shower.

Nearly half the prisoners in four-block stood gripping their cell bars, watching. They knew what time it was. Most of the men wanted to shake George's hand and wish him luck, while the rest just wanted to see the expression of a man who had been locked up for forty years straight and was now going back to court, hoping to win his freedom. Either way, George paid them no attention. He was too busy fighting to get his mind focused on the task ahead of him. After showering, he rushed back to his cell to get dressed. On his way, he barely felt the pats on his shoulder and back from men reaching through their bars to wish him well. The words of encouragement the men spoke hardly registered.

After he finished dressing, George stepped from his cell dragging two hulking duffel bags with his right hand and hugged a stack of legal documents to his chest with his left. Before he continued up the catwalk, he stopped and looked into the face of young Nathaniel. George's heart sank as he thought about the future of the child prisoner if he happened to get released. He was not willing to let anything stand in the way of his freedom, yet he felt so much anguish in knowing the boy would be fair game in the minds of the sadistic child predators after he left.

Nathaniel's tiny hands gripped the bars as he looked up at George with a wide grin on his face. "Good luck, George," he said, simply mimicking the chant of the other prisoners up and down the rock. Nathaniel had no idea that George, the last bulwark that stood between him and a fate unimaginable, might not return.

George placed his thick fingers over the child's hand. "You stay strong, son. If you ever need anything, just ask one of the members of BTT that I've introduced you to and let them know." He gave the boy's hand one last squeeze, grabbed the straps of the duffel bags, and moved on up the catwalk.

George nodded and showed his teeth affably at the reassuring touches and supportive words the men blurted as he walked by. He stopped again as he arrived in front of Never Black's cell. The young man stood at the front of his cell, smiling broadly, and George saw genuine enthusiasm in his face. "George, man, you take care of your business when you get there. Don't even worry about us in here. You know this playa from the south side of Chi-town can hold it down," Never Black said, laughing. "You've put in enough years, mellow. It's time for you to go."

George reached up and took Never Black's proffered hand. "There's no guarantee that I'll be leaving, but if I do, you know who to stick with. You watch your back and Nathaniel's too. You know what type of perverts are out to get you.

"And beyond that, you keep studying what you need to know about yourself and your history. Learn and remember what it means to be a black man, and you will always do the right thing. I have to go now, but we'll see each other again, one way or another." With that, George released Never Black's hand and marched toward the bulkhead, this time with the guard lending a hand with one of the duffel bags.

As he and the guard trekked across the yard, George felt the exhilaration of anticipation churning inside him. The prison backdrop blurred while new and exciting possibilities blazed to the forefront of his mental vision. His heart tried to beat a hole through his chest. More than four decades had passed since he set foot outside the walls of Jackson Inside. When George and the guard arrived at the control center, two sheriff deputies handcuffed and shackled him, then they all three stepped outside the prison doors.

Without thinking, George stopped after only two steps and inhaled deeply. It was a fairly warm morning, the azure sky cloudless. Although the entire week had borne beautiful weather, now the air somehow smelled different, as if he had just staggered from a burning building and inhaled his first coveted breath of fresh air. The newly grown leaves seemed to sparkle, reflecting the light of a sun that seemed to shine that much brighter.

George felt a slight tug from the chain clamped around his waist, and he started again with the baby steps the ankle restraints forced him to take until he made it to the deputy transport vehicle. Once inside, George found that he relished even the smell of the car leather and exhaust fumes.

After the second deputy shut the trunk on the large duffel bags, he got into the passenger seat, and the car pulled up to the front gate, preparing for inspection before it left the prison. George looked to his left and saw the hobby craft store displaying the prisoner-made items it sold and the prison newspaper building. Not once had he ever seen these two buildings that had such a dramatic influence on everyday prison life. He tried to burn the image on his memory. Then he thought of how useless the attempt would be, for he would try to consume every second of this journey.

They turned left on Cooper Street. There was quite a bit of traffic, at least from George's perspective. About a hundred yards down the road, he saw the Jackson parole camp. The camp housed over one thousand minimum-security prisoners, most of whom were close to their parole date. Just beyond the camp, he saw a large Victorian-style home. He had heard stories about this place: the warden's house. Behind it and to the left sat the trusty division, which housed fifteen hundred more minimum-security prisoners.

The sights coasting by captivated him. Each time he turned in one direction, he immediately mourned the loss of the opportunity to see what was in the other. His head rotated constantly, soaking up every detail: the different models of cars; a woman walking up the street with her child; the restaurants; a state-police post; office buildings. He felt as if he had been beamed to a different planet.

Traffic was light on Interstate 94. George wished the deputies would slow down. The fields, ponds, and farms with horses, cows, empty cornfields that seemed to rush by. Other cars on the highway moved just as fast, but that didn't calm his unease. Traveling at anything faster than a quick sprint now felt extremely unsettling. Not accustomed to feeling fear so acutely, George sat plastered to the backseat. He still looked left and right, but nothing moved except his neck. The rest of his body sat motionless.

George had seen many of the newer models on TV and in magazines, but when he looked to his left, he saw a car so awkwardly shaped, a loud guffaw exploded from his throat. The driver looked at him through the rearview mirror and the other turned halfway around in his seat. The deputies looked at each other knowingly, smirked slightly, then fixed their eyes back on the road. George didn't notice the exchange. His attention stayed riveted on the world around him.

They had been on the road for about twenty minutes when suddenly George yelled,"Look!"George leaned toward the right-side window, his nose hovered a mere inch from the glass "Over there. It's a deer!"

The second officer looked out the window and saw the deer drinking from a small rivulet. "Yep, that's a deer," he said with a smile."There're lots of 'em out this way."He turned back to the road once again.

About forty-five minutes into the trip, after having marveled at how Jackson's surrounding countryside transformed into the bustling urban populations of Ann Arbor and Ypsilanti, George gazed out the window to his right and watched, stunned, as the immense Detroit Metro Airport rolled into view. While George gaped in wonder, a mammoth 757 passenger plane shrieked raucously overhead, speeding toward the tarmac, looking as if its underbelly would peel the roof off the deputy transport vehicle. George cringed in alarm.

Remembering the stories of the historical, gargantuan twelve-ton Uniroyal tire—the biggest tire in the world—that rose, forsaken, eighty feet skyward on the edge of Allen Park, George looked ahead with almost childlike excitement. As he'd heard it, the behemoth served as a Ferris wheel at the 1964-65 New York World's Fair. Twenty-four gondolas traveled around the tire where the treads were, carrying nearly two million people before it was moved to Allen Park in 1966. The tire appeared, and George smiled widely.

As the car raced through the west side of Detroit, he surveyed the horizon. On both sides of the highway, stubby residential buildings appeared sporadically. The grassy knolls rolling alongside the freeway obscured much of the view to each side. The deputy, uninhibited because, George guessed, he was an officer of the law, sped unabashedly toward downtown Detroit. George eagerly anticipated the sight of downtown again.

Emerging several miles outside of the heart of downtown, George could see off in the distance the tops of tall glassy buildings. He could only guess that it was the world headquarters for General Motors corporation, a building that was previously known as the Renaissance Center, he had read about. After a while, he saw Comerica Park, the home of the Detroit Tigers, Ford Field, the Lion's Den, and other structures just recently built within the last three decades or so. The view stunned him. The walls of Jackson forbade any such beauty. People with the look of having somewhere to be strode purposefully on the walks. Clean restaurants and respectable businesses lined the boulevards. Countless possibilities and unlimited opportunities flashed through his mind like lightning. If only he could get another chance, Detroit would remember George Evans.

A few moments ago, George and the two deputies entered the doors of the Wayne County third circuit court, located in the Frank Murphy Hall of Justice in downtown Detroit. They locked George in a holding tank behind the judge's courtroom. Afterward, the officers returned to their car and removed from the trunk two large green stuffed canvas bags full of George's exhibits and loaded them onto a transport dolly then wheeled them to the courtroom.

When George stepped into the tank, he saw several other men from the Wayne County jail dressed in all green, sitting on three wooden benches. One bench lined the back wall; another stood parallel to that one in the middle of the room, with two more against the wall on either side of the door. A small partition in back left-hand corner of the room blocked off a small stainless steel toilet. The deputies removed George's restraints, and he sat on the bench to the right of the door.

George felt intoxicated. A calmness descended over him, and his focus sharpened to a point. The exhilaration of being in this environment—an environment governed by the state and federal constitutions and amendments, higher court precedents, court rules, and regulatory statues: the law—washed away the trepidation from his nerves the ride to the courthouse brought on.

"George," a man standing in the corner talking to two other men blurted aloud. "Is that you?"

George stared at the man, trying to recognize the man before he responded. Because the lights in the holding tank were dim, he had to squint to bring the man's face into focus. The man left the wall and moved unhurriedly toward George. "It's me, Scarface," he said hopefully.

Recognition sprouted in George's mind. The speaker and his two friends had been paroled within the last year. Now it seemed they were all on their way back to prison, likely with new convictions. After chatting it up with the men for a few minutes, he found out that his assumption was true; all of them were on their way to trial for crimes they committed while on parole. The conversation inevitably turned to a question-and-answer session regarding those prisoners the men knew back in Jackson. Thereafter, the conversation segued into law. The men damn near pleaded with George to give them loopholes to beat their cases. "Beat their cases?" George thought to himself. "For what? So they can get out and commit more crimes and come back with even longer sentences?"

The men made the emptiness in George's stomach burn. The thought of men squandering their freedom for no good reason chewed at his senses. In the middle of one of their questions,

George stood and made his way over to the bench nearest the toilet, where no other men were present. The men he left behind looked dumbfounded, but they all knew George well enough to know not to follow.

George rested his legal documents on the bench next to him, grabbed a small stack, and flipped through it. He made himself focus and read for a half an hour before he rearranged the paperwork and rested his head against the wall behind him. Ten minutes to go, just enough time for a power nap.

The deputy's keys entering the lock wrested him from his siesta. "You, you, you, and you," the deputy said, indicating George, two other black men, and two white. The handcuffs the deputies put on the men held securely but not to the point of discomfort. George, the last man in the single-file line, marched the short distance down the corridor and into the courtroom with a face devoid of emotion, a facade belying the rush of excitement bubbling underneath.

The men were seated side by side on a long bench behind a table reserved for the defense. A moment passed before the bailiff entered the room and intoned, "All rise!"

Everyone in the courtroom stood, including the prisoners and several attorneys sitting to their right, the prosecutor, his assistant, and a paralegal, along with several spectators and a group of twenty fifth-grade students and their teacher sitting directly behind George in the audience.

The judge, a middle-aged white man garbed in his pleated black robe of office, walked through the door adjacent to the judge's bench then sat and stated, "You may be seated." The bailiff announced, "The court of the Honorable James Linbush is now in session."

Mad, bad, and dangerous to know.

—Lady Caroline Lamb

Chapter 15

Jackson released its population from lockdown status. Many men hustled from their cells in a ravenous search for food. The restlessness built up from being confined in the small cells for so many days, and the cold fares of beans and Jell-O left the men hungry, frustrated, and testy.

Scrap Iron left his cell and searched out a few of his men. He was hungry. His insides felt hollow. He would've sworn his stomach was about to touch his backbone. He handed a grocery list of food items and two hundred dollars worth of tokens to one of his men and told him and a couple others to go see if the store was open. If it was, they were to cut to the front of the line and get what's on the list. It was time to eat some real food.

Scrap Iron turned to another one of his henchmen and instructed him to find out if the rumors were true: if George Evans went back to court. If so, he told him to find out where Never Black and Nathaniel were then report back. As that man turned and trotted off, Scrap Iron turned and ordered one of his men to find Samuel Davis.

"I want to know where he is at all times," the big man grumbled. "Matter of fact, put two men on 'im, and every time he moves, one of 'em is to report to me." Scrap Iron was foolish. One could even go so far as to call him ignorant. And although he was himself a very dangerous, ruthless, savage man, he had enough sense to be wary of Samuel Davis.

Years prior, Samuel Davis had once mistakenly left a folder in the law library that contained the transcripts of a hearing held on remand from the Michigan Court of Appeals to the Recorder's

Court of Detroit. One of Scrap Iron's men picked up the folder and delivered it to Scrap Iron.

Originally, the prosecutor charged Samuel Davis with two counts of first-degree murder for the killing of a federal agent and a Detroit police officer, who were transferring him to another jurisdiction, and assault for shooting a bystander.

At the evidentiary hearing on remand, three men from the Pentagon testified that it was the belief of many inside the Pentagon and the United States Army that Samuel Davis's sentences were too harsh and should be reduced. The Pentagon officials testified to Davis's military training and his extraordinary service to his country.

"Samuel Davis," the transcript of one the officials' testimony read,"volunteered for special services and for two tours of Vietnam at the height of the war. He was put through the most ruthless training the army had to offer. Once, during basic training and while on furlough to a small town near base, he got into a fight in a bar, broke a man's jaw, two ribs, and dislocated an arm. He was placed in jail, and the next day the MPs picked him up and took him to a country road and, while Davis was handcuffed, beat him until he was unconscious then placed him in the trunk of the car, drove him to base, and put him in the brig for thirty days without light and with very little food and water, filing charges because he fought and did not kill his opponent.

"You have to understand the goals of the United States at that time,"the testimony continued."We were not trying to conquer North Vietnam. We were trying to assist South Vietnam in stopping the spread of communism. To accomplish this goal, the US relied mostly on B-52 bombers and'search and destroy'missions to achieve its aim. Sgt. Samuel Davis was an integral part of the 'search and destroy' mission. He was the best of the best. He ran a headhunter squad, a trained assassin spearheading a queue of trained assassins.

"Once, while three of his men were wounded and held under fire in a shack by eight Viet Cong, Sgt. Davis took a .50-caliber machine gun and crawled through a swamp only to get shot in the left leg and have the entire left side of his jaw blown off. Nevertheless, he continued to advance on the enemy. After the ammunition ran out, he continued to crawl through the swamp. Eventually, he crawled into the enemy camp and, with a knife, killed all eight heavily-armed Viet Cong and rescued his trapped men.

"Sgt. Davis sewed a white lion patch onto his shirt, over his heart. So notorious and ruthless were his deeds during his two tours of Vietnam, he became known as the White Lion throughout North and South Vietnam. When the North Vietnamese Army put out a murder contract on Sgt. Davis, he killed at least sixteen men who tried to collect the white lion patch.

"Sgt. Davis held the dual position of running his own headhunter squad while acting as chief interrogator for the United States Army and all US allied forces in Southeast Asia.

"We once had a Vietnamese informant tucked in at a base camp near Da Nang. At the time, we had no way of distinguishing him from the seven South Vietnamese allies staying with us at the base. The informant and his actions cost a soldier his life. Many suspected him of having jeopardized several missions, but those allegations were never proven. Either way, we were not in a position to take any further chances. Too much was at stake. We were getting word of the Tet Offensive and were preparing to counter that. We got authorization from Field Commander, General William C. Westmorland, to call in Chief Interrogator Sgt. Samuel Davis. We located him deep within the jungles of the Mekong Delta, just south of the Annamite Range, with his headhunter squad. While flying in on a Huey, Sgt. Davis called base command and ordered a fire built in the center of camp and to have all of the Vietnamese sit around the fire. He ordered us to give all of the Vietnamese men pencils and paper. Near the fire, he wanted one Vietnamese tied facedown naked, spread-eagled.

"When the Huey landed, Sgt. Davis did not say a word. He simply walked to the fire, broke down his M16, separated the barrel, and stuck the tip into the fire. When the tip turned white from the heat, he pulled it from the fire and shoved it into the bound man's rectum. Immediately, talking and writing broke out among the seven other Vietnamese men. Sgt. Davis was sure that this strategy would work, but as it turned out, the Vietnamese simply started pointing the finger at each other randomly. We were right back where we started.

"Sgt. Davis lined the men up, shoulder to shoulder, took another soldier's M16, and executed all the Vietnamese men on the spot."

The Pentagon officials went on to testify about how General William C. Westmorland called in Sgt. Davis and his headhunter squad after the killing of the seven Vietnamese. In all, the Pentagon officials testified for two days.

"In short," the testimony concluded, "Sgt. Samuel Davis is a killing machine built by the US army who was taught to kill any and all who might take him captive, the *reason* for the captivity being immaterial. And that is why an FBI agent and a Detroit police officer lay dead in the street that day. We don't, to this day, know how to simply turn off these machines. For these reasons, and for the testimony given in the past two days, and on behalf of the Pentagon and the US Army, we request that Sgt. Samuel Davis be given a lesser sentence than double mandatory life."

The court thereafter reduced the two first-degree murder charges, for which life without parole was mandatory, to two second-degree charges, leaving Samuel Davis with the hope of one day getting out.

Scrap Iron had once looked Samuel Davis in the eyes, and there he glimpsed death waiting. Throughout his entire life, the big fellow had feared no man, up until he met Samuel Davis. He had to know the whereabouts of Samuel Davis at all times so that when the opportunity presented itself, he could make his move on Never Black and Nathaniel unimpeded.

Tina Brown, the beautiful black female law student from the University of Michigan, sat alone in her classroom on the second floor of the subhall, catching up on some of her work. Normally, she would be working with a class full of prisoners during this time of day, but when she entered the prison this morning, the female guard securing the arsenal up front told her that the lockdown status would continue throughout the entire day.

Every day she worked, Tina found herself instructing a room full of potentially dangerous men. The thought made her think about the day she told her parents that Jackson Inside had hired her temporarily to teach within the prison walls. They urged her not to take the job. Yet Tina assured them that the rigid security at the prison guaranteed her safety. That same belief in Jackson's security was the reason why she refused to wear her personal protection device today. She only carried her communication radio with her.

When Tina found out that the institutional lockdown would last for the rest of the day, she insisted that she didn't need her PPD and argued that she would only be working in her classroom anyway. That damn plastic box was so inconvenient, always getting caught on stuff, sometimes triggering false alarms and causing swarms of guards to rush the classroom, scaring the shit out of her. Finally, the guard acquiesced, realizing that the risk of something tragic happening was minimal. But then, while she sat in her classroom, the control center announced over the loudspeaker that the facility would be returning to semi normal operations. Tina promptly stood up from her desk and moved to the window. There she could see men beginning to trickle out of one-, two-, three-, four-, and five-blocks. She immediately walked back to her desk, picked up the phone, and dialed the three-digit code for the control center. The guard at the desk told her that all school classes were canceled and that no prisoners were allowed in the subhall for the day. That's good, she thought. That way, she wouldn't have to return to the arsenal just to pick up a PPD.

After she hung up the phone, Tina sat wondering what she should do next. Presently, she thought about the VHS video she received from a New York theater on an Irish dance she had been practicing. Not yet having found the time to watch it, she thought that maybe this would be the perfect opportunity. When she first received it, she stuck it in her brief case, hoping that maybe an opening in her busy schedule would present itself. She loved dancing as much as anything else in her life. Anything beyond raising her son, working, and school involved dancing. As a matter of fact, in her free time, she choreographed her own dance troupe. Since the age of nine, she'd at least once danced nearly every contemporary dance popular at the time and even some not so contemporary. She danced in school gymnasiums, university auditoriums, theaters, upscale nightclubs. Once, she was invited to participate in a Zulu dance competition in South Africa. She performed on small clearings of red clay in the middle of rubbish dumps and shanties under the clear African sky. This year, the New York dance troupe invited her to perform *indlamu*, the traditional Zulu war dance, in Nigeria and South Africa. She had, for the past three months, gotten out of bed at 4:00 a.m. and danced. After work she danced for two hours more. When she first moved into her own home, she told her father that she didn't need him to buy her new furniture or appliances, but it was a must that he design her a burnished maple dance floor like the one in the old Savoy Ballroom in Harlem. Her father took two months off work to lay down the floor.

Tina shook herself from her reverie. She sighed, knowing that she didn't have time to watch the video. She had too much work to do. Removing a CD player from the desk drawer and slipping on the headphones, she began listening to a lecture on the current trend of the constitutional Fourth Amendment search-and-seizure law. She pushed her chair back and reclined enough to cross her legs on top of the desk, situating herself for the two-hour-long discourse.

I had always harped on the apartheid of South Africa as compared with the constitutional apartheid I perceived in the American way of life. In a lecture at the New York Law School on the disparity in sentencing and the harshness of sentences imposed on blacks and Hispanics, as opposed to those imposed on whites, I commented on the change in the population of the state's prisons in recent years from white to black and Spanish.

—Bruce Wright, New York,
Supreme Court Justice

Chapter 16

George felt pretty good. Things had been going quite well lately. First, the court had brought him back on a writ several weeks ahead of schedule. Maybe this was a sign that the hearing would end with a favorable judgment and prompt release date. Another detail that he welcomed as an absolute positive was that a relatively young white man presided over the hearing. In George's over forty years of dealing with the law, he found that black judges penalized black defendants with significantly harsher sentences than their white counterparts. This phenomenon occurred so often that black defendants commonly prayed to be assigned a white judge. A *Detroit News* survey found that on average, black judges in Detroit sentenced black defendants to ten times more years in prison than white judges, no matter if the white judges were racists or not.

"Next case is *People v. Biegajski*, Your Honor," intoned the bailiff, pulling George's attention to the front. "Mr. Biegajski is here for sentencing."

"John Burnside, Your Honor, retained counsel appearing on behalf of Mr. Biegajski." A well-dressed middle-aged man stepped from the audience and stood before the podium. The first white prisoner on the bench, a young man who looked to have been about twenty-five, with a shaved head, stepped forward and stood next to his attorney.

"Let the record reflect," announced the judge, barely looking through the wire-rimmed glasses that rested on the end of an impressive snout, "that Mr. Biegajski is present with his lawyer.

Today is the day for sentencing. Counsel, do you or your client have anything to say before the court imposes sentence?"Tilting his small head forward, causing a few strands of predominantly black hair to dangle in front of one eye, Judge Linbush showed no emotion. He wasn't a stern-faced man, but rather, he had the look of a man forced to sit through the most onerous of lectures.

"Yes, your Honor," the neatly-dressed attorney stated, "I have spoken with my client, and he feels deep remorse for his crimes. And I would like for the court to take notice that Mr. Biegaski's family is present today and that his parents are extremely distressed over this matter. His parents support their son, and they pray that the court would exercise leniency and impose a short sentence or maybe even probation so that the defendant and his family can get on with their lives."

The attorney stepped to the side, and Biegajski, shackled and scrawny, leaned toward the microphone. "I just wanted to say I'm sorry, Your Honor," he began, "and that I don't believe that I should have to go to prison for these crimes."

"All right. Let the record reflect that both Mr. Biegajski and counsel have had an opportunity to address the court. Now the court is obligated to state the facts of the case before sentencing.

"Mr. Biegajski was convicted by jury of first-degree criminal sexual conduct, child cruelty, and child torture. The victim is the son of Mr. Biegajski's eighteen-year-old girlfriend. While living together, Mr. Biegajski attempted to burn off the victim's penis by pouring rubbing alcohol on the penis and groin area while the victim lay naked on the bathroom floor. Over the next few days, scabs and chemical burns formed on the child's penis, scrotum, and groin area. At this point, Mr. Biegajski again poured rubbing alcohol over the victim's penis, scrotum, and groin area.

"The victim was twenty-four months old at the time.

"Lastly, Mr. Biegajski sodomized the tiny child.

"These horrific crimes for which you have been convicted do not warrant the smallest show of leniency. For the child-cruelty conviction, for trying to burn off the child's penis, the court imposes a sentence of not less than two years and no more than four years. For the child torture conviction, where you again tried burning off the child's penis after the formation of scabs and chemical burns, the court imposes a sentence of not less than four years and no more than ten years.

"Lastly, for the conviction of first-degree criminal sexual conduct, where you sodomized the twenty-four-month-old boy, the court imposes a sentence of not less than four and a half years and no more than twelve years."

"That's too much damn time, Your Honor!" hollered the white prisoner. "I won't be eligible to get out for at least ten years."

"Well, that's not quite true, Mr. Biegajski," the judge corrected. "The child cruelty and child torture sentences will be served concurrently with the criminal sexual conduct sentence. Which means that in reality, you'll do absolutely no time at all for the first two counts. And according to the disciplinary credit statute, you should be home within three and a half years or less."

Mr. Biegajski went on to appeal his case, which was published in volume 122 Michigan Appeals, page 215.

Before Scrap Iron sent two of his men to the prison store, he had sent word throughout the blocks for the few men in his inner circle to bring all the food in their cells so that they could combine it and maybe get a meal that way. Sadly, the turnout was only a few bags of chips and some salted crackers. Even still, the crew devoured every crumb on their way to the store.

Meanwhile, the men Scrap Iron had sent to the store were having a hard time of it. When they arrived, at least 150 other men were already loitering around the store entrance, waiting for it to open. After about five minutes, a rookie guard appeared from around the corner and announced that the store would not open because the institution was still on lockdown status. Several of the men tried explaining that the control center lifted the lockdown and that the store was supposed to be open. Others requested that the guard call the control center and see for himself. The guard, because he was new to the job, disregarded the men's appeals, knowing that prisoners were manipulative, and walked off without another word.

The moment the guard rounded the corner, one of the men in the sea of agitated prisoners picked up a rock and hurled it through the store window. "Let's break in this bitch!" came from the midst of the crowd, followed by, "Yeah, if they don't want to open it, let's take all that shit!"

* * *

Scrap Iron, with his henchmen in tow, arrived at the back dock of the kitchen. His plan was to buy some food from one of the kitchen workers. Men who worked in the kitchen hustled extra money by sometimes preparing food using the stoves, grills, and ovens in food service, packaging it up, and selling it to men on the yard. Other times they left the food raw and sold it to men who would rather prepare the food themselves. Scrap Iron was prepared to take it any way he could get it. And if the men didn't want to sell him anything, he told his men to strong-arm whatever they had.

Before the men could step up on the back dock, a man exited the back dock with a sandwich in his hand. The whole group recognized the man, a very serious young black activist from Detroit who called himself Truth, a name he gave himself that acknowledged the words he spoke to the men on the yard. The man looked up and eyed Scrap Iron. Scrap Iron sighed heavily, hoping that this wouldn't take long. Scrap Iron would've liked to slap the guy, but he just couldn't bring himself to do it. A few times, Truth had actually given him something to think about. Even still, Scrap Iron hated to see the man coming.

Truth hopped off the dock and stood in front of the men. "The recent statistics don't lie," he said. "Blacks constitute only 13 percent of the population but make up 37 percent of all abortions in the United States." He nodded once, turned, and walked off.

Shaking his head in disgust, Scrap Iron climbed onto the back dock of the kitchen. His men fanned out, some approaching the kitchen workers directly, asking to buy food, while others searched through boxes, cabinets, freezers, ovens, behind dish racks, looking for the food that the kitchen workers no doubt had stashed in preparation to smuggle back to the block.

The kitchen workers, knowing that their stash was lost already, decided to sell what they had. In all, Scrap Iron and his men procured a large pan of cinnamon rolls, which they stacked into a large plastic bag, several large packs of tuna, four bell peppers, four big onions, a tub of salad dressing, and ten loaves of bread. Tuna sandwiches would make a meal tonight.

Over in a corner, two of Scrap Iron's men who were looking for stashed food lifted two large bags of powdered potatoes and found two bloated fifty-gallon garbage bags full of homemade wine. The spud juice had been fermenting since before the institutional lockdown. The kitchen workers to whom it belonged didn't have the chance to secure it before the alarm sounded. The men called over to Scrap Iron and showed him their plunder. Scrap Iron smiled and waved the men over. The look on the faces of the kitchen workers was one of pathetic resignation. They watched miserably as the brutish men carefully dragged the swollen bags over to the edge of the back dock.

Scrap Iron yelled for one of his guys further inside the dock to grab enough cups for everyone. He punctured one of the bags, and the pungent odor of rancid orange juice slugged him in the face. He smiled ecstatically. *Food and wine, not a bad start,* he thought. He sent the other bag of wine and a couple sleeves of cups around to the men waiting in front of the store.

Already reckless, the men guzzled the appalling brew haphazardly. If just one of the guards caught wind of the events happening at that moment, they would have taken swift and immediate action. Intoxicants and the state's most dangerous prisoners did not mix well, and the guards knew it with a frightful certainty.

One of Scrap Iron's cronies came and tapped him on the shoulder. Draining the rest of the wine from his second cup, and after the involuntary grimace from the bitterness of the wine subsided, Scrap Iron looked at the man who then cupped his mouth and whispered something in the big man's ear. Once again, Scrap Iron's face lit up like a kid on Christmas morning. Scrap Iron prodded the man on the shoulder, urging him toward the corner where they could snatch a moment of privacy.

Out of his pocket, the man pulled a plastic bag the size of his palm. By the look of it, Scrap Iron estimated that it had to contain somewhere between 350 and 400 rocks of crack cocaine. Scrap Iron snatched the bag and examined it more closely. Top-notch, just like he thought. The other man pulled out another bag, which held two brand-new syringes and nine grams of China white heroin. Scrap Iron could not believe his luck. The merchandise he held in his hand was easily worth close to forty thousand, prison value. Scrap Iron suddenly seized the man in a bear hug, laughing. "My nigga. I love you."

The four men moved down one chair, and Biegajski rotated to the end of the bench next to George. George watched as the man's parents left the courtroom. How much money had they spent on his lawyer? he wondered. The man's parents didn't seem at all surprised nor upset at the sentence. In fact, it was almost as if they expected it.

"Next case is *People v. Donald Miller*, Your Honor," the bailiff announced. "For sentencing."

"H. Goldstein here, Your Honor. Retained counsel appearing on behalf of Mr. Miller." An almost scrawny white-haired man approached the podium. Donald Miller rose from the bench of prisoners and stood next to his attorney.

George eyed the attorney again, noticing the largest diamond he had ever seen set in a ring on the little man's pinky finger.

"Let the record reflect," said the judge, "that Mr. Miller is present with his lawyer, Mr. H. Goldstein, Esquire, of Goldstein, Goldstein and Furman.

"Today is the day set for sentencing. Counsel, do you or your client have anything to say before the court imposes sentence?"

"Your Honor, earlier today I spoke with you in your chambers concerning sentencing in this matter, and I will stand by my statements."

"Very well. And you, Mr. Miller, do you wish to address the court before it passes judgment?"

"Your Honor," Miller began, "I just want to say that I'm sorry for committing those crimes. My family, who is of course in the audience today, has hired several psychiatrists to examine me, and they all concluded that I was not at fault. I mean this in the sense that there was no specific intent on my part to commit those crimes.

"It's my understanding that Mr. Goldstein has furnished you with the necessary papers. Other than that, I want to express my regret and sorrow to the families of the victims."

"Okay," said Judge Linbush. "Let the record reflect that Mr. Miller and counsel have spoken. Now let the court, pursuant to statute, state the facts of the case before sentencing.

"Mr. Miller pled guilty to one count of murder in the second degree. In exchange for the plea, the prosecutor has agreed to drop seven other counts of murder in the first degree, along with reducing the instant charge from murder in the first degree to murder in the second degree.

"The facts of this case are particularly gruesome. By your own admission, you are a serial killer. A book by a woman named Sue

Young called *Lethal Friendship: A Mother's Battle to Put—and Keep—a Serial Killer Behind Bars* chronicled your crimes. There has been public protest and outrage with numerous groups lobbying for Michigan to enact the death penalty. To that end, they are gathering signatures at this very moment.

"Over a period of two years, eight women were found brutally murdered: all of them found in fields or woods, some buried, some not. Again, by your own admission, Mr. Miller, prior to death, many of the women you tortured and all of them you raped and sodomized.

"Five of the women were shot in the head at pointblank range with a .38-caliber handgun, another beaten with a pipe, and one other killed with a hatchet.

"All of your victims were between the ages of eighteen and twenty-eight years old.

"Because of the heinous nature of your crime, this court must set an example and show you and those like you that society will not tolerate such conduct from any of its citizens.

"For the crime of second-degree murder, the court hereby sentences you to the custody of the Michigan Department of Corrections for a period no longer than fifty years and no less than thirty years."

"Your Honor," Miller stated almost stoically, "how much time will I have to serve on this sentence before I'm eligible to be released?"

"With good behavior, you will be out in seven and a half years, Mr. Miller," the judge answered, slamming the gavel down, closing the case.

Donald Miller, prisoner number 157793, moved to the end of the bench. George looked back and studied the faces of Miller's parents. For the first time today, George felt a tremor of unease in his gut. Miller had kidnapped, raped, sodomized, tortured, and murdered eight women, and still he could possibly get out in less than eight years. Yet that didn't disturb George as much as the fact that neither he nor his parents seemed the least bit surprised at the sentence. A disturbing realization that dampened the store of confidence George had built up inside.

All animals are equal, but some animals are more equal than others.

—George Orwell

Chapter 17

"Next case is *People v. Derick Anderson,* Your Honor. Defendant is here for sentencing." The bailiff handed the file to the judge and resumed his post near the rear wall.

Before the young black man could stand erect from the bench, a tall young white man with a shaved head bolted from his seat in the audience. Instinctively, the bailiff stepped forward, his hand moving quickly to the holster on his side. A shocked silence fell over the courtroom. The youth stopped at the podium, and the bailiff slowly retreated.

"I'm here to be sentenced, and I want to be sentenced with my own kind," said the young man.

Watching the exchange, George studied the man's clothes. He sported a pair of scuffed-up cowboy boots, some dingy jeans, with a wrinkled T-shirt under a tattered blue-jean jacket that had a giant swastika splayed over the back. The young boy was a skinhead no doubt. George figured that he had probably gotten out on bond, so he didn't have to appear in the jail getup or the shackles.

"I remember you," the judge intoned. "John Grimmet. Your trial was two months ago. You were found guilty of ethnic intimidation for pouring blood on a black child and her mother while verbally abusing them with derogatory racial slurs. You were also charged with, but acquitted of, drawing the swastikas found on the sidewalks of a local synagogue. Am I right?"

"Yes, Your Honor."

"So what's your problem now, Mr. Grimmet?"

"Well, Your Honor, today I'm supposed to get sentenced. I've watched you sentence two of my Aryan brothers, but now you're moving on to the inferiors. I don't want to be sentenced behind one of them." He flicked his thumb toward the bench holding the chained men.

"I have no money," he continued, "no attorney, and no family here to support me. I'll represent myself. I'm exercising my constitutional right to be sentenced with my own people."

"First off, Mr. Grimmet, you have no constitutional right to be sentenced in any specific order. Secondly, this court will not tolerate your referring to anyone as inferior, for your implications are false and have no place in this court. Under the laws of this land, all men are equal. No man is better than any other. Our great constitution is blind to color. Is that understood?"

"Your Honor, with all due respect, I think your facts are a little off. These watermelon seeds here," the skinhead stated, indicating George and the other black men on the bench, "were excluded from the original constitution."

As soon as the teacher in the audience heard "watermelon seeds," her eyes bulged. Shocked motionless, it took her a second to turn and hurriedly instruct her students to cover their ears.

"At the time the constitution was written, we still legally owned slaves in this country. We wrote the constitution for ourselves, the pure race. We didn't let these"—he looked back at the bench with a sneer—"these coons run free until many years later, after we amended the constitution."

George looked at the judge, expecting him to bang his gavel at any second and order the man arrested for contempt of court. Yet the judge just sat and listened with convincingly suppressed amusement simmering under his skin.

"You said everyone is equal, but you know that's a lie," the young man continued. "Our police handpick blacks and other inferi—I mean, *minorities,*" he spat the word with as much scorn as he could muster, "to arrest. Blacks get convicted and sentenced more severely, and everyone knows that the police pull them over and search their cars just because they're black. The police know that all of them are either breaking the law or are about to. Everyone who's ever dealt with the system knows that whites get better plea bargains than blacks, that the courts give whites lighter sentences than blacks for the same exact crimes, and that the parole board denies parole to blacks more often than whites, even when their criminal histories are the same.

"Everybody in this country—*our* country—knows that blacks get sent to higher security levels more frequently than whites and do harder time than whites. To pretend that blacks, Mexicans, or Jews are equal to white men is like pretending that a shit-eating fly is equal to a soaring eagle. Just because they both have wings don't make them the same."

The audience stared dumbstruck. Several members sat poised on the edge of their seats, jaws gaping. An old Mexican man in the back row had stood up, appalled, eyes blazing in protest, but speechless. A Jewish woman had moments ago quickly hustled her young son out of the courtroom.

The convicts along the bench were silent also, staring as if the skinhead had just grown two heads and a tail. Abruptly, one of the white men started laughing, and as if that was a signal, the black man sitting next to George laughed nervously right along with him.

George listened with half an ear to the young idiot at the podium. He had heard the same garbage spewed in prison for too many years to count. Nevertheless, the fact that the judge had allowed the guy to continue ranting for so long disturbed him profoundly.

"Consider this: we invented the telescope, and blacks invented the crack pipe. We flew rockets to the moon while they drove Cadillacs to the welfare office. We eat ham and chops, they eat intestine and pig nuts. While we—"

A loud crack cut short the boy's harangue. The judge withdrew his gavel and sat forward in his high-back brown leather chair. "Mr. Grimmet, you will shut your mouth right this moment, or I will have you escorted from this courtroom."

"Why, Your Honor? Is it because I speak a truth that you feel and believe in your heart? A truth that you're afraid to speak because of politics? Well, Your Honor, I'm not a politician, so I don't have to play at politics. I have a right to address the court before sentencing, and I intend to speak my piece."

The judge inclined his head to the side slightly, almost thoughtfully, and watched as the young man plowed on.

"If you're afraid that I'll let them in on the big secret, then don't worry, Your Honor. We've played this game for years, but the dumb fuckers are too stupid and lazy to do anything about it. All we have to do is throw them a bone or two disguised in so-called civil rights, and they'll lie down for another four hundred years, just like the good little doggies they are.

"We built this nation on the backs of blacks. Plantations were the best idea since the invention of the wheel. And now that the plantation has run its course, we get the same results from the prisons. From the plantation to prison—it's the same game, different rules."

The youth looked at the black prisoners on the bench and then into the audience. After a moment, he shook his head in disgust then turned back to the judge and continued. "What's even sadder and more convincing of their inferiority is the fact that they let us send their dumb asses over to other countries to fight for us. Hell, they sign up by the thousands to go and protect their masters. Like I said, good little doggies.

"In the book of John chapter 18, verse 38, Pilate asked jestingly at the trial of Jesus Christ, 'What is truth?' I'll tell you what today's truth is: this country has one set of laws for the white man and a whole other set for the inferior races. And that is as it should be. This is our Manifest Destiny. To attempt to put blacks on equal footing with whites is a sin against God. Look at how they live in Africa. They're barefoot, malnourished, underdeveloped, plagued with AIDS, and they screw in bushes. They're animals, and they should be grateful we enslaved them.

"I know that you're going to try and tell me that I'm wrong and that my thinking is backward, but I also know that when you take off that black robe and drive home to have dinner with your white family, you're going to tell them what happened today, and you're going to laugh about it. You're going to tell them that a real white man stepped up in your courtroom and said what you only wish you could. You're going to smile because you know I put these heathens in their place, these niggers, that spic in the back, and those money-sucking Jews.

"I could go on and on, but for what? You already know the rest. It's a simple case of the master and the slave, the ruler and the ruled, the conqueror and the conquered. I sometimes fantasize about the good-for-nothing beasts one day standing up for themselves so that the master race can show them openly where the power truly lies.

"So, Your Honor, I don't want to hear that equal-opportunity, affirmative-action crap. The laws discriminate against blacks for a reason: they're intellectually inferior, lazy, deceitful, roguish, and depraved. White men should be treated better under the law. I want to be sentenced before these savages, and I want less time than you would give to one of them. That is my birthright.

"Now I've had my say, your Honor. The floor is yours."The young white boy remained standing.

The judge sat completely still for seconds, his face beet red. Instead of exploding, the judge said, slightly irritated,"Mr. Grimmet, how nice of you to give me my courtroom back. As I said before, I will not tolerate outbursts in my courtroom. If you say another word without permission, you will hear about your sentencing in a jail cell.

"Nevertheless," the judge continued, "in order to prevent you from disturbing this courtroom again, I will move you up on the schedule." The judge turned to the clerk and motioned for him to hand him the next case file. "Defendant Anderson," he said to the black man who still stood waiting to approach the podium for sentencing, "return to your seat. I'll get to you next." Anderson sat down without protest.

"Let the record reflect that Mr. Grimmett has refused counsel and has represented himself through all adversarial proceedings against him. As is prescribed by law, I will recount the facts of this case before I pronounce judgment.

"Mr. Grimmet, you're the leader of a local skinhead organization promoting Aryan brotherhood and Aryan superiority. A jury convicted you of ethnic intimidation. The charges stem from an incident you took part in at a local mall with four other unidentified skinheads. You all surrounded a young black woman who was pushing her infant daughter in some type of baby buggy in the parking lot of the mall. After surrounding her, you and your followers began taunting her and spouting racial slurs at the pair. The victim asked you to stop repeatedly. Witnesses testified that while crying, she tried to run back into the store. At that point, you and your four companions again surrounded her, and you, Mr. Grimmet, removed from a coat pocket a large bottle of blood and poured it all over the child and splashed some into the mother's face. Now—"

"But it was only chicken blood, Your Honor. Nothing wrong with that. Some of these porch monkeys drink the stuff like Kool-Aid. It's like a delicacy to them."

"Mr. Grimmet, this is your last warning. One more outburst and you'll be spending a few hours in a jail cell. And what you're saying is not only beside the point, it also reinforces the jury's correct judgment in rendering a guilty verdict.

"The ethnic intimidation law is new, albeit one that's an abiding eyesore on the state's justice system. Despite that, it is a law, and because it's a law, I must follow it.

"A civilized society cannot suffer violations of its laws, regardless of what I or anyone else may think of them. Therefore, the court hereby imposes a sentence of no more than one year of probation with an allowance for discharge in six months with good behavior. Now, Mr. Grimmet, leave my courtroom and report to the office of parole and probation to be assigned an officer.

"Good riddance, Mr. Grimmet, and I hope to never see you in my courtroom again."

"Before I leave, Your Honor, can I say one more thing?"

The judge sighed heavily, "Make it quick, Mr. Grimmet. I have other cases to tend to."

"Okay. Thank you, Your Honor. I just wanted to let you know that while I was waiting for the courthouse to open this morning, I saw two sheriff's deputies escorting a shackled black man through the front of the building. When he stood up out of the back of the car, I noticed something strange about him. I couldn't put my finger on it until he started walking. Arrogance, that's what it was. He walked with his chest stuck out and his head held high like he ruled the world or something. I wanted to run up and spit in his face.

"Before the three men could make it to the doors, I hurried up and stood close so I could get a better look at his face. When I looked into his eyes, Your Honor, I saw no fear. He didn't cringe or cower like a lot of them niggers do. I asked one of the deputies who the man was, and he told me that he was a prisoner from inside the walls of Jackson. He said that he was back for some kind of hearing.

"It was that one right there, Your Honor." The skinhead pointed directly at George. "Yeah, he looks like a real troublemaker. The kind of nigger that we would've drawn and quartered on the spot back in the good ol' days. Keep a close eye on him."

"Your Honor, this is outrageous," screamed a black man from in the audience, vaulting from his seat, too appalled to sit and listen any longer. "How could you let this man talk like this in a court of law?" That question snapped the aghast audience back to life, and a chorus of protests arose from the crowd.

The judge banged his gavel thunderously. "Order in the court!" he barked. "I want order, or I'll have this courtroom cleared, so help me."

Only after several minutes did the judge regain control of the courtroom. Instead of leaving, though, the skinhead returned to the audience chamber and sat in the front row behind George.

With a smirk on his face, George turned and regarded the moron behind him. This guy was pretty funny, he thought, then shifted back around to watch the rest of the proceedings.

"The next case is *People v. Derick Anderson*, Your Honor, and defendant is here for sentencing," announced the bailiff.

"Dwight Schmidt, Your Honor, of the public defender's office, appearing on behalf of the defendant." A primly dressed huge white man stepped up to the podium. His coffee-colored suit stopped about a half-inch short of completely covering his wrists and ankles and fit rather snugly over his huge barrel chest and tree-trunk arms.

"Let the record reflect," stated the judge, "Defendant Anderson is present with counsel, Mr. Dwight Schmidt. Counselor, do you or your client have anything to say before the Court imposes sentence?"

"Your Honor, at first glance, my client would appear to be a career criminal, having already been to prison twice before. A careful review of his record, however, indicates that his first sentence was for a nonviolent, petty shoplifting conviction. He, along with three other youngsters, got caught stealing a camera from a local store. He served two years on that sentence. For the second offense, the police found a washing machine, stolen from a warehouse, at his mother's residence. For that, though, there were mitigating circumstances. It was Christmastime, Your Honor, and the man had no money. He stole the appliance to give to his mother as a gift.

"We are here today for yet another nonviolent offense. None of the defendant's actions made the six o'clock news, nor were they reported in the local newspapers. These crimes are not worth the cost of locking Mr. Anderson up, Your Honor. Therefore, defendant prays for this court to show mercy.

"Actually, Mr. Schmidt," stated the judge, "I have this as defendant's fourth felony conviction. He was convicted for stealing the camera, a serious property offense, breaking into the warehouse, another property offense, and then he escaped from prison camp while serving time for breaking in the warehouse. Now defendant is back to get sentenced after his fourth felony conviction. That's why the prosecutor has filed a fourth-felony-offender notice."

The attorney opened a leather-bound folder and thumbed through a thin stack of papers. "That may be correct, Your Honor," he remarked, quickly scanning several sheets of paper. "Ah, here it is." He snatched one sheet of paper out of the folder and waved it at the judge. "A fourth-felony supplemental, life being the maximum penalty.

"You see, Your Honor," continued the lawyer, "the original attorney appointed to this case is sick, and I'm just a stand-in. I really haven't had time to thoroughly review defendant's case file. I beg your pardon."

"Yyyyuh-yuh-yuh-your Honor, I'm ssssuh-suh-suh-suh-sorry I sttuh-stttttuh-stuh-stuh-stuh-stole a hhhhhham, bbbbbu-buh-buh-but I wwwas hungry. And—"

"There are many people out there that are hungry, but they don't resort to theft," interjected the judge. "People who want to eat work for a paycheck and then buy their food."

"I wwwwuh-wuh-will work, sssssir, bbbbut people wwwuh-wwwwuh-woh-woh-won't hire mmme 'cccccuh-cause they ssssay I cccccuh-ccccuh-cuh-cuh-can't talk."

Ignoring Anderson's last remark, the judge moved on. "Let the record reflect that Defendant Anderson and counsel have spoken. Now let the court state the facts of the case before sentencing.

"Defendant Anderson, a fourth-felony offender, was convicted by jury of petty larceny from a building." Anderson may as well have not been in the room the way the judge talked over him to his attorney. "He was caught stealing ham from a local grocery store. The stolen item is not much to consider. However, considering this is his fourth felony—"

"No, Lord Jesus, no! Oh, dear God, no no no!" A heavyset dark-skinned woman came barreling through the audience partition. As she reached Anderson, she fell to her knees, hands together in supplication. Anderson bent and tried to put a shackled hand on her shoulder.

"Who is this woman?" the judge demanded of Anderson.

"It's my mmmuh-muh-mamma, sir."

"Well, tell her that she can't disrupt my courtroom like this and that she needs to return to her seat."

The bailiff stepped forward and, with both hands, gripped the heavy woman's upper arm. Vainly, he tried to tug her erect. Over the radio, he called for two more officers to come and assist him.

Turning his attention back to Schmidt, the judge proceeded. "The court hereby orders that Defendant serve no less than thirty years and no more than seventy-five years in a state correctional facility."

Before anyone could say anything further, the woman sprang to her feet screaming. She shook the bailiff off and launched herself at the attorney. "Please don't let them take my son away for the rest o' his life," she cried uncontrollably, seizing the sturdy man's lapels. The attorney recoiled in surprise but caught the stout woman by her elbows to support her against sending them both sprawling.

The attorney tried to comfort her, but the sobbing woman was hysterical. Two more bailiffs entered the courtroom from the front. As they approached up the aisle, the original bailiff broke off from the woman and began escorting Anderson toward the rear door that led to the holding tank.

The two made it about four steps before the woman peered around and saw her son being taken away. Swifter than her bulk would have seemed to allow, she released the lawyer, turned, and dashed after her son. Three quick strides later, she fell to her knees and clutched at her son's legs.

Looking up at the judge with tears glistening on her fleshy cheeks, she prayed, "Oh please, God, no, don't take my son away from me. He's the only thing I have left."

The two backup officers had just now reached the bawling woman. As they struggled to pry her grip free of her son's shackled legs, she implored the judge urgently. "Please, Mr. Judge, he ain't never hurt nobody. Please don't take his whole life from him. I need him at home, sir."

"Look, lady, I haven't taken your son's life. I didn't tell him to go into that store and steal from hardworking citizens. Those were his fingers, not mine. Now let go of that man and return to your seat or leave my courtroom.

"I'm getting sick and tired of these interruptions, and if they don't stop, I'm going to start handing down fines and jail sentences."

To pry the woman loose, the two bailiffs squeezed pressure points on her wrist, wrenching a long pain-filled shriek out of her. When she let go, the two bailiffs restrained her on the spot, as the third bailiff tugged a struggling Anderson toward the rear door. When he heard that last scream from his mother, Anderson fought mightily against his captor, trying to return to his mother's side, unable to protest aloud because the anxiety and distress of seeing his mother manhandled exacerbated his stuttering.

When the bailiff finally dragged the struggling man through the rear door, the mother seemed to calm down instantly, as if the closed door had stolen the last of her resolve. The two bailiffs on top of her slowly eased up and helped her to stand. Shrugging her arms free of their grip, she straightened her clothes, her hair and, without another word, wearily trudged toward the exit. The entire courtroom watched as she paused with her hand on the door handle and turned to face the judge once more. Her mouth opened, and for seconds, nothing came out. Finally, her mouth shut with a click. There was nothing left to say. She pushed open the door and left the courtroom, and any hope of saving her son, behind.

A black and a white man stood on the first-gallery bulkhead of four-block arguing raucously over a seven-year-old gambling debt from a football game. Both men contended that the other owed him a dollar. The dispute had gotten so loud, the clamor drew the attention of the guards on base.

One of the guards got up to investigate. As he approached the men, the guard yelled for them to keep the noise down. Because the two men ignored him, he stepped closer, almost in between them, and smelled the spud juice a second too late. Both prisoners turned on the guard, and an argument heated up rapidly. The officer reached for his radio to call for help but instead caught a left hook to the jaw. He staggered to the side a couple steps before catching his balance and launching a right cross at the lanky white prisoner, sending him tumbling. The second prisoner rushed the guard against the bars of the bulkhead.

Spotting the commotion, the other guard pushed the button on his personal protection device to summon backup, taking the stairs two at a time. Prisoners gathered on base to watch the two guards battle the two drunken prisoners. The young prisoners, both in their midtwenties, caught the worst of it; the second guard's knuckles held thick calluses from years of bar brawling. Forty-five, with a huge beer gut, a smoker's cough, and a cheap tattoo across the back of his neck that read "100% Honky!" the second guard landed blows that sounded like thunder.

When the first member of the response team crashed through the four-block entrance, the door swung and knocked one of the prisoners standing on base into another prisoner. Like a lit match into a dry wheat field, the base exploded into a violent melee. Although the prisoners outnumbered them three to one, the guards still held their own—even the two female guards—against the inebriated convicts.

Tina Brown faded in and out of consciousness, trying her hardest to focus on the droning monotonous voice as it attempted to explain the subtleties of constitutional law. The snug headphones filtered out nearly all other sound.

"Next case," the judge directed the bailiff.

"The next case is *People v. Billy Walker*, Your Honor. The defendant is here for sentencing."

A black man of about forty stood up, walked to the podium and stood next to the same muscle-bound attorney who represented the last defendant.

"Dwight Schmidt, Your Honor, public defender's office, appearing on behalf of Defendant Walker," the attorney uttered.

"Let the record reflect that Defendant Walker is present with his attorney, Mr. Dwight Schmidt. Today is the day set for sentencing. Counselor, do you or your client have anything to say before the court imposes sentence?"

"Your Honor, my client understands what's going on here. He has been to prison for armed robbery, then after his release, he successfully completed a two-year parole and now has been convicted of another armed robbery.

"Those are the few bad points, Your Honor. But contrary to what one might think, my client does have some redeeming qualities.

First, my client has never been suspected in nor convicted of a crime where actual violence occurred. Secondly, in neither robbery was the weapon loaded.

"Furthermore, my client is a family man. He has taken care of his family by providing for them life's necessities, that is, food, clothes, and shelter. My client's wife and two children are here in court today to support their husband and father. I urge the court to consider these facts upon sentencing.

"The combined amount my client claimed from the two robberies was likely less than five thousand. To spend thirty thousand dollars a year to keep my client incarcerated for an extensive period of time would be against state interests. Instead of prison, the court can elect to fine my client a guesstimate of what he took during the robbery and an additional fine for punitive reasons as allowed by statute. On top of that, the court could order my client to attend outpatient counseling and employment workshops, eventually at his own expense. I ask the court to consider the mitigating factors previously mentioned and use its judicial discretion to impose a lighter sentence than is customary. Society should reserve the harsher sentences for those persons who commit crimes that are actually violent, not just those classified as violent, as is the case with my client."

The two guards patrolling the dining area of the chow hall had heard, over their mobile radios, the distress call from four-block. Because shift command had not assigned them to the response team, their duty was to remain vigilant over their assigned section of the prison. Warily, they walked through the metal tables, keeping their ears open for any sign of trouble. With all the violence over the past week, the entire staff was on edge.

As they neared the back dock, the guards heard more voices and laughter than the three men working the area would account for. Stepping in sight of the back dock, the guards beheld a vigorous crowd of about fifty men loitering, shoving, or wrestling with one another.

One of the guards walked toward the edge of the horde and ordered the men to leave the kitchen. The men who had not noticed the guards approach now turned and converged on the two men. The prisoners nearest the guard laughed wildly at the demand. Drunken mirth rippled through the pack of men. The fringes of the crowd slowly began to flank the guards. Knowing that the situation could detonate at any second, the guards laughed along with the prisoners and casually retreated from the area. The nearest exit soon appeared, and the guards took it posthaste.

The prisoners, for some reason, chose not to follow, and the first guard out of the door called over the radio for backup. The captain responded that all available personnel were tending to the disturbance in four-block and that they were to leave the area immediately. Seconds later, the emergency siren blared over the loud speakers, drowning out all radio communication and forcing the staff to maintain radio silence until shift command killed the alarm.

"Your Honor, I've been to prison before," Walker began, despair flattening his deep voice, "and I've made the same mistake twice. I'm remorseful, but I know that don't really mean anything. I'm a two-time loser, and I know that."

Walker paused, dropped his head for a second, looked up again, and continued. "I know the court is going to throw the book at me. I won't stand here and try to fool myself by thinking different. All I ask is that the court don't take the rest of my life from me. I know I've done wrong and I have to serve my time, I just don't want to die in prison. That's all I ask."

"Let the record reflect that defendant and counsel have had the opportunity to address the court. Now the court will state the facts of this case before sentencing.

"Defendant, a second-felony offender, pled guilty to robbing a liquor store while armed and stealing an undetermined amount of cash. Just before the attendant closed the store, defendant, wearing a ski mask, walked into the liquor store and pulled a gun on the cashier and demanded all of the money in the drawer. After getting the money, defendant left through the front door. Officers caught him walking through an alley less than three blocks from the store.

"Now counsel wants me to consider as mitigating factors that the defendant has never actually harmed anyone and that the gun was never loaded. I hardly find these facts compelling. I will not reward a criminal for not harming someone. Had defendant not been captured, it would have been only a matter of time before he hurt or killed someone. Then before this Court, he would stand a convicted murderer. The only way to stop him and people like him from harming innocent victims is to keep them off the streets.

"Therefore, the court hereby imposes a sentence of not less than sixty years and no more than ninety years in prison."

"Objection, Your Honor, on two grounds," Schmidt said, shocked. "First and foremost, the sentence exceeds my client's life expectancy. The law prohibits sentencing judges from giving defendants sentences that they cannot serve. It would be tantamount to telling a man to jump in the air and not come down. It's impossible. Secondly, claiming that my client might hurt or kill someone in the future, well, you're sentencing him for something he might do, which the law also forbids. For these reasons, I implore the court to reduce the sentence to at least one that my client can actually serve."

"Take it up on appeal, counselor. Next case," the judge concluded as the gavel clacked with finality.

The bailiff stepped forward. "The next case," he intoned, "is *People v. George Evans*. Defendant is here for an evidentiary hearing."

There is in this world no such force as the force of a man determined to rise.

—W. E. B. Dubois

Chapter 18

Scrap Iron and his cronies laughed uncontrollably as they watched the two guards leave the kitchen. The big man himself fell back on a long table clutching his stomach and wiping tears of glee from his eyes. One of his men came over and told him that a bunch of prisoners was fighting guards in four-block, which ripped an even louder bout of laughter from Scrap Iron's stomach. He was still laughing when the emergency siren blew.

The sound of the siren sobered the big man up enough to pull himself together. He rolled over and pushed himself off the table, gathered his men, and left the back dock. The gang of men cursed and complained loudly over being called to lockdown once again. Their fury swelled with each step they took toward the blocks. More Jell-O, more hunger, more frustration; just the thought of it pissed them off even more.

As the group rounded the corner, Scrap Iron looked over at four-block. A crowd of men stood just outside of the doors while a fight just inside choked off the entrance.

Scrap Iron, with about twenty of his men, made a detour for four-block. The potent spud juice and the injustice of two lockdowns in a row had the men primed for a fight. The men assumed that that was the reason Scrap Iron led the men toward the brawl. However, Scrap Iron had a different motive for the detour. Where were Nathaniel and Never Black? he wondered. Since this disturbance created the perfect diversion for him to handle his business, Scrap Iron surreptitiously scanned the crowd ahead of him, searching for the man he dispatched to find the two young boys earlier.

Scrap Iron leaned to his right and told the man next to him to take with him another man from the crew and find the two young'ins and deliver them to the big pedophile. Two men on his left, he directed to go find Samuel Davis and report back on his whereabouts and, while they were at it, to locate the first two men he had sent earlier, right after the lockdown status had ended, to locate Samuel Davis. Those two men had never reported back.

Guards were pouring from the subhall now. Nearly twenty-five guards raced across the yard to four-block. The gathering in front of four-block had swollen to nearly three hundred bodies. When they arrived at the fringes of the fidgeting crowd, the guards had to push a path through to the doorway. Just as the guards neared the center of the group of men, a battery of kicks and punches fell upon the guards from all sides. Taken by surprise, the guards crumbled into panic. After a moment, though, the guards regrouped and fought their way into a tight circle, trying to match the prisoners blow for blow.

Up on the roof, the best marksmen from among the guards on duty manned the gun towers. Other guards tromped from the control center to the roofs garbed in full riot gear, some with rifles, some with camcorders in hand.

About ten minutes earlier, two relief officers rushed to collect the riot gear from the arsenal. The arsenal guard gathered every can of pepper spray and tear gas in the room and loaded it into a cart designed for transporting chemical weapons. A sergeant checked all the rifles, shotguns, and pistols, making sure they functioned properly, and loaded shells into those that needed them. All available guards took a set of equipment and rushed to their preassigned details.

Meanwhile, the records office supervisor instructed all twenty-three secretaries under her command to immediately shut down all systems, clear away all desktops, and bring out all red-tagged files: the files of the most dangerous prisoners inside the walls. Department procedure required that these files be readily accessible during a major disturbance—and this, no doubt, qualified as a major disturbance.

In the middle of the large office, isolated and ominous, squatted an ovular red table. No one other than the records office supervisor or her superiors could touch the thousands of pages of court transcripts, psychiatric files, and black-and-white and colored photographs dating back to the early sixties stacked in ragged piles on the table's surface. Some of the images depicted a man in full military regalia, others of him in street clothes, and a few of him in prison clothes on the yard of Jackson Inside. Because the information on the table had to remain accessible at all times, the warden authorized the menacing display about three decades ago, and it had not moved since.

In accords with procedure, the records-office supervisor contacted the director of psychiatric services. When the phone rang, the director picked up the phone and listened intently. After about fifteen seconds, he placed the phone back on its cradle with a slightly trembling hand. No more than a heartbeat later, he stood up and hastened to the small dolly situated in the corner of his office. On it sat a small file cabinet with the name Samuel Davis stenciled on the sides in large white letters. He tilted the dolly on its wheels and, as he rolled it past his secretary toward the door, pointed to the side of the cabinet and uttered,"Priority 1 call."

The records office supervisor called the deputy warden, who in turn called the captain of the guards. The captain immediately dispatched two guards to the roof of the prison with orders to find Samuel Davis and track his every move with a camcorder.

Two young secretaries each wheeled in a gray file cabinet containing the personnel records of all staff employed by the prison complex. Every secretary on hand extracted a stack of files and started placing calls to staff members on the second and third shifts, those at home on their regular days off, and even those on vacation, alerting them to the disturbance and putting each one of them on standby. One of the inspectors notified the Michigan State Police and the nearest National Guard post, placing them on standby also.

At home in the shower, the warden's phone rang insistently. He hopped out of the shower, dried off haphazardly, and strode to the phone. Ten minutes later, he was in his car racing toward his prison.

George had moved from the bench to a chair behind the defense table. He watched as people in the audience tried to help the wife of the man who got sentenced to sixty years. She had fainted. The judge ordered a ten-minute recess, during which the woman was revived and, along with her two children, escorted out of the courtroom.

"The next case is *People v. George Evans,* Your Honor. The defendant is here for an evidentiary hearing," the bailiff announced as the proceedings reconvened.

George stood, took a deep breath to steady the residual jitters he felt from the excitement of being in court, and declared, "George Evans, Your Honor, in propria persona, in his own person."

At Jackson Inside, the prisoners could feel the tension against their skin like the humidity of a muggy afternoon in July. A horde of nearly two hundred white prisoners rallied in Peckerwood Park, with more arriving by the second. Three contract killers—Gary Wolfe, Augie Contie, and James Brown—herded the men together, knowing there would soon be a need for an organized defense. On the tennis court adjoining Peckerwood Park huddled roughly a hundred Latinos, led by twice-convicted murderer Rubin Herrara, preparing for the inevitable. Even a large knot of the usually disjointed blacks assembled about fifteen yards to the opposite side of Peckerwood Park, between the subhall and the Big Top. Several smaller factions of mixed races huddled together between Peckerwood Park and the entrance to the subhall.

On the other side of the yard, about fifteen men from Chicago's Robert Taylor Projects, with Johnnie Razor-bey, founder of the MDOC branch of the Moorish Science Temple of America, at their head, rushed into four-block, searching for a place to take up a defensive position. The group encountered four guards standing behind their desk arguing with a group of prisoners. The prisoners were demanding the guards relinquish their keys, but the guards stubbornly refused and repeatedly ordered the prisoners to lockdown. If a guard voluntarily handed over his or her keys, that guard would be dismissed outright. However, if it happened during a riot, the guard would be fired then possibly brought up on felony charges. Giving up their keys was out of the question.

The four guards remained unyielding despite being grossly outnumbered—until they noticed Razor-bey and the rest of his men rush into the block. The band's arrival seemed to drain what little resolve the one female guard had left. She swore crudely then bolted for the exit, running recklessly. Pushing her way through the plugged entrance, ducking under fists and kicks, dodging around falling men, the guard tore down the short sidewalk across the old road and through the card tables on the yard. Too surprised by the fierceness of her crazed flight, the men gathered on the yard merely watched as she zipped by.

When she crossed the sidewalk leading to five-block, she chanced a look back and saw that the other three guards had abandoned post also and now sprinted right behind her, fleeing for the subhall. On their heels, the same group of prisoners ran, still demanding the guards' keys. This time, with all of them gripping long shanks in their hands.

The female guard swung away from five-block onto the short sparse grass of Peckerwood Park. With burning lungs and weakening thigh muscles, she headed left where the fence ended. She itched for the safety of the control center. All she had to do was turn right at the fence, hurry down the old road, and veer left into the subhall. Once there, a few more steps onward would take her to gate 15, the entrance to the control center, blessed safety. From her many hours of training, she knew that at least fifty guards stood ready at the control center gate with shields, helmets, pepper spray, and tear gas. Thirty more yards to sanctuary.

Rounding the end of the fence, she realized that she would not make it. The three male guards overtook her, leaving no one between her and a mob of rabid prisoners. Panic swelled in her chest; her lungs heaved and sucked at air that suddenly seemed too thin to satisfy her need. She pumped her legs as fast as she could. As soon as she hit the old road heading for the subhall, she heard drunken voices no more than two or three meters behind her yelling, "Give us the keys, mothafuckas!" Her heartbeat stuttered, yet she ran on.

With tears of dread pouring from distended eyes, she cried out miserably, "Help me, pleeeease! Please don't leave me!" To her horror, not one of the male guards even glanced rearward. From the corner of her eye, she saw several shadows, elongated from the late morning sun, the shadows of men bent on violence. The silhouette nearest to her had an arm raised high with what she knew was a deadly blade in its grasp, poised to strike with brutal force. Screaming in desperation, she squeezed what little thrust she could from her fatigued legs and leaned her upper body forward, clenching her shoulder blades together, tensing every spare muscle, preparing for the blow she knew would soon chop her down.

Up ahead, one of the male guards named Jeff Hanson, desperate himself in his flight for safety, heard the terrified scream for help behind him. He knew the woman it came from too. Her name was Carolyn Marsh: a coworker and a dear friend. Her dilemma had broken through the swathe of terror surrounding his senses. Looking back, he saw her plight and almost wept. Confronted with the choice of losing his job or saving the life of a friend, guard Hanson envisioned his wife and his four young children. Having recently purchased a new home—a home that his wife so devotedly took care of—the mortgage and down payment had left only two thousand dollars in the bank. If he lost his job now, he could lose his house, his car, and maybe even his family. Finding another decent-paying job in this economy would be hell because Michigan had the highest unemployment rate in the nation. His compassion grappled with his logic; how would he take care of his family? How would he be able to live with himself if he let Carolyn be killed?

Hanson's inner struggle lasted the span of about two heartbeats. The next second, he ripped his keys from his hip clip, took aim over his shoulder, stopped after a few more paces, turned, and flung the keys as hard as he could at the prisoner poised to stab Carolyn. Carolyn, leaning forward like a sprinter for the finish line, her face pallid and frozen in a rictus of horror, was on the verge of stumbling when the heavy ring of keys zipped over her head and connected noisily with her pursuer's face.

Caught by surprise, Murder Rap flinched back from the impact. He slowed to a stop when he realized what had hit him. A few yards ahead, guard Marsh stumbled along a few more strides before crashing painfully to the pavement. "Dumb-ass cops," one of the prisoners remarked as he recovered the keys and, along with the rest of the clique, turned and headed toward five-west, the hole.

Guard Hanson rushed to Marsh's side and helped her up carefully. He winced at the horrendous gash on the left side of her face, running from her eyebrow to her lower jaw, a jaw the fall had broken in two places. Hanson supported her the rest of the way into the subhall and through gate 15.

A guard watching the incident from the roof of five-block radioed the captain and notified him about the keys. The captain called the warden, who had just arrived at the prison, and relayed the information to him. After ordering the captain to fire Hanson immediately, the warden instructed him to set up central command in the visiting room, where the brass would go to monitor the disturbance.

The warden phoned Lansing, getting the director of the MDOC, Patricia Caruso, on the line. After the warden briefed her, Caruso called Jennifer M. Granholm, the governor of the state of Michigan.

The man who recovered the keys handed them to the leader of their small but lethal crew. Burns Culver, or Murder Rap as he was known throughout the system, had seven men with him as he marched toward five-block. He had a plan. If this didn't get him where he wanted to be, nothing would.

Ever since he set foot inside Jackson, Murder Rap had longed to join up with Namen Travis. He idolized the man. Anything Travis asked him to do, he would do it simply because he knew Travis wouldn't be on bullshit. Everything the man did had a purpose, and if Murder Rap could do something to further his cause, he wouldn't hesitate. That's why he and his crew now stalked toward five-block. They were going to let Travis and the rest of his boys out of the hole. Travis definitely wouldn't want to miss out on what was going down.

As Murder Rap unlocked the rear entrance to segregation, he and the rest of the men met with no resistance, for the five-block guards had long ago abandoned post. And as always, the din inside matched that of any made by an arena full of basketball fans. The men fanned out on the base, yelling Travis's name. A man in one of the cells on base directed them to the first quiet cell.

Murder Rap entered the antechamber alone to unlock the inner door. A few seconds later, after Murder Rap called out to him, Travis emerged from the dismal and oppressive darkness, blinking to adjust his eyesight. Murder Rap quickly explained what was up in the prison and about how he and his men had strong-armed the keys from one of the guards and that Travis was the first man they freed. He asked Travis what he wanted him to do next. Instead of giving instructions, Travis confiscated the keys and walked purposefully from the quiet cell.

The eight men followed Travis as he moved from base all the way up to the fourth gallery, freeing all the men who came to the hole with him. Pulling one of his men to the side, Travis explained the situation to him and told him to go to every cell and free every man who wanted to join Travis's crew until the riot was over and leave the rest locked up.

Namen Travis walked and sat behind the guards' desk. Swinging his boots up onto the desktop, he reclined back and tried to organize his thoughts. Some serious shit was jumpin' off, so he had to proceed carefully. He had the keys to the prison, and in minutes, he would lead the largest crew to ever stomp the grounds of Jackson Inside.

Oblivious to the shrill squalling of the emergency siren, Tina Brown, still lounging groggily in her chair, had one hour left before the lecture coming out of the headphones ended.

The warden, inspectors, and several guards looked on as an army of secretaries and on-call staff members hauled in and organized tables, files, phones, coffee, cups, fax machines, and copy machines, transforming the prisoner visiting room into central command.

The disturbance sprouted much too rapidly for the healthcare personnel to react in time. The entire medical staff had gathered in the hallway of their offices. Since traversing the one hundred yards to the control center entailed the risk of being caught in the middle of the riot, the administrative heads had authorized the health care unit manager to implement plan B.

The pretty short petite HUM led the way as the queue of nervous professionals trotted behind, heading for the back hallway of the top floor. After about ten minutes, they arrived at their destination with all infirmary personnel accounted for. Standing toward the end of the hallway, the HUM opened a mop closet and turned on the light. She walked to the far wall, opened a wooden cabinet, and with her right hand, slipped a key into a small lock in the wall behind the cabinet. Seconds after she turned the key, the entire wall slid to the right, revealing a dusty set of stairs. Without hesitation, the frightened team rushed up the stairs and out onto the roof to safety.

Travis could not think. That goddamn siren was too loud. Frustrated, he swung his legs off the desk and slid out a thin slab of wood right under the lip of the desk, just above the top drawer. A single sheet of paper taped to the surface displayed the three-digit codes for every phone inside the prison. Travis picked up the phone and dialed the number for the warden's office. Ten rings sounded before the secretary, sounding out of breath, picked up the other end.

"Warden's office," answered a feminine voice.

"This is Namen Travis. I'm calling to let you know I'm in charge of Jackson Inside now, and if you don't want me to kill this guard I got hostage, you'll kill that alarm within the next sixty seconds." Travis hung up the phone without waiting for a response.

Up front in the warden's office, the secretary kept the phone to her ear as the other end disconnected, stunned at what she just heard. The guard in the five-block gun tower had said nothing about a hostage. Nevertheless, her training told her that during a crisis, there was no room for assumptions. She got a dial tone then called the warden in the visiting room turned command center.

With his arms folded across his chest and his legs back up on the desk, Namen Travis counted the seconds as the siren continued to caterwaul. He made it to thirty-two, then the noise ceased. A vicious crooked smile curved up one side of his face.

On the sentencing issue, the disparities in sentencing, I don't argue that an element of racism is not involved.

—Justice Fred L. Banks Jr.

Chapter 19

George stepped forward and stood before the podium, leafing through the documents in his folder, setting those most important to the side. He let his arms drop to his sides and briefly looked toward the prosecutor. Turning back to the bench, he met the contemptuous gaze of the judge. Leaning forward, with his crossed arms resting on the massive bench, the judge stared bullets through George's skull.

Judge Linbush prided himself on three things: his extensive knowledge of federal and state constitutional law, his adherence to those laws, and his ability to read men. He considered it part of his job to be able to read the parties who stood before his court. The man who now stood before him was an open book. Although he based his assessment on more than just appearance—Judge Linbush had subpoenaed George's file weeks prior—paperwork couldn't fully define a man's person. From the file, the judge concluded that George was a very intelligent man, having earned his GED, an associate's and a bachelor's degree, as well as a degree in paralegal studies all while incarcerated. In each of those endeavors, he ranked among the top one percent of all aspirants in his class, graduating summa cum laude to obtain his bachelor's. The prisoner was a thinker, a doer. The judge found a thirty-eight-page term paper in his file entitled "The Moral Premise of Law throughout the Ages." A work of art, the judge concluded. Considering Evans's accomplishments, the judge figured that he didn't watch much TV or waste time listening to music or playing games.

The man now in front of his bench has done more than just survive forty-plus years in prison; he has exceeded the limits of his restraints. According to block reports written by prison guards, Evans naturally fell into the leadership role. He had engendered that self-determined spirit in other prisoners, organizing think tanks, charity drives, and other altruistic undertakings. By the composition and construction of the self-prepared legal pleading sitting before him, Linbush could tell that Evans had been studying the law for decades and was very familiar with its subtleties. All in all, Evans was a dangerous man. The judge had best step carefully, and smartly, with this one.

"Before we begin, Mr. Evans, I would like to take this opportunity to ask if you would like the court to appoint you an attorney to represent you in this matter?" said the judge.

"No, Your Honor. I motion the court to allow me to proceed pro per," George responded."

"Anticipating the possibility that you may want or need an attorney, I have enlisted several attorneys—several very efficient attorneys—who have already researched and have prepared briefs in support of your issue. They are ready to assist or represent you right now."

"I'll pass."

"Well then, the next order of business—determining whether you're qualified to represent yourself. Expecting this, you have submitted a letter to the court attesting to your capability, letters from numerous appellate attorneys and a couple of state and federal judges, all of whom emphatically assert that you are more than capable of representing yourself."

Some of the signers of those letters, for example, federal district judges John Enslen and Arthur Tarnow, Ingham County Circuit Judge James R. Giddings, and the director of the State Appellate Defender Office, James Neuhard, along with appellate attorneys James S. Lawrence, Laura K. Sutton, and Susan J. Smith, line the back and side walls of the courtroom. Their entourages included clerks and legal researchers, paralegals, and legal assistants. A few other paralegals and legal assistants present represented other firms whose attorneys could not attend.

"Have you been furnished with a copy of those letters, Mr. Sturtz?" the judge asked, addressing a middle-aged man garbed in an expensive suit, standing at the podium representing the state. Douglas Sturtz served as the director of the Appellate Division of the Wayne County Prosecutor's Office. At a table to his right sat his assistant prosecutor and a paralegal.

"Yes, I have, Your Honor," he answered, his voice funereal.

"We have the signers of those letters in the courtroom today, ready to be sworn in as expert witnesses to testify to Mr. Evans's qualifications. Would you like an offer of proof?"

"No, Your Honor. I'll stipulate to the qualifications." The ingratiating slow inflection of the prosecutor's voice annoyed George, but he ignored it and focused on the proceedings.

The judge turned to George. "Mr. Evans, the court will grant your motion for self-representation. Would you like a thirty-minute recess to go over your pleadings?"

"No, sir."

"Are you ready to proceed?"

"I am ready, Your Honor."

"Mr. Sturtz?"

"I am ready also, your Honor."

"Mr. Evans, state your issue."

The courtroom was packed. Several minutes after the bailiff announced George's case and after the other prisoners' families had cleared out, the judges, attorneys, law students, and their professors began filing into the courtroom. Students from the law schools at the University of Michigan, Michigan State, Thomas Cooley and Wayne State now sat shoulder to shoulder on the benches. The class of fifth-grade students remained seated on the front row of the right column of benches. Everyone else—except for the few local citizens who attended court proceedings out of sheer boredom or morbid curiosity—attended the hearing on invitation from Judge Linbush himself. A novel issue, one bearing public and state interests, was before the court. By order of the court, several firms had filed briefs as amici curiae.

George felt good today. He thought the pressure of the hearing would have his nerves more on edge, like they were during the ride to the courthouse. However, the moment the judge called his case, all apprehension evaporated; a calm spread throughout his system like fresh blood. The ambience of professionalism soothed him and freed his thoughts. The courtroom was where he belonged; this was his domain.

George's voice rumbled clear and strong when he responded to the judge."Racial disparity in sentencing, Your Honor."

Prisoners had complete control of four- and five-blocks.

Namen Travis had two of his men posted as sentries outside of the quiet cell from which Murder Rap had recently released him. The men stood just out of range of the inside gun tower, knowing better than to give the guards any hope of a target. Travis had a hostage in the quiet cell. While the men were off on different missions, he found the man hiding in a place he wouldn't disclose, beat him up, and locked him in the quiet cell. He refused to tell anyone the guard's name. Travis instructed the men standing outside the cell to not look inside it and, if they did, to expect a most harsh and immediate punishment.

The prisoners looted both stores on the compound and were raiding the property room and the quartermaster presently. They had control of the Big Top, pillaging the large freezers and food coolers, the cabinets and storerooms. Over two hundred prisoners were tromping through the subhall toward the south complex to free the rest of the twenty-five hundred men housed in six-, seven-, eight-, eleven-, and twelve-blocks who weren't already out of their cells.

Big Will was hurrying down the bulkhead of the hole with at least forty men, whom he had just freed from their cells, in tow. The majority of the men he had already released tarried by the showers on base, where he instructed them to wait until he returned. Sprinting back down to the shower area, Big Will told the men that they were going to strike out as soon as he got the order, which wouldn't be long.

Only 26 men refused to join Namen's gang, and they all remained locked in their cells. Led by Big Will, the other 224 men hustled to the other end of the block where Namen Travis sat behind the guards' desk, facing them. As the men got within ten yards, Namen stood. Having had his clothes fetched from the property-storage room in the hole, Travis had donned his trademark green army fatigues, his immaculately polished shin-high army boots and capped it off with a midnight black beret slanted sideways. Every original member of his gang had on the same uniform.

Travis held up his right hand, and the men halted immediately. "I sent a man out to check on the situation outside, so I can know, before we walk out, the status of the prison. I'm also going to leave two men posted in front of the quiet cell and rotate them every two hours. I have a bargaining chip in there. If the staff get out of line, or if I don't get what I want, I'll drag him out to the yard and fuck him up right in front of the cameras."

Travis went on to tell his men that he had a plan, a plan that would only take a few hours to implement but that would make national headlines, making the front pages of magazines and newspapers across the country, and even find a place in the history books. As he explained the details, the men interrupted his telling with questions about the potential of getting caught up in criminal prosecutions or about how they were going to stay fed. Travis explained that although other men had likely looted the store already and for that, it was going to be difficult to keep everyone fed, still he had figured out a way to solve the problem and make money for all of them. Then he walked over to the phone, picked up the receiver, and dialed a three-digit number. The warden answered in central command.

"Namen Travis here, warden," he proclaimed loudly so that all of the men present could hear him. "Get a pencil and write this down." After a short pause, he continued. "I want three thousand of the biggest and best pizzas in the city with assorted toppings. I want three thousand boxes of KFC, along with 10,000 pops—no, make that 25,000 pops. I also want 750 apiece of Pall Malls, Kools, and Camels, 10,000 pints of assorted-flavor ice cream, and find us some apple and pumpkin pies. Yeah, I haven't had homemade pie in a while. I want some pies . . . and some lobster, too.

"I want it all delivered within the next five hours and brought through the front gates and up to gate 15. I'll have some men waiting to take it from there. When the food arrives, have someone announce it over the loudspeaker. Have them say, 'Namen Travis, you're food is ready.' Have them say it twice.

"If you do not have my food here within five hours to the minute, you and whoever else is up there monitoring the roof cameras will witness an execution worse than what them Arabs do to your American soldiers." With that, Travis slammed the phone back on its receiver.

The men in front of the desk hooted, hollered, and cheered raucously as if Travis had made a game-winning basket. The men knew the warden had no doubt that Travis meant what he said and that everything Travis had demanded would be there within five hours. One of them walked over to the quiet cell and hollered into the short, dark hallway. "Thanks, muthafucka!" Savage laughter erupted from the crowd.

Travis, seated once again behind the guards' desk, watched the excitement and smiled. When the clamor subsided, he told the men that he had demanded so much so they could sell what they weren't going to keep to the rest of the population and make some money. Out of the corner of his eye, he spotted Big Will walking toward him with the man he sent out to scout the yard. Travis stood and huddled off to the side with the two men. After a minute or two of whispering, Travis returned to the desk, raised his hand for quiet, and said, "Our first order of business will be to send fifty men to the maintenance department in the basement of the gym to pick up some cutting torches and some tools we can use as weapons. Meanwhile, a few other men will dig out the knives my crew has hidden around the prison. Bring everything you find back here."

Big Will started selecting the fifty men for the task before Travis had finished talking. The men stood to the side ready to go. "I'm going to need another fifty men to comb the yard and take money, drugs, weapons, or anything else of value from men in groups of five or less. Again, bring everything you find back here. We will divide our take when we get everything together.

"A note of caution: do not approach anyone in Scrap Iron's crew or anyone belonging to BTT, especially Samuel Davis. Matter of fact, I need two men to keep track of Davis and let me know what he's up to at all times." Two eager young fellows stepped forward and accepted the task. Big Will stood the men to the side then finished counting out the second group of fifty.

"Now," Travis continued, "we're going to hit the yard. Everyone who doesn't already have an assignment will come with me. We're going to blue-hold card protective custody. All of the rats, snitches, and bitches, you can do what you want to 'em. Just remember, take anything of value and bring it back here when we're finished.

"You already know who I'm after. That piece of shit on protective custody. Leave his ass to me." Travis said this last statement with a sneer and a faraway look in his eyes.

If one took a survey limited to the black prisoners, male and female, in every state and federal penitentiary in the United States of the most hated prisoner in the system, the overwhelming response would name the man Travis was intent on now.

Twenty-seven guards trained rifles on the yard from the roofs of every block inside Jackson. Ten other guards—one to each block—stood on the roofs holding camcorders, recording every second, trying to cover every square foot of the yard.

Namen Travis, with fifty men on his heels, burst through the front door of five-west, sprinting toward six-block protective custody. The guard in the overhead gun tower phoned central command and informed the warden of the situation. The warden contacted the director of the MDOC, who ordered all power to every television in every prison across the state shut off. In March of 1981, a riot broke out at Jackson Inside, and prisoners at several other prisons watched its broadcast on the news. As a result, riots ended up breaking out at several other prisons. That was not going to happen this time.

All off-duty guards, inspectors, deputy wardens, and other security staff employed by the MDOC, who were within the state, were called to report to the prison nearest their location. Once there, other staff members briefed them on the riot and the statewide lockdown. Eventually, they all boarded the Greyhound buses in the parking lots of each facility and then transported to Jackson Inside.

Two arsonists broke into a maintenance supply room and seized twenty gallons of paint thinner and ten gallons of gasoline.

A Vietnamese prisoner named Giang Troung Ngo sat in his cell in four-block monitoring his radio. It was an old multiband FM radio, modified so that he could listen in on staff in central command communicating with the guards on the roof and outside the prison, the local and state police posted around and throughout the prison.

Scrap Iron and a few of his men sat on the metal tables in the corner of three- and four-blocks. Some men perched, eating food stolen from the Big Top and the prisoner store, while others smoked crack-cocaine-laced marijuana, injected heroin into their veins, or guzzled spud juice. A few of the men laughed and waved at the cameras on the roofs on the buildings.

Tina Brown winced. She removed her headphones and sniffed the air. A strange odor stung her nose. Rising from her seat, she sniffed the air again and traced the smell to the classroom door. Smoke? Why the hell did she smell smoke, and where was it coming from? She opened her door, walked across the hall and through the door of another classroom. Approaching the window, she saw prisoners everywhere—hundreds of them. She looked up and saw smoke billowing from the roof and windows of the Big Top. She scanned the yard, looking for the response team of guards she knew would, any second now, be rushing toward the disturbance. After seeing not one guard around the Big Top, she searched the rest of the yard. *That's strange, not one guard in sight,* she thought. Something made her look up, and when she did, she saw more guards than usual on the roofs with rifles and camcorders. Something wasn't right. She turned and trotted back to her classroom and snatched her mobile radio from the desk. Depressing the call button, holding the radio close to her mouth, she uttered,"This is mobile 13 in the school. I need some information. Copy?"

Tina waited a few seconds, but no response came. She tried again, and still nothing happened. Dropping the radio on the desk, she picked up the phone and dialed the control center. When the female voice answered the other line, Tina pronounced,"Yes, this is Tina Brown in the school. I'm having a problem . . . ." Before she could finish, Tina heard the woman scream "Oh my god!" and then the phone clattering to the floor.

"Hello!"Tina yelled."Hello!"

Seconds later, a male voice picked up the line."Hello."

"Hello? Who is this?"

"This is the warden, Ms. Brown. Please tell me exactly where you are calling from."

"I am standing behind the desk in my classroom in the subhall, room 1, on the second floor. I saw smoke coming from the chow hall, and I can smell it from here. What's going on?"

"Ms. Brown, why did you not evacuate the building when the emergency siren sounded?" asked the warden, trying to keep his voice level.

"I had my headphones on. I didn't even know the siren blew. Why? What's the problem?"

"Listen carefully, Ms. Brown. Are there any prisoners around you?"

"No."

"Is the door to your classroom locked?"

"No, it isn't. It's open like always."

"Ms. Brown, I need you to go over and lock the door, right now. Please hurry."

"Would you please tell me what's going on?"

"Please just go and lock the door."

"Okay, but I want to know what's going on."

"Ms. Brown . . . ." The Warden's voice grew stern, his calm beginning to crack. "I will tell you what's going on soon enough. But right now, I need you to go over to the door and lock it. That's an order!"

The warden's tone had risen to a shout. Before she realized it, Tina had dropped the phone and was almost to the door. The door shut with a loud thunk. When she heard the lock click automatically, she ran back to the phone and reported, "It's locked. Now what's going on?"

"Now, Ms. Brown, I want you to pick up your radio and switch it to the emergency frequency. The normal frequency may have been compromised." Tina picked up her radio and changed frequencies. The radio sprang to life.

Tina picked the phone back up. "Okay. It's done."

The warden's voice came through the radio. "Ms. Brown, this is the warden. Do you copy?"

Still holding the phone, Tina picked up the radio with her left hand. "I read you. But would you please tell me what's going on?"

"Hang the phone up, go to your closet, and lock yourself in. We can communicate through the radio."

"Excuse me, sir, but I'm kind of confused. Will you please explain to me what's going on?"Tina pleaded.

"In a minute, but first I need you to step into your closet and shut the door. Hurry now."

Apprehension began to creep its way into her system. She looked at the radio in her hand and noticed a slight tremor. As she moved toward the closet, she said into the radio, "You're starting to scare me."

"I apologize for that, but I just need you to follow my instructions. Everything will be okay, we have everything under control," the warden assured her. "Are you in the closet yet?"

"I just shut the door. I can't see a thing in here."

"Stay calm, Ms. Brown, and let me explain the entire situation before you ask any more questions."

"Okay." By now, Tina knew that something had gone terribly wrong. This was not normal procedure, hiding in closets and such. As she readied herself for whatever news the warden would give her, the vilest of scenarios crept into her mind. Maybe it was another terrorist attack. But that wouldn't make sense, why would they attack a prison? Or maybe there was an explosion and a pipe or something was leaking toxic fumes. *Oh shit, am I going to die?* That thought summoned a vision of her son's beaming face. Dear lord, what would he do without her? Apprehension morphed into panic. Her heart skipped a beat when the warden's voice buzzed through the radio again.

"A full-scale riot is in progress, Ms. Brown. The prisoners have taken over and now have control of the inside of the prison. What we're going to—"

"Did you say the prisoners have taken over the prison?" This last the warden could not hear because he still had the call button depressed when Tina tried to break in.

"Ms. Brown, you have to wait until the radio is clear before you speak. Otherwise, all I will hear is noise. Again, let me explain the situation fully before you ask questions. I will answer all of your concerns then.

"As I was saying," the warden continued, "the prisoners have taken over the prison. I am in central command, in the prisoner visiting room. The majority of the staff, official and civilian, have evacuated the building. Only two staff remain inside the prison: you and a guard. From our understanding, a group of prisoners led by Namen Travis has taken the guard hostage. As far as we know, he hasn't been harmed, and he is being held in one of the quiet cells in the hole."

The warden released the call button just long enough for Tina to scream in the radio."Did you say Travis? Namen Travis?"

"Yes, I did, but—" the radio screeched as Tina depressed the button again. The warden let up and Tina hollered,"The same guy that beat up the counselor the other day and runs around the prison in army fatigues? With a large group of very violent men as his followers, all dressed the same way? The crazy one?"

"That's correct."

"Send some guards to escort me out of here. I'm ready to go."

"I'm afraid I can't do that, Ms. Brown. At least not yet. Things aren't quite that simple. We first have to assess the situation fully before we take action. We have the local, county, and state police with us, as well as the National Guard on its way, so the situation is contained. Things are under control and—"That last statement would have made Tina laugh hysterically at any other time, but now it made her want to curse. However, instead of cursing, she depressed the call button and shouted into the radio.

"The hell you do! If you had control, you'd send someone to get me out right now. You wouldn't need to *assess* the situation." She infused that last with as much sarcasm and venom as she could muster."When I took this damn job, you told me that the classroom doors are security doors and that prisoners couldn't break into them once they're shut. Was that a lie?" She released the button.

"Well, no, that wasn't a lie, but the situation is much more complex than usual. In theory, the prisoners can't get in once the doors are closed, but that theory is contingent upon the prisoners not having keys."

"What! What the hell do you mean that theory depends upon the prisoners not having keys. Are you telling me that the prisoners have the keys to the prison? Is that what you're saying? What the hell do you people get paid to do around here?"

"Ms. Brown. Let's just settle down. I understand your frustration, but your insults will not help us any at this point. Right now my job is to keep you safe. I can't do that if you do not listen."

The warden's words penetrated her fear and distress just enough to allow her a moment of clarity. He was right. Whatever the situation, blame was not the way to resolve it. She had to calm herself and allow these people to do what they can to help her. "Okay, sir, I apologize for my outburst. It's just that I'm really scared right now. What do you need me to do?"

"First, I need you to listen. You need to know that we are positive that Namen Travis has a set of keys, and we suspect that Scrap Iron may also have a set. At the moment, that's all I can tell you, but I promise you, no harm will come to you.

"However, for me to be able to keep that promise, I'm going to need your cooperation. You see, we know that some prisoners can modify their FM radios to pick up our mobile radio traffic. That's part of the reason why we switched to the emergency frequency. Even still, given time, they likely can pick up this one too. I don't believe that any prisoners are aware of your location or that you are even still in the building, but in order to be sure, I'm going to need you to maintain complete radio silence unless it is an absolute emergency. And the same will go on my end. I will be in touch whenever the situation changes. Copy?"

Tina sat there for seconds, pondering what the warden had just proposed. He wanted her to sit there in a dark closet and what, sing songs to herself? Her stomach churned. Oh, why didn't she listen to her parents?

"Ms. Brown, do you copy?" the warden uttered through the radio.

"I copy, sir."

"One more thing. If prisoners just so happen to find your location, which we don't expect, contact us immediately, we'll come storming in.

"I'm not going to lie to you, this thing may take awhile. But you will be fine, I promise. Until then, you be brave for me. Now cut your radio down to the lowest possible setting, and monitor just in case I call you. But it is very important for you not to call out unless it is absolutely necessary. Are you with me?"

After a short pause, Tina muttered "Gotcha" and turned the radio down. So distracted was she by the madness that seemed to suddenly bloom around her, the click of the radio shutting off escaped her notice. Oblivious, she slipped the radio into its leather case on her hip.

The warden clicked off his radio, turned, and grabbed a computer printout one of the secretaries held out for him. It was a photograph of Sgt. Gary Moore, a white guard who worked at the prison for eight years. He had punched in at 0500 hours but was now unaccounted for. Shift command had assigned him to the backside of five-west, the hole. His station was the desk where Namen Travis now sat making his demands. This was the man they suspected Travis was holding hostage.

As far as I'm concerned, when you lose that many males of a particular race in one generation to the so-called criminal justice system . . . that's genocide. It's a quiet kind of genocide.

—Justice Joseph B. Brown Jr.

Chapter 20

Despite Judge Linbush having been on the bench for ten years now, no case had ever appeared before him that would allow him to put his own stamp on the law. He had sat in on a few important cases from time to time, but nothing that would make national headlines or have a substantive impact on a public issue of note. It was never his intent to force his way into the spotlight or to impose his will as a judge onto society, yet he felt somewhat defrauded at having had no opportunity to wield his extensive legal knowledge and exhibit his strict adherence to constitutional law.

When Linbush received George Evans's appeal, with racial disparity in sentencing being one of his issues, the judge knew without question that the chance that he had so subconsciously coveted had arrived; this issue embodied the perfect fact situation. The big case was now before his bench.

Over the years, many prisoners had appealed their cases, with some of them arguing racial disparity in sentencing. However, all those cases were prepared by the prisoners themselves and never by attorneys. An unwritten policy of appellate lawyering impelled attorneys to forego briefing issues that dealt with racial discrimination by judges. Any attorney who dared speak about arguing racial disparity in sentencing issues for their clients was labeled as a bleeding-heart liberal or dirty-nigger lover. Racial arguments of that nature were a tinderbox waiting to get kicked over in a barn full of hay. They could irreversibly damage the lawyers' careers who argued them and the judges' standing or reputations who ruled on them. For that reason, Linbush had rubber-stamped those appeals, denying relief on either procedural grounds or for "lack of merit," as did all other judges across the nation.

Judge Linbush believed that the political climate was now stable enough to weather this issue. "Your argument, Mr. Evans."

George cleared his throat and looked up from his paperwork. "Because of the racial structure of the criminal sentencing laws," he began, "I was given a more severe sentence for my murder conviction than would have been given to a white person with the same or similar circumstances. This racial disparity in sentencing not only affects me, but it also affects thousands upon thousands of blacks across the nation and—"

"Objection, Your Honor." Prosecutor Sturtz stood briskly and raised one hand to the judge. Sturtz, a red-faced man with a slight stoop to his shoulders, had a few wisps of snowy white hair crossing over the crest of his balding pate with a thick band of neatly cropped strands on the fringes. Except for a pale mustache, his face was clean shaven, exposing sagging jowls that gave him a perpetually lugubrious expression, as if the years had siphoned away all traces of gaiety. "On two grounds," he continued. "First, the doctrine of finality prevents our system from getting bogged down by endless appeals. It has been more than forty years since this man was convicted by a jury of his peers. His initial appeal was denied decades ago. Yet now, like a cold sore, he's back again. At some point we must say enough is enough. That point is now.

"Secondly," he continued, "The defendant is arguing racial disparity in sentencing for all black prisoners nationwide. This is not a class action, and such an argument is impermissible. There is only one appeal before the bench, so let's stick to that one."

George beckoned to the judge. "Your Honor, if I may." Linbush nodded. "To your first objection," George stated, addressing Sturtz, "a claim of actual innocence waives all procedural bars."

"Your Honor," chimed in the prosecutor's paralegal, a young man no more than five-seven, with neatly trimmed dark hair and a thin goatee, "the prisoner has misapplied the law. He's referring to MCR 6.508(D). That waiver is limited to the actual innocence of the conviction, not the sentence."

"Actual innocence," responded George, "includes 'of the sentence imposed.' *Jones versus Arkansas*, volume 929 Federal Reporter, second edition, page 381, 8th Circuit 1991."

"Your Honor," a homely-looking young woman interjected, "that supporting law is simply too far removed from our circuit to have any bearing on these proceedings." She was dressed in a tan pantsuit with a thin gold chain hanging from a short thick neck. Her fingernails flaunted no polish that George could see, and her blond-streaked brown hair hung in a ponytail to the middle of her back."And eighth-circuit precedent is not binding on our circuit, nor has it been adopted in our state," the assistant prosecutor finished.

Without a trace of emotion, George replied, "*Jones v. Arkansas* was based on the ruling in *Murray versus Carrier*, volume 477 of the US Reports, page 479, of 1986, a ruling by the United States Supreme Court, which is binding on the whole country."

"Again," the paralegal countered, "*Carrier* held that actual innocence means of the conviction. There is no mention of any application towards sentencing."

When George didn't smile, his face looked severe. It wasn't the same expressionless grimace worn by the hardened men on the yard of Jackson Inside but the look of a man thoroughly focused on the task before him; he sported the look of a surgeon on the last leg of a triple-bypass operation."You can find your answer fifty-eight pages after *Carrier*, in *Smith v. Murray*. That ruling, relied upon by the *Jones* court, held that actual innocence means 'of the sentence imposed.' The Supreme Court ruled on *Smith* later in the same day as it did *Carrier*. Justice Sandra Day O'Connor delivered both opinions."

"In spite of that ruling, it—"

Judge Linbush cut the prosecutors response short with a raised hand."Enough of this useless quibbling," he announced."Mr. Sturtz, the court addressed your argument two months ago in your *motion to dismiss*, which was denied without prejudice. The only avenue open to you at this point is to produce new evidence not available to you at the prior closed hearing. Since you have not produced that evidence, you do not get two bites at the apple. Therefore, your first objection is denied. Proceed to your second objection."

Sturtz, whose countenance remained just as somber as ever, did not protest further. Instead, he said,"The defendant is arguing racial disparity in sentencing for minorities across the nation. He's not allowed to do that. The statute only permits him to appeal his own case. He cannot use this opportunity as a platform to fight for the rights of prisoners across the nation."

The judge looked at George, nodding for a response.

"I am fighting for racial disparity in sentencing for others because when word got out on the prison yard that I was returning to court on that issue, nearly two hundred men asked me to present their racially disparate sentences to the court. I am arguing racial disparity in sentencing for people across the land because I have the honor of being a cofounder and the president elect of BTT, which stands for the *Black Think Tank,* a prison organization whose sole purpose is to uplift disadvantaged black communities across the nation. BTT is made up of black individuals, mostly prisoners, who have harmed black communities in some way. A few months ago, our national newsletter contained an article informing everyone that the Honorable James Linbush had granted a hearing for oral arguments on the issue of racial disparity in sentencing on my case and that I would be returning to court to argue that issue. The response was staggering. We received thousands of letters from men and women incarcerated nationwide, begging me to argue their sentencing issues. Additionally, thousands upon thousands of supporting letters poured in from the fathers, mothers, husbands, wives, children, and friends of those incarcerated under racially disparate sentences, all pleading for my support. In a special supplement to all penal institutions and free world agencies we're affiliated with, I promised to argue their cases. So I am here today, as president of BTT, to fulfill that promise.

"Furthermore, I'm fighting for the victims of racial disparity in sentencing because I am too a victim of such. Because my suffering and destiny is connected to theirs, what affects one, affects all. When—"

"Let's back up here a moment," Linbush cut in. "I need some clarification. You mentioned an organization called BTT, a think tank I think it was. Anyway, who exactly makes up the membership?"

"We are black men who have taken away from black communities in some way, whether it be by robbery, murder, drug selling, or whatever. These same men have grown to understand that if they are ever going to regain their dignity and self-respect, they must contribute positively to the communities they victimized."

"When you say, 'men who have taken away from the black communities,' what exactly did they take?" the judge asked.

"We took away respectable role models, the aspirations of some potential leaders, the ability of the community to grow. We, as black criminals, by our negative actions, swept from our communities such things as hope, self-confidence, integrity, vision, and so on."

"And how is this connected to the reasons you're in prison?"

"It's connected because we were all links in a chain of nonentities. Because most of us didn't know how to think. Because of our criminal mentalities and behavior. Through our ignorance and stupidity, we forewent the chance to uplift one another. Instead of taking our children to libraries and on picnics, we left them at home alone to learn life's lessons through television and music. Instead of nurturing healthy family units, we created dysfunctional families by not being there for our children and their mothers. Instead of creating and supporting positive community functions, some of us brought in drugs, poisoning the morale and retarding the intellectual growth of black communities. We didn't encourage activities that promoted healthy lifestyles and an ethical culture. Instead, we promoted, through our actions, black-on-black crime, which often sent our communities spiraling in the wrong direction.

"We at BTT—"

"All right, Mr. Evans," interrupted Linbush. "That's enough. I understand. Sounds like a very interesting and sorely needed organization you're involved with. I wish it much success.

"Now, Mr. Sturtz," the judge said, turning to the prosecutor, "your second objection is overruled. Mr. Evans—"

"But, Your Honor—" the prosecutor blurted, but the judge promptly forestalled his appeal. "No buts, Mr. Sturtz. Let's move along.

"Mr. Evans, go right ahead," the judge directed George with a flick of a hand, "fight for your people."

Fifty-year-old Giang Troung Ngo, a small man, around five feet five inches and around 130 pounds, serving a fifteen- to forty-year sentence for rape, stood behind the stage in front of three-block and watched sixty-four-year-old serial killer Danny Ranes and his brother Wolfgang exit four-block and hurry through the crowd, moving in his direction. He hoped they had every token of the four hundred dollars he had asked for. That was more money than he could make in a year. The anticipation made his hands tremble, so he stuck them in his pockets to conceal his excitement.

"Here it is,"bellowed Danny Ranes as he approached, extracting a cloth bag from his pocket that clinked heavily when he dropped it in Ngo's eager hands. Wolfgang withdrew two similar bags and handed them over, also. Ngo greedily stuffed all three sacks into his pockets."Now where's the woman?"Wolfgang demanded.

"All I know is that she's in the closet of her classroom with the door locked. I asked around, and I found out that she runs her class out of room 1 on the second floor of the subhall. They have big wooden security doors, so you'll probably need something to knock it down."

"Don't worry," Danny Ranes declared, pulling up his right pant leg, exposing a long crowbar tied against the side of his calf muscle, "I got it covered."The top of the bar curved through a hole in his front pants pocket."I stole it from maintenance about an hour ago. Let's go, Wolfgang."

Giang Ngo stood there a while after the savage pair ran off. He stuck his hands in his pockets and fingered the bags of tokens. God, did that money feel good, he thought. The fate of the young student he had just possibly doomed was the furthest thing from his mind at that moment.

Not long after the warden had declared the situation at Jackson Inside a full-scale riot, aides and assistants informed their Michigan and US senators of what was transpiring in the state. Calls went out to the Michigan legislators also. Congress took no overt action in the beginning; however, some simply assigned one of their aides to monitor the situation from their offices. Several hours later, after receiving an update stating that a University of Michigan law student and a prison guard remained trapped inside the prison, Michigan Senate Majority Leader Mike Bishop announced that mass transportation would be available in the capitol building parking lot within the hour for anyone who wanted to go on site and monitor the riot. US senators Carl Levin and Debbie Stabenow rushed to their own offices in Washington to monitor the situation. The House and Senate shut down all official activities, their leaders advising those members who opted not to go on-site to keep track of the situation regardless.

The Michigan state police set road blocks and detours to divert the traffic within a five-mile radius. Local and county police officers went door to door evacuating residents who lived within a one-mile radius of the prison and shutting down all schools until further notice.

"Most of you already know me, and if you don't, you know of me. I'm Namen Travis, and I'm running this prison now." Travis, along with about fifty members of his makeshift clique, huddled around the guard's station in six-block. He spoke through the intercom, addressing the men who stood at their bars looking and listening. "And for all of you who've never heard of me . . . well, let's just say that after today, you will never forget me."

When the laughter of the men surrounding him subsided, Travis continued. "I have a few members of my crew with me, and I have the keys to every cell in this block. If you don't want more pain than is necessary, I suggest you save us some trouble and take all of your tokens, jewelry, and anything else that's worth something and put it all on a blanket in the middle of your floor. Don't think you can hide anything because remember, we know where all the stash spots are.

"Oh, and before I forget, when we make it to your cell, please step out onto the catwalk. We have weapons you really don't want us to use. Things can get kind of nasty if you resist. But I don't think that will be a problem because most of you are rats and cowards anyway. If you're not in here because you were scared you would get butt fucked, then you're in here because your bitch ass couldn't pay back some money you owed.

"You may have ran to the guards once and let them save you before, but now there's nowhere to run. I can't promise you that this process will be completely painless, but I can tell you this: the less you resist, the quicker this will be."

Travis shut off the intercom long enough to disperse his men throughout the block. When the men started toward the galleries, he pressed the call button and spoke into the receiver again.

"One more thing before I go. I got a special treat for that piece of shit at the end of third gallery. Yeah, you know who I'm talking about. I'll be up there to see you in a few. I thought I'd give you a minute to send up a prayer or two." With that, Travis released the button and marched, with the five men he kept behind, up to third gallery.

Stopping in front of a security door at the end of the third gallery, Travis unlocked it and stepped through. In front of him stood a brown-skinned man, five feet six inches, around 135 pounds, trembling in fear. A second before the man dropped to his knees, Travis glimpsed in the man's eyes terror so absolute it nearly evoked a twinge of sympathy inside Travis. That lasted for about half a second, then he stepped forward and began threading a rope between the unresisting man's legs, then over his shoulders and around his waist and neck. All the while the man prayed, "Our Father, who art in heaven, hallowed by thy name, thy kingdom come . . ."

The rope now tightly secured around the abject convict, Travis looped a span of the rope from his hand around his elbow and then kicked the supplicating man onto his side. After dragging him from his cell and as Travis tugged him down the gallery, his captive began to holler, "Give us this day our daily bread. Forgive us our trespasses, as we also forgive those who trespass against us . . ."

The prisoners still in their cells watched, horror-struck, dread as evident on their faces as the tone of their skin. Some of them stood silent while others yelled and prayed along with the bound man as his body thumped down the metal stairs between the galleries.

Finally, as Travis descended the last flight of steps, he turned and pulled backward, towing the man across the base and out of six-block. Parked just outside, the prison ambulance—the Meat Wagon—which Travis had sent a man to commandeer on his way to the block, waited uncomplaining for its cargo. Travis let the rope unravel from around his elbow and fastened it to the back of the Meat Wagon. The tethered man began to sob loudly. Travis, along with Carl Rogers, climbed into the front seat while Big Will stepped onto the back and smirked as the man begged and blubbered on the ground behind the cart. Turning the ignition, Travis put the cart in gear and drove attentively—so that the rope wouldn't snap—up the old road. As the cart exited the other side of the subhall, Rogers turned on the blinker. Laughter erupted from the crowd of men ambling nearby. Rogers smiled and waved like the president of the United States.

When the Meat Wagon neared Peckerwood Park, Travis took a left in the yard. Everyone on the yard turned to watch the spectacle. Even the guards on the roof looked on, revolted yet captivated.

Some of the men who recognized the human sack raking the dirt behind the wagon hurled rocks at him, while others chased and either spit on or kicked the pathetic man.

The warden watched the scene from the big screen in central command. He snatched up the microphone to the prison intercom system. "Namen Travis, please do not do this," he yelled as he depressed the call button. "This is the warden. I'll work with you. Call me, and we'll talk about it."

For the first time in his career, the warden felt powerless. Travis had called him and said that he had stationed his men at fifteen-yard intervals starting from outside of the quiet cell in five-block east and ending next to the stage outside of three-block. Travis also told him that if anyone decided to storm the prison or if his food was late, he would have the order to execute the guard relayed to the men inside. On top of that, he had his orders from the governor: *under no circumstances are you to allow the law student or the guard to be injured. Their safety is top priority.*

So the Warden watched, impotent, as the scene unfolded. The men at the card tables stood as the Meat Wagon wheeled around them and stopped just in front of the stage. Travis and two other men got off the Meat Wagon and untied the poor soul fettered to the back.

Lifting the battered and bloody man, Travis and the other two men, who had been identified as Elvis Williams and Carl Rogers, dumped the body onto the stage. The prisoner lay on his side, his bloody face turned toward Travis.

"Joseph Skipper," Travis bellowed, standing a foot away for the prone man, "in 1994, you broke into an old woman's house. You struck her, knocked her to the floor, and robbed her."

"But I didn't know who she was," the man pleaded.

"You're lying!" Travis roared back at him. "You knew who she was, you bitch-ass crack head, you knew. Everybody in Detroit knew her house. It has been the city's most famous landmark for over four decades."

"I swear I didn't know who she was, sir," Skipper blubbered.

"You knocked her to the floor," Travis continued to shout. An ever-growing ring of men swelled around the stage, listening intently to Travis's harangue.

"Sir, I swear I didn't know who she was . . . p-please believe m-me, sir." Skipper's voice cracked several times as he begged.

"She was an old woman!"

"But I didn't r-recognize her." Tears were now pouring in a steady stream across the bridge of Skipper's nose, only to leak off the side of his face onto the stage. "Sir, I swear I didn't."

"With your fist, you beat her," Travis hissed, kneeling down to place his face inches from Skipper's. "You knocked her to the floor!"

"But I swear I didn't recognize her. I was high, sir. My m-mind wasn't right."

"Bullshit!" Travis roared. "You're a lying bitch. How in the fuck could you not recognize one of the most famous black faces in the world? Ever since December 1, 1955, she has been an icon. She sparked a historical movement. You sound like a fool, claiming that you didn't recognize the face of Rosa Parks."

With those last words, Travis spit in the man's face and grabbed him up. He dragged the sobbing and shuddering man to a nearby light post and held him there while Rogers took another length of rope and began lashing it around Skipper's waist, legs, and belly. Once he had him secured to the pole, Travis reached back for a rubber tire someone held out for him and draped it around Skipper's neck. Travis called for the gas can he had confiscated from the maintenance garage. He intended to employ the same death-by-torture method invented by the natives of South Africa against the traitors who cooperated with the hated South African apartheid government by pouring the gasoline into the hollow of the tire and igniting it. An excruciating execution called *necklacing*.

Abruptly, just as Travis prepared to grab the gas can from a man on the side of the stage, the warden's voice blared, "Namen Travis, your food has arrived," three times in succession out of the loud speakers. Travis halted the execution immediately. He turned to Skipper and growled, "You got a short reprieve, my man, but I'll be back."

After posting a few men around the condemned man, Travis headed toward the three green four-wheel Gators—the ones the maintenance workers used to transport equipment throughout the prison grounds—parked nearby. He got into the driver side of the lead Gator then led the other two vehicles to gate 15 to pick up their food.

Tina Brown huddled in a dark corner of the closet, terrified. She could hear the relentless thrum of someone shouldering the wooden security door, trying to gain entrance. The thumps came one on top of the other, too fast for one man to do alone. There had to be at least two. Realizing that, she hunkered down a little further in the corner.

From time to time, the pounding would cease, only to be replaced by a sharper impact and, after that, a scrapping, as if a huge bear were trying to claw its way in. It didn't matter what the warden said; Tina knew that these prisoners didn't need a key to get to her. That door would not hold out for much longer.

A couple hours ago, the urge to pee had come on strong. Tina sat in the closet wondering, for long minutes, what she was going to do. Inspiration hit. The warden did say that no prisoners had made it into the school building yet. She remembered that a vase with artificial flowers sat on a table in the far corner of the room. The point was fast approaching where she would not be able to hold her water any longer. And she refused to sit or stand in a puddle of pee, not even her own.

At first she peeped her head out of the door cautiously. When she saw no sign of any prisoners, she stepped and moved warily toward the back of the room. Once at the table, she snatched the flowers from the vase. Abruptly, she heard voices and footsteps. Without waiting to see if her hearing held true, she turned and bolted for the closet. The moment she took off, she stubbed her toe painfully on a table leg. Her eyes watered immediately. Despite her agony, she continued running. Just as she passed her desk, the telephone cord seemed to reach up and grab her by the ankle. She went sprawling and hit her head wickedly on the wall next to the closet door. She looked around quickly and saw that her trip had torn the telephone cord from its socket.

Seeing as there was nothing she could do, she grabbed up the plastic vase and dove for the closet. Tina's heart hammered against the empty vase as she clutched it to her chest. After an anxiety-filled minute, the notion came to her to report what she thought she heard to the warden. Setting the vase down quietly, she felt along the cold floor for her radio. When her hands felt nothing, unease sent a wave of goose bumps prickling over her skin. Three times she searched every square inch of the closet. Nothing. What in the hell did she do with her radio? The moment she thought it, the answer jarred her spirit: she probably left her radio on the table on the other side of the room from where she had gotten the vase. The radio was her only connection to the civilized world, and just when she determined to chance another trip out, she heard the first thump and the vulgar curse words that followed. The prisoners had found her.

Now she sat wondering how much longer she had before the door gave in, and a fate she could not bear to imagine enveloped her life.

Truth leaped onto the stage in front of three-block. To the men milling around the stage, he shouted, as he read from an article out of the July 19, 2007, *Detroit Free Press,* "Blacks in the United States are imprisoned at more than five times the rate of whites, according to a study released Wednesday by a criminal justice policy group. Michigan's rate per one hundred thousand people: four hundred and twelve whites, two thousand two hundred and sixty-two blacks." When he finished, Truth refolded the newspaper article and slid it into his pants pocket just before he hopped down from the stage and strode off.

I think that we should be men first, and subjects afterward. It is not desirable to cultivate a respect for the law, so much as for the right.

—Henry David Thoreau

Chapter 21

George spoke for two hours. He articulated to the court that in order to clearly understand the role of blacks in today's judicial system, one had to first understand the judicial system's history in relation to black people. George chronicled the history of racial discrimination against blacks, all of which the law had sanctioned.

His commentary began in 1619 with the first blacks brought to this country aboard a Dutch trading ship that anchored at Jamestown and exchanged fourteen blacks for food and supplies and where the so-called settlers forced blacks to work the tobacco fields and do whatever else whites told them to. The transatlantic slave trade, where millions of blacks were bought and stolen from Africa then squeezed into the dark, damp, filthy hulls of ships and brought to this land and sold on auction blocks. Slave codes, which denied blacks any legal status besides that of property of whites. Plantation life, where families were broken up, members sold, women and children made sexual victims at the whim of perverted whites. The Fugitive Slave Act, which placed harsh penalties on those who helped runaway slaves. The Dred Scott decision, where Roger Taney, the chief justice of the US Supreme Court, held that blacks were an inferior race, unfit to associate with whites, and so inferior that blacks had no rights, which the white man was bound to respect. Black Codes, state laws holding that free blacks were legally subordinate to whites. Lynchings, which were used to maintain the status quo of white superiority. Jim Crow laws, the system of laws that enforced racial segregation and discrimination throughout the country. The Scottsboro case, a case that epitomized the racism and injustice of this country's racist court system, where two white women falsely accused nine blacks of raping them and the men had to spend a total of more than a hundred years in the jails and prisons of Alabama before they were freed.

George continued his assault on this country's justice system by citing, among other examples, the struggles of black Americans against the racist segregation laws of the south. Delving into the civil rights movement, he recounted the Montgomery Bus Boycott, where the laws mandated that blacks had to relinquish their seats so that whites could sit. The Little Rock Crisis, a desegregation issue that started when Arkansas National Guardsmen with bayonets turned away a fifteen-year-old girl from Central High School and ended when President Dwight D. Eisenhower ordered paratroopers of the 101st Airborne Division to escort the little girl into the school. Student sit-ins, Nashville, where black and white students protested segregation in hotels, motels, libraries, theaters, and restaurants. *Brown v. Board of Education,* where the US Supreme Court ruled that the doctrine of separate but equal as applied to education was unconstitutional. German shepherd dogs and fire hoses of the Birmingham Police Department were turned on civil rights protestors in violation of their First Amendment right to peaceful assembly and protest. Current stop-and-search laws, used by many policemen across the nation to stop cars driven by blacks, searching and harassing them for no other reason than because they are black, a new form of racism termed driving while black.

CNN and MSNBC interrupted regular programming with breaking news of a major disturbance at the world's largest walled prison: the maximum-security penitentiary in Michigan known as Jackson Inside. In the background hovered an aerial view of the prison. Thousands of men milled around the yard, looking like ants on a mound. The camera swiveled to take in the thick plumes of smoke billowing from several different buildings. The reporter was saying that prisoners had taken complete control of the interior of the prison. The view of the prison disappeared, and in its place, a photograph of a grinning prison guard with the name Sgt. Gary Moore printed underneath flashed on to the screen. The anchor reported that Sgt. Moore was being held hostage in the segregation block of the prison known as five-west or the hole in a soundproof room without light or water. Seconds later, a photograph of Namen Travis sprouted next to that of Gary Moore, as the news anchor reported that Namen Travis, the leader of the largest gang within the Michigan Department of Corrections, held Sgt. Moore hostage. The woman read portions of Travis's criminal and prison records to the viewers. "According to prison authorities," the anchor reported, "a group of men had broken gang leader Namen Travis out of the segregation unit known as five-west, or the hole if you choose to use prison vernacular, where he was being held for major assault of a counselor, earlier in the day. Only demands for food have been made so far. Travis has told officials that further demands would be forthcoming."

When the photographs of Moore and Travis faded, a picture of Joseph Skipper replaced them. The prison kept Skipper, the reporter went on to say, in the most secure protective custody cell in the prison, due to the nature of his crime. Joseph Skipper broke into the home of civil rights matriarch Rosa Parks before assaulting and robbing her. Since his arrest, men detained in the county jail had assaulted him numerous times. He had been under protective custody since entering the prison system. "Somehow," she said, "Travis took the prisoner from his secure cell, tied him to the rear of a small prison ambulance, and dragged him across the prison yard then tied him to a light pole and has given what he termed a blood oath to execute him for his actions against Rosa Parks, a black woman he called a crown jewel of the black race."

Thereafter, a smiling image of Tina Brown popped up on the screen; the broadcast used the picture from her student ID. "A civilian, a young graduate student from the law school at the University of Michigan, is also trapped inside the prison."

No civilians outside of those in central command were officially privy to this information. The fact that it now made breaking news on networks across the nation indicated a major leak.

"Tina Brown is a student teacher who, as part of a field study, instructs classes on the law for inmates inside the prison. At this moment, we have her father live from his home."

The view on the screen split from the newscaster on the left to the ebony skin and salt-and-peppered hair of Tina Brown's father sitting next to his beautiful wife on the right. He sat and nodded solemnly as the anchor addressed him.

"Mr. Brown, our hearts go out to you and your family in this moment of crisis, and we know that you have a lot to worry about right now, but can you tell us what you know about the situation so far?"

As the father spoke, he hugged his wife closer. She, even with her tawny-colored eyes puffy from recently shed tears and her straight ink black hair slightly disheveled, sat silently as her husband addressed the camera, her Native American beauty radiating through her pain.

"I spoke on the phone with the warden of the prison," Mr. Brown said in a strong, deep voice, dampened by distress. "He told me that they had declared the situation a full-scale riot. He said that there were no other staff inside the prison except one guard, who had been taken hostage. He also told me that no prisoners knew that my daughter was trapped and that she had a mobile radio with her and was in direct contact with him. He said that a full squad of guards would rush the building if anything directly threatened her safety. That's about all we know. Now we're just waiting and praying."

"Were you told her exact location within the prison?"

"I was told that she is in her classroom, behind a security door. The warden said that the prisoners could not break through the security door. It's said to be the latest in high tech security."

"Mr. Brown, can you tell us how it was that your daughter came to be trapped inside the prison while all other staff were evacuated?"

"I asked the same question. I was told that the details were unclear right now."

"One of her instructors at the University of Michigan informed us that your daughter is not only a top student but quite the dancer, Mr. Brown."

A fond smile spread involuntarily across Tina's father's face. "She's actually a professional dancer." He pointed across the room, and the camera panned to the right and zoomed in on a three-tier display case holding myriad trophies, ribbons, and plaques.

"Dancing is Tina's passion," he continued. "She has her own troupe and has danced all over the US, Europe, and Africa. When—"

"She's teaching me how to dance," exclaimed a little girl who had been standing behind the couch with two teenage boys at her sides.

"Excuse me, I didn't get that," the anchor woman stated.

"I'm Carice, Tina's sister."The little girl had walked around to the front of the couch and forced her way in between her mother and father."She's teaching me how to dance," she repeated.

As the interview proceeded, footage of Tina dancing on stage played in the lower right corner of the screen. At the time, she was teaching dance at the Ecole des Dances Latines-Tropicales in Paris. Next, the screen switched to her dancing ballet with her troupe at the Russian Academy of Theatre Arts.

"Anyone who is around my daughter for any significant amount of time will be taught how to dance," said the father.

"And your daughter looks to be such a beautiful dancer, Mr. Brown. We look forward to seeing her dancing again soon, once she is safely returned to her family."

"I think I'll do a little dancing with her myself," said the father, smiling while the three children laughed.

"I'm sure you will, Mr. Brown. And thank you again for your time, sir."

Progress was slow, but the security door was definitely giving in. Ranes and Wolfgang continued ramming the door in turns, trying to bend the door inward enough to get the crowbar between the door and the jamb. Perhaps then they could pry the lock loose.

The constant shouldering and striking of the door had caused the bolts that fastened the door to the jamb to slip slightly. The damage done so far was negligible; however, if they kept ramming . . .

Although Danny Ranes's sixty-four-year-old body stood only five-nine and weighed only 175 pounds, it was powerful. Years spent in the weight pit and doing calisthenics left him with hard, taut muscles under slightly loosened skin. His brother Wolfgang was younger and much stronger. When they noticed the door yield that one bit, they renewed their efforts twofold. Instead of taking turns, they decided to batter the door simultaneously. Before each impact, they stood on the other side of the four-foot-wide hallway and, on the count of three, crashed the wooden door with all their considerable strength.

After several impacts, the serial killers stopped and examined the top hinge. The bolts had loosened a speck more. Wolfgang excitedly tried to force the crowbar in the fissure, but there was not yet enough room. Just a few more rushes.

A table sat in the center of the cement stage in front of three-block. On top of the table, lobsters, pizzas, pies, sodas, and more rested awaiting their fate. Namen Travis stood directly behind the table, arms crossed over his chest, listening to one of his men as he spoke quietly next to Travis's shoulder. Several more twenty-five-feet-long tables, arranged in front of the stage, held more viands. The men positioned behind the tables bartered and traded the food nonstop, yet it seemed not to put a dent in the line of prisoners in front of the tables.

Medical patrols, which Travis had set up, scouted the yard in the green Gators, looking for the sick and injured. Anyone they found they carried to gate 15 and left them there with the notice that a bill for services rendered would come due in the weeks to follow, and if they didn't come back to Jackson Inside, they would be found no matter which of the state's fifty or so prisons they ended up in. Word had spread that all men not affiliated with a gang had to pay to receive medical attention. Travis imposed a toll for any nonaffiliated man approaching gate 15 for medical treatment. The four men posted at the entrance to the subhall made sure that everyone complied.

As Travis watched the food and money change hands at the tables, a man walked up to the stage and handed him a bullhorn. One of the guards had lowered it in a basket from the roof of three-block with instructions to give it to Travis so that he could communicate with the guards on the roof whenever he wanted to.

Travis retrieved the bullhorn and straightaway strolled to the rear of the stage. He scanned the rooftops until he found what he was looking for. Pointing the bullhorn directly at the CNN camera crew, he bellowed, "One hour to execution!"

"So we are here today, seven years into the twenty-first century, still fighting for our basic constitutional rights. This time it's for our Fifth Amendment right to equal protection at sentencing. In short, regardless of our crimes, we should be given the same sentences as whites who have been convicted of the same crimes. Because my sentence is racially disparate, this court should vacate it and resentence me. *Res ipsa loquitor*, the issue speaks for itself. And with that, Your Honor, I rest my case." George gave the faintest perception of a bow, which was more of a slight bending of his head.

Initially, Prosecutor Sturtz thought that he would spot the anger and hostility in the defendant's face the moment he stood to respond to his argument. Throughout his entire career, he had learned to recognize the drawing up of men's features, the poorly controlled fury. Not once had he stood up to contest a case, and the bitterness was not there.

Now, however, all he could discern from the look on Evans's face was smugness. The man had an air of superiority so thick that Sturtz nearly found himself grimacing in irritation. Amusement and self-assurance flitted across Evans's face in turn. Why did he figure himself in such a superior position? wondered Sturtz. Did Evans believe himself superior in his knowledge of the law? Or did he think the facts of his case were so far in his favor that the strength of his issue lay beyond reproach? Sturtz intended to find out what lay behind this criminal's store of confidence.

"Objection, Your Honor. The defendant is off base here," Sturtz began. "His life sentence falls within the statutory range. His crime is what we call a floater, which means that the law allows the sentencing judge to give him anywhere between one year and life in prison. That the court decided to give him the high end of the statute, well, that was at that court's discretion. The sentence is well within the boundaries of a law that has been on the books for close to one hundred years. Its legality has been tested, and it has endured. Therefore, I ask that this court deny the prisoner's motion for resentencing."

"Is it your position," the judge asked George, "that the statute itself is racist and therefore unconstitutional?"

"No, Your Honor," George responded, "and I'll tell you why. First, however, I want to respond to the prosecution's reliance on the legality of my sentence." He had remained standing at the podium from the moment he started arguing his case several hours ago.

"Your Honor, as a very close friend of mine once said in one of his most famous speeches, this, what the prosecution speaks of, 'is the terrible myth of organized society, that everything that's done through the established system is legal—and that word has a powerful psychological impact. It makes people believe that there is an order to life, and an order to a system, and that a person that goes through this order and is convicted, has gotten all that is due him.

And therefore society can turn its conscience off, and look to other things and other times.

"'And that's the terrible thing about even trials in the past, is that they have this aura of legitimacy, this aura of legality. I suspect that better men than the world has known and more of them, have gone to their deaths through a legal system than through all the illegalities in the history of man.

"'Six million people in Europe during the Third Reich? Legal.

"'Sacco-Vanzetti? Quite legal.

"'The Haymarket defendants? Legal.

"'The hundreds of rape trials throughout the South where black men were condemned to death? All legal.

"'Jesus? Legal.

"'Socrates? Legal.

"'And that is the kaleidoscopic nature of what we live through here and in other places. Because all tyrants learn that it is far better to do this thing through some semblance of legality than to do it without that pretense.'"

George paused for a moment to let the gravity of William Kunstler's "The Terrible Myth" speech settle on the minds of his listeners.

"Now, Your Honor, I don't see anything wrong with a law that allows the sentencing judge to give a convicted felon any sentence from one year up to and including life. The crimes that allow for indeterminate sentencing are very serious. In the cases of serious drug offenses, kidnapping, brutal robbery and assault, rape, child molestation, murder, and so forth, the stiffest penalties should be available for the judge to impose. Under those scenarios, the indeterminate-sentencing statute is a just law. However, when that same law is used to target blacks and other minorities who appear before sentencing courts, that's when it becomes unjust. This double-standardizing of the law is nothing new to American jurisprudence. In fact, earlier, I mentioned such a law when I spoke of the 'parading without permit laws' that the police used—and the courts upheld—to arrest those involved in peaceful assembly and protest."

George paused to leaf through the documents in his folder. He pulled out a single sheet of paper and began to read."'There are two types of laws: there are just and there are unjust laws. I would agree with Saint Augustine that"An unjust law is no law at all."

"'Let us turn to a more concrete example of just and unjust laws. An unjust law is a code that a majority inflicts on a minority that is not binding on itself. This is difference made legal.

"'There are some instances when a law is just on its face and unjust in its application. For instance, I was arrested Friday on a charge of parading without a permit. Now there is nothing wrong with an ordinance which requires a permit for a parade, but when the ordinance is used to preserve segregation and deny citizens the First Amendment privilege of peaceful protest, then it becomes unjust.'"

When he finished, he replaced the sheet back in the folder."That quote,"George said, looking up at the judge again and then over the entire room,"was from a famous letter the Reverend Martin Luther King Jr. wrote in 1963 from the Birmingham City Jail, where he had been arrested after marching in protest against the racist segregation laws of Alabama.

"For more current examples, examine some of today's housing and employment laws that are just on their face but often racially discriminatory in their application. That's why people open up newspapers every day and see courts and juries awarding blacks and other minorities monetary awards for violations of the various fair housing and employment statutes.

"Another example that I spoke on earlier is the stop-and-search law. Again, this law certainly appears just on its face. There's nothing wrong with affording the police the authority to stop and search suspicious vehicles. Any modern civilization needs that jurisdiction to control the flow of illegal drugs and to combat the manifold criminal activities that occur on streets and highways. Yet when racist police officers use the stop-and-search law to stop and harass people of specific ethnic heritage or skin color, then the stop-and-search law becomes unjust.

"So, in following that logic, I am compelled to conclude that the practice of indeterminate sentencing is unjust when used to preserve discriminatory sentencing policies of racist judges and to deny blacks and other minorities their Fifth Amendment right to equal protection under the law.

"The racist sentencing practices allowed by indeterminate sentencing are what Reverend Martin Luther King, Jr. referred to as 'difference made legal.'

"Blacks and other minorities should be given the same sentences as whites because it is simply the right thing to do. Applying the law equitably to everyone engenders a high respect for the law, and it is to this end that we must all work. We are the architects of the law, and we must assume responsibility for its design. Because the—"

"Objection, Your Honor." The prosecutor surged from his seat with surprising celerity. The reason for George's aplomb had just dawned on him. It wasn't about who had the stronger factual basis or who had superior knowledge of the law. The prisoner's smug attitude stemmed from something entirely different: the prisoner believed in his own moral superiority—Evans believed he was the better man.

"This whole argument is moot," Sturtz declared, brandishing a stack of papers. "When prisoners get themselves into serious trouble in prison, they're written major misconducts, more commonly known as tickets. What I have here is a stack of these tickets I subpoenaed from the prison. There's eighteen total, all of them for fighting or serious assaults the defendant committed over the years. I'm not talking about horse playing either, Your Honor. My—"

"Mr. Sturtz," interrupted the judge, "are you going to rehash your entire motion to dismiss, something that we've already covered? I really don't have time for this."

"No, no, Your Honor," Sturtz replied almost apologetically. "I will get to the focus of the matter, nothing frivolous this time." Sturtz's demeanor had suddenly shifted from an apparent indifference to something bordering on hysteria. "My position is ironclad," he continued. "My foundation's being laid right now. This prisoner's not a better man than me. Even should—"

"Wait a second," blurted the judge. "What did you just say, Mr. Sturtz?"

"Uh . . . Your Honor?"

"Repeat what you just said."

"Uh . . . what . . . I'm laying my foundation?" That came out more a question than a response.

"No, bring it up a bit. You just said, 'This prisoner is not a better man than me.' That's what you said, wasn't it?"

"Ah, well . . ."

"What did you mean by that?"

Sturtz harrumphed and sorted the stack of papers in front of him unnecessarily, unable to maintain eye contact with the judge at the present moment. "Ah, well . . . I just misspoke. I didn't mean it. Anyway, let's move on. Where was I?" Sturtz straightened his lapels then tugged at the hem of his jacket. "Oh yeah, here we are. If the court did go so far as to vacate the life sentence, because of the prisoner's exceptionally violent institutional record, the people would strongly urge the court to reinstate the life sentence. He was a violent man in 1964 and has not changed since then. The people believe that if the court were to examine these misconducts, it would agree. Yet, your Honor, I believe that to vacate a life sentence only to reinstate the same life sentence is an exercise in futility and something that would undermine the public's confidence in this state's judicial system. Therefore, I move to dismiss."

"Mr. Evans, is this true? I have your institutional file, but I haven't seen any tickets for fighting. Because there was nothing there, I assumed that you had not acquired any misconducts. Now here it is that the prosecutor claims to have a whole stack of them. Can you explain that?"

George didn't answer immediately. Looking straight into Judge Linbush's pale gray eyes, he announced, "Yes, it's true."

"You have eighteen tickets for fighting?"

"That's correct."

"And all of them were serious?"

"Very serious."

"Did anyone get seriously injured or need treatment or hospitalization afterward?"

"In every single one."

"Your Honor," spouted the prosecutor, now offering a self-satisfied smile of his own, "let me interject if I may. I would like to read an excerpt from one of his tickets. It was written by a guard who was manning the gun tower on the roof of the theater inside the prison.

"'At o'six forty-five hours, I returned to my post from a bathroom break, and upon looking out of the out slot, I witnessed a fight just outside of the six-block entrance. Two prisoners were facing each other and swinging their fists. One of the men was George Evans, 97855. After the other man stopped fighting, Evans continued hitting the man until he fell to the ground, unconscious. Another man was behind Evans on the ground, who I later found out was also beaten unconscious by Evans."

After finishing, the prosecutor flung the ticket to the table in front of him and declared, "This is the man we have before us today, Your Honor, asking for a lighter sentence."

Before the court could comment, the prosecutor read from another ticket.

"'While working three-post, I observed prisoner Evans stomping a man in the face who lay on the ground. The man on the ground appeared to be unconscious. While stomping the man's face, two other prisoners attacked Evans from behind. The men knocked Evans down and began beating him. Somehow, Evans managed to get to his feet, and once upright, he ran over to the man lying on the ground and resumed stomping the man in the face.'

"Your Honor, of the eighteen fighting tickets, Evans had been convicted seven times of stomping men in their faces while they lay on the ground. In fact, I have one ticket here where Evans knocked a man out and actually rolled him over so that he could stomp him in the face. This prisoner does not qualify for resentencing simply because of his character. He's entitled to nothing. I don't want Evans living in my neighborhood, and I don't think anyone else here does, either.

"He's an extremely violent man, Your Honor, and he's already in for murder. I believe wholeheartedly that the only time that Evans should be released from prison is in a pine box."

Now this is the Law of the Jungle—as old
and as true as the sky;
And the Wolf that shall keep it may prosper,
but the Wolf that shall break it must die.

—Rudyard Kipling

Chapter 22

Down on all fours, with his right side braced against the wooden security door, Danny Ranes supported the ponderous weight of his brother Wolfgang on his back. Wolfgang, working feverishly, had managed to jam the flat end of the crowbar in between the door hinge and the jamb.

Now Wolfgang pried and yanked at the hinge with abandon. The crowbar slipped noisily from the cleft a few times, but after a while, the head of one of the hinge bolts snapped off with a metallic pop and fell to thump Ranes on the back of his neck. That seemed to give Ranes the excuse he needed because he collapsed to the floor, sending his brother lurching.

However, the real reason for his collapse was because his brother was just too damn heavy. Ranes's shoulders felt afire from the incessant ramming, and now he had to support this big bastard on his back. Exhaustion gripped him like a snake, and he felt a migraine coming on.

Wolfgang picked himself up off the floor but didn't utter one reproachful word, for he understood. He was on the brink of total exhaustion too. Yet unlike Ranes, Wolfgang, driven by an inordinate lust, ignored the fatigue, snatched up the crowbar, and began hammering the safety glass fiercely. The glass spider-webbed with every blow, but it held strong. The window seemed only to stretch with each impact, no matter how hard or how long Wolfgang pummeled it.

What the killers didn't know was that the thick security glass, called 'sandwich' glass, comprised alternating layers of a strong plastic material, flat panes of glass, and crisscrossed wire mesh. Bought for the very purpose of creating an impenetrable safety chamber for staff members caught in a riot or to shield themselves from attacking prisoners, the prison spared no expense in purchasing and installing the glass. As the latest in bulletproof technology, the windows could resist a large-caliber slug at close range. Two men with a crowbar didn't stand a chance.

Ranes continued to lie on the floor, too exhausted to move. Standing over him, his brother continued to smite the window. Abruptly, Wolfgang gasped sharply, and the crowbar clanged to the floor, missing Ranes's head by mere inches. Wolfgang nearly chocked trying to get his brother's attention.

"Danny, there she is! There's that bitch!"Wolfgang ejaculated, his voice infused with childlike excitement.

Ranes continued blustering profanities at the close call with the crowbar for a few seconds before Wolfgang's statement registered. "What," he said as he popped his head up to peer through the mangled window. He watched her silhouette dart across the room to a back table. From there she ducked under other tables and moved chairs, searching frantically for something. She looked rabid. Her hair, disheveled and matted to her face, had lost its usual sheen, sweat glued her blouse to her two alluring heaving breasts, and her golden brown cheeks flaunted dried streaks of mascara from recently shed tears. She had never looked more appealing.

All weariness forgotten, Ranes leapt to his feet and bolted to his left to get a better view through the picture windows. For a while he watched anxiously as she searched the barren classroom for who knows what. Suddenly, an urge stronger than his minuscule store of patience could hold back welled up inside of him. He had to have her. All these months he had been watching her, imagining what he would do to her if he could just get her alone. He had pleasured himself night after night to thoughts of raping her unmercifully and then looking into her eyes as he choked the life out of her.

Ranes beat the window hungrily. The wench's head reappeared from under a desk. Their eyes met. In that brief moment, he knew that his fantasy was about to come true. Wolfgang lunged in front of the window beside his brother to behold their prey more clearly. That's when she screamed a melody of terror that delighted the men's ears before she fled back into the closet.

Ranes and Wolfgang wrapped their arms around each other as they hurried back to the door. "God, she's beautiful, isn't she?" Ranes said laughing.

When they reached the door, Ranes quickly fell to all fours. "Hurry, Wolfgang, climb on." He couldn't contain himself any longer; his elation bubbled over as tears and flowed across the deep hollows and sharp angles of his time-worn face.

As Tina sat slumped and trembling in the far corner of the closet—fear, hopelessness, and frustration taking turns ravaging her psyche—she wondered how her end would come. Would it be at the hands of those brutal beasts hammering at the door or from cardiac arrest? Her heart drummed wildly against her breastbone; sweat seeped copiously from her pores. The lump on the crown of her head throbbed like a second heartbeat and hurt something fierce. She felt no real hunger or thirst, for fear trumped all other sensations, but she knew in the back of her mind that food and water remained critical in whether or not she remained lucid.

All the while she sat there on the brink of hyperventilating, she berated herself for being so stupid and leaving the radio on the other side of the classroom. "Tina, Tina, Tina," she chided herself, "how in hell could you forget to grab the damn radio?" With the phone dead and the chances of escaping slim to not even close, the radio was her last hope. She could feel the walls mocking her. Instead of protecting her, they seemed to have changed sides and were now holding her prisoner until the animals raging against the door could come claim her.

The pounding and scraping on the door had been going on for close to five hours now. Even still, every time one of them hit the door, her body jerked involuntarily. It was only a matter of time before the so-called security door became not quite so secure. The next blow could be the one to cave it in completely. She was willing to bet that when the prison installed the doors, they didn't count on monsters as determined as these having as much time as they did to test their worth.

During the first couple of hours, she had fancied her would-be assailants getting tired and eventually abandoning their hunt or maybe even just taking a break to go grab a bite to eat or something to drink. And in that short respite, she would be able to pelt out to the back of the room and retrieve the radio. That hope had slowly rotted into despair as time wore on. She knew that the men were not going to stop. If she was going to act, she would have to do it in spite of their presence. It's not like they didn't already know she was in there. The door had held this long, so maybe it would hold long enough for her to run out and get the radio, she reasoned.

She gathered herself up enough to stand. Her head swam, and she staggered to the side a step or two. It didn't help that her legs and back felt cramped from crouching in the same position for such a long time either. After catching her balance, she stood still for a moment then stretched her body to work blood back into her extremities. She approached the door. Minutes ago, the pounding had started anew, but now she willed herself to ignore it. Taking several deep breaths, she unlocked the door and turned the knob slowly. Once she felt the latch release, she paused again. "Let's go, Tina. You can do this," she told herself, firming her resolve.

Before she could lose her nerve, she pushed the door open and dashed for the rear table. She hadn't even made it halfway across the room before her heart fell to her stomach again. From there she could see that the radio was not there.

Nevertheless, she kept going, making it her business to not look in the direction of the door or the windows; she did not want to look into the face of those ruthless savages. When she arrived at the table, she saw the fake flowers scattered everywhere but no sign of the radio. She examined the table and noticed that it sat askew. Remembering that she had stubbed her toe when she ran for the closet hours earlier, she knew now that it must have been the table that her foot caught. Ducking underneath the table, she searched the floor in the immediate area. When the radio didn't turn up, she started sweeping the room feverishly from back to front, scattering chairs and upending trash cans. As she approached her desk, a surge of desperation ran through her. She got down on her hands and knees, scanning underneath her desk, and suddenly, a pounding on the window jerked her eyes in that direction. She froze, horrified, for what seemed like eternity.

Tina recognized the hideous sweaty face in the window. She wanted to turn away, but before she could, another appalling face appeared, this one huge and nearly as repulsive as the first. The scream that wouldn't come seconds ago exploded out of her now.

With all thoughts of finding the radio dispelled, Tina scrambled back into her hideaway and locked the door.

Danny Ranes, his was the face of terror. She recognized him because he attended one of her law classes. Whenever she taught his class, he would arrive early and appropriate the rearmost table. Even though all her students watched her as she instructed the class, she always thought there was something a little too intent in his gaze; when he watched her, she saw nothing of an interest in law in his eyes.

Her gut coerced her to go to the control center one evening and read his file. Tina found out that he was serving three life sentences for three counts of second-degree murder, one count of assault with a dangerous weapon, and a gun charge. The media referred to him as the Kalamazoo serial killer. The police suspected him in as many as fourteen killings where each female victim was kidnapped, raped, tortured, and then murdered, but they lacked sufficient evidence to try him.

The other man Tina did not recognize, but the similar characteristics of the face and body and she knew—they were brothers, both serial killers of women. If those two ever got their hands on her . . . In a panic once more, Tina glided both hands across the cold floor, desperately searching for a radio she knew was not there. She didn't know what else to do; it had to be somewhere.

"Mr. Evans," Linbush said, leaning forward, peering over his glasses, elbows planted on the bench before him, "please explain to me," the judge's voice turned to iron, "why I shouldn't ship you right back to a prison cell right now? And make it good."

"Child rapists, sexual predators, drug dealers, and extortionist, Your Honor, all of them," George answered coolly. Just then, he realized how long it had been since he'd had a drink. Three hours of debating and not a sip of water left his mouth dry and made his stomach burn.

Surreptitiously, George looked around for anything that resembled water. His eyes fell on a metal pitcher and a glass sitting on a flat six-inch-wide projection on the side of the podium. Now that he noticed it, he could remember a small older woman placing it there and mumbling something about a cold drink while he was listening to the prosecutor's rebuttal. But that was quite a while ago. He put a huge hand to the side of the pitcher. It was still cool.

George hoisted the pitcher with two hands and turned the stainless steel lip up to his mouth. The liquid tasted like paradise as it ran smoothly down his throat.

Silence descended over the courtroom. Everyone, including the judge, gaped at George. The teacher in the audience chirped "Oh my!" and covered her open mouth with a hand.

Jackson Inside forbade the use of glass vessels or bottles within the prison. The administration deemed them dangerous contraband because prisoners could easily modify them into weapons. Because over four decades had passed since he had even touched a glass, it never occurred to George that the woman placed it there for him to use.

For George, the courtroom and the people in it had vanished. Whatever elixir that blessed little old lady put in this pitcher invigorated every inch of his being. Never had he tasted something so delicious and refreshing. It was so different than the orange, rusty, polluted, and filthy water at the prison. This must be one of those new energy drinks he'd heard about. He gulped and swallowed noisily until the last drop rolled down his throat, then, with mild regret, he set the pitcher back down on the podium. Not yet realizing that everyone in the courtroom had their eyes fixed on him, he smothered a belch that came unbidden from his satisfied gut. He looked toward the clerk who sat next to the judge's bench and asked, "What was that?"

"What was what, sir?" the clerk responded, still a bit perturbed.

"In the pitcher. That drink, what was it?" George said, indicating the stainless steel pitcher.

"Uh . . . it was . . . water, sir," the clerk answered hesitantly, not knowing whether or not George was serious.

At first George looked skeptical, but then when he remembered that for so many years, he had to imbibe the scarcely potable water at Jackson Inside, he knew that he had just tasted fresh clean water. The taste seemed otherworldly.

Just then, George noticed the staring faces surrounding him. At the same time, he became conscious of the moisture that had dribbled from his mouth and down the front of his shirt while he was drinking. He wiped at the moisture on his chin and lips and said, "Excuse me," slightly embarrassed. If his skin wasn't so dark, those watching would have witnessed a pint of blood color his face. He still didn't realize that he was supposed to use the glass.

Instead of letting his embarrassment linger, he dispelled it by turning back to the judge and continuing his explanation. "I was protecting the weaker prisoners, most of them only boys, from sexual predators, extortionists, and drug dealers, Your Honor. Had I not done what I did, most of them would have been raped and exploited in every way for the rest of the time they were in prison."

The prosecutor flinched as if George had slapped him when he heard his explanation. "I object, Your Honor," the prosecutor whined. "It's just not right. No matter what I say, no matter what evidence I present, this prisoner brings forth some incredible prison story to counter it.

"These tickets are incontrovertible proof of the defendant's violent character. They solidify my position. But now here he comes with convenient answers for everything. He's slipperier than an eel in baby oil." Sturtz's pink face turned crimson as he ranted.

"The defendant is appealing to the national outrage against child molesters that stems from the 2005 abduction, rape, and murder of nine-year-old Jessica Lunsford in Florida by forty-seven-year-old pedophile John Couey."

"You're referring to the Jessica Lunsford Act?"

"That's right, Your Honor. The act was named after her and mandated tighter restrictions on sex offenders and increased prison sentences for pedophiles.

"As we all know, Lunsford's brutal murder sparked a national outrage against pedophiles. The defendant is trying to ride the same wave. It's appalling, Your Honor. His tactics—"

"All right, all right, Mr. Sturtz," the judge broke in. "Slow it down for a minute. Now, Mr. Evans, let's take this one step at a time. Explain to the court exactly who these men are that you fought and assaulted. Be specific."

"They were all pedophiles, rapists, and extortionists. If they didn't come to prison for it, they had no problem getting hip to the practice once they got in. Most of them were convicted of the most horrifying crimes imaginable, so horrible that the media would not touch the stories. Being officers of the court"—George paused and looked toward the prosecutor and then back at the judge—"you know exactly who these men are I speak of."

"But," the judge stated, "those men operated individually, not in groups. The prosecutor insinuated that you often fought more than one at a time."

"It's the 'birds of a feather' scenario, Your Honor. In prison it's common to see them form into groups. We call them packs or crews. They're all cowards, and they find strength in numbers."

"Well, how do you get involved? Do the young men come to you?"

"Sometimes they do. Other times they come to BTT, and either myself or some other member will confront the pedophiles. But you must also understand that BTT is not the only organization that the youngsters approach. They approach the Sunni Muslims, the Moorish Science Temple of America, the Nation of Islam, and other religious organizations. In fact, they'll approach any organization or anyone if the need is great enough.

"Furthermore, there are times when the victims don't approach anyone but nevertheless are saved because someone on the yard who's watchful enough to notice the telltale signs notifies one of the prisoner organizations. Or a guard may even report it to us."

"Why would a guard report such an incident to a prisoner? Why not handle it himself?"

"They usually do handle it themselves. The guards generally get first crack at it. Regardless, they are still limited in the level of help they can offer. Officially, the guards' power is limited to them either writing a ticket or putting someone in the hole or on protective custody. Eventually, the predator will be released from the hole and be right back to doing what it was he went to the hole for. And as for protective custody, most young men do not think highly of protective custody, Your Honor. Protective custody, or PC as it is known in the system, will kill all chances of a young prisoner gaining the respect of other prisoners. Most will refuse to go on PC, and many times, the prison can't force them to. Prisoners and guards follow different rules, and the guards are excluded from engaging in the more effective deterrents."

"If the guards know what's happening, then why do they write tickets when they know it's to save a young man from rape or exploitation?"

"Only a select few guards are bent on writing tickets. For example, if you examine the last five tickets I received, you will see that all of them were written by the same guard, Mike Richardson. He's known throughout Jackson Inside as the ultimate racist. He's one of a group of officers who're known as the good ol' boys. It's an unofficial league of neo-Nazi-type officers who've been around for decades. Even though they aren't in every single prison of every state, the problem is still nationwide. Plainly put, they are nothing more than a group of racists out of the Aryan brotherhood who get together to make minorities' lives miserable. It's a game to them."

"Why doesn't the prison system do something about them?" Linbush even managed to look sincere with this question.

"They try, but there isn't much they can do because there are no laws to prevent them from writing tickets. There are no checks and balances. Just as a judge, in many cases, has the authority to give any length of years to a convicted felon who appears before him, the guards are allowed to write tickets unrestrained. The former allows for racial disparity in sentencing, and the latter for racial disparity in ticket writing."

"Why the excessive force though? Why not stop when the threat is removed? It seems as if the stomping is a bit superfluous."

"Each pack or crew has a leader, the alpha male. Without him, there is no pack. Destroy the leader and you've destroyed the pack. Yet simply killing him won't work. The only way to destroy the alpha male is to discredit him. There is no better method of discrediting a man in a maximum-security prison than to knock him out and stomp his face on the prison yard, in full view of the population. Once that is done, that pack will never reform."

"Isn't that dangerous?"

"Very dangerous, especially the stomping part." George's demeanor hardened, and his voice plunged several degrees. "Once you begin stomping their leader's face, the pack transforms into a school of sharks who've caught the scent of blood. They lose all sense of caution and attack like maniacs, blind and mercilessly. They see their own demise tied to the neck of their leader, so they fight for their own survival. While I was stomping their faces is when I'd suffered my more serious injuries. I've been hit with boards and pipes, I've been cut more than fifteen times and stabbed more times than I can remember. The last fight I had, I came out of it with a punctured lung from a shank. I was hospitalized in intensive care for five days. I had a two-inch tube inserted between my ribs to drain fluids from the left side of my chest."

Never Black and little Nathaniel Abraham had been watching the disturbance since the beginning from the windows of the law library. They watched a man get brutally stabbed and left in the road right in front of where they knelt. They stared as the first wisps of smoke drifted on gusts of wind from the roof of the Big Top and then burgeon into dense clouds of rolling black smoke. However, the most disturbing moment came when they witnessed Namen Travis drag a man on the ground, hooked to the back of a maintenance Gator, screaming and bawling, out of the subhall, through the yard, all the way to the corner between three- and four-blocks. It was at that moment when Nathaniel broke down. His curiosity floundered and his terror prevailed. He begged Never Black to hoist him up so that he could hide above the drop ceiling. Despite Never Black's attempts to dissuade him and assure him that he would be okay, Nathaniel would not relent. Finally, Never Black acquiesced and helped the boy into the ceiling. When he had found a secure place to roost, Nathaniel slipped the fiberglass square back into its slot.

Earlier, before the riot broke out, Never Black had convinced Nathaniel to walk to the library with him. Never Black knew that the men that worked in the law library always kept a box of scrap paper in the office, and since there wasn't much else to do, he wanted to show Nathaniel a little of what he had learned from an origami book he had read. While they were flying some of the paper planes Never Black had managed to teach Nathaniel how to make, the emergency siren sounded. As they hurried to clean up their mess and leave, Sandra Girard intercepted them and told them to hang back a minute. When the library cleared of all other inmates, Sandy explained that something serious had happened and that they would probably be safer if they remained in the library, promising them that no one could break down the new security door. They agreed to stay as long as they wouldn't get into any trouble. Sandy promised that they wouldn't.

Now Never Black knelt alone at the window, watching the action out on the yard. There were guards everywhere on the roofs. He could see real policemen, the National Guard, cameras, and reporters.

When Travis returned with a cart full of real-world food, Never Black yearned to be out there. He wished George was there, then he would definitely go out and enjoy the festivities.

As Never Black looked on, a cluster of Scrap Iron's men staggered into view, making their way up the old road, nearing the law library window. Never Black sniggered. They were probably looking for him and Nathaniel. He didn't bother ducking out of sight because it didn't matter if they saw him or not; they couldn't get past the security door anyway.

Before the pack could pass by, Never Black stood up and banged loudly on the window. All faces promptly turned toward him; Never Black waved at them. Stunned motionless for only a second, the mob broke into an all-out sprint toward the subhall. In less than thirty seconds, a gaggle of men crowded in front of the door.

Never Black capered tauntingly before the door chanting, "Can't get in. You can't get in. You can't get in!" When he finished dancing, he squished his nose up against the window, stuck his thumbs in his ears, and wiggled his fingers. The men on the other side of the window laughed at his antics.

In the midst of his gibing, Never Black heard the lock click. With his face still plastered to the window, he cut his eyes toward the door handle. The man still gripping the key as it rested in the unlocked door smiled ominously. Before Never Black could react, the key turner shouldered the door with such force, it knocked Never Black across the room into a bookshelf, where he slid down to the floor, dazed.

Scrap Iron's men poured into the room.

The first man to reach Never Black snatched him up by his collar and boomed, "Where's the boy?" two inches from Never Black's nose. His breath smelled like shit, but Never Black didn't have time to consider such things. He was too busy wondering how the situation had come to this.

When Never Black didn't answer right away, the man held Never Black at arm's length with one hand, reared back, and struck him hard enough to bubble his vision with black spots and leave his ears ringing.

The man struck him a few more blows and asked again, but still, Never Black refused to talk.

"Go get Scrap Iron," the man growled. One of the men near the door left at a run.

Wolfgang stood inspecting the middle hinge of the door. The bolts were loosening. The two brothers had kept up the last ramming session for about half an hour. Prior to that, the bolts from the top hinge had all broken off. That's what ignited the most recent round of fierce battering. Nevertheless, the men were completely exhausted. They were both running off pure adrenaline spiked with a fiendish lust.

Tiredly, Wolfgang bent over and picked up the crowbar. He wedged it about five inches below the ruined top hinge and pulled mightily. The top of the door bent almost six inches outward. Wolfgang, stretched up on his toes, barked through the opening, "We're coming, bitch!" and guffawed raucously.

In central command, the warden paced the floor anxiously. He was concerned about Tina Brown. Many men had entered the subhall since the riot began, but the warden only cared about the two individuals whom a guard spotted entering the building more than seven hours ago. Danny Ranes and his brother Wolfgang, two serial killers, had entered the building and haven't been seen since. The warden knew that if Ms. Brown was in trouble, she would have no doubt contacted him at once. So instead of jumping the gun, he had set a small contingent of officers to keep a watch out for the two murderers. Moreover, he did not want to further jeopardize her position by using the unsecured radio, so he had decided to wait it out. Now, however, his store of patience was beginning to flag.

He picked up the radio. "Mobile 99 to 5 [the guard on the roof of five-block, the closest to the library]."

"Go ahead, 99."

"Anything on the Ranes brothers yet? Over."

"Nothing yet, over."

"Copy that, 5. Keep your eyes open."

"Copy that, 99. Over and out."

The warden paused for a moment before pressing the call button again.

"Mobile 99 to fire marshal [on top of five-block monitoring the smoke entering the subhall]."

"Go, 99."

"What's the status on the law library? Over."

"Status unchanged, 99. Minimal amount of smoke entering law library. All should be well. Over."

"Copy that, fire marshal. Keep watching. Over."

"Copy, 99. I got it covered. Over and out."

A table had been positioned right next to the light pole where Joseph Skipper sagged against his bindings. Climbing on top of the table, Namen Travis looked up at the clusters of people on top of four-block. After a moment, he held up his hand for silence. In a voice heavy with scorn and rage, he yelled through the bullhorn, "I want the world to know that I have the man who broke into the home of Rosa Parks, beat her, and then robbed her.

"I call to witness the reverends Jesse Jackson and Al Sharpton, the minister Louis Farrakhan, Dick Gregory, Nelson Mandela, Colin Powell, Bill Cosby. I call Oprah Winfrey, Nikki Giovanni, Condoleezza Rice, and Sheila Jackson-Lee. I call out to all the blacks of the world."

Travis turned back toward the crowd of prisoners and shouted, "What is your will? Should I set him free to walk amongst us? Should I let our shame stroll freely in our faces? Or should I send him on his way into the next life?"

A few "free him's" could be heard throughout the crowd, but the chorus of "Kill him! Kill him!" swallowed all other protests.

Travis turned again and raised the bullhorn to the media. "My name is Namen Travis. I want the world to hear me. Rosa Parks earned the right to live in this world, to live in a black neighborhood free of crime. The punishment for the filth who would dare violate that sacred right is death by torture!" The roar from the prisoners behind him was deafening. No one but Travis could hear the doomed man resume his recitation of the Lord's Prayer.

Feeling the caress of death along his spine, Joseph Skipper writhed in his bindings, trying desperately to turn toward the cameras. His invocation grew loud; his voice teetered on the edge of delirium. "Our Father! Pleeeease help, oh, God, pleeeeease! Who art in heaven . . . hollowed . . . be thy . . ." His prayer trailed off into chokes and sobs.

The warden's voice rang thunderously over the loudspeaker, and the captain of the state troopers shouted through a bullhorn, all in a last-ditch effort to dissuade Travis.

Ignoring their pleas utterly, Namen Travis, with a cold, grim face, lit a stem of rolled up newspaper and tossed it into the hollow of the tire.

The scene was one that any who watched would not soon forget. Flames engulfed the man's head completely and flickered skyward. The piercing shriek that issued from the dying man's lungs silenced even the heartless prisoners of Jackson Inside. Many of the men in the crowd flinched back, and some even doubled over and hurled their recently ingested vittles onto the hard-packed dirt. The rest scattered, some racing for the safety of the subhall and others just finding some other place to be. Watching a man bleed to death or seeing a skull caved in did nothing to prepare the men for what they witnessed this day.

It took long minutes before the shrill of death quieted, and the furious blaze settled. The sight that remained, most people had only seen in movies. A blackened smoking skull lolled to the side, the lipless mouth frozen in remembered agony. The flames had chewed through his upper torso and exposed a scorched clavicle and a few ribs. Flecks of charred flesh fell intermittently from Skipper's flame-eaten remains. The sickly sweet smell of death would permeate the grounds of Jackson Inside for a long time to come.

Not caring that most of his spectators had abandoned the scene, Travis once again turned to the cameras. "The will of the people has spoken! The law of the jungle prevails!"

Infant mortality rates are 146% higher for blacks; chances of imprisonment are 447% higher; lack of health insurance 42% more likely; the proportion with a college degree 60% lower. And the average white American will live 5½ years longer than the average black American. Just as it is nonsense to postulate that race cannot be considered in remedying race discrimination, so it defies common sense to think that race is not a factor in continuing disparities in black/white life chances.

—Julian Bond

Chapter 23

CNN's latest breaking news: As the anchorman gave a brief account of the life of Ms. Rosa Parks, a photograph of Ms. Parks sitting in a bus covered the screen. Seconds later, an image of her being booked after her arrest replaced the first. Lastly, footage of the wake procession in the White House rotunda, which allowed hundreds of people to pay their last respects, played for a few seconds.

The disembodied voice of the anchor was stating that Rosa Parks possessed one of the most notable black faces in history, equating her with the likes of Reverend Martin Luther King Jr. and Nelson Mandela. "She was the granddaughter of slaves," the voice continued, "and on December 1, 1955, police officers of Montgomery, Alabama, arrested her for refusing to surrender her bus seat to a white passenger; her refusal kicked off a movement to desegregate public transportation. Rosa Parks's courageous act turned the tide in the black struggle for civil rights. Thenceforth, she was known as the Mother of the Civil Rights Movement."

The wake procession faded, and a 1994 booking photograph of Joseph Skipper appeared next. The caption near the bottom of the screen read Rosa Parks's Assailant Executed.

"In 1994, drug addict Joseph Skipper broke into the Detroit home of Rosa Parks and, while robbing her, assaulted her and knocked her to the floor. Even before his conviction, black prisoners nationwide expressed their outrage in the form of curses and death threats.

He became a pariah among the nation's black prison population. During the greater part of his incarceration, the state of Michigan had to afford him protection from the rest of the prisoners.

"That protective custody seems to have failed him recently. As we reported earlier, prisoners have overrun Jackson Inside, the largest walled prison in the country, located in Jackson, Michigan, and Joseph Skipper fell victim to the chaos that ensued. At the onset of the disturbance, a group of prisoners dragged Skipper from his cell then, after tethering him to the back of a small utility cart, towed him across the prison grounds. Only minutes ago, Joseph Skipper was executed on the prison yard, in the area known as the Killing Grounds.

"Gang leader Namen Travis, a man convicted of second-degree murder, draped a tire around Skipper's neck after binding him to a light post then poured gasoline inside of the tire and ignited it. Joseph Skipper died minutes later. It was a form of execution called necklacing, the very same method used by the South African Zulus to punish those who cooperated with the former South African apartheid government.

"Gang leader Namen Travis is also holding Sgt. Gary Moore hostage in a secluded, lightless, soundproof cell without running water or toilet accommodations. We have been told that Travis told the Warden that if the guards or any law enforcement officials storm the prison or fire live rounds onto the yard or in any of the blocks, he would behead Sgt. Moore."

The voice went on to describe the layout of Jackson Inside while a computer generated diagram formed on a large screen. The display highlighted five-block, otherwise known as the hole. A meandering tail of fifty dots ran from a cell inside five-block that was labeled Sgt. Gary Moore, all the way outside of the block to the last dot labeled Namen Travis. The flashing dots inside of the block remained stationary, but the line outside of the block undulated every so often, seemingly tracking the movements of the Namen Travis dot.

"Gang leader Namen Travis told the warden that he had a 'fifty-headed dragon,' and the second he gave the order, that dragon would bite the head off of the hostage.

"It has been approximately ten hours and still no update on the status of the University of Michigan law student Tina Brown, who's trapped in a secluded area of the prison."

At the beginning, Tina Brown pitied herself. She wondered what she had done to deserve a fate such as the one she faced. For a long while, life had seemed as if it had turned against her. Now, however, after long hours of reflection, flashes of the many black women, past and present, who'd been in situations far more hopeless than hers yet survived, invaded her mind. After a while, they started to help her put things in perspective. She let herself imagine the weary faces of the black women who had to labor from dawn to dusk, picking cotton in the sweltering heat of an unforgiving sun then, after that, had to return to the plantation only to suffer rape at the whim of their slave masters and any other white man who got up in his head that he wanted some slave sex. On top of that, they also had to watch as their children were sold on auction blocks and their husbands drawn and quartered. Yet, through all this, they survived.

Before now, she could only marvel at such resilience. Tina never had to actually understand what those women had gone through. To survive that and remain, for the most part, whole seemed beyond her. How did they do it? How deep were their wells of strength? Could she have made it through all that?

Her thoughts drifted forward. During the civil rights era, black women marched until the skin on their feet blistered and bled. They suffered attacks by hoses that sprayed water at pressures so high, it peeled the bark off trees and sent children sailing over parked cars. When vicious police dogs finished ripping and tearing at their clothes and flesh, they were arrested and housed in overcrowded, filthy jails, and they survived.

Black mothers saw their daughters (Denise McNair and Cynthia Wesley, both eleven years old, and Carole Robertson and Addie Mae Collins, both fourteen) blown to pieces while they sat in Sunday school at Birmingham's Sixteenth Street Baptist Church, by white racists. Oprah Winfrey and Maya Angelou suffered sexual abuse and betrayal at the hands of male relatives they trusted. Through all this, they survived.

Suddenly, her self-pity transformed into a sense of shame. How dare she show weakness in the face of hardship when her ancestors left her a legacy of incomparable strength and dauntless perseverance. At that moment, she recalled the words of a poem her grandmother had gifted her when she left home for college. She had given it to Tina framed in glass and told her to read it whenever times got tough, that it would give her strength. When she moved into the dormitory at school, that poem was the first thing she unpacked and hung on the wall. It went from there to her apartment wall after graduation, and it now hung from her bedroom wall at home.

Though she had long since committed the poem to memory, she kept it framed on her wall as a memento. And as her grandmother recommended, she recited it whenever she needed strength. The last time she remembered reciting it was just before she took her last exam.

If there was ever a time that she needed strength, it was now. The poem her grandmother called the black woman's poem, by Maya Angelou, started in a whisper but gained force as the spirit of all those black women who had suffered infused her with the determination to survive.

Still I Rise
You may write me down in history
With your bitter, twisted lies,
You may trod me in the very dirt
But still, like dust, I'll rise.

Does my sassiness upset you?
Why are you beset with gloom?
'Cause I walk like I've got oil wells
Pumping in my living room.

Just like moons and like suns,
With the certainty of tides,
Just like hopes springing high,
Still I rise.

Did you want to see me broke?
Bowed head and lowered eyes?
Shoulders falling down like teardrops,
Weakened by my soulful cries.

Does my haughtiness offend you?
Don't you take it awful hard
'Cause I laugh like I got gold mines
Digging in my own back yard.

You may shoot me with your words,
You may cut me with your hatefulness,
But still, like air, I'll rise.

Does my sexiness upset you?
Does it come as a surprise
That I dance like I've got diamonds
At the meeting of my thighs?

Out of the huts of history's shame
I rise
Up from a past that's rooted in pain
I rise
I'm a black ocean, leaping and wide,
Welling and swelling I bear in the tide.

Leaving behind nights of terror and fear
I rise
Into a daybreak that's wondrously clear

I rise
Bringing the gifts that my ancestors gave,
I am the dream and the hope of the slave.
I rise
I rise
I rise.

From the moment Tina found herself trapped in the riot, she believed herself cheated and defeated. And though the men only outnumbered her two to one, she felt the odds were insurmountable. She felt like a newborn mouse cornered by two alley cats.

Now, however, after reflecting on the passion her ancestors had shown for life, the strength and courage they displayed when no succor seemed forthcoming, she realized that inside, she possessed that same passion, that same strength and courage. History had proven that as a black woman, she could endure the unendurable. She would not defeat herself before she even had the chance to fight.

The tears that seemed to well up unbidden every minute or so, she wiped away determinedly. She refused to give one more tear to those sons of bitches. When Tina lifted herself from the floor, it felt as if she had climbed through the cold wet soil of a newly dug grave and had just broken through to daylight and fresh air. She knew that she wanted to live, and she would either survive or die trying.

Her mind had already begun to formulate a plan even before she became conscious of it. Turning and walking to the rear of the closet, she groped along the wall until she found what she sought. Lifting the long wooden broom from a hook on the wall, she positioned a foot on the handle about six inches above where the bristles fanned out and kicked downward, snapping the handle near the bottom. She inspected the broken end and found it jagged and sharp, just as she intended: a killing spear, her equalizer.

As she gripped her weapon with both hands, she rallied her courage for what she knew she had to do if she would have any chance of survival. The big man, Tina didn't know, but she knew that she was at least thirty years younger than Ranes and maybe just as strong, and a lot faster too. All her years of professional dancing kept her in extremely good condition. That, added to the fact that they would be completely spent by the time they made it through that door, increased her chances considerably, she thought.

Lastly, she had the element of surprise on her side. Those rapists wouldn't expect her to attack first. They probably thought she would go to her doom like a meek kitten. She would show them soon enough just how dangerous it was to assume. Because dealing with two attackers, even fatigued ones, might prove too much for Tina, she planned to even the odds. As soon as the first man showed his ugly face in the closet doorway, she would put all her weight and strength behind plunging the jagged end of the broom handle deep into the soft spot below his Adam's apple. Her aim would be true because their eyes would need time to adjust to the lightless closet. In that brief span, she would act without mercy. The law student was going to kill a man.

Scrap Iron and two of his men rushed into the law library and stopped a few steps in. A few of the men already present greeted him, but Scrap Iron ignored them. Truth be told, he couldn't even hear them. His eyes were riveted on the far wall, where Never Black stood trembling.

Without a word, Never Black bolted to his right and disappeared down an aisle of books.

"Huh," belched Scrap Iron, a bit thrown off but still not giving chase. He knew there was no escape. He and his men laughed at the futility of Never Black's flight.

A loud thump that emanated from the direction of Never Black had cut short their laughter. The men trotted through the aisle to see what was up. There they saw Never Black sprawled on the floor, holding his head. The damn fool had dived head first into the cinder block wall, probably trying to kill himself.

Scrap Iron seized a fistful of the seat of Never Black's pants and hoisted him up. He carried the pitiful young man to the nearest table and flung him on top of it.

The massive pedophile raised a giant paw and cuffed Never Black on the side of his head. Never Black skidded off the table. Scrap Iron grabbed him up and shoved him against a wall. Clapping him several more times on the head, Scrap Iron snarled, "Bitch, where's the boy?"

"I object, Your Honor. I move for an offer of proof." Prosecutor Sturtz looked at George and shook his head contemptuously, an almost imperceptible smile of triumph flickering at the corners of his mouth. "The prisoner is depicting himself as some sort of hero, a regular Mr. Goody Two-shoes. For Christ's sake, he had a prison work assignment entitled 'cleaner of blood.' Give me a break.

"It's all a bit much for me, Your Honor. This convicted murderers going around the state's highest-security prison fighting men for being sexual predators, drug dealers, and extortionists and then getting beaten and stabbed by the bad guys. When will this nonsense end, this prison drama, or whatever you wish to call it.

"Just who does he think he's talking to?" The prosecutor had walked from behind his desk and stood between the judge and George. He looked directly at the audience as he spoke. "This isn't the prison yard where anything goes. What we have here is a court of law, the centerpiece of justice for the legal disputes of our nation. Truth, not lies, is the foundation upon which our judicial system is built. No high school dropouts here, no quitters. Our courts are manned by overachievers, men and women who dared to burn the candle at night to reach for the better life.

"At my table, Your Honor," said the prosecutor, turning and pointing at one of his assistants, "is a graduate of the Thomas Cooley school of law. Six years on the dean's list.

"Myself, I am a proud Wolverine, graduating fifth in my class." The prosecutor was confident now, on comfortable ground. He stopped, pointed to a framed degree behind the judge's desk, then looked at George. "That, my friend, is a sheepskin from Harvard, JD, cum laude, if you will, now over on that wall—"

"Enough of this Mr. Prosecutor. I don't know where you're going with this, but let's get back on track here."

"My point, Your Honor, is that the man's story is patently unbelievable. The story is just a touch too fantastic, too contrived, a bit too pat. On the one hand, you have all of those prison battles, and on the other you have that man," Sturtz said, pointing a shaky finger at George, "in the middle of those battles, just a swinging, punching, and stomping away to save someone he doesn't even know. Well, I'm just choked up with emotion. The cuts, the stabbings, the big tube in the side of his chest, well, if he wouldn't have gone that far, I probably would've bought some of it. Nevertheless, since he did, I would like to see evidence of these wounds. A two-inch tube would have left a fairly noticeable scar, not to mention all of the other cuts and puncture wounds he spoke of."

The prosecutor raised his voice and glared at George. "I motion the court to order the prisoner to strip from the waist up."

The prosecutor continued his glare. While George simply stood there impassively watching for the judge's reaction. Surprisingly, Linbush's attitude during George's hearing had not been what he expected. He thought he would face a two-front attack from the judge and the prosecutor. Linbush had actually been pretty fair so far. George didn't know what had changed during the course of the day, but he thought it better to just ride it out and not question his good fortune.

Sturtz, however, was on the verge of apoplexy. He jabbed his index finger at George again and said, "I intend to prove that man a liar and a fake. Since we've heard so much about the man's skin today, let's see some of it. I don't believe any of the crap spewing from his mouth, and I don't expect that anyone else here today does either.

"As an advocate for the people, I'm not going to allow just anyone to walk into this courtroom and run any type of a cow-dung story on us. The citizens of this state deserve better, and I'm here to see that they get it." Sturtz raised his chin pompously. "Order the prisoner to strip from the waist up. The people invoke their right to confront the evidence put forth. I'm moving for an offer of proof." He finished with a nod and another finger thrust.

George felt no surprise when Linbush, citing a rule of evidence, granted the prosecutor's motion. With no objection, and not even waiting for the judge to finish explaining his ruling, George began to unbutton his prison-issued blue and orange shirt. When he finally laid his undershirt on the podium, he heard a voice cry, "Oh, my God!"

The judge had blurted the exclamation upon seeing what lay hidden underneath George's prison uniform. At the same time, Linbush had vaulted to his feet and leaned as far as he could over the bench, peering at George's bare torso.

Nearly in synch with Linbush's outburst, George heard a woman shriek in the audience. He glanced around and watched as the elementary school teacher shot erect and grabbed an arm of a little girl sitting next to her. "Get out, all of you kids. Move it! We're leaving."

As the last of the children filed out of the courtroom, the teacher turned around and hissed at the prosecutor, "That sure was extremely stupid. They're just little kids, you know." Then she vanished through the door after her students.

"What?" snapped the prosecutor defensively to the audience with his arms spread wide. "What did I do?"

"Asshole," someone else yelled from the audience.

Excited whispers and shouts filled the courtroom. Several audience members tried to move forward in order to get a closer look at George's body. Seeing the bailiff having a difficult time trying to restrain them, the judge banged his gavel against the bench and ordered the audience members to return to their seats.

Linbush himself descended the steps of the bench and approached George. Circling George, the judge examined the clumps and clusters of distended scars, some long and vicious looking, others convex and puffy. A few of the longer ones looked to extend up to twenty-four inches, snaking around his body from front to back, covering his chest and abdomen. His trunk resembled a mass of grotesque snakes frozen in motion.

Judge Linbush's expression betrayed his scandalized senses. He moved closer. The scars splayed across the man's body teased at Linbush's memory. The sight took him back to his college years. Inside of a black-history book one of his professors had taught from, black men in the nineteenth century wore those same scars as regularly as white men wore suspenders. They called them welts and most often resulted from the blows of a leather whip or strap. Wincing, Linbush stepped away from George, somewhat dismayed.

"What the hell happened?" Linbush uttered.

One of the transport staff that transported George to the prison spoke. "About eight years ago, a small gang of men tricked George into a small maintenance room in the basement of the gym. They beat him with their fists and clubs until he was unconscious. They then stripped him and strung him up in the middle of the room from a support beam. They flogged him with a leather whip spiked with nails they had fabricated in the hobby craft program for just that purpose."

"Who were they, the men that did this?"

"Sex offenders, Your Honor, mostly, then there were some drug dealers and extortionists. Your common prison gang, only several of them had combined together to accomplish this act."

"Why did they do it?"

"They were trying to discredit BTT. In their minds, they had become too adept at preventing sexual attacks, stopping the exploitation of younger prisoners and so forth. They were trying to destroy BTT."

"But why did they single George out? It seems like they went out of their way to get him."

"Because he was the leader, the head. They thought if they chopped the head off, the body would die."

"Okay. But then why didn't they stomp his face in view of the rest of the prisoners as he's often done to them?"

"Good old-fashioned fear. Except, Your Honor, it wasn't him they were afraid of. They feared one of his cofounders. As he's told you, stomping a man's face on the prison yard is the gravest of insults.

They did not want to take the chance that the sight of stomping his face on the yard would be taken as a personal attack on his cofounder."

"Why would they fear him more than George? He must be a very dangerous man."

"He is, Your Honor."

"Who is he?"

"His name's Samuel Davis."

"So, I take it, none of the perpetrators were ever caught?"

"That's right."

"No one could make any identifications I suppose?"

"Correct."

"Couldn't or *wouldn't* identify them?" the judge asked knowingly, speaking directly to George now.

"It was pretty dark down there."

The judge leaned forward, his mouth mere inches from George's. "When people live by the criminal's code of silence in the face of crime, they sharpen the razor that cuts their own throats. You're a smart man, Mr. Evans. Keep that thought in mind."

The judge straightened, never taking his eyes from George then, for the prosecutor's sake, instructed George to show him where the tube had been inserted to drain his chest cavity. George lifted his left arm. The two-inch scar rested about an inch below and two inches to the left of his nipple.

"Over here, Prosecutor Sturtz." The judge turned to the prosecutor's table. "You wanted to see it, now come take a look. And while you're at it, take a look at all the scars from the prison wars you so adamantly claimed did not happen."

Sturtz sat at the table, scrupulously studying a document he had in his hands. Without looking up from the paper, he mumbled, "Uh, well, that's quite all right, Your Honor. Let's move on to more serious matters. The defendant claims that he's the victim of racial disparity in sentencing. Let's—"

"That isn't true," George interrupted, putting his clothes back on as he spoke. "Don't limit the issue to me being the only victim."

"Oh yes, that's right. Let me rephrase. It's the prisoner's position that a large number of minorities in prisons all over the country are victims of racial disparity in sentencing. Now let's—"

"Again, that's not true," George broke in anew. "You grossly oversimplify the case. When you limit the victims, as you're doing, you undermine the scope and severity of the issue. Let me make this as clear as possible so there will be no misunderstandings: Racial disparity in sentencing is a significant impediment in the progress of black Americans, and its place in history must be exposed to the world abroad.

"Race-based sentences keep blacks in prison for many more years than whites for the same or similar crimes. Blacks suffer in dark cold cells while their white counterparts are set free to become productive citizens and to nurture their communities. Whereas white prisoners are released on parole to raise their children, black prisoners are limited to speaking with their children over the phone by expensive collect phone calls after the parole board continues their sentences. Babies are left to grow up without fathers, breadwinners are absent from the home, dysfunctional family units are created by this systematic plague. The ecology of the black community becomes unbalanced and unhealthy.

"Racial disparity in sentencing is a bitter spice that seasons the black community with hopelessness and helplessness.

"To take it a step further, let's look at the criminal justice and sociology departments of your higher educational institutions across the country, which take the number of incarcerated blacks—a number blown greatly out of proportion due to race-based sentencing—then use those figures as evidence to teach their students that black communities have a disproportionate number of people who exhibit criminal mentalities. In that way, educational institutions indirectly become victims of race-based sentencing, for when they miseducate their students, they subvert their primary goal. After that, those same students take that nonsense home with them and teach it to others who hang on every word of the 'college educated,'" George said, signing quotation marks as he did, "thereby corrupting entire communities. All of that engenders a false sense of superiority in whites and a false sense of inferiority in blacks.

"When the state sentences black people based on their skin color then points to those same sentences to show a dysfunctional black culture that cultivates crime, the state mimics a sick dog that returns to lap up its own vomit.

"The majority of incarcerated blacks across the nation who are victims of racial disparity in sentencing have family and other loved ones. The parents of the prisoners are victims, as are their aunts, uncles, and cousins. Some of them have wives, husbands, and children. Prisoners' extended families are connected to and victimized by these race-based laws in the same way that the Jews who escaped the Warsaw ghettos and Nazi Germany were connected to and victimized by Germany's race-based laws when that government gassed, shot, hung, raped, starved, and tortured their fathers, mothers, husbands, wives, aunts, uncles, cousins, and children in the death camps of Auschwitz, Belzec, Chelmno, Majdanek, Sobibor, and Treblinka. Though the names have changed to San Quentin, Pelican Bay, Huntsville, Marion, Sing Sing, Joliet, Graterford, Attica, and Jackson Inside, the tumor that links these places—racism—has remained unchanged.

"Just as blacks in this country, in Europe, in Africa, and all over the world were aware of and felt the pain of the victims of the racist apartheid laws of South Africa, blacks all over the world are aware of and feel the pain caused by the racially disparate laws of this country. In that sense, racial disparity in sentencing has global implications.

"Additionally, there—"

"Excuse me, Mr. Evans. Just hold up a moment." Judge Linbush held up a hand. A clerk had entered the courtroom and ascended the bench to speak close to the judge's ear. George's suspicions bubbled straightaway. To interrupt court proceedings in this manner could only signal an emergency.

After a brief back-and-forth with the clerk, the judge announced, "I'm not exactly sure of what's going on, but a statewide directive has been issued addressed to all state courts from the office of the director of the Michigan Department of Corrections. It states that all prisoners out on writs may be ordered returned to their respective prisons without further notice. We are on standby. Considering this, Mr. Evans, you may wish to sum up your argument."

I love those who yearn for the impossible.

—Johann Wolfgang Von Goethe

Chapter 24

Crumpled on the floor in a battered and bloody heap lay Never Black. The unbridled violence Scrap Iron had inflicted upon him, attempting to bludgeon out of him the whereabouts of Nathaniel, left Never Black a broken ruin.

Just before Scrap Iron's murderous explosion, he had asked Never Black for the umpteenth time where the boy was. The answer Never Black offered sent the giant pedophile into a seething rampage.

"You know what," Never Black had said defiantly when Scrap Iron had demanded, after several blows to Never Black's head, to know where Nathaniel was hiding, "you're nothin' but human garbage. Your breath smells like shit, and your body smells like a week-dead corpse."

Never Black knew that his words would infuriate Scrap Iron. In fact, he was counting on it. Because he had failed to kill himself when he dived headfirst into the wall, he thought if he provoked Scrap Iron enough, he'd finish the job for him. With that in mind, Never Black continued, "You like to rape people that's weaker than you because no one else will touch you—" A heavy blow made Never Black's ears ring.

"Shut the fuck up!" Scrap Iron bellowed.

Even before his vision could refocus, Never Black started again. "You're a bitch, a loser, and a pedophile, and that's all you'll ever be. Your family don't care about you—" Another blow dazed him.

"And you're going to die alone inside these prison walls, then you'll burn in hell forever." After that, it seemed like the punches and kicks would never end.

Now, still alive, his jaw fractured in two places, most of his front teeth scattered somewhere on the library floor, several ribs cracked, and his eyeball dangling by the optic nerve from its socket, Never Black struggled for every painful breath.

Like a horrific, perverted comic villain, Scrap Iron stood akimbo over the mangled form of Never Black and roared with contemptuous laughter.

Despite their exhaustion, the killers were certain that the security door to the law classroom would yield soon. Ever since Wolfgang wedged the top hinge loose, the remaining two bent slightly each time one of the murderers rammed the door. Now, however, they faced another complication; the smoke seeping from the classrooms across the hall—those nearest the Big Top—was getting thick, making it difficult to breath. The flames had engulfed most of the roof of the chow hall, and helicopters were flying over, dumping thousands of gallons of water and tons of fire-retarding chemicals onto the blaze. The chemicals and steam created a potent mixture.

Tina, bedraggled and weary, stepped resolutely out of the classroom closet. The killers stopped their ramming to watch her. To the middle of the room, she walked and cleared a large space, dragging chairs and pushing tables against walls. When she finished, she returned to the middle of the room and paused for a second before she started dancing. It was a comical yet spirited dance—with kicks and hops—called the hornpipe. Ship captains used to dance it on deck when the seas were calm and the winds were good. Tina and her troupe had performed the dance many times for audiences of children.

Through the window, Tina could see the two men glance at each other dubiously. The last time Tina had stepped out of the closet, the men stopped trying to break the door down and watched her. She thought she'd try it again, maybe buy herself a little more time. It worked. Bewildered expressions or no, the men looked on, blessedly still.

While the average convict, in the early stages of the riot, had raided the prisoner store and the Big Top for food, the infirmary for drugs and syringes, or the property room for TVs and radios and such,

Samuel Davis had targeted the butcher shop. He stole the longest sharpest knives he could find, and the ones he didn't take, he took and snapped in half using a door jamb then hid the fragments. His instinct, honed by years of training and combat, wouldn't allow him to leave any weapons behind for his enemies. He had no need of hoarding food; a man with a weapon could always eat.

Hid away in the mop closet on the fourth-gallery bulkhead in three-block, Samuel, swiftly and expertly, prepared himself for war. With his shirt off, he lined his waist with thick issues of *Field & Stream, Black Enterprise,* and *Ebony*, then cinched a belt tight through the loops of his pants and another around the tops of the magazines, securing in place his knife-proof vest. To complete his battle gear, he slid several knives between the magazines and his pants waist. The remaining blades he took and rolled up in a pillow case and shoved between the magazines and his lower back.

Outfitted and ready, Samuel opened the door to the mop closet and peered down the gallery. He spotted no one. Flicking open the wings of his mirrored sunglasses, he slipped them on and pulled the bill of his cap low over his brow. He rushed down the gallery bulkheads and trotted across base, stopping just in front of the heavy doors leading out of three-block. There, he pulled out of his pocket a small sack of homemade wine and a cup. He filled the cup with wine and sloshed the rest over the front of his shirt. Flinging the bag to the floor, he pushed open one of the doors and staggered outside.

Just beyond the doors, Samuel stumbled against a couple of men, one of who promptly shoved him away and yelled, "Watch where you goin', you old-ass drunk."

"*Excusé moi*, gennellmen," Samuel slurred, belched, then tottered off and disappeared into the crowd.

On top of four-block, near the roof's edge, guard Mike Richardson sat beside a table and watched the prison yard through a pair of binoculars. Every few minutes, Richardson would turn to a legal pad that lay close by on the table top and jot something down.

The legal pad held several pages full of six-digit numbers. Richardson was gathering numbers from the shirts and pants of prisoners on the yard. He planned on writing them all major misconducts, the most serious sort: inciting a riot and possession of a weapon.

Every major misconduct affects the receiving prisoner's release date. However, the charges Richardson aimed to stick the men with would have the gravest consequences of the all, aside from serious assault or homicide tickets. With a ticket for inciting a riot or possession of a weapon, the prisoner could look forward to losing at least two years of accumulated good time and getting a two-year pass over from the Michigan Parole Board, totaling at minimum an additional four years in prison for each ticket.

Richardson would be careful to only get the prisoners serving indeterminate sentences and were therefore eligible to have days taken away from them. He wouldn't waste time with the lifers right now, for tickets would have no effect on them getting out of prison. Oh, but be sure, he would deal with them later.

At the moment, Richardson's focus was on the men idling against the wall of five-east. Most of the men belonged to different religious organizations, none participating in the riot; all of them were black. So far he had scribbled 267 inmate numbers on the legal pad.

With two misconducts each, those black men would have to spend a total of 2,134 extra years in prison, 2,134 years families and communities would suffer the absence of those black men. Not one of those years the men will have served for any crime they committed; rather, those centuries will have been lost at the whim of a racist prison guard, who was allowed free reign over the lives of prisoners because of a glitch in the system. The MDOC's method of processing major misconducts is grievously flawed, flawed to the point of absurdity. A credo etched in the hearts of all MDOC employees holds that under all circumstances, a guard's word is sacrosanct. There is no litmus test for verifying the accusations of prison guards, and such a condition allows bigoted guards to act unchecked and with impunity.

Opposite Richardson, on the other side of the table, sat twenty-two-year-old guard Jane Austin. An average-looking young lady with average ambitions. She planned to remain a prison guard until she retired. She was also the newest recruit to the"good ol' boy" network. Up to that point, she had secured 111 guilty findings on bogus major misconducts she had written on black prisoners. She had another twenty-nine years and five months to go before she retired.

* * *

"Because the United States of America is arguably the most powerful country on earth and definitely the most influential, it is considered a world leader. What this Court's ruling will do in the matter of racial disparity in sentencing will not only set an example internationally of how a world leader enacts and enforces its laws, it will also help to define our future as a nation. Every country in the world keeps a watch on our laws, our laws send forces rippling through the world's social ether. If we are to properly assume the position of world leader, then we must consider and guard our conduct as a nation. Whether we are viewed as a just or unjust leader, a righteous or corrupt nation, is a matter left up to us. When—"

George had been speaking for less than five minutes when a clerk hurried into the courtroom and spoke to the judge urgently.

"That's it," the judge pronounced as he stood and faced the deputies who had transported George to the courthouse. "The directive is finalized. All prisoners out on writs are to be returned to their respective prisons immediately. Those from Jackson Inside are to be handcuffed, black-box restrained, and shackled."

Before the judge even finished his statement, the guards had the cuffs around George's wrist and were working on the belly chains.

"What's going on?" George asked Judge Linbush.

"I'm not sure, sir, but it's serious. No one has any details at the moment, just hearsay, but it sounds like something major."

"Will I get a chance to finish presenting my case?"

"There's no need. I've heard enough. The only thing left now is the ruling."

As the deputies prodded George gently but firmly toward the door, the spectators, lawyers, and others in the audience patted George on the back, congratulated him on his presentation, and wished him luck. When the three men approached the door, Linbush raised his voice over the crowd.

"What do you want done with the duffel bags?" The judge was referring to the two bulging duffel bags the deputies had toted into the courtroom on a dolly. The bags contained the thousands of letters George received from incarcerated black men and women across the nation victimized by racial disparity in sentencing.

"I move for their admission as my exhibit B," George responded as he and the deputies neared the door.

"But what's exhibit A?" yelled the judge, perplexed.

"My life!" George shouted as he shuffled through the doorway.

At the prosecution's table, Sturtz screwed up his face and asked the judge, "What 'life' was he talking about, Your Honor? Was he talking about his 'life' as a black man or his life sentence?"

"Oh, just shut your mouth, Doug," snapped the judge.

Every man alive has a breaking point; that point comes whenever life places upon a man's shoulders more weight than he can carry. When a man breaks, it's not his body that comes apart; it's the soul, that essence people call the substance of man, that shatters.

When Scrap Iron's brutes opened the door to the law library, Never Black's soul fractured. Moments later, when Scrap Iron lumbered into the library, Never Black's innerself crumbled. For that reason alone, the young man decided to take his own life. He would end it before the nightmare he had narrowly escaped so many times overtook him. He wanted to escape the pain and humiliation of the gang rape he knew would soon follow.

Someone said that a man's life flashes before his eyes whenever he nears death. What lay ahead of Never Black was worse than death. His miserable life scrolled through his mind, a life epitomizing the dreadful existence of the black man in the United States, a life forged by the fires of poverty, familial dysfunction, an impoverished neighborhood; a life shaped by the hammer of an incompetent public school system, alcohol, drugs, then pounded against the anvil of racism. Each factor, in turn, aided in knocking him to the floor.

Above all, though, Never Black blamed himself. Regardless of the obstacles, a man was supposed to step up and take possession of his life. That's what men do, that's what men have done since the dawn of history, and that's what men will do until the end of time. George had constantly reminded Never Black of that fact. George called it manning up.

Had Never Black spent more time focused on school and less time kicking it with his homeboys, he probably wouldn't be in this situation. But it was so much easier to just hang out and loaf around. If hitting the books meant "manning up," then to "man up" meant to work, to take control and accept responsibility for your own life and actions. That was hard to do. Being responsible meant thinking, and thinking was hard to do when you were always drunk, high, or both.

Never Black felt the sharp regret that accompanies despair. The most poignant regret he felt was dropping out of school. In the free world, he never allowed himself a lot of time to dwell on it, but he knew that a job in this age of technology was nearly impossible to get without an education. Moreover, being a dropout, having no skills to brag of, being black, an alcoholic, a drug addict, and a slacker added up to a life full of loss, failure, and misery.

Instead of drinking and drugging, he should've taken part in beneficial and commendable activities like the other teenagers his age who were now successful, respectable citizens. In his folly, he used to laugh at them, but now he realized that they had "manned up," something he had not the courage to do. Instead of spending so much time playing basketball and watching rap videos, he should've stayed home and spent that time with his children. He felt a piercing stab of shame and guilt when he thought of his children. Even for them, he failed to "man up." What was the opposite of that, "man down?" If so, he sure was an expert at that, "manning down." At the moment, he had it down perfectly. He was the man down on the floor in the corner of a room in a prison, broken and bloody, who was about to become a human receptacle for the abominable lust of depraved men. A sardonic chuckle tried to escape his tattered lips, but his throat was too weak and dry to even begin vibrating. Yet the effort managed to push a drop of blood through the slit of his lips to trickle down to the edge of his lower lip and dangle there like a black man hung from a poplar tree.

"Bitch, where's the boy," Scrap Iron thundered, towering over the hapless young man. "Last chance, muthafucka. Where's my little boy?" A swift, powerful kick followed that question and broke another one of Never Black's abused ribs.

If Never Black could've been granted one wish in life, he would've chosen to be reborn white. God, how beautiful life would be as a white man.

Scrap Iron hoisted the defeated youngster by his collar and the seat of his pants and launched him into the wall. Never Black connected hard and flopped to the floor like a pile of dirty clothes.

"I want the boy!" The giant sounded like a wounded elephant.

If he were reborn white, Never Black thought, life's road would be paved in gold. He would have no troubles, everyone would love him, he would have rich friends. His blond-haired white wife would cook for him and their white children every day. Each morning, he would leave his white house, in his white car, with his white family and travel up that gold-paved road to anywhere he wanted to go.

Scrap Iron grabbed Never Black again and lifted him up, but this time he dumped him on a table so he lay flat on his stomach with his legs draped over the edge. Never Black struggled pathetically, but Scrap Iron's men restrained him easily. Helplessly, he felt hands claw his belt buckle loose and yank his pants down and off his ankles. The searing pain that blasted through Never Black as the perverted men commenced their gruesome, horrific work demanded recognition and got it in the form of a cutting, discordant scream that rebounded off the walls, through the hallways, and eventually dissipated into nothingness. The gang rape of Never Black had begun.

Little Nathaniel clung desperately to the insulated ceiling pipes. The pipes were his only salvation. With each agonizing scream Never Black let out, Nathaniel's body jerked in terror. But what frightened him even more were the obscene peals of laughter booming through the ceiling tiles. If he was ever unlucky enough to hear him laugh, he would bet that that's what the devil would sound like.

I wish to live because life has within it that which is good, that which is beautiful, and that which is love. Therefore, since I have known all of these things, I have found them to be reason enough and—I wish to live. Moreover, because this is so, I wish others to live for generations and generations and generations.

—Lorraine Hansberry

Chapter 25

The security door to the classroom was breached. The middle latch had broken from the frame. Now all that was left to do was bend the bottom latch inward. For added security, the bottom latch was twice the size of the middle and top latches, but it would only take fifteen minutes or so to bend it now that the other two hung free. After that, the serial killers could enter the room and go about doing what they knew best: torture, rape, murder.

"It won't be long now."Wolfgang's head poked through the wide gap as Ranes forced the top of the door forward. His voice, cold and callous, reached out for Tina."We're coming, bitch!"

On the ride back to Jackson, George's plan to take in all the sights he had missed on the way to court had fled, driven out by anxiety over the hearing. Did he cover all the important points? Was he adequately prepared? Was it a fool's move to represent himself instead of accepting an attorney? And was his presentation professional? He had never argued orally before a court. His considerable experience dealing with the court system consisted of submitting legal briefs and petitions. In his experience from the many legal parlays he had engaged in with different attorneys, he believed that he had done pretty well. But was "pretty well" enough? He felt the burden of all those thousands and thousands of incarcerated blacks and their families depending on him to succeed. Did he let them down?

Though it was difficult to manage things with the shackles and the black box on—which limited hand movement to the upper section of his thighs—George managed to leaf through his papers as the deputy's vehicle coasted down the highway. If he could improve his argument in any way, he could easily prepare a supplemental brief and send it in. So far, however, he didn't think it would be necessary. He was confident that he had covered all bases.

So intent on his review of the legal documents, George failed to notice the roadblock, at which the car had to slow down to get through, a mile out from the prison, and he didn't hear the helicopters "thwuping" back and forth over the area. Finally, his eyes lifted abruptly when the car stopped before the front gate of the prison.

Thousands of National Guardsmen stippled the perimeter of Jackson Inside. The countless blue and black shirts of state, county, and local police officers clogged the area in a flurry of activity. Television crews lined the far side of the road behind George, and hundreds more armed and civilian bodies dotted the roofs of the cell blocks. Black plumes of smoke rose from numerous parts of the prison, the thickest of them concentrated near the center where the chow hall sat.

"A prison riot," George heard himself utter. The documents fell from his hands. An overwhelming sense of dread enveloped him.

It was a struggle, but Never Black managed to lift himself from the floor. He had lost track of time and his surroundings about thirty minutes into his suffering. It hurt to move, yet he forced himself erect. His body trembled in pain. Still disoriented, he stumbled a bit but regained his balance. With his one good eye, he scanned the room. The place was empty. How long did it go on? How long had Scrap Iron and his men been gone?

A few feet away, he saw his clothes and shoes scattered in a small area. That's when he became aware of his nakedness. Instinctively, he moved to recover his clothes but then thought to hell with it. What did it matter if he was clothed or not? Dead men don't need clothes.

Never Black limped agonizingly slowly out of the library, staggered down the short hall, and turned right into the subhall. As he passed gate 15, medical staff rushed to the bars and begged, "Sir, please, don't go that way. Come this way, we can help you." The words could not penetrate the quiet surrender within Never Black. It's funny how now that he knew his life was forfeited, a sort of peace consumed him. A peace that put the world in one place and himself in another. He staggered on.

Ordinarily, it took a person about three minutes to walk from the subhall to four-block; however, with several cracked ribs, which made breathing a battle, and injuries in places he had never dreamt could hurt so bad, Never Black's circumstances were anything but ordinary.

After exiting the subhall, he had to rest, hanging on to the fence in Peckerwood Park. Taking short breaths, all of which seemed just short of enough, he felt a little strength return. None of the pain went away though. Ignoring it, Never Black started out again, staggering down the old pock-marked road. Five minutes passed . . . fifteen minutes . . . thirty minutes, still he limped on. He stopped every few yards to check his bearings. The effort of walking diminished almost all secondary functions; he could barely walk and breathe at the same time. A migraine blurred the vision in his one good eye—if distended and bloodshot could be considered good—and the other hung uselessly. Up ahead, he could just make out the doors to four-block through the small slit left between his swollen eyelids.

Never Black's legs failed as he turned left in front of three-block. The few times he had fallen before, he had mustered enough strength to push himself upright, but not this time. His body seemed someone else's right then. He negotiated a knee up under him, and then another. He managed to get his palms flat on the concrete, pushed his face off the ground, and began a slow, painful, agonizing crawl down the old winding road in front of three-block.

Never Black's difficult journey down the old road was marked by a trail of blood.

The encouraging words and sympathetic utterances men shouted from the yard never hit their mark. The offers of help shouted over the loudspeaker and from other prisoners, as well as the caustic jeers and mocking laughter, fell upon deaf ears. Never Black had enough of everything, especially enough of the life as a black man. It was time to call it quits.

Someone, he didn't bother to see who, held open the door to four-block, allowing Never Black to crawl inside. A sad and disturbing sight, still he crawled on. Ever so slowly, he inched across base, up flights of stairs, and around bulkheads until he reached fourth gallery. Just as he curved onto fourth gallery bulkhead, arms trembling, knees ablaze, he slumped against the safety wire mesh that stretched from the side of the steps to the ceiling. His dangling eye slipped inside a crevice left between a support pipe and one of the plastic ties that held the mesh against it. When he moved to recover, the eye stretched grotesquely, and the pain that exploded inside his brain chased all consciousness away.

Like a prisoner in a cell, the Warden paced the floor of central command. Two seven-by-nine-feet flat-screen LCD monitors hung from the front and the back walls. A lieutenant stood at the small control panel near the front of the room. The panel could pull up on the screen any area of the prison where the more than one hundred yard cameras were focused. A crowd of staff members huddled before the LCD screen on the back wall, which an assistant deputy warden controlled, watching as a camera scanned the prison yard. The camera was searching for Samuel Davis. He had not been seen since the beginning of the riot.

The location of Samuel Davis was a top priority. A priority first coming in the form of a request from someone in the United States Army. The second request coming only moments later and this in the form of a directive straight from the Pentagon: EXTREME URGENCY! LOCATE-REPORT-MONITOR SAMUEL DAVIS!

Currently, however, the warden's focus and top priority were the events taking place on the stage in front of three-block. An image of Namen Travis, wearing nothing but boxing trunks and boxing shoes, dancing around a motionless body covered the screen. The warden had just watched as Travis pummeled the man with a whirlwind of taped knuckles. The view panned left, showing an older man struggling against three of Travis's men who were dragging him onto the stage. The warden rubbed his eyes in irritation. He was supposed to be in control of this prison, but all he could do now was watch. And wait.

The man that lay at Travis's boots, Kevin Morgan, had once bragged to other prisoners that once, just for fun, he had forced a crack-addicted black woman to perform oral sex on a dog. For his insult to the dignity of black women, Morgan lay unconscious on the stage, with a broken nose, jaw and all his front teeth smashed out.

Another man lay in a similar state over in a corner. He was twenty-two-year-old Edward Bradley, a black man from Detroit who made national headlines for savagely beating and carjacking ninety-one-year-old Leonard Sims outside a Detroit party store.

Lamont Marshall, bald, plump, with short gray stubble crowding his cheeks, wrestled mightily against the three huge men tugging him onto the stage. Marshall was already serving a life sentence for the 1980 attempted murder of a woman when the Metropolitan Cold Case Team of Grand Rapids produced the results of a new DNA test that linked blood evidence preserved from the 1975 murder of Laura Jean Ellis to him. Lamont Marshall was also being investigated as the sole suspect in the 1970 murder of Shelly Mills, the 1976 murders of Kathryn Darling and Nancy Sweetman, the 1977 murder of Ida Mae Luchie, and the 1980 murder of Catherine Fingleton, all strangled and stabbed to death. For murdering women, a prison sentence wasn't enough; Travis had his own form of punishment to deliver.

As Marshall struggled, he glanced over at the light post shooting up out of the right corner of the stage. Tied to the poles was fifty-five-year-old serial killer Coral Eugene Watts. Marshall had watched Travis beat the man unconscious, tie him to the pole, then go to work on him with a baseball bat, breaking both of his feet, legs, and arms. Lastly, he seized each of Watts's fingers and wrenched them backward, bones and connective tissue crunching and ripping noisily. Coral Eugene Watts was the most notorious black serial killer in history, serving life sentences for killing two women. Experts believed that Watts had killed more than Jeffrey Dahamer, John Wayne Gacy, and Ted Bundy combined. His spree ended in 1982 when he ran up against two Texas women, twenty-year-old Loris Lister and her eighteen-year-old roommate, Melinda Aguilar, whose escape from Watts led to his arrest.

Less than an hour before Travis was released from the hole, he had just finished reading *Evil Eyes* by Corey Mitchell, a book depicting the Watts murders. Even before Travis assaulted the counselor, he knew a little about Watts's case and disliked him from the start. However, after learning more of the lurid details, Travis's dislike morphed into hate. Only arrant cowards harmed women. For a man to prove his worth, he had to fight other men, dangerous men, in hand-to-hand combat. He must earn warrior status, the status that all men should strive for. Namen Travis was a proven warrior.

Studying Watts's shattered aspect—limp and unclad with the wooden handle of a small plunger shoved so far up his rectum that only the reddish rubber suction cup could be seen—Marshall fought even harder to get loose. Horror-struck, Marshall yelled to the people looking down from the roof, begging them for help, as the men hoisted him onto the stage.

After Never Black came to, he had to gingerly work his eyeball free of the narrow gap. As soft and malleable as an olive, the eye slipped from his fingers several times before he could finally mash, squeeze, and pull it loose. Once free, Never Black had to rest again before he moved on, exhausted from the painstaking process. Fifteen more minutes slid by before he made it to his cell. He had to lie on the catwalk five times to rest.

"Look!" shouted one of Scrap Iron's men, his outstretched arm pointing across the yard.

Scrap Iron, sitting on one of the metal card tables in the corner of four-block, looked in the direction the man indicated. There he saw George Evans descending the ramp leading out of the subhall.

The warden told the lieutenant to zoom in on the roof of the subhall. Five maintenance workers, on their knees reading blueprints and taking measurements, came into view. The warden knew that they were trying to determine the best place to drill a pencil-sized hole from the roof down through the ceiling of the law classroom because he had given the order to do so. The hole would allow the crew to insert a five-millimeter snake camera into the room. His concern about the law student had steadily risen since the two murderers had entered the building and not returned. For assurance, he had contacted the company that built and installed the security doors. The company confirmed that it was impossible for two men to break through that door. Besides that, Tina Brown had the radio and knew to contact him if there was trouble. But still, the warden felt uneasy.

Never Black clutched the bars and pulled himself upright. He staggered the last few steps to his locker, opened it, and dug his state-issued leather belt out from the bottom. Slowly and carefully, after looping the belt around his neck, he stepped up onto the cold porcelain toilet. He reached up to thread the other end of the belt through the overhead vent.

George hurried across the yard, trotting and walking alternately, heading straight for four-block. As he passed through the metal card tables, Travis spotted him, leaped off the stage, and jogged to catch up to him.

"What happened in court, bro?" Travis asked excitedly.

"Nothing yet," George responded distantly, his attention focused on four-block.

"Someone told me that you argued racial disparity in sentencing for everyone?" Travis had trouble keeping pace with George.

"I did."

"Do you think the judge will give a ruling in our favor?"

"Too early to tell."

Just then, George arrived at the entrance of four-block and entered without looking back. Behind him, Travis yelled, "Maybe I can apply a little pressure," as George disappeared through the doors. Travis lifted the cordless phone that the guards on the roof had lowered to him so he could have direct contact with the warden and pushed a button. The warden answered the line immediately.

"Get the governor on the line within sixty seconds, or I'm going to behead the hostage," Travis demanded coldly then clicked off the phone.

"Never Black!" hollered George as he ran across base.

Many men still occupied some of the cells in four-block, not wanting any part of the riot. Most of them stood at their bars, talking and squinting, trying to watch the events on the yard through the tiny window panes. When they heard George's desperate cries for his friends, they all spun to watch as he ran across base.

"Never Black! Nathaniel!" George continued to yell as he raced up steps, around bulkheads, and up more steps. When he reached fourth gallery, he sprinted up the catwalk. "Never Black! Never Black!"

As he stopped in front of Never Black's cell, his heart almost did the same. "My God!" he blurted.

Never Black lay in a puddle of blood. Blood loss had stolen the little strength Never Black had left, and before he could loop the belt through the vent, his body collapsed to the floor. With the belt still looped around his neck and his head propped at an awkward angle against the toilet, he lay motionless. George rushed into the cell. Carefully, he worked his hands underneath his friend's legs and neck. When George lifted him from the floor, Never Black's head rolled toward him, revealing the full extent of his grievous injuries. George's face contorted with the effort of containing his rage and sorrow, veins snaking his forehead. He felt the slow drip of blood on his left arm, and his eyes traveled down Never Black's body in order to find the source. What he saw horrified him more than anything he had ever seen. Where Never Black's genitals were supposed to be, ragged and tattered flesh remained. His penis and scrotum had been cut off.

"No, Lord, no. This cannot be." George's vision blurred as tears welled up along the bottoms of his eyelids then tumbled down his face.

George backed Never Black out of the small cell. Through his grief, he remembered little Nathaniel. He stepped down to the boy's cell and saw it empty. Conflicting emotions ravaged his heart: the straits Nathaniel could be facing now made him want to scour the prison straightaway, yet he couldn't leave Never Black in this condition.

Without further thought, George rushed down the steps and bulkheads then across base.

"Help! Somebody help! Man down!" he shouted as he exited four-block.

The crowds of men outside turned and watched George as he ran with his young friend cradled in his arms. No one responded to George's pleas; in fact, those watching fell silent.

George continued to run, yelling for help. "Man down!" he yelled up to the people on top of five-block. "Man down, damn you!"

Then George felt the stir of the body in his arms.

"Stop, George . . . it hurts too much . . . ." Never Black grimaced as he forced his fractured jaw and battered throat to form words.

"But I've got to get you some help," George said, but it came out more like a request than a statement.

"Bro . . . no need . . . . I . . . won't make it . . . . It's over for me . . . I know it."

George didn't want to admit it to himself, but he knew Never Black was right. Slowly, he sank to his knees. Considering Never Black's condition, as it was, it surprised George that the young man had survived for this long.

Never Black's voice emerged as a whisper. "Hey . . . buddy . . . how'd it go in court?"

"The judge said he'll let me out soon," George lied.

A little life flowed back into Never Black. "That's good," he said in a somewhat stronger voice. "Go home . . . and live free." Never Black tried to smile, but a spat of gurgling coughs racked his worn body, snatching the happiness from his lips. The coughs continued a bit too long, and George thought the end had come. However, after a few more spasms, Never Black settled down again.

"Are . . . you going to . . . to dance . . . ," Never Black asked when he was able, "and sing the . . . Langston Hughes poem . . . when you walk out them doors?"

"You know I am, little buddy," responded George. "I'm going to sing the poem and do a dance on the day I walk free." All men in prison dreamed of the day they'd walk free. They dreamed of the day they could make love to a woman, eat a succulent home-cooked meal, and just enjoy time with their families. George had no woman and no family, and because he had eaten the garbage served in the chow hall for so long, he had lost even the capacity to fantasize about a decent meal. His dream of freedom was not typical. He dreamed of performing an African dance, a dance of his people, while he sang "Dream Variations," his favorite poem, by Langston Hughes, something he would do within hours of his release.

For the first time since George found him, Never Black's eye opened; it resembled a large peeled orange with a section removed. The eye fluttered before focusing on George. The question that followed, George knew, came from Never Black's unending despair at the plight of black people in this country. "Why . . . are there so many . . . liquor stores . . . in the hood? Why so many?"

"The liquor stores will leave black communities when strong, intelligent black people decide that they should leave. It'll take work, but it'll happen."

"Really?" said Never Black as he attempted another unsteady smile.

"I promise."

"That's good."

"Now listen, my friend," George said, not wanting to disturb Never Black's peace but needing to find out something before the young man left this world for good. "Who did this to you?"

Never Black's body shuddered in remembered agony. He said nothing for long seconds, then he muttered, "Scrap Iron and his nasty crew."

George knew, but for his own conscience, he needed confirmation. He felt horrible for making the young man relive his nightmare for even a second, but he pressed on. "What about little Nathaniel? What happened to him?"

"He's in the ceiling."

"He's in the what?"

"The law library. We moved . . . we moved a ceiling tile . . . and I stood on a table . . . ." Never Black's eye closed, and his breathing slowed alarmingly.

"Never Black!" George spouted, fearing the worst.

Never Black stirred a moment later. His eye blinked open. He found his voice again and continued. "In the ceiling . . . . He's on top of the pipes . . . I left him . . . safe . . ."

"So Scrap Iron never found him?"

"No. But he . . . he wanted him bad."

"He tried to get you to tell him where Nathaniel was?"

Never Black's face contorted in pain and rage. "They . . . beat me bad, George. They did horrible things to me." A tear glistened at the corner of Never Black's eye before trickling down to mingle with the dried blood stiffening his hair.

"Even after they beat you, you didn't tell them where Nathaniel was?"

"I couldn't . . . . I'd rather die than let . . . that pervert . . . touch little Nate."

"So you manned up, huh? On the biggest, strongest guy in the prison, you manned up? You went against the whole pack, and they still couldn't break you."

A light flickered in Never Black's eye as he grasped the implication of what George was saying. "I . . . I . . . I guess I did . . . didn't I?" he breathed.

"You sure did, buddy," George said with genuine pride in his voice.

George bent and kissed his friend on a bloody cheek. One corner of Never Black's ravaged mouth twitched: a doomed man trying to fend off death's touch with a smile.

With a last valiant effort that took the rest of his depleted strength, Never Black raised his head mere inches. The exertion drained his face of blood, his skin turned deathly pale. Nevertheless, he fought and won his last battle when his lips arrived to kiss George lightly on the forehead. The touch was soft and exhilarating, like a butterfly's wing brushing against one's skin on a summer day.

George withdrew slowly. He couldn't stop the flow of tears.

"George . . . oh, God, George . . . I don't wanna die." With that, Never Black's head fell back and thumped against George's chest. His muscles went slack, and his last breath escaped in a hiss. As Never Black died, his swollen eye remained open to give George one last look at a once cheerful soul as it escaped its prison forever.

> Prison is a very negative environment. When employees punch out for the day, they must not take any of the prison with them. I am a recovering alcoholic who relapses every two or three days. I cannot maintain a healthy relationship with a man and I have no kids, which is devastating for a woman whose lifelong dream was to have a husband and children. At family reunions I find myself standing with my back to a wall, wide eyed, searching the men in the crowd, trying to determine from whom the violence is coming from next.
>
> —Ruby Daniels, Career MDOC employee,
> Special Activities Director,
> Jackson Prison

Chapter 26

CNN interrupted the current news program and returned to the top story: crisis at a Michigan Prison. "Gang leader Namen Travis has raised the stakes in the hostage crisis at Jackson Inside by commanding the governor of Michigan to enact a law ending racial disparity in sentencing in Michigan within twenty-four hours, threatening to behead the suspected hostage, prison guard Sgt. Gary Moore, if his demand is not met.

"We have the Reverend Jesse Jackson with us to comment on the situation. Reverend Jackson, can you explain this racial disparity in sentencing issue that has been thrust before the world as a result of the prison riot in Michigan?"

The screen split to show Reverend Jackson seated in a small studio on the right, with the anchorwoman in the CNN studio on the left. The bottom right-hand corner of the screen displayed an aerial view of Jackson Inside.

"It's a national tragedy," the reverend began. "Blacks are often given much longer sentences than whites for the same crimes, causing them to serve additional years and sometimes decades more in prison because of their skin color. The problem is as simple as that.

"The black men and women who spend those additional years in prison are only a part of the problem. The larger picture includes parents, children and other family members who are affected because their parents, children, brothers, and sisters are suffering in prison. Entire communities are derailed.

"Racial disparity in sentencing is a racial nightmare for blacks. It is a reverberation of slavery that has slithered down through the generations, only to flare up again and whack black people in a different manner."

Reverend Jackson pontificated for a while longer, and afterward, the anchor returned to the developing story. "There is still no update on the young law student trapped in a secluded part of the prison."

After several miserable silent minutes passed, George scooped his young friend's body off the ground and began his march toward gate 15. He ignored the men around him as he trudged across the five-east walkway and onto Peckerwood Park. Before he made it halfway through the field, a young man swung a small branch and cracked George across the back of his head. "Bitch, it's your fault!" he shouted as he ran by George.

The blow staggered George, and he fell to one knee, still supporting Never Black's remains. Shaking off the dizziness, he stood back up and resumed his trek.

Another young man ran up to George and spit in his face angrily. "You self-righteous muthafucka! You the one killed 'im, you phony son of a bitch." A gob of mucus oozed down the side of George's face, but he didn't bother to wipe it away.

Instead, he said, "Yes, I did," staring straight ahead. "And I'm sorry. I should've done more to protect him before I left. I didn't think . . . . I didn't know." George continued to rebuke himself as he walked up the ramp and disappeared into the subhall.

A guard opened gate 15 as George walked into the subhall. George stopped before the gate and laid the shell of his friend on the floor. Swiftly, several nurses and a doctor rushed to check Never Black's vitals. George stood, hesitated, then whispered, "I'll miss you, my young friend, my best friend. God, how I'll miss you."

"And so will his wife and his daughters," murmured one of the nurses sadly as she knelt beside the body. Another nurse, noticing the blood caked on George's face and arms, handed him a damp cloth.

"He had no family," George responded as he wiped absently at his hands and face.

"Oh, you're mistaken, sir," said the nurse, still absorbed in her work. "I've treated him on numerous occasions in health care, and he was so talkative and proud of his wife and daughters, twins I think. They were a close family. They would come to the prison and visit him every week, sometimes two or three times."

"Frederick Brown's wife and daughters died eight years ago in a car accident. He was the driver. He had been drinking. Frederick was serving time for three counts of vehicular manslaughter."

"A drunk driver?" gasped the nurse as she looked up at George.

"He was a FAS [fetal alcohol syndrome] baby," said George as he turned and began walking away "and he and alcohol didn't get along well at all."

Just inside the subhall exit, George glanced at but didn't pay much attention to a wheelchair parked against the wall. A handicapped man sat slumped in the seat. "Can you push me outside, brother?" the man asked as George passed.

George kept walking.

"Black man!" The disabled man's voice grew forceful, almost commanding. "I'm talking to you."

George stopped and turned around. He studied the man's lowered head. A black knit cap stretched down over his crown to nearly his eyes. George could just make out a large black patch covering his right eye. The man's left arm shook uncontrollably, and drool ran from a corner of his mouth, down onto his chin, and dribbled off the edge like a slow IV drip. George suspected the man had Parkinson's disease.

George hurried back and grabbed the handles of the wheelchair. When he started rolling the man, he said, "I can only push you outside, my man. I've got some serious business to take care of right now."

"Thanks, brother," muttered the crippled man.

George pushed the wheelchair out of the subhall and down the ramp and stopped where the end of the ramp met the road.

Duane "Beast" Harris, Ed Hill, Robert "Double R" Rimmer, Ron Jordan, Terry "T-Young" Young, Larnel "Baby J" Johnson, Lamont "Killer Miller" or "Money Mont" Miller, Marvin "Al Capone" Holden, and a growing number of BTT members and their allies stood in the road, watching George expectantly. Almost every one of the men standing there were in for murder in some degree, and not one of them was accidental.

George released the wheelchair handles and approached the crowd of men. "Good brothers, I'm about to destroy the most dangerous, out-of-control ring of pedophiles, sexual predators, and sweepers I've ever known. It's about to get ugly, and there's no need for any of you to risk your lives or your chances of going home for me. I can handle this alone."

"Come on now, George. You know better than that." Beast stepped from the crowd and walked over to George. "It's going to take more than one man to handle that big freak. And besides, it's been a while since I had the chance to stretch my muscles." Beast smirked as he flexed and rotated his shoulder joints.

"I'll wipe that nasty little bugger!"

Something in the man's voice, the sincerity and strength behind it, made George whirl around. For a second, he almost recognized it, until he saw who had spoken. A couple of the men behind George smiled. He even gave the man in the wheelchair a small smile himself.

"Thanks for the support," George said, "but I don't think you can offer much help right now."

Before George could turn, the debilitated man leaned forward abruptly and stood out of the wheelchair. Drawn and shrunken shoulders spread wide and powerful. A hunched back straightened. While in the wheelchair, the man huddled in on himself so much, George had failed to notice the man's barrel chest and thick limbs. The tremor in his arm had vanished, and no more drool ran from his mouth.

With his head inclined forward, the one-eyed man removed the knitted cap and tossed it aside then ripped the patch from his eye, letting it drop to the pavement. When he raised his head, George flinched as if he'd been slapped.

"I'll wipe that nasty little bugger," Samuel Davis repeated, still using the voice of his disguise, and smiled dangerously.

"Positive ID! Positive ID!" yelled the deputy warden monitoring the LCD monitor on the rear wall of central command. "We've got a positive ID on Samuel Davis!"

Everyone at the front of the room turned to look at the screen. The warden rushed to the back of the room.

On the road just outside of the subhall stood Samuel Davis, talking to George Evans as an expanding crowd of men watched nearby. The view zoomed in on Samuel and enlarged to cover the entire screen. The men and women in the room stared, stricken, as Samuel stripped off his coat and lifted his shirt, revealing a frightening array of lethal blades. A few in the crowd shivered as they saw George Evans reach and pull twelve inches of gleaming steel from Davis's waistline.

"The blood war is about to begin," murmured the warden.

In the Pentagon, the two old men sat in luxurious chairs arranged in front of the Ancient One in his wheel chair. Stacks of old military files littered the table next to them, along with empty doughnut and pizza boxes and half-empty coffee cups. While the men gabbed about the old days, a green light flashed on the conference phone that sat in the middle of the table.

"Sir, we have a confirmed visual of the live wire," said a voice over the speaker. When the military's trained assassins experienced intense, deadly combat in war and were brought back to the states but were unable to readjust to societal standards, the military classified them as "live wires." Samuel Davis was a live wire.

"Current status, please?" asked one of the men.

"Subject is talking with another prisoner in front of the subhall. He has what appears to be an assortment of knives around his waist."

As the voice described the events in the prison, a uniformed man across the room aimed a laser pointer at the security overlay of Jackson Inside the old men had pulled up hours ago. The overlay covered most of one wall. The red dot landed on a spot indicating the front of the subhall where the "live wire" was standing. To the far right of where the men stood, a green light flashed on and off, which indicated where the man whose voice issued from the conference phone was located—on top of four-block. Another blinking red light, this one back near the group of men on the area designating the subhall, represented the location of Tina Brown.

"Current status of the law student?"

"A maintenance crew is drilling a hole through the roof to drop a snake camera into her classroom for a visual."

"Are we set?" asked the Ancient One.

"Affirmative, sir. On your command."

On the Ancient One's command, the US Army sniper sitting next to the military officer on top of four-block, with his high-powered, special issued rifle mounted on a tripod, with Samuel Davis in the crosshairs, would pull the trigger. The military couldn't afford to allow Samuel Davis to draw negative attention to the US military by allowing him to kill civilians. The times were politically incorrect. Such negative national attention from this much-decorated Vietnam veteran headhunter squad leader had the potential to reactivate international coverage and outrage of the search-and-destroy missions conducted by the headhunter squad leader Lt. William Calley at My Lai and My Khe in Vietnam in 1968 where between 350 and 500 unarmed old men, women and children were massacred. This would be a special hotbed after the national media discovered that Samuel had shot a female civilian and killed an FBI agent and a Detroit police officer in the early seventies. Even then, the army had a difficult enough time brushing off the activists and milksops crying foul to Washington. Only now, the stakes were much higher, with the military under so much pressure from growing domestic and international unrest over the wars in Iraq and Afghanistan. Davis would have to be neutralized.

Scrap Iron examined the knives on the table. He wanted only the longest and strongest. The sharpness of the blade didn't matter much, but the point and the length of the handle did. He had ordered his men to lay their best "shanks" in front of him.

He selected one with a ten-inch rubber handle and a nine-inch rusted blade. In prison, men called a knife that size a bone crusher. But it wasn't George's bones Scrap Iron wanted to crush; he wanted to hit the flesh underneath the rib cage and plunge the knife with all his might upward to bust his heart.

Tina Brown grunted softly as she touched her forehead to her knee, stretching to get every muscle in her body as limber as possible, preparing, because only moments from now, she would face the most traumatic event of her life: hand-to-hand combat with two serial killers. If she lost, she would be beaten, gang-raped, tortured, killed. If she won, she would be wounded, scarred, but alive.

George examined the blade in his hand for a moment and then handed it back to Samuel Davis. "No, I'll use these," he said, holding up his heavily scarred fists.

"Are you sure?" Samuel Davis asked doubtfully.

"Positive," George answered. "Where?" he demanded, glaring at Samuel.

Samuel pointed to the tables in the corner between three- and four-blocks. In one motion, George snatched his T-shirt over his head and threw it to the ground. Then the eighteen-year Golden Gloves heavyweight champion of Jackson Inside began jogging to the most important bout of his life: a bare-knuckle fight to the death.

One of Scrap Iron's men shouted, "He's coming!"

Scrap Iron shoved men out of the way, rushing through the crowd to meet George.

Eight Bengal tigers—Samuel Davis, Beast Harris, Double R, T-Young, Baby J, Killer Miller, Al Capone, and Chuckie "Taboo-Bey" McGee—stalked, side by side, toward Scrap Iron and his men. Behind them, the rest of BTT and its allied members brought up the rear.

Off in the distance, Scrap Iron's men surged from the corner tables to meet the oncoming army.

The guards on the roofs watched the scene unfold. Over the radio, the warden spoke to the captain of the guards on the roof of four-block. The captain ordered two guards to raise their rifles.

The captain shouted into the bullhorn. "You men in the crowd, move back! Prisoner George Evans, stop where you are. Prisoner Evans, you are ordered to stop!"

George kept jogging. The gap between Scrap Iron and George had narrowed to about sixty yards.

"Mobile 15 [guard manning gate 15] to 99."

"This is 99, go ahead, fifteen."

"The black prisoner brought to gate 15 by George Evans has been pronounced dead. I repeat, we have a dead prisoner. Copy?"

"Copy that. We have a cold one at 15."

Men vacated the area around the card tables, and Namen Travis had ordered his men to move away from the upcoming fight and assemble on the stage; it was not their beef. Travis drove off in the Meat Wagon, with it lurching twice as the wheels rolled over the smoldering body of Joseph Skipper. Two Gators, driven by his men, sped after him.

The bullhorn on the roof blasted again. "George Evans, I order you to stop. I order all prisoners to stop where they are, or I shall order the guards to fire their weapons." The warning boomed through the bullhorn twice more, with no more effect than the first.

The warden scooted to the edge of his chair. All eyes in central command stared fixated on the LCD monitor.

The captain's voice blared through the audio. "Fire! Fire your weapons!" he shouted to the armed guards.

A volley of bullets pelted the ground, tiny dust plumes erupting between George and Scrap Iron. Everyone on the yard froze.

"BTT, I order you to move back. Proceed through the subhall and report to the south yard. Move now!"

The warden winced and flung himself at the radio. Squeezing the call button, he roared, "Hold your fire, goddammit! Hold your fire!" He hoped that Travis wouldn't decide to take that as a breach of his conditions for the safety of the hostage. He told the captain to threaten the prisoners, not to shoot at them. The blood coursing through his veins sounded like a raging river in his own ears. Nervously, he waited for the phone to ring.

George and the rest of the men behind him hesitated, not knowing what they should do. The guards had already fired warning shots. The next volley would kick up more than just dirt.

After only a moment, the decision was made for them. Samuel Davis came striding forward.

The warden and everyone one else in central command shot from their chairs and scurried closer to the monitors. The lieutenant had split the view between an enlarged shot of Samuel Davis and a smaller one of the man garbed in a military uniform on the roof of four-block. No other images cluttered the screen.

Before George and his men left the area near the subhall to meet Scrap Iron and his men, Beast Harris, on orders of Samuel Davis, had painted two-inch circles on Samuel's face, head, back, and around his lower sides, with watered, non-clay-based pastel paints taken from the prison art class that Samuel had secured in plastic bags in his pockets. Each circle stood for a head that Samuel had taken in the jungles and swamps of Vietnam, a macabre combination design taken from the headhunters of China, India, Indonesia, Japan, the Philippines, Taiwan, and Africa. The circles were bright red outlined in white. The first one located in the middle of his forehead and an inch separated that one from the next, which was directly in back of it. The circles went over the top of his head, down his neck and spine, and at his lower back, the circles spread in both directions, ending almost at his belly button. There were thirty-six circles total. Starting at the hairline on Samuel's forehead and going down the sides of his face were two long white fangs representing those of the African male lion. This was how Sgt. Samuel Davis and his men of the headhunter squads dressed in the blistering insect-infested heat of the death jungles of Vietnam when on their search-and-destroy missions.

"Sgt. Samuel Davis, this is Lieutenant Col. John Hollingsworth," the man in military uniform shouted over a bullhorn,"United States Army, 82nd Airborne Division, Company B, Second Battalion, 508th Parachute Infantry. Stand down, Sergeant Davis. This is not your detail. I am your commanding officer, and I order you to STAND DOWN, Sergeant Davis!"

Samuel Davis was going to kill Scrap Iron; in that, he would not be deterred. They wouldn't fire live rounds into a crowd of prisoners as long as it was just prisoners killing prisoners and no staff got hurt. Plus, he knew that Travis had already warned them that if they fired any live rounds in the prison yard, he'd kill the hostage. The warden must have felt like he had bees up his ass after those warning shots. Samuel wouldn't be surprised if whoever ordered those shots fired got fired themselves. Staff safety had been a priority ever since the September 13, 1971, Attica prison riot, when 1,500 troopers and officers stormed the penitentiary and shot to death thirty-two prisoners and nine guards. The threat of firing live rounds at live targets was a bluff.

Lt. Hollingsworth and the marksman next to him were jokes. Samuel had spotted them hours ago. As long as the potential to compromise civilian lives never arose, Samuel was safe. There were no civilians inside the prison, or so he thought.

Samuel closed to within about fifteen yards of his target; picking up his pace, he pulled out two long blades.

"Can anyone here read lips?" the warden asked the cluster of bodies.

"I can," said a state police detective.

"What's he saying?" the warden asked, pointing at Samuel Davis.

The detective studied the monitor for a few seconds before answering, "He's reciting Psalms twenty-three: four and five. 'Yea, though I walk through the valley of the shadow of death, I will fear no evil; for You are with me; Your rod and Your staff, they comfort me. Thou preparest a table before me in the presence of mine enemies: though anointest my head with oil; my cup runneth over.'"

Following suit, the seven warriors behind Samuel pulled out their weapons: an assortment of monstrous-looking knives, metal pipes, aluminum bats, and wooden stakes. Farther away, Travis yelled to his men, "Strap up!" Dozens of men around Travis pulled out weapons just as ugly as the men behind Samuel.

George watched how confidently Samuel moved toward the oncoming battle. Knowing his friend was no fool, he realized that Samuel knew the officers on the roof weren't going to fire live rounds into a crowd of prisoners. He took off.

Opposite George, Scrap Iron, noticing George's hands were empty and that he had no shirt on to hide any other weapons, threw down his knife and ran to meet his foe.

George caught Samuel off guard when he sped past him.

A long war cry rumbled from deep within George's chest—"Aaaaaaaaaaaaaahhhhhh!"—as he picked up speed. The two men closed to within five yards.

"Aaaaaaaaaaaaaahhhhhh!" Scrap Iron's coarse roar echoed his enemy's, sprinting as fast as he could toward George.

Violence and injury enclose in their net all that do such things, and generally return upon him who began.

—Lucretius (Titus Lucretius Carus)

Chapter 27

The heat was becoming oppressive, and the smoke was beginning to squeeze the oxygen from the small closet. Yet despite her problems, Tina remained focused; her ardent desire to live kept her alert.

In front of the locked door, Tina stood practicing her killing thrust with the broken broom handle. She pictured the soft indentation where throat met collarbone and stabbed at it, alternating different heights for the two men. She was at least five inches taller than Danny Ranes and nearly the same height as the other. Rolling the broom handle in her grip, she rehearsed, again and again, lunging for throats she imagined would soon appear in front of her.

Whichever of the ill-fated men opened the door first would feel the brunt of her anger and frustration, concentrated on a single delicate spot. Both she and the man would likely hit the floor together, he falling rearward and she following. Thereafter, she would roll to the side, snatching the broom handle as she went, and put the wall at her back, in case the second man rushed at her.

Moments earlier, Tina had removed her shoes and socks and swept the floor with her blouse and sweaty palms. She tested the grip of her bare soles on the cold floor; her soles clung to it as if cemented there. That would put more power behind her strike. "Come on, you sons of bitches," she whispered hoarsely. "I'm ready."

Like a head-on collision between two semi trucks, the two combatants slammed into each other at top speed. A sickening thud rent the air. Two heavy bodies recoiled from each other, tumbled to the dirt, and lay still. Seconds ticked by before the onlookers watched the unconscious men begin to stir. On unsteady legs, still dazed, both George and Scrap Iron stood and raised clenched fists.

George crouched low as he moved in close to try and slug it out with his enemy. The moment he threw his first punch, George realized that he had either underestimated his opponent or that the years had slowed him down. George didn't have time to figure out which, though, for Scrap Iron moved like a viper, a three-hundred-pound viper, with anvils for fists. Sidestepping George's left jab, Scrap Iron landed two of his own to the side of George's face, staggering him painfully.

A crowd of over two thousand men encircled the two fighters, all silent except for a few murmurs and groans. The people lining the roofs of the cell blocks stared in morbid astonishment.

Recovering quickly, George rushed his opponent, a strategy that in the past led him to numerous victories in the ring. Scrap Iron smirked as he danced to the side, anticipating George's slowness, and landed a three-punch combination to his chin. The blows straightened George's back. Shaking his head clear, he charged forward again. This time a quick right opened a gash over his right eye. George charged right back in.

Seeing Scrap Iron's left arm tense, readying to launch another jab, George ducked underneath it, coming up to the right with a quick powerful hook to the left side of the pedophile's jaw. Surprised, the big man shuffled back a few steps. George strode forward and tried another hook, but Scrap Iron sidestepped it and landed a solid overhand right to George's nose, followed by a flurry of punches to the body.

The light fled and darkness descended. George tried blocking the blows with his elbows, buying time to allow his vision to clear. Needles stabbing at his face and warm, sticky blood running into his mouth and down his chin told him that his nose was broken. He ignored it. Blinking his eyes into focus, George released two quick hooks and a jab that slowed Scrap Iron a step, enough time to get his bearings. When Scrap Iron came forward for the kill, George planted his feet and stood toe-to-toe with his foe, exchanging blow after devastating blow.

Both men were tiring, but George's swings slowed just a bit faster than his enemy's. Meanwhile, Scrap Iron's assault on George's rib cage continued. Every blow took that much more energy out of George's body.

Scrap Iron saw that George's guard had slackened, which meant it was time to finish him. The big man spread his legs and sent what felt like hammers at George's face. Every single punch landed. As each one landed, George staggered back a step. Scrap Iron was right on him, affording him no retreat. Stumbling into one of the metal card tables was the only thing that saved George from crumpling to the ground when a left hook from Scrap Iron buckled his knees.

George regained his footing but for only an instant. A crushing uppercut lifted him off the ground and sent him skidding in dust. There he lay, out cold and on his back for the first time in his life. His eyes felt glued shut, and his mind journeyed into what Muhammad Ali called his "dream room." He saw orange and green neon lights flashing erratically, bats blowing trumpets, alligators playing trombones, snakes screaming.

Scrap Iron threw his fists in the air, roaring in celebration as he turned to the crowd. "I told y'all he couldn't fuck with me! I'm the champ around this muthafucka!" he bellowed, pounding his chest like an irate gorilla.

In order to earn your stripes at Jackson Inside, one had to murder a dangerous man on the prison yard. A young black man from Detroit known as Point Blank had decided months ago to earn his stripes before the year's end. His reputation would exceed all others before him and would be talked about long after he left. All he had to do was kill Samuel Davis, and the riot presented the perfect opportunity.

The young man stood amid the crowd, ignoring the fight but watching Samuel Davis's every move. Samuel Davis slowly made a circuit around the two fighters. As he neared Point Blank's position, the young man crouched behind the shoulder of another man. Moments later, Point Blank slid from within the crowd, pulled out a rusted blade, and rushed toward the wide back of Samuel Davis. If things went as planned, Davis would die with a blade stuck in his throat.

Samuel Davis heard the swift scrape of footfalls on gravel and knew that the young man had finally decided to make his move. Long ago, he noticed the boy watching him. Owing to his reputation,

Samuel had to remain vigilant at all times. Scared or ambitious, it didn't matter; men would try him from time to time. Quite a while had passed since the last attempt, yet his combat experience kept him wary. His eyes took in everything but gave away nothing.

Estimating the distance by the sound and the number of paces the boy took, Samuel Davis timed his approach perfectly. Just as Point Blank neared close enough to strike, Samuel Davis ducked suddenly and spun to his right. As shock morphed into terror, Point Blank's expression revealed that he knew he had fucked up. But before he could recover, a knife that hadn't been in Samuel Davis's hand a second ago arced toward the young man's face. Point Blank had time enough for a panicked scream before the knife plunged deep into his right eye socket. The scream died instantly; his body crumpled to the ground and convulsed briefly before his soul departed.

Seeing what happened, five of Scrap Iron's men stampeded toward Samuel Davis like a herd of enraged bulls.

"Mobile 18 to 99."

"This is 99. Go ahead, 18."

"There's smoke coming out of two second-floor classrooms in the subhall, copy?"

"Copy that, 18."

"Mobile 14 to 99."

"Go, 14."

"George Evans is up, and they're going at it again."

Jack Johnson, Joe "the Brown Bomber" Louis, "Smokin'" Joe Frazier, and Muhammad Ali stood over George. "Get up, big boy," Louis said. "We're the great ones, and if you want to be like us, you have to get up, son. Finish the fight."

George laughed. He laughed because he *was* one of them, one of the greatest heavyweight boxers of all time, and he knew it.

"If I hadn't come to prison, I would have gotten with you, Smokin' Joe," George said to the stocky brawler standing over him. "And you too, Muhammad Ali. You were fast, but I was fast too. Even if you would've beaten me, I would've made you respect me as a fighter and as a man."

"I believe you would have," Muhammad Ali said as he reached down to help George up.

"Stay down, old man," growled Scrap Iron as he turned to see George pull himself up from the dirt.

When George made it to his feet, a smile teased at the corners of his bloody mouth, and determination burned in his dark eyes. He moved toward Scrap Iron, a hunter stalking his prey. Scrap Iron, his confidence somewhat shaken by look on George's face, danced back a few steps. George followed. Scrap Iron jabbed at George's face. George dodged. The next blow from Scrap Iron flew harmlessly to the side after George slapped it away. Scrap Iron let loose a barrage of punches, with several landing but none able to stop George.

Frustrated, Scrap Iron rushed George, fists flailing. George shuffled to the side the instant Scrap Iron got in range. With the precision of Muhammad Ali, a left jab clipped Scrap Iron on the chin and dazed him. Scrap Iron would never recover.

Combination after combination staggered the big man. His guard fell lower and lower as George pursued him back toward the ring of spectators. Finally, George relented and watched as Scrap Iron teetered on his heels. Taking aim, George reached out with a quick left jab and followed it up with a devastating overhand right. The pedophile's head jerked skyward as he toppled back like a falling redwood. The crowd parted and let Scrap Iron hit the ground with a thud, moaning like a wounded elephant.

"Kill him! Kill him!" the crowd chanted.

Samuel Davis had dashed away from his five pursuers and now crouched underneath one of the metal card tables with his back against the central pole that supported the flat surface above and the four projecting metal seats. Having dragged the dead boy, Point Blank, with him, he used his corpse as a shield. Two attackers lay across the table top, kicking at Samuel's arms and shoulders but unable to do any real damage. Another two kneeled in front trying to stab Samuel that way. The fifth man lay dead between Samuel and his two frontal attackers after Samuel drove a knife under his rib cage when the man got close trying to crawl under the table to get at Davis.

George drew near and stood next to the fallen pedophile's face. Scrap Iron's head lolled slowly left and right on the hard-packed dirt. George raised his right foot as high into the air as he could and, with all the force he could muster, force intensified by memories of Never Black, by thoughts of all the helpless victims tortured by this monster, brought his heel crashing down on Scrap Iron's face.

Groans of revulsion buzzed through the crowd. Several men flinched back from the violence of the impact. Scrap Iron's eyes opened wide the second George's foot pulverized his nose, but he had not the time nor the wits to defend himself.

Another crushing stomp sent the pedophile fleeing back into unconsciousness. Yet that didn't stop George. Stomp after stomp ripped skin and muscle from Scrap Iron's face. George paused for a minute and stared down at the mess he'd made. Abruptly, he leaped into the air, heaving both knees to his chest, and slammed down all his rage, anger, and body weight onto the destroyed man's face. Blood and flesh splattered in all directions. Bone crunched appallingly. George lost his footing and fell on his backside.

Those of Scrap Iron's men engaged with Samuel Davis and the rest of BTT turned and rushed toward George when they realized he was stomping their leader's face. Samuel Davis scrambled from beneath the table the instant his attackers withdrew. The men of BTT rallied around George and formed a protective wall of knives, poles, and bats. As strong and powerful as they were, George's protectors were hard-pressed to keep the frantic men away from him.

The battle raged; men fell. Suddenly, the barrier at George's back collapsed. The circle tightened quickly to close off the gap, but not fast enough. In that brief span, one of the enraged attackers lunged at George desperately and managed to thrust a knife into his lower back. The blade punctured a kidney. Pain exploded throughout his body. Stumbling against a metal card table, George clutched at the knife, trying to stanch the blood gushing down his side.

Everywhere around him, the fight boiled chaotically. A few members of BTT broke away to chase and put down wounded enemies. So far three lay dead, two at the hands of Samuel Davis. Two, sometimes three, severely wounded men were slung across the flatbeds of the Gators before Travis's men drove them to gate 15 for medical treatment. After, of course, first securing fifty-dollar promissory notes from the victims or a cosigner.

A young brute, mid twenties, six feet six inches, 270 pounds, charged recklessly at the circle surrounding George. Three men went sprawling in the dirt, scattered by the sheer ferocity of his onslaught.

In two huge strides, the behemoth reached George, who lay face down on a table, nearly paralyzed from pain. Smelling blood, the young man raised a blade high into the air and drove it, with both hands, down at George's back.

A thunderous sound exploded right next to Tina's ear, it seemed, when the door to the law classroom came crashing down. The blast jolted her insides, sending her heartbeat into a panicked frenzy.

The killers' footsteps clattered toward the door fast, much faster than she wanted. Tina thought she had prepared herself for the moment that was fast approaching. However, now that it was upon her, her bowels liquefied and her knees turned to jelly. She tightened her grip on the broken broom handle, but her arms still trembled. Her thoughts raced in all directions, scenarios of failure, of missing her target by just that much, congested her mind.

Forcing herself to breathe deeply, she firmed her resolve once again. She would not let fear cause her to blunder. Life or death, those were the stakes. The instinct for survival took control, and a primitive calmness overtook her being. Her legs tightened for action, muscles flexed, mind cleared. The hunted became the hunter as she raised her weapon and held it steady. "Won't be no fun, you sicko rapists," said a voice in her mind. "when the rabbit's got the gun."

No sooner than she steadied herself to confront her demons did the door swing open with so much force, one of the metal hinges dislodged from the wooden jamb. The war had begun.

The blur of a man appeared in the doorway. Tina didn't see a face, a body, clothing, or anything else besides the neck, her attention hyper focused on her target.

Danny Ranes didn't even have time to flinch before something sped out of the darkness of the closet, and he felt a sharp agonizing pain at his throat. The next second, something knocked him to the floor, gasping and bleeding.

Tina rolled off the man, still clutching her spear, and prepared to defend against the attack she knew was on its way. As she turned and tried to bring the spear to bear on her attacker, a large meaty fist hit her in the right eye, sending her rebounding off the wall behind her. Still conscious but dizzy as hell, she scrambled to get away. She made it to her knees and was rewarded with a slug to the side. The pain that shot through her body and sizzled her brain told her that a rib had broken.

Knowing that escape was next to impossible, Tina abandoned her attempts at flight and turned with all speed and stabbed wildly in the direction from which the last blow came. She didn't know whether she was the luckiest woman on earth or if her hand had been guided, but when she felt the broom handle encounter slight resistance, she thrust harder and felt it sink into flesh. An exquisite sense of relief and a profound feeling of revulsion at once surged through her. With all her strength and using her body weight as leverage, she shoved her spear into the belly of her attacker.

A strangled"Uuhhhh!"issued from her attacker. Without wasting time to see how effective her strike was, she tore the spear free and galloped for the exit. With tears of pain blurring her vision, she misjudged the width of the exit. Her shoulder collided with the jamb, and the impact and her momentum sent her spinning at an angle to the other side of the hallway. Wincing in pain, she regained her feet immediately. She couldn't afford to baby herself. Those murderers chasing her didn't care two flies about how much her body hurt. Hunched over somewhat, she raced down the smoky hallway.

Through the putrid cloud of smoke that had her gagging with every other breath, she could see the top of the stairs up ahead. She slowed just enough not to overrun the steps and maybe go tumbling headlong. That delay would cost her. A heavy bulk suddenly struck her from behind, sending them both tumbling down the concrete stairs.

Though blessedly short, the tumble down the stairs assaulted almost every inch of her body. At the bottom, Tina ended up face down on the floor. The man who had tumbled with her released her. However, before she could struggle free, a flurry of punches and kicks seemed to come from everywhere. She could do nothing more than curl up like an infant and protect as much of her body as possible.

With her sufficiently beaten, a pair of hands yanked at her wrists, and another pair grabbed at her ankles. Struggling weakly, Tina, on the verge of tears, grappled with despair as the two killers hauled her back up the hallway and into the classroom.

Samuel Davis stepped in the front of George's young would-be killer and seized the knife by the blade as it descended toward George. The young man tried to snatch the knife free and was shocked when it didn't budge. He tried a few more times, thinking maybe he just needed to pull a little harder. The hand held the blade firm, blood streaming down its length, dripping onto a semiconscious George. The big youngster jerked the knife from left to right, baffled.

Finally, not being able to comprehend why Samuel Davis just stood there clenching a blade that had to be cutting his fingers to the bone, the young man glanced at Samuel's face.

The whites of Samuel Davis's eyes showed blood red, as if the vessels running through them had all burst simultaneously. The pupils had dilated so far they looked like black pits, gateways to death.

Samuel Davis knew that he had to do something to get the enemy away from BTT's leader, or they would kill him. He had to do something fast, something big, something that would stop the show, like dropping a shock grenade in a hooch.

With the swiftness of the mamba, Samuel's free hand grabbed the man's other wrist and pulled the struggling man to him. Twisting his victim around, he wrenched the knife free, and now had the blade at the man's throat. Behind the man now and with the knife held tightly at his throat, Samuel scuffled backward and dragged the man with him, ascending the seat and then to the top of the table.

What Samuel did drew attention from Scrap Iron's men and from his own men. When Samuel jammed his head down and his teeth into the jugular vein in the man's neck, many of those men who fought nearby moved away, and some stopped altogether.

The warden shouted over the loudspeaker for Samuel to stop, and as he spoke, he knew his words were lost. Lt. Col. Hollingsworth shouted orders at Samuel, but they too fell short of their goal. All the people on top of the blocks, the prison employees, law enforcement personnel, National Guardsmen, newscasters, and everyone else had their eyes riveted on Samuel. Nearly all the cameras had turned and focused on the former headhunter squad leader.

Like a monster from a science fiction movie, Samuel growled and chewed viciously on the jugular vein as the man writhed and struggled to free himself and moaned and wept in pain. Agonizing and torturous sounds gurgled from his lips.

"No, Samuel, no." moaned George, bent over from the knife in his kidney and taking a step from the table. He watched as blood poured from around Samuel's mouth and down the man's chest.

While Samuel's jaws and teeth continued their hellish work, the knife in his right hand dug deep into the man's left side and slid across the right side, shooting blood everywhere. The most bloodcurdling scream ever heard on the yard shot from the man's mouth.

Again, another deep and vicious cut from the left side to the right. Deeper this time. Much more blood. Then another penetrating cut and another. Finally, Samuel dropped the knife and reached deep into the man's stomach and pulled out guts and held them high. He then lifted his head and let it fall back, the shock of the tangible horror knocking everyone backward, their eyes locked on Samuel's bloody, demonic face as blood erupted from his mouth like volcanic ash and hot magma. The sharp, piercing cry that followed, overpowered everything inside the Killing Grounds.

All was silent. The rioting prisoners had fallen back at least fifteen yards from the table upon which George had fallen and where Samuel now did his hell.

Law enforcement personnel, criminal justice students, and the media stood on top of the blocks horrified, an appalled silence holding descending over the group. Those that could speak did so in a whisper. It was only months later and through the investigation of a government task force investigating the riot that it was revealed that the actions of Samuel Davis had not only sent many of the prisoners into a mild state of shock, but the law enforcement personnel, criminal justice students, and media as well.

Though all the cameras had continued to record the actions of Samuel Davis, the public's viewing had been locked out as being too graphic for any audience. Only the military camera broadcast the gory details to the wide screen watched by the three old men in the Pentagon. They did not speak. Occasionally, the head of the Ancient One would nod.

For thirty more minutes, Samuel continued his slaughter. The men fell back further. The warden and Lt. Col. Hollingsworth were hollering and giving orders over the intercom. But nothing could stop Samuel. Two people on the roof had fainted. Many of the people on the blocks had turned their backs while others vomited. A woman screamed hysterically while a nurse attended another woman who was a newscaster for a major TV station. The newscaster stood on the edge of four-block. Her eyes had been locked on Samuel but now stared past everyone, her gaze vacant and empty, and her body trembled noticeably. Her camera crew were unable to communicate with her.

Acute post-traumatic stress from the Vietnam War shoved the live wire over the edge again. He positioned the huge man's corpse over the top of the table, and with a meat cleaver, commenced hacking at the dead man's neck until his head parted ways with its body.

His right hand clutched hair, as Samuel held the severed head high.

Samuel roared in Vietnamese. "Tôi là Hunter trưởng và tôi để sợ! Các sư tử trắng đã nói!" (I am the Headhunter and I am to be feared! The White Lion has spoken!) Later, George found out that this was the man who had mutilated Never Black's genitals. The government assassin, the 108th Airborne Division's executioner, felt at home amid the chaos. The smell, the taste of blood, the death of his enemies heightened his senses. His reflexes were on edge, his mind locked in survival mode. Among all the murderers at Jackson Inside, Samuel Davis was the alpha killer.

Like Jason Voorhees, Scrap Iron, mangled and mutilated, sat up stiffly. Two of his men, Gerrel Barnes and Kenneth Spears, ran up and helped him to stand. Scrap Iron brushed them off. "Stay here," he commanded in a slurred, nearly incoherent rasp. The risen monster stumbled off through the crowd and across the yard.

In pain but not really feeling it, Scrap Iron plodded up the old road. Anger and rage consumed him. He could feel the tattered flesh dangling from his face. George had stomped his face on the yard, one of the most disgraceful insults a man could receive. And he did it in front of the entire prison population. More than that, though, he had done it in front of cameras that were broadcasting all over the fucking world. As hurt as he was, Scrap Iron's pride would not let that humiliation go unanswered. He would have his revenge immediately and decisively.

It was hard to breathe through his crushed nose and aching windpipe. He sucked in short breaths rapidly, trying to take in enough air. His chest cavity wouldn't expand far enough for deep breaths. Yet he marched on toward his destination.

Just past the gym, he turned right and walked down a short flight of stairs leading to the old maintenance room—the same room where George had been hung by his arms and beaten damn near to death.

Scrap Iron's mind was a confusion of madness. What George had done to him severed any connection to reason he had left. His blood churned hot; he couldn't see anything other than revenge. Scrap Iron was insane.

Even still, he had a plan. From the maintenance room, he would drag the cutting torch along with its fuel tanks back to the corner of four-block. After that he would have his men tie George to the top of one of the metal card tables. With the torch, he intended to burn open George's chest cavity, rip his heart out with cruel fingers, and watch it, still beating, in the palm of his hand as it spilled the last of George's lifeblood to the hard dirt of the Killing Grounds. This he swore to do on the life of his mother.

Still in central command, the warden was screaming into the radio at the maintenance men on top of the subhall. "What the fuck is taking you assholes so long? We have a civilian trapped in there, goddamit! I want that camera dropped into that room right fucking now!"

The warden tried to pace his frustration and anger under control. Minutes ago, he had tried to contact the law student over the radio. A sense of foreboding had tickled the pit of his stomach, the feeling one got when something wasn't quite right. Too much time had passed, and he knew that by now, if out of nothing but pure frustration, the law student would've ignored his warning to not use the radio and contacted him.

When he got no response, he tried dialing the three-digit code to the classroom phone. He got no answer there either. His anxiety intensified, and his stomach began to churn. That's when he radioed maintenance again and politely told them to move their asses. If anything happened to that girl . . . No, nothing would happen to her. When they dropped the camera into the classroom, it would reveal that everything was fine and that he was just paranoid. He prayed.

Abruptly, Tina kicked out, and one of her captors fumbled and let loose her legs. With her feet on the ground, she tugged wildly and wrenched her hands free. Immediately, she dashed away, going once again for the exit. She didn't make it. Behind her Danny Ranes hooked an arm around her neck and tried to muscle her to the ground. He had expended so much energy trying to get into the classroom that his strength was failing. Now he had the thick smoke depriving him of oxygen and a goddamned hole in his neck where the bitch had stabbed him. He was losing blood fast. The girl wasn't weak in any sense of the word, but under normal circumstances, he would've been able to overpower her easily. None of the women he had ever kidnapped, raped, tortured, and killed had fought so fucking hard. Why couldn't she cringe and cower in terror like the rest of them? This bitch had courage, that's what it was. She had heart. The black woman wanted to live. The thought sent a thrill of excitement through his spindly body. "I love you, Tina," he whined hungrily in her ear.

In a panic, Tina let her body drop straight down. When she felt Ranes's grip loosen as he tried to catch her, she wrenched her body sideways. Her head came free. She rebounded off the floor and bolted for the desk. Snatching up a suction-adhering pencil sharpener from the desktop, she turned hurriedly and smashed it into Wolfgang's face, who was dogging her heels.

Wolfgang, also worn out from their assault on the classroom door and struggling through the agony of the wound in his middle, reeled back and grabbed his face. His hands came away bloody. And his front teeth felt jagged, chipped. "Fuck!" he yelled. "You stupid bitch! I'm gonna bite your fucking nipples off!"

Wolfgang tracked Tina to a corner, where she stood with the sharpener poised for another strike. In a mad rush, Wolfgang threw himself at Tina, hoping to take her down with sheer bulk. Tina sidestepped, and he felt the pencil sharpener connect with the back of his head and his forehead connect with the wall. She raised the sharpener and hit it against the top of his head; again and again she struck the rapist. "You're the stupid bitch," she yelled.

Wolfgang's vision doubled for an instant, but he still saw a fist come flying at an unwary Tina. It was his brother; he had hit the silly bitch in her neck and knocked all the fight out of her. Two more blows to the solar plexus crumpled her to the floor.

One foot in front of the other, thought Scrap Iron as he dragged the heavy fuel tanks away from the maintenance room. Off in the distance, he saw five men running toward him. Because only one eye functioned properly, and that one just barely, he couldn't tell who the men were until they got within about fifty feet.

Instantly, Scrap Iron turned around and dragged the tanks as fast as he could back down the stairs. He needed a weapon. Reaching into his pocket, he searched for matches to light the torch but came up empty. Frantically, he scanned the room and spotted a downed pipe a few feet away.

The slaughter of Johnny Hanks by Scrap Iron's men beneath the bleachers had infuriated the gang from Chicago's south side. Scrap Iron's gang was too large for a direct confrontation, so the men had bided their time, waiting for an opening. Now they had the pedophile trapped.

Scrap Iron, still crazed with vengeance but lucid enough to recognize his peril, reached desperately for the pipe and, in that same instant, felt the first knife slip into his flesh. The gang from Chicago's south side went to work.

Tina Brown fought on rather than just giving up. But there was nothing much else she could do. Breath came with effort as her head lolled against the wall. Her eyes were swollen nearly shut, and her body ached badly. She swung at the men feebly, like a newborn fighting off the cold of the outside world. As she pulled each arm up to swing, it felt as if she were swinging against the strongest current in the deepest part of the deepest ocean. She fought blindly, without even the strength to close her fists or her mouth. With no hope of fending off her attackers, she slapped weakly at the air. She refused to surrender in any way to the horrors about to befall her. Even still, she felt the shadowy fingers of despair closing around her heart.

When a few of his friends offered, George refused to be carted off to gate 15 for medical attention. Instead, he had Samuel put duct tape around the wound and knife to stop the bleeding and prevent it from causing more damage. He didn't remove the knife because he knew that it was likely the only thing keeping him from bleeding to death. He wanted to go one more round with Scrap Iron.

The two serial rapists had ripped off Tina's blouse and bra. She now lay on the desktop naked from the waist up with two savages poised over her like jackals over a carcass.

The monster Scrap Iron swung frantically, hollering for his men, but they were at least eighty yards distant and couldn't hear him. Hit after hit he took, falling to his knees, still screaming. The five men continued their grisly work, stabbing, punching, kicking.

Minutes later, the five men tromped back up the steps. As they filed past the back dock of the kitchen, one of them dropped a black garbage bag into one of the dumpsters. Their task completed, not one of them missed a step, melting back into the crowd of men on the yard. The cold dish had been served.

Wolfgang, standing at the edge of the desk, spread Tina's legs and reached to unfasten her belt. A sudden jolt of pain where Tina had speared him tore through his abdomen, bending him over double. He groaned in agony.

With strength born of desperation, Tina turned her head and clamped her teeth into the flesh of Danny Ranes's forearm. Howling in pain, Ranes clenched his free hand and clocked Tina on the side of the head. She bit down harder. He slugged her again and again, but she held fast. Ranes reached desperately for a stapler a foot from Tina's head, grabbed it, and whacked her on the cheek. After the third strike, a gash opened up across the side of her face, and she finally let go.

Beast Harris rushed up to Samuel Davis. "I just got word that the Ranes brothers are in the law classroom raping the teacher Tina Brown."

Without a word, Samuel Davis turned and bolted for the subhall.

"Isn't he headed towards the subhall?" One of the old men in the Pentagon watching the riot via satellite stood up from his plush leather chair. The view had never left Samuel Davis. The three old men had sat watching as Samuel Davis butchered several prisoners on the prison yard. No one had commented on the unconstrained violence the man exhibited.

"That's affirmative, sir," Lt. Hollingsworth on top of four-block answered through the speaker phone.

"We may have a situation," uttered a second old man, still seated at the semicircular table.

"What are your orders, sir?" asked Lt. Hollingsworth.

"If he makes that turn up that ramp to the subhall . . ." The old man paused.

"It's your call, sir," the lieutenant's voice crackled.

"How much further?" the old man asked.

"About fifteen yards and closing very fast . . . ten yards . . . five . . . . Affirmative! He has turned!"

"Take him out!" The old man's voice echoed around the secure room.

"Kill him!" Lt. Col. Hollingsworth shouted to the sniper.

"Dead man," whispered the sniper as he squeezed the trigger of the high-powered rifle, the crosshairs of which were locked on Davis's back the whole time.

Big Will ran up to Travis and told him that someone had overheard a man tell Samuel Davis that the law student Tina Brown was trapped in her classroom in the subhall with the Ranes brothers and that they were raping her. "No the fuck they ain't! Not on my watch!" Travis boomed as he took off for the subhall.

Truth picked up the abandoned bullhorn that Travis dropped when he fled for the subhall. Walking toward three-block, he stood in the middle of the old road. Into the raised bullhorn he yelled toward the CNN cameras, reading a headline from the front page of the *Detroit News:* "'We must stop killing us.'" Truth signed quotations and continued, "This is from Detroit Mayor Kwame Kilpatrick in his State of the City address this year.

"We have come to a point in our community where this is no outside conspiracy doing this to us.

"'This is us killing us. This is mostly African-Americans killing African-Americans . . . and we, as a community, have to stop it now. Nobody's coming to save us.

"'Men of Detroit, the time is now for us to take the openhearted and courageous way. It's time for you to make the first move. It's time for all of us to lead.'"

Truth tossed the newspaper on the ground. "It's not just black men in Detroit killing black men in Detroit. You have to turn the binoculars around and look through them the right way. Blacks are killing blacks anywhere you find large populations of blacks. Look at Los Angeles, Denver, Dallas, Houston, Chicago, Cleveland, Gary, Boston, Philadelphia, Atlanta, Miami, New York. Then look at what we have here." Truth turned and swept his arm in a wide arc, indicating the entire prison yard, stopping momentarily on the smoldering remains of Joseph Skipper, the tire still looped around his neck, the mutilated body of Coral Watts bound to a light pole on stage, the four dead men stretched out near the card tables, three of whom were slain by Samuel Davis, and another left lying across the old road. All of them black, all of them killed by blacks.

"Some say it's a cultural thing born out of centuries of slavery, poverty, no education, miseducation, alcohol, and drugs. Whatever the cause, the result is practically an entire race that views itself as uncivilized heathens, who refer to themselves as niggers, a word conceived and cultivated for the sole purpose of exploiting, denigrating, subjugating, and belittling the black race. It's the reason why many black men refer to their own mothers, sisters, wives, daughters, aunts, and nieces as bitches and hoes, those beautiful black women that Harlem Renaissance author and folklorist Zora Neale Hurston referred to as the 'mules of the world.' There was once a time when African empires would have declared war on any nation that disrespected its black queens. Now, however, black men try to *outdo* any other nation in disrespecting their own.

"This type of backwards thinking creates self-destructive patterns that led to what Malcolm X termed 'self-hate.' And because of it, other races around the world look down on blacks as the shit floor mat of the world, as animals only good for entertainment, a few jokes or some nice music once in a while." Truth paused for a second. Suddenly, he jabbed a finger at the CNN camera and shouted, "Better man up, black man! We are a race in crisis!"

With that, Truth pivoted, handed the bullhorn to one of Travis's men, and walked away.

Expecting Excellence Everyday

—Motto, Michigan Department of Corrections

Chapter 28

Every eye in Central Command followed the Warden as he paced the floor, some wary as if they expected him to explode any second. His head swiveled from one LCD screen to the other, watching intently. Sweat soaked the front and pits of his shirt and dripped from the hand that gripped a mobile radio fiercely. Every few seconds, he called the maintenance crew on top of the subhall.

"How much longer, dammit?" he yelled into the radio again.

"About forty-five seconds, sir," a nervous voice returned over the radio. "We've broken all the way through the ceiling of the classroom, and we're pulling the drill up now. We'll be dropping the camera down any second."

"Get it done, damn you. Damn all of you to hell. The entire world is watching, and we will, I repeat, we will save that civilian!"

As he watched Travis sprinting toward the subhall, Big Will stood confused, trying to figure out what Travis had yelled to him on his way by. Something must have been going down, and he must have yelled for him to bring the gang. That must have been what it was, but even if it wasn't, he'd rather go and be not needed than be needed and not go.

Turning to face the restless throng of men idling near five-block, Big Will yelled, "Everybody to the subhall, now!" He himself leaped off the stage and bolted for the subhall without waiting to see if any of the others were following. The footfalls of over six hundred men, a good chunk of them Travis's men, with the rest made up of men and gangs who had agreed to a temporary alliance, shook the ground as they surged for the subhall.

"It has to happen. I think it has to go down," shouted the warden. "It" meant American Eagle, code for the operation to rescue civilian Tina Brown. When the Warden gave the order, five hundred guards would rush through gate 15, up the subhall steps to the law classroom. That troop would spearhead the strike. Five hundred more guards in a space in front of central command and over two thousand guards in the prison parking lot awaited the Warden's command. Standing next to the fence inside the parking lot was five hundred state troopers. Outside the fence and surrounding the entire complex were five hundred National Guardsmen.

With the muscles of his jaw tightening, wishing he could smother the words he must next say, the warden raised the radio to his mouth and squeezed the call button. "Red alert! Red alert!" The cue to prepare for American Eagle blared over radios all around the institution. Squads inside the prison and in the prison parking lot ranked up in lines two men abreast, ready to storm the prison.

"Look!" a secretary in central command shouted, pointing at an LCD screen on the rear wall. The warden's head snapped around, leaving his body to catch up. The screen had gone blank. Suddenly, a blurred image emerged of dusty pipes, spider webs, and beams passing out of vision as the snake camera was lowered through the roof of the subhall.

Wolfgang had managed to unfasten Tina's pants and was yanking them down her legs when he heard a strange noise coming from the opposite end of the room. The two rapists along with Tina turned their faces toward the sound.

The sound of the ruined door moving underfoot was what attracted their attention. The source of the noise drained the blood from Wolfgang and his brother's faces. Samuel Davis stood dangerously on top of the fallen wooden slab.

On his way to the subhall, Samuel Davis never forgot about the sniper on the roof. He gambled on the fatal shot not being fired until the last possible moment. A risky bet, but it worked. He realized that the men on top of the roof knew the civilian was inside the prison and was there to make sure that if she were injured or killed, he had nothing to do with it. If any harm came to the woman while he was anywhere in the vicinity, the heat would fall on them.

While he raced toward the subhall, the prickly hairs on the back of his neck stiffened. He didn't know how close he could cut it, but he had to time it perfectly. He glanced back hastily to take measure of the snipers position once more. The turn up the ramp into the subhall, he decided, was the key. As soon as he turned up the ramp, there would've been no doubt as to where he was headed. And that would've left the sniper and his commanders no choice. That's when he would have had to die, or so they planned.

Instead of turning the bend, he vaulted mid stride to the side and rolled several feet before promptly slithering the rest of the way into the subhall. A split second after he dived, the first shot hit the wall ahead of him, and by the time the second and third shots came, he was inside the subhall sprinting for the stairs.

"Now, now, you naughty little boys," Samuel said, shaking an index finger on a raised right hand, smiling maliciously as he stepped through the doorway."It doesn't look like Santa will be bringing you bums anything for Christmas."

Before either man could move, someone else burst through the doorway, coughing. Samuel Davis showed no signs of surprise when Namen Travis stepped up on his left. He spied Travis behind him on the run to the subhall.

The warden hesitated just outside the doorway to central command, holding the door open with one hand and the radio to his lips with the other. With his eyes, bloodshot and glassy from anxiety and frustration, riveted on the rear wall's LCD screen, the warden waited. An image of a woman splayed across a surface with two men standing over her blinked into view. He delayed no longer. "American Eagle! American Eagle!" he barked into the radio as he ran, leaping down the three steps to the muster room.

Two men out front swung open the wings to gate 15, allowing hundreds of queued guards to spill through in a rush to the subhall.

When the warden glimpsed the image of Tina lying flat on her back, half-naked, he felt his world crumble to dust, the universe constrict around. Images of himself ruined and shamed before the world flickered within his mind. Yet the picture he saw up ahead as he shoved his way through gate fifteen showed him just how wrong he was. The universe hadn't come for his career or his pride;

it wanted his soul. And he almost gave it up when he saw the tide of men, led by Big Will, flood into the opposite end of the subhall. The two masses collided head-on in the narrow corridor leading to the stairs to the upper-level subhall, where the civilian awaited rescue.

With only a moment's hesitation, Namen Travis chose his target. He clinched his fists and lunged for Wolfgang, the man nearest to violating a black woman. So mad was his rush and blinded was he by rage and indignation, Travis didn't see Danny Ranes extract a zip gun, the most deadly weapon in the system, from the small of his back. A loud pop, like the sound of a firecracker, issued from Ranes's hand. Travis stumbled forward a few more steps and stopped, a confused look replacing the fury that twisted his face seconds ago. He looked down at his chest and saw a small hole in his shirt and a spot of blood blossoming wider as he watched. A spray of crimson spurted from his lips as he fell to the floor and toppled over, dead.

Samuel Davis marched forward, stepping over Travis's lifeless body.

Wolfgang, fueled by anger and frustration, pulled out a knife and lunged at Samuel Davis. Davis, extracting a blade of his own from his waist, raised it, preparing to meet his enemy head-on. What happened next, he didn't expect from the likes of Wolfgang.

Just before Wolfgang made it within striking distance, he dived recklessly to the floor. Thinking that the man had slipped and fallen, Samuel growled in shock when he felt the knife part the thin leather tongue of his right boot and slice into his foot. The pain blinded him for only a fraction of a second, but it was long enough for Wolfgang to roll to his feet and drive his knife into the back of Samuel's shoulder.

Another wave of pain rushed through Davis's body, laced with disbelief at how fast Wolfgang moved. It seemed impossible. Samuel Davis knew he had no time to waste and expelled his surprise. Glancing over his shoulder, he saw that Wolfgang gripped the shank with both hands, trying to force the entire length of the blade into his back.

In one motion, Samuel Davis reached over his shoulder, and the moment his hands clutched the back of Wolfgang's head, he dropped to one knee and, with a mighty heave, wrenched his arms downward, slung the man over his shoulder. Before Wolfgang could settle from the impact, Davis had a knee in his throat. Without hesitation, the United States-bred assassin gripped Wolfgang's head with freakishly strong hands and twisted it violently. A muffled disgusting crunch signaled the end of Wolfgang's life.

One task complete, Samuel lifted his eyes to an empty desk; Danny and Tina were gone.

Once the guards encountered the prisoners, they had to initiate plan B of American Eagle—stopping any advancement of prisoners onto the second floor of the subhall.

The subhall corridor was constructed to accommodate comfortably three men abreast. As the hundreds of prisoners and guards battled in the narrow confines, the corridor seemed to have shrunk to the width of a doorway. The fight boiled ferociously, spilling through the hallways and up the stairs. Bloody faces sprouted everywhere, broken noses, busted lips, lacerations.

The smoke in the hallways was overwhelming. Neither the warden nor any of his staff had anticipated the dense smoke in the hallway, and they were unprepared. The prisoners, however, most of whom had some type of makeshift mask on their faces, were less affected.

One bright spot the warden had noticed was that the prisoners weren't using any weapons. He couldn't guess whether it was because they didn't have any, a theory he doubted himself, or because the prisoners wanted to feel the anger and frustration they were giving to his officers. Whatever the reason, he felt a small sense of relief for at least that much fortune, especially when he had to fight his way through to the second floor. Even still, he could feel his face swelling in certain places, and he could taste blood, things he hadn't felt since his youth.

To stanch the suffocating smoke the warden snatched a torn pillow case off the face of a prisoner that lay unconscious then wrapped and tied it around the lower half of his face and proceeded up the stairs.

Springing from the floor, Samuel Davis turned and saw Ranes yanking a struggling Tina through the doorway. Ranes froze when he saw Samuel's face, the painted circles, the white fangs, the bloody mouth. And those eyes. Death eyes.

"Hey, tough guy," Samuel began, "I'll make you a deal. Let her go and I'll let you live, your life for hers.

"But if you choose not to, then I'll come take her from you. And if I have to do that, I'm going to punish you for it. First I'll beat your brains loose, drag you back over to this desk, and break your back. That won't kill you, though, just paralyze you. After that I'll flip you on your back, cut your stomach open, reach inside, and pull your fucking heart out. I'll ram your heart up your anus.

"Then again, maybe I won't. Maybe you'll beat me and get to keep the girl. Do you think you can beat me, Danny Ranes? Do you?" Ranes's eye flicked from left to right; his tongue slid over ashen lips as he slowly edged out the door. He was on the edge of fleeing, Samuel saw, so he turned his attention to the girl.

"Now, Ms. Brown," he said, "listen carefully. I'm going to count to three, and when I hit three, he is going to let you go. I want you to run back into the classroom and get behind the desk. I promise no one else will touch you."

Tina was beyond panic, dread, or terror. It was as if her world had been flipped on its head. She saw and understood what was happening, but it was happening to someone else, she felt. Before Samuel Davis even made it to three, Danny Ranes released her, and automatically, her body responded; she ran, ran away from the man who would ravage her soul.

Tina knew that she could trust Samuel. Despite the gruesome aspect that appeared before her, her instinct tugged her towards the grim-faced, bloody horror of a man.

Wary as a tiger, Samuel Davis crouched low and stalked toward Danny Ranes, prepared to counter whatever other surprises these bastards had for him. After three steps, he saw Ranes's face relax, all blood rushing away from the surface, leaving his face a pallid ghostly white. The man swayed for a moment and fell hard on his face, dead from blood loss.

A masked man stepped silently into the classroom and stopped just inside the doorway. On the floor lay several still bodies. From the way they lay motionless, the man could tell they were dead. Life could never appear so . . . dead. He recognized them all too. Stepping over Danny Ranes, who had blood stains darkening most of his clothes from neck to ankle, he saw Namen Travis not six feet ahead of him, sprawled, pale disbelief frozen on his face. Beyond him, the man saw Wolfgang's body and winced; Wolfgang's neck was twisted at an impossible, revolting angle.

The dead men didn't concern him at the moment. He looked toward the desk and saw two more bodies unmistakably living, and a queer feeling flowed through him—elation spiked with sharp sickles of apprehension.

Samuel Davis, leaning against the desk, weary, haggard, his own blood and the blood of the men he fought and slew on this day and probably the blood of the three dead men here covering him, cut a gruesome aspect. Shirtless, Davis had blood-soaked magazines lining his waist with a plethora of knives—very real and very sharp—encircling the periodicals. And then all those painted circles and white fangs smeared with sweat and blood now. It was all too much. The sight turned the man's blood cold for a second, causing him to shiver involuntarily.

In Davis's left hand, he clutched a long, thin filleting knife, and in the right he gripped a heavy meat cleaver that he had used to behead the man on the yard. A makeshift garrote, fashioned out of piano wire strung through the handles of a jump rope, dangled from his left hip. On his right side, Davis carried what the man could only guess was supposed to be a knobkerrie, the same weapon used hundreds of years ago to crack skulls by African Zulu warriors. This one was fashioned with a billiard ball secured by leather strips to the end of a broken hammer handle.

Standing next to Samuel Davis was the person he came in search of. His heart felt as if it wanted to beat its way up out of his throat. The law student was barefoot and wearing her torn and bloody blouse. He winced again when he looked upon her face. A long gash traveled the length of her jaw, beginning from her left ear and ending just below the corner of her mouth. Both of her eyes were swollen nearly shut; he could see bruises on her face and neck and knew that her bloody blouse hid more. He wondered how far her assailants had gotten before Davis showed up.

With her right hand, Tina pressed her bra to the wound in Davis's shoulder and clutched a broken broom handle in her left. Suddenly, a fit of coughing seized the man.

Davis pushed off the desk and spread his legs, knife gripped and cleaver raised, ready to kill. Tina hastily dropped her bra in order to wield her weapon with both hands. She held the spear high, just above her shoulders, the pointed edge aimed at the soft indenture in the man's neck. Her muscles tightened, and her feet braced. Adrenalin shot through her veins like pure nitrogen.

"Come on, motherfucker!" she screamed maniacally.

"Bullshit," said the intruder, removing the torn pillow case from around his face and taking a step back. "I'm the warden."

The prisoners fought hard, but from the start, most knew they would eventually lose. While the guards were replaced by fresh combatants whenever they tired, the prisoners had no such reinforcements. When a prisoner went down, they were simply short one more man. Hundreds of guards waited their turn to get at the unruly weakening prisoners. There seemed no end to the guards, yet the prisoners fought on.

"Ninety-nine to fifty." The warden stood in the doorway of the classroom and peered down the hall. At the top of the steps stood several wardens from different prisons throughout the state, along with his deputy warden and his assistant deputies. After forty-five minutes of intense fighting, it was finally over. All prisoners in the subhall had been secured with handcuffs and leg irons, chained to one another and laid facedown with an officer kneeling on their backs, pepper spray in hand. Things were safe and clear now for the medical staff to enter the prison.

"I'm in the law classroom," ordered the warden. "Bring immediate medical attention for one female civilian and one prisoner. ERT, main speakers, five times. I repeat, ERT, main speakers, five times. Move!"

The ERTs, or the emergency response teams, comprised of volunteer guards from all prisons in the surrounding county. This particular team, however, included the specially trained volunteers from among facilities throughout the entire state, martial arts experts or sharpshooters all.

Two hundred and fifty ERT members, wearing riot helmets with plastic face guards, some holding plastic shields that protected over half their bodies, marched in two columns down the hall and up the stairs. Attached to their belts, pepper spray and tear gas canisters dangled at the ready. Twelve-gauge shotguns and .45 caliber and nine-millimeter semiautomatic pistols peeked from behind shields and nestled in holsters. A few men without shields carried a pistol in each hand.

All prisoners knew that, by policy, the ERT carried firearms, safeties released. No warning shots; the ERT shot to kill.

In the middle of the ERT, medical personnel, toting supplies and equipment, shuffled to keep up. When the procession arrived at the classroom, medical staff continued in, but the ERT reversed directions. They marched back down the stairs, maneuvered through the prone prisoners and down the subhall ramp, leading to the prison yard. One file went left, the other right, and queued up shoulder to shoulder on the old road behind the fence, partially surrounding Peckerwood Park. All faces and cameras turned to stare at the ERT as they prepared for their next mission: storm the prison and rescue Sgt. Gary Moore, if he still lived.

A week after the riot and in a room hidden from the general custom, the full "good ol' boys" network gathered at a small redneck bar in Jackson, Michigan, to observe their annual celebration, honoring their statewide member achievements.

"Prison guard Mike Richardson, come on down!" shouted a half-drunk portly eighteen-year veteran of the MDOC from the front of the room.

A tall man with fiendish blue eyes stood up to the cheers of the other seven members present. He swaggered to the front of the room and turned to address his cohorts.

"Six months ago," he started out, "during the riot at Jackson Inside, I wrote 1,010 major misconducts for assault and fighting on 1,010 monkeys and wetbacks. The warden deducted two years' worth of good time and disciplinary credits for each misconduct, which totaled 2,020 years. Multiply that by the 31,000, it costs to house each man per year, on that day alone, I made our race wealthy to the point where we'll be able to build at least a hundred new homes and send hundreds of our children to the best schools in the state. Furthermore—"

"That's enough, Mike," laughed the emcee, slapping Richardson on the back. "We've had enough details." He handed Richardson a four-inch statuette carved out of soap, a painted monkey with a gold prison-guard cap on its head.

"The golden boy award," the pudgy man bellowed. Clapping and whistling and cheering erupted from the small crowd of guards and their spouses and companions. After Richardson returned to his seat, the emcee held up a hand for silence.

When the room quieted, he said, "Guard Jane Austin, come on down!"

A cute petite little thing stood up from the crowd. Fully grown but looking no more than fifteen years old, weighing just under a hundred pounds, and standing no higher than four-eleven, Jane Austin blushed as she stepped shyly to the front of the room. "While sitting at the table on top of three-block," a timid yet pleasantly sweet voice barely made it past the front row, "during the riot, with my coworker, Mike Richardson, I wrote eight hundred major misconducts for assault, fighting, rape, and arson on eight hundred people. For that, the warden deducted sixteen hundred years worth of good time and disciplinary credits. Times that by thirty-one thousand, and I guess that's why you have me standing here." She paused briefly then added, "And I have twenty-nine years to go before I retire." Another round of applause.

The emcee handed Austin an exact replica of the statue handed to Richardson, except this one had the golden cap turned backward. "Rookie of the year," the man blurted, followed by more clapping and shouts of approval.

"Don't forget, now," the emcee continued, "we consider only bogus misconducts for the award. None of the valid tickets were tallied. And of equal importance, remember that the parole board will issue a minimum of two-year continuations for each misconduct. With 1,810 misconducts written, that's an extra 3,620 years in good time and disciplinary credits. That gives us a grand total of 7,240 years counting parole board continuations. These fine officers here did a hell of a job, don't you think?"

"Yes, sir," someone shouted.

"Damn right," another voice exclaimed.

As silence descended on the crowd, Austin remained standing at the front of the room. Slowly, she raised downcast eyes and gazed into the crowd. For long seconds, she stood staring into the eyes of her fellows. Then her right hand moved toward the flowing blond hair sprouting from her head. Entangling her fingers in pale locks, she gripped a handful of hair and pulled. A blond wig came off to reveal a clean-shaven crown. She dropped the wig on a table, and the crowd exploded with shouting and fist pumping.

The women in the crowd followed suit and removed wigs—brown, auburn, black, golden—faces beatific, delighting as if the fake hair had weighed a ton.

Suddenly, Austin's small body went rigid as if struck by lightning, her small breasts straining against her shirt as she thrust out her chest, shoulders pulled back. A slender leg shot out to the side then reversed directions and slammed against its opposite; her right arm shot stiffly into the air, hand straight as an arrow. When she spoke this time, everyone heard her.

"Hail Hitler!"

"Hail Hitler!" The small crowd echoed her words and stood at attention, bodies rigid, hands stiffly extended forward.

Remember to play after every storm.

—Mattie Stepanek (thirteen-year-old, best-selling author of books of poems about love, hope, and peace, who, along with three older siblings, died of a rare form of muscular dystrophy)

Chapter 29

The prison was in the seventh month of a twelve-month lock down. George had lost his blood-spill detail and received two years in the hole for fighting and inciting a riot. With the hole filled to capacity, he had to serve his time in his cell.

Samuel Davis was prosecuted for ten counts of second-degree murder—the young man who attacked him from behind, the two men beneath the card table, he who severed Never Black's genitals, and Wolfgang Ranes. After the riot, during the clean-up phase, guards discovered two bodies, the bodies of the men Scrap Iron had sent after him at the onset of the riot, in the butcher's shop, hanging from meat hooks with their heads hanging grotesquely from broken necks. In the mop closets of three- and four-blocks, two of the three pedophiles who'd tricked George into the maintenance room years prior and beat him near to death with a spiked leather whip, pipes, and fists were found with their throats opened wide. The third man, the one who was the originator of the plan to whip George, was found in a closet, tortured to death, with his belly cut open, heart pulled out and stuffed up his anus.

At a closed evidentiary hearing in a Jackson County courtroom, three men from the Pentagon testified for two and a half days on behalf of Samuel Davis. The judge dismissed all charges; the prosecutor did not appeal. Still, for the sake of propriety, the warden sentenced Samuel Davis to the hole for one year.

George, with a leg propped on the rail of his bed, pushed back and balanced on the two back legs of his chair as he read his favorite passage from one of his favorite novels, *Crime and Punishment* by Fyodor Dostoyevski. The policeman was interviewing an ex-law student, the prime suspect in a double murder/robbery. He asked the ex-student, who had no idea he was a suspect, what he thought of the unknown murderer's conscience. The suspect replied, "If he has a conscience, he will suffer for his mistake. That will be his punishment—as well as the prison."

George had a conscience and had suffered for more than forty-four years for killing that man in his mother's bedroom in 1964. In fact, no other thought had occupied so much of his time. Though he had only been sixteen at the time, had just witnessed his mother dead from an overdose on drugs supplied by George's victim, and saw that same man trying to force heroin into the veins of his eight-year-old sister before selling her for sex to the pedophile in their living room, not even all that justified or helped to mitigate his crime. He did not have to kill the man. Murder was a sin, a violation of one of the Ten Commandments. Yet George believed his sins forgiven. Decades ago, he'd accepted the light of Christ into his heart, ensuring him everlasting life.

Even when George lost himself in the fury of battle against Scrap Iron, he heard the men chanting, "Kill him! Kill him!" Yet no matter how hurt he was from the death of his best friend, he never intended to kill the man. He wanted only—

Two bodies appearing before his cell interrupted his musings. George looked up and saw Sandra Girard, director of Prisoner Legal Services, standing next to a stern-faced guard as he unlocked his cell door then turned and strode back up the catwalk. George's heart hammered against his sternum. No cell doors had been opened since the end of the riot months ago; the guards and temporary workers passed out meals. He watched Sandra apprehensively. For her to appear suddenly at his door at a time like this, without notice, could only herald something urgent. In which direction, good or ill, George couldn't guess.

She stood at the door for a moment. George saw a tear well up in a corner of her eye and trickle haltingly down the slightly loose skin of her face. He lowered the front legs of the chair to the floor and stood slowly. Sandra was a close friend of his, and anything that could bring her to tears in front of him was cause for concern.

The slender woman stepped nervously into the cell. She cleared her throat before reading from the top of a stack of papers gripped tightly in her hand. "Flash memo," her voice thick with emotion, "from the warden." She cleared her throat again.

"Attached to this memo is a forty-one page opinion and a one-page order from the Honorable James Linbush."

George froze, unable to even moisten his suddenly dry mouth. Standing there, he waited for Sandra to continue, not even daring to hope that the words that followed would bring anything other than the sting of disappointment he had so often felt over the years. Memories of the argument he presented to the court that seemed so long ago flooded his mind, all the places he wished he'd had time to develop further, the things he later decided he could've done without. He tried to steel himself against the bitterness he knew would try to swallow him if he heard the words he expected. *Man up,* he chided himself silently. Face grim, he tried to steady his heart. Just another order, one no more different than the others. That last thought was a lie, he knew, but a necessary one. He could not afford to leave himself vulnerable to a letdown that threatened to shred the rest of his hope.

"For reasons that will be apparent, I do not have time to read the opinion," Sandra continued. "The order states, 'In the case of the *People of the State of Michigan v. George Evans,* the defendant was found guilty, by jury, of murder in the second degree in 1964 and subsequently sentenced to life in prison. In appealing his sentence in 2008, defendant Evans asserted that his sentence was constitutionally defective under the Equal Protection Clause, as it was racially disparate with sentences given to white prisoners for the same or similar crimes.

"'After having reviewed the briefs of both parties and sitting through oral arguments, this court finds that defendant's argument has merit.'"

George's mouth fell open. Sandra lifted her eyes from the paper and stared into George's. A hint of a smile curled the corner of her mouth as she looked down and read the rest of the order.

"'It is hereby ordered that one, defendant Evans's life sentence is vacated; two, defendant is resentenced, in absentia, to a term of twenty years to forty-four years in prison, with credit for time served; and three, Defendant Evans is hereby discharged from any sentence owed to the state of Michigan.'"

Before she even finished the order, George had stumbled back, knocking the chair out of his path to slam against the rear wall of his cell. He stood there trembling, eyes vacant, one hand clutching the sink for support. Sandy stepped into the cell and let the stack of papers slip from her hands to the floor. Rushing the last few steps, she flung arms around George and pulled him from the wall.

When the tears came, they came in a rush. Sandy's embrace jerked him from his stupor, and a flood of emotion washed over him, tears coursing down his face like the rushing current of a mighty river, soaking the hair and blouse of his friend. Both of their bodies shuddered against the other, their sobs growing more insistent, feeding off each other.

After a while, Sandy released George. Him having regained a hold of himself, she peered happily into his eyes. Suddenly, her hand darted out and clasped his, offering the strongest and most courageous man she had ever known her strongest, firmest handshake."Well-done, Mr. Evans."

"It took a few days, but I guess I did get it done,"George joked, at which point they both laughed. Sandy knew that George had been fighting for his freedom from the first day he had entered prison. "How long before I can go?"

"According to the order, you had sixty minutes from the transmission of the fax to vacate the premises.The three verifications the order the warden required took a few minutes, so now you have about ten minutes to pack your things and leave."

George was packing before she could get the last word out, pulling out his footlocker from underneath his bed, dumping the contents of his wall locker unto his bed, sorting through it all, and selecting only things of practical importance and sentimental value.

Meanwhile, Sandy was back outside the cell door, asking whether he wanted a bus ticket and, if so, to where, whether he had money, and where he was going to live. Her inquiry turned out to be a labor in futility, for the big man was a flurry of movement, his words tumbling forth so fast she could scarcely catch a single word.

The packing didn't take long. He never owned a tape player, television, or radio. One pair of free world pants, a shirt, several T-shirts, and three pairs of athletic shoes was the only clothing he owned. He donned one of his Love Black T-shirts before packing the rest. From the outside of the wall locker, George removed photographs of his heroes: Muhammad Ali; Nelson Mandela; Marva Collins, the teacher's teacher; and Dr. Jarvick, the inventor of the plastic heart. George regarded a man's heroes as windows to his character, aspirations, spirit, and heart.

He placed everything in a black plastic garbage bag. After he finished packing, George stood in the center of the cell and looked one last time over the cell he had spent the majority of his life in. This day seemed a fantasy just yesterday. As he looked over the cracks in the walls, the paint drips on the floor, a too-small mirror, and the porcelain toilet and sink, he realized how long and how deep he had buried his hatred for this place. Over the years, he couldn't risk letting his loathing for this cell, this prison, dominate him; otherwise, he would've risked allowing despair to defeat him.

Now, however, he felt no fondness for this ten-by-six-by-eight-foot *Skinner box*. Standing there, he realized he would not think back upon the memories of the last four and a half decades with fondness, regret maybe, but never fondness.

In the corner, he spied the manual typewriter on which he had won his freedom. That machine, and others before it, had carried him through the years, the medium that translated his hopes and desires into tangible form. Next to it sat several five-hundred-sheet reams of paper stacked atop each other, and next to that, pushed up against the wall, were five stacks of personal law books that nearly reached the ceiling. Though the tools had served him well, he would yet leave them for the next man. Maybe they will bring him the same blessings as they did George.

The black garbage bag, he hefted and turned to leave the cell. Before George could leave, Sandy darted past him and pulled an old sheet of paper, yellowed from age, from the wall. "I'll keep this," she said, smiling. The paper read as such:

The Autobiography of George Evans

> I am the old mule making its way up the mountain. The years of heavy loads has bent my aching back. Still, I inch my way up the jagged, narrow, and dangerous paths.

My motto:
I shall keep on keeping on!

A horrible thought struck George just before he took the first step from his cell, and he looked at Sandy. "What about little Nathaniel?"

With a knowing smile, she said, "I knew you'd ask. When I received word of the order and while the warden was awaiting verification, I contacted the director and called in a few favors." She backed away from the door to let him through and, with an outstretched hand, guided his eyes up the catwalk. "Look," she said.

From the direction of the bulkhead, a familiar solid figure came strolling up the catwalk, with a green duffel bag slung over a shoulder and a bedroll under the other. George's apprehension washed away in a tide of relief. Nathaniel's new protector, he who would occupy the cell George was presently vacating, was Samuel Davis.

"I'll see you in the control center," Sandy said, squeezing George's forearm as she turned and glided past Samuel Davis.

As Davis approached, George turned to little Nathaniel, who was standing with an arm reaching for George through the bars of his cell. He had the biggest, most innocent smile on his face, showing small snowy white teeth.

"George, I love you, man," Nathaniel squeaked in a voice not yet deepened by puberty. "Would you tell my mamma I love her for me?"

"No problem, little man," George replied. "But you have to promise me something first."

"What?"

"You have to promise to participate in all of the educational programs the system has to offer, to put in your best effort, to live your life the right way, to become a strong, independent man, a man who cares about himself and a man who cares about his people. I know you're young right now and that unfair circumstances put you here, but you are here, in prison. The system is forcing you to grow up fast, and that's exactly what you have to do if you want to make it through this prison and this beautiful thing called life. Can you understand that?"

"Yeah, George, I got you, man," Nathaniel said, still grinning.

George stuck his hand through the bars and palmed the young boy's head and shook it playfully. "You take care of yourself and listen to the old geezer," George said, gesturing toward Samuel Davis, who had been standing listening for a minute or so.

George dodged a blow to the short ribs from the old geezer. "Watch it now," Samuel said. "You're not too fresh yourself."

Smiling, George held out a hand to the man he had named one of his closest friends.

"Go," ordered Samuel gravely as he took George's hand. George knew that the man wanted no awkwardness. Love and respect had always remained unsaid but understood between the two men.

With one last clench, George released Samuel's hand and started up the catwalk. That's when he became aware that the clamor reverberating throughout the cell block was actually cheers and howling for him. Up and down the catwalk, fists stuck through the bars pumped and reached out to touch him as he passed. Cell doors shook so hard, George thought many would surely break loose any second. Opposite him, all four galleries showed men at their doors raging their encouragement and approval; he even spotted some men whom he knew didn't like him celebrating his good fortune.

As he walked down the gallery, he didn't shy away from the shoulder clenches and the pats on the back the men gave him. Some men may have sincerely wished him well, others may have imagined themselves receiving good luck from one who seemed the luckiest man at Jackson Inside, and yet others may have simply wanted to say they touched the man who had snatched his own life from the mouth of hell. Whatever the case, he did not want to rob these men of their victory, for in truth, it belonged to them also. Black men had received in the past and continued to receive disproportionate sentences, and maybe now things would change. He was the first of many to receive a small taste of justice.

George walked across base and pushed open one of the heavy metal doors and stepped onto the yard. Cutting across the old road and through the yard, he walked past the stage, still scorched where Joseph Skipper burned to an agonizing death. Soon, he came upon the patch of ground where he stomped Scrap Iron's face in. He lingered long enough to spit in the dirt then kept moving.

George knew that news spread through Jackson Inside like voltage through wires, but how word had spread to the other blocks during a lockdown was beyond him. It didn't matter though; he was beyond caring anyway. The nearly five thousand voices ringing from all the blocks on the north and south yard melded to create a cacophony of wild, thunderous approval. Toward the Big Top, George spotted the temporary food-service workers, hired to replace the locked-down prisoner workers. They stood outside of the building to watch the famous George Evans stride across the yard. On the roofs, even the guards manning the gun towers abandoned their posts to lean out over the railing and watch.

Impossible though it seemed, as George crossed the sidewalk leading to five-east, the noise level grew even louder. Men of all races had been swept up by the excitement and added their bellows and hoots to the clamor. Even still, George could pick out a few individual voices from the tumult, and he knew that the men from Detroit's east side ghetto were the loudest. Born and raised in the Brewster Projects, George embodied their home, and in him they saw a small piece of themselves leaving. George could hear wall lockers slamming, cell doors rumbling. The prison had gone mad again, but this time from elation and hope and not from despair and misery.

Glancing to his left, he stared at the gym where he had won eighteen heavyweight titles, the first at age sixteen. "That's right," he said, nodding once at the gym. Twenty more yards brought him to the ramp of the subhall, and the last image the men of Jackson Inside ever saw of George Evans was of him raising a clenched fist and giving a quick jerk of triumph as he turned left and disappeared into the subhall. The men said that George never looked back.

It took more than six months for Judge Linbush to finish his opinion for *People v. Evans,* dealing with racial disparity in sentencing. It was a very troubling opinion. Defendant Evans presented some extremely unsettling facts. On top of that, about a week after the hearing, the judge received a letter from Evans questioning some of his own sentencing practices Evans had witnessed the day of the hearing. He articulated clearly and pointedly his issues without falling into logical fallacies.

The judge was willing to admit that many of Evans's observations were correct; Linbush intentionally sentenced minorities, namely Hispanics and Blacks, to longer periods of incarceration. However, he had his own set of logical reasons for his practices. Unlike other judges, Linbush cared for the welfare of the ethnic communities of minorities. Because minorities engaged in more criminal activity than whites, he handed down harsher penalties, hoping to wake them up. They were not only destroying their own lives, their criminal mentalities were also shattering their families and wreaking havoc on their communities.

And it seemed as if most minorities didn't mind being incarcerated. In fact, it seemed as if most considered prison as either a rite of passage or a natural consequence in the course of their lives, especially among young black males. If that line of thinking continued, Linbush knew that their lives and the lives of future generations would continually decline. It had to stop, and he was in a position to force some type of change. Harsh penalties for one, in his mind, should serve as a warning beacon for others that would elect to follow.

Yet after the completion of the hearing, Linbush was forced to reconsider his position. Maybe his approach did do more harm than good. Up until the end of the Evans hearing, the judge had never chosen to examine the effect his practices had on the current state of minority communities. When he decided to undertake such an objective examination, he found that despite the harsher penalties, minorities continued to flow in and out of the penal system in droves. That's when he decided upon a change. Nevertheless, he refused to castigate himself too severely, for many a great man in history had chosen to do the wrong thing for the right reason. He had a judgment call to make on the way he would confront a social crisis. He did what he felt at the time would have the most substantial effect. As it turned out, he was wrong.

In any event, he still had time to alter his approach and set right what lay within his power.

Another unsettling issue, which at first irritated Linbush, that Evans mentioned in his missive dealt with his comments and demeanor surrounding the ethnic-intimidation sentencing. The implication that he was a racist put his back up initially. He continued through the letter anyway, and after Evans analyzed his reasoning, the judge sat pensive and shaken. Without hesitation, would he admit the devotion and affinity he felt for his own race? A man who wouldn't was either no man at all or a confused fence sitter and couldn't be trusted. But in no way did he believe that the observers would view his tolerance of his youth as racism. Nor his comments about how he personally felt about the ethnic-intimidation laws. Evans, in his letter, placed the issue in the context of slavery, a subject Linbush hadn't dealt with his entire career. Slavery was a dead issue as far as the United States was concerned, or so he thought before he read Evans's letter. As intelligent and erudite as the judge bethought himself, he felt woefully out of touch with the state of the nation after finishing Evans's thought-provoking words.

Even still, he needed to gain some objectivity, and after combing through the transcripts of the sentencing hearing himself, he submitted them to State Judicial Tenure Commission and requested an investigation on himself.

Pending that, he completed his opinion in the Evans case. It was his best work ever. He sat in his chambers, reclined in his tall leather chair, and read the opinion once more before he gave it to his clerk for filing. He began the composition with a quote from the US Supreme Court Justice John Marshall Harlan in the dissenting opinion of *Plessy v. Ferguson*, penned in 1896.

> In view of the Constitution, in the eyes of the law, there is in this country no superior, dominant, ruling class of citizens. There is no caste here. Our Constitution is color-blind, and neither knows or tolerates classes among citizens . . . all citizens are equal before the law. The humblest is the peer of the most powerful.

It was dark outside, and the rain fell in sheets upon the streets; lightning and thunder, one dogging the other in rapid succession, shook the city of Detroit.

Fresh off a sparsely populated Greyhound bus, George stood just inside the glass doors of the station, with his nose an inch away from the windows. He watched the rain patter the roofs of cars as they crept by cautiously, tires squirting waves of water into the air from puddles collected in potholes. Up the street, in the parking lot of a corner store, he saw a couple huddled underneath a black umbrella scrambling for the shelter of a white compact car. *So many cars*, he thought. He had never driven one in his life, and now here he was, thrust back into an alien world, a grown man expected to be as familiar with driving as he was with tying his shoes. And the lights, there were so many lights. Downtown Detroit blazed, colors bouncing every which way. The many designs danced up and down the sides of skyscrapers and winked in and out on the fronts of more modest buildings. All of it he soaked in. He promised himself that he would relish every second and every breath until the day he parted this earth.

Four and a half decades he'd spent in a world so utterly different than the one now confronting him. Now, as his breath frosted the window in front of him, the discordant, melodious thrum of life excited a sense of hope and dread within his heart. The initial rush of adrenaline had subsided, leaving behind a mute disbelief.

A place to rest his head and gather himself was what he needed. Half an hour had passed since he stepped off the Greyhound bus. With his meager savings, the balance left from his prison account that the institution had given him in the form of a check for three hundred dollars and seventy-five dollars in cash, he would catch a city bus to the east side and find a cheap motel. Tomorrow he would begin a new journey.

Far up the street, George spotted the top of a bus riding high over the squat automobiles around it. About fifteen blocks away he estimated, which meant it would take at least ten to twelve minutes to get here—plenty of time to do what he had to do.

George pushed open the bus-station doors and stepped out into the rain. Heading for the bus stop across the street, he stopped in the center of the grassy median and let the small plastic bag fall to the ground with a wet plop. Every dance step Tina Brown taught during the breaks between her law classes, George remembered. He stood straight but loose, his body angular like the lines of a Brancusi sculpture. Summoning his inner strength, he focused his thoughts and blocked the world out. He lifted his right foot, resting its baby toe on top of the big toe of the left, crossed his right arm over his chest, and bent his left arm behind him and across his lower back. Twisting his torso to the left, he prepared to begin the traditional victory dance of the Barabaig of Tanzania.

Slowly George unwound. His arms rose to shoulder level and he began to whirl. A song, soft and pregnant with emotion, floated from his mouth.

To sling my arms wide
In some place of the sun
To whirl and to dance
Till the white day is done
Beneath a tall tree
While night comes on gently
Dark like me

That is my dream

To sling my arms wide
In the face of the sun
Dance, whirl, whirl
Till the quick day is done
Rest at pale evening
A tall, slim tree
Night coming tenderly

Black like me

George danced for the painful memory of a sister named Mary, in dedication to the memory of his friend who called himself Never Black, for an end to ignorance, fear, apathy, indifference, racism, drugs, the criminal mind set and raw injustice, and for a new beginning and a new life.

The dark form of the dancing man was silhouetted by the golden flashes of the city's neon lights; his lungs breathed in deep gusts of fresh air as the black man danced and sang in the heavy rain pouring on the city.

Furtive rhythms Of Sex Fleck the distance between us,
With sparks of Africa,
Like poppies scattered upon a desert
Fragments of archaic beauty
Thrust forward
Like moist lanterns
Lighting a faded world . . .
Teach me, O little black dancer,
The forgotten Art of Living!

—Aubrey S. Pierce, Harlem dancer

Chapter 30

Ten years later, Tina Brown went on to found her own law firm. In time, her staff swelled to fourteen attorneys, five paralegals, and six secretaries. Sitting behind the desk in her private office on the top floor of the General Motors building in downtown Detroit, formerly known as the Renaissance Center, she hosted three of her firm's most important clients arrayed in a half-circle before her. For two hours they had been discussing the recent merger of her clients' companies where they reaped enormous profits. Tina Brown was the architect and director of that merger. At the close of the meeting, the three corporate officers surprised her with a check for 750,000 dollars, a token of appreciation for her outstanding work.

The now president of the merged company she represented sat in a chair on her left hand, admiring the elegance of Tina's private office. A very expensive sofa, which looked to be handmade from imported Italian leather, with huge ostrich-leather pillows at each end, crouched near the wall to his right. Her desk, medium in size yet expensive, gave the impression of teak imported from Asia, tailored just for her he was sure. Then there was the beautiful burnished maple floor. Highly unusual for an office on the top floor of a modern skyscraper, the floor gleamed as if a sheet of glass lay on top of stained wooden slats. The floor and the furnishings themselves had to have cost the young lady a mint. In contrast with the opulence of the rest of the office, the chairs the president and his two associates sat on were the wooden fold-out types one could buy for a few dollars at a flea market. The wooden chairs wore rubber shoes, obviously to protect the luxurious maple floor.

His gaze drifted to the wall behind Tina's desk, which was actually a huge rectangular slab of glass, that allowed one to take in the rest of downtown to the Detroit river and beyond for miles into Windsor, Ontario, on the other side.

Five beautiful paintings adorned the two side walls. One was in pastel, an African warrior by Hershell Turner, and the other four—a Gino Severini, a Rufino Tamayo, a Gilbert Stuart, and a Franz Marc—were original oil on canvas, not prints. Behind him, on the wall opposite Tina's desk, he found something that singly destroyed the flowing color schemes and enchanting decor of this otherwise flawless sanctuary. Framed by stained wood and floating behind nonreflective glass and bisecting a poster-size copy of the poem "Still I Rise" by Maya Angelou that hung behind it, whatever the thing was assaulted the harmony of the office's meticulous layout. "May I?" he asked, his curiosity spilling over.

"Sure," Tina said.

The president rose and strode over to stand before it. For several minutes, he studied it but still couldn't determine what it was. Slender and about three feet long with one jagged end, it looked like a thin broken quarterstaff. But why would she have a piece of a stick hanging on her wall in the middle of a poem? he wondered. He turned and looked at Tina. "What's the reddish brown color on the jagged end?"

"Blood," Tina answered.

That gave the president pause. He considered for a moment then asked, "Animal?"

"Human," she responded.

"Burglar, thief?

"Serial killer."

The president turned and examined it again. He noticed something at the bottom he missed before. Words scrawled so small he had to squint to see them read "Zulu Killing Spear."

"What's the story behind it? Why have it here?"

Tina fell silent, glaring at the spear a moment before saying, "It's there as a reminder."

"A reminder of what?"

"It's a very long story, Mr. Abraham. I'm sure you all don't have time to listen to my boring stories."

"Sure we do, Ms. Brown," the President said. "You're an extraordinary individual, and I'm pretty sure I speak for all here when I say that nothing that involves you, a spear with dried blood on one end, and a serial killer could be considered as boring."

"Well, okay," Tina sighed. She adjusted herself in the plush leather and began to recount the most horrific day of her life. "One day, while sitting behind my desk, sort of like this." She pushed her chair back, lifted her legs, and crossed them on top the desk. Leaning back, she retold every gruesome detail of her nightmare.

When she finished her account, her clients gaped at her, incredulous.

Amazed, the woman perched on the front of her fold-out chair said, "Wow. I'd heard that Jackson is an awfully dangerous place. What made you choose Jackson prison to do your work study? How could you teach at a place they called the Killing Grounds?"

"Law students at the University of Michigan's school of law work with prisoners from time to time on cases that may prove challenging or espouse important principles of law. After reviewing many of the cases, I determined that many of this nation's prisoners were treated extremely unfairly by the courts, mainly because many prisoners lacked knowledge of their rights. I wanted to do my part to change that."

"I wonder," the man sitting on the far chair blurted, "whatever happened to Sgt. Gary Moore? Did they rescue him?"

"Now that was interesting." Tina smiled. "As it turns out, months before the riot, Namen Travis and his so-called soldiers had been investigating the prison guards that worked the hole. Somehow they discovered that Sgt. Moore and a coworker were manipulating the system. On certain days, Sgt. Moore would have his coworker punch him in but would not show up to work. And other days it would be vice versa.

"Anyway, Travis found out, and from then on he began blackmailing both of them. Travis had the men bringing him a pint of cognac and other small things like cologne every month to keep his mouth shut. On the day the riot started, Travis knew exactly where Sgt. Moore was, and it wasn't at Jackson Inside. Sgt. Moore was up north in a cabin with no radio or television, camping with his family. Travis squeezed all he could from that knowledge."

"Hah," the man spouted, "I know the warden's guts really twisted over that one." They all laughed at that.

"What about Scrap Iron? Did he survive?" the President asked.

"That Chicago gang decapitated him and threw his head in a dumpster," Tina answered gravely.

After a moment of silent contemplation, the lady in the middle raised her hand hesitantly and hung her head to the side pensively as if she didn't want to but had to voice a nagging question. "Your radio, did it ever turn up?"

"Now that's a real jewel there," Tina said, blushing. "You see, most noncustody staff members kept their mobile radios on the desks or somewhere close at hand. Although we're given a holder to attach to our belts, we rarely used them because it was too awkward and inconvenient. Well, that day, I guess that I was so distracted I put the radio in its holder" Tina paused and eyed her clients.

Realization bloomed on the woman's face. "You had it on you all the time," she gasped.

"I'm afraid so," Tina said, smiling. "I had it on my hip the whole time."

"I don't know whether to laugh or cry," the man on the right said.

The four of them chatted a few moments longer. Afterward, she escorted her audience to the door. The parting was more personal than usual. Instead of handshakes and good-byes, she received warm embraces and words of praise. The president kissed the scar on her left cheek and hugged her fiercely.

Once her clients had departed, Tina sent the rest of the firm's employees home.

After locking the lobby area Tina returned to her office and locked the door. From a drawer she pulled out a CD and slipped it into a player sitting next to her desk. Warm rhythms and euphoric Irish melodies filled the room. Flutes, fiddles, bouzouki, acoustic and electric guitars, button accordions, bass drums, Eulian Pipes, low whistle, orchestra, and keyboards mingled into an arousing harmony. With the music playing, she folded the three wooden chairs and carried them across the room to lean them against the wall. Removing her shoes and her glasses, she placed them on the desk then let her hair down. Next off came her shoes and socks then her pants and blouse down to her underwear. When she finished, Tina stood nude in the center of her exquisitely polished hardwood floor.

Her back to the poem and the killing spear, she looked through the window out at the Detroit skyline. She raised her left foot until it rested on the tip of its big toe; she pressed the knuckles of her left hand against the firm muscle of her left buttock, palm facing out. With her right shoulder raised slightly, she lifted her right arm and held it straight in front of her, fingers straight, palm down. She dropped her head and closed her eyes, pausing to empty her mind. Then, in an explosion of energy, the lawyer bolted halfway across the room and leaped into the air and kicked and twirled as she began to dance Michael Flatley's"Celtic Fire."

Afterword

The Negro writer stands surrounded by the whirling elements of this world. He stands neither on the fringe nor utterly involved: the prime observer waiting poised for inclusion.

O, the things that we have learned in this unkind house that we have to tell the world about!

Despair? Did someone say that despair was a question in the world? Well then, listen to the sons of those who have known little else if you wish to know the resilience of this thing you would so quickly resign to mythhood, this thing called the human spirit . . . .

Life? Ask those who have tasted of it in pieces rationed out by enemies.

Love? Ah, ask the troubadours who come from those who have loved when all reason pointed to the uselessness and foolhardiness of love. Perhaps we shall be the teachers when it is done. Out of the depths of pain we have thought to be our sole heritage in this world—O, we know about love!

And that is why I say to you that, though it be a thrilling and marvelous thing to be merely young and gifted in such times, it is double so, double dynamic—to be young, gifted and black. Look at the work that awaits you!

Write if you will: but write about the world as it is and as you think it ought to be and must be—if there is to be a world, Write about all the things that men have written about since the beginning of writing and talking—but write to a point.

Work hard at it, care about it.

Write about our people: tell their story. You have something glorious to draw on begging for attention. Don't pass it up. Use it.

Good luck to you. This nation needs your gifts. Perfect them.

—Loraine Hansberry

References

Gerritt, Jeff. 2006. "Dying Inmates Deserve System with More Compassion." *Detroit Free Press*. A. 8.

Gerritt, Jeff. 2006."Inmates Aren't the Only Ones Who Pay for Poor Medical Care in Prison Unhealthy Confinement; Long-Term Costs Will Be More for Everyone." *Detroit Free Press*. A. 8.

Gerritt, Jeff. 2006. "Inmates Die When State Corrections Officials Don't Learn from Mistakes Neglect in Custody." *Detroit Free Press*. A. 10.

Gerritt, Jeff. 2006. "Mentally Ill Inmate Dies in Isolation; State Reviews Case; Lack of Care, Heat in Cells Are Issues." *Detroit Free Press*. A. 1.

Gerritt, Jeff. 2006."Needless Death Sentence; Level of Care in State Prisons Is Putting Health of Inmates at Risk." *Detroit Free Press*. A. 10.

Shellenbarger, Pat. 2006."Sentenced to Die?" *Grand Rapids Free Press*. A. 1.